Linda Fairstein is an Assistant District Attorney and head of the Manhattan Sex Crimes Unit. Her first novel, *Final Jeopardy*, introducing Alex Cooper was published in 1996, and this was followed by *Likely to Die*, *Cold Hit* and *The Deadhouse*. She lives in New York.

Likely to Die

LINDA FAIRSTEIN

A *Time Warner* Paperback

First published in the United States in 1997 by Scribner

First published in Great Britain in 1997
by Little, Brown and Company

This edition published by Warner Books in 1998
Reprinted 1999, 2000 (twice), 2001
Reprinted by Time Warner Paperbacks in 2002

A CIP catalogue record for this book
is available from the British Library.

ISBN 0 7515 2120 5

Printed and bound in Great Britain by
Clays Ltd, St Ives plc

Time Warner Paperbacks
An imprint of
Time Warner Books UK
Brettenham House
Lancaster Place
London WC2E 7EN

www.TimeWarnerBooks.co.uk

For
ALICE ATWELL FAIRSTEIN,
the best

LIKELY TO DIE

1

The answering machine kicked in after a fourth irritating echo from the insistent caller. I listened to my recorded voice announce that I was not available to come to the phone right now, as little hammers pounded furiously inside my head. The last Dewar's of the evening had been unnecessary.

I cocked an eye to glance at the illuminated dial glowing an eerie shade of green in the still dark room. It read 5:38 A.M.

"If you're screening, Coop, pick it up. C'mon, kid."

I was unmoved, and mercifully not on duty this morning.

"It's early and it's cold, but don't leave me dangling at the end of the only working phone booth in Manhattan when I'm trying to do you a favor. Pick it up, Blondie. Don't give me that 'unavailable' stuff. Last I knew you were the most available broad in town."

"Good morning, Detective Chapman, and thank you for that vote of confidence," I murmured into the receiver as I brought my arm back under the comforter to keep it warm while I listened to Mike. Too bad I'd cracked open a window for some fresh air before going to sleep. The room was frigid.

"I got something for you. A big one, if you're ready to get back in the saddle again."

I winced at Chapman's reminder that I had not picked up any serious investigations for almost five months. My involvement last fall in the murder case of my friend, the actress Isabella Lascar, had derailed me professionally. It had prompted the District Attorney to direct the reassignment of most of my trial load, so I had taken a long vacation when the killer was caught. Mike had accused me of coasting through the winter season and avoiding the kinds of difficult matters that we had worked on together so often in the past.

"What have you got?" I asked him.

"Oh, no. This isn't one of those 'run it by me and if it's sexy enough I'll keep it' cases, Miss Cooper. You either accept this mission on faith, or I do this the legitimate way and call whichever one of your mopes is on the homicide chart today. There'll be some eager beaver looking to get his teeth into this—I can't help it if he won't happen to know the difference between DNA and NBC. At least he won't be afraid to—"

"All right, all right." Chapman had just said the magic word and I was sitting straight up in bed now. I wasn't certain if I was shivering because of the bitterly cold air that was blowing in from outdoors, or because I was frightened by the prospect of plunging back into the violent landscape of rapists and murderers that had dominated my professional life for almost a decade.

"Is that a yes, Blondie? You with us on this one?"

"I promise to sound more enthusiastic after some coffee, Mike. Yes, I'm with you." His exuberance at this moment would be offensive to anyone outside the family of police and prosecutors who worked in the same orbit as he did, since it was fueled by the unnatural death of a human being. The only comfort it offered was the fact that the particular murder victim in question would be the undistracted focus of the best homicide detective in the business: Mike Chapman.

"Great. Now, get out of bed, suit up, take a few Advil for that hangover—"

"Is that just a guess, Dr. Holmes, or do you have me under surveillance?"

"Mercer told me he was in your office yesterday. Got an overheard on your evening plans—Knicks game with your law school friends, followed by supper in the bar at "21." Elementary, Miss Cooper. The only thing he couldn't figure was whether we'd be interrupting any steamy bedroom scene with a call at this hour. I assured him that we'd be the first to know when you gave up on abstinence."

I ignored the shot and welcomed the news that Mercer Wallace would be part of the team. A former homicide cop, he was my best investigator at the Special Victims Squad, where he caught all the major serial rape cases and pattern crimes.

"Before you use up your quarter, are you going to fill me in on this one and give me a clue about how to sell it to my boss?"

Paul Battaglia hated it when detectives shopped around his office to pull in their favorite assistant district attorneys to work on complex criminal matters. For the twenty years that he'd been the District Attorney of New York County, he had operated with an on-call system—known as the homicide chart—so that for every twenty-four-hour period, every day of the year, a senior prosecutor was on standby and ready to assist in the investigation of murder cases in any way that the NYPD considered useful. Questioning suspects, drafting search warrants, authorizing arrests, and interviewing witnesses—all of the tasks fell to the assistant D.A. who was "on the chart" and had the first significant contact with the police.

"You're a natural for this one, Alex. No kidding. The deceased was sexually assaulted. Mercer's right—we really need your guidance on this one." Chapman was referring to the fact that I am the bureau chief in charge of the Sex Crimes Prosecution Unit—Battaglia's pet project that specializes in the sensitive handling of victims of rape and abuse. Often, since many of those crimes escalated to murder, my colleagues and I were designated to handle the ensuing investigations and trials.

I was stretching across to the drawer of the night table to find this month's homicide chart, to check whether I'd be stepping on the toes of one of the D.A.'s fair-haired boys, and how much flak I'd be heading for. "Well, until eight o'clock this morning, Eddie Fremont is catching."

"Oh, no, you gotta save me from him," Mike responded. "Son of a senator. That's about as useful as having my mother at the station house. Fremont's a whackjob of the first order—I don't think he'd know probable cause if it bit him in the ass."

Chapman often did a stand-up comic routine at the bar at Forlini's, the courthouse watering hole, with the monthly calendar and chart in his hand, calling out the name of the assigned assistants and reliving some embarrassing episode from the career of each of us as he rolled off the dates. Fremont was an easy target, one of those brilliant students with impeccable academic credentials that simply failed to translate to the courtroom. Everyone assumed he had been hired as a "contract," because his father, the former senior senator from Indiana, had been Paul Battaglia's roommate at Columbia Law School.

"Or if you wait until a few minutes after eight, you can have Laurie Deitcher," I countered, aware that she would be responsible for decisions on anything coming in during the next twenty-four hours.

"The Princess? Never again, Blondie. The only time I had a high-profile case with her, it was a disaster. During the lunch hour, instead of prepping witnesses and outlining her cross-examinations, she'd make us wait in the hallway while she plugged in her hot rollers and troweled on some more makeup. Then she'd belly up to the jury box like she was Norma Desmond ready for her close-up. She looked great for the cameras, but the friggin' perp walked. Nope. You just call Battaglia and tell him Wallace and I woke you up in the middle of the night because you were the only person who could answer our questions. Hang tough with him, Cooper. This is *your* case."

"Like what kind of questions, Mike?"

"Like can you tell if she was raped before she was killed or after? Like does establishing the time of death have anything to do with the speed at which the sperm deteriorates, because of interference from her body fluids?"

"Now you're talking my language. Of course he'll let me keep a case like that. What do you need from me?"

"I think you'll want to get down here as soon as you can. Have your video guys meet us, too. The Crime Scene Unit has already processed the room and taken photos, but they had to move really fast. I'm just worried we all may have overlooked something that might turn out to be important, so I'd like your crew to go over the whole area and record it. Once the story breaks, the place'll be crawling with press and we won't be able to preserve it."

"Back up, Mike, and start at the top. Where are you?"

"Mid-Manhattan Medical Center. Sixth floor of the Minuit Building." East Forty-eighth Street, right off the FDR Drive. The oldest and largest medical compound in the city.

The victim must have been transported there for an attempt at treatment after she was found.

"Well, where shall I meet you? Where's the scene?"

"I just told you. The sixth floor at Mid-Manhattan."

"You mean the victim was killed *in* the hospital?"

"Raped and killed in the hospital. Big wheel. Head of the neurosurgery department at the medical college, brain surgeon, professor. Name's Gemma Dogen."

After ten years at my job, there were very few things that surprised me, but this news was shocking.

I had always thought of hospitals as sanctuaries, places for healing the sick and wounded, comforting and easing the days of the terminally ill. I had been in and out of Mid-Manhattan countless times, visiting witnesses as well as training medical personnel in the treatment of sexual assault survivors. Its original redbrick buildings, almost a century old, had been restored to recapture the look of the antiquated sanitarium, and generous patrons of more recent times had lent their family names to a handful of granite skyscrapers that housed the latest in medical technology and a superb teaching facility—the Minuit Medical College.

The familiar knots that tied and untied themselves in my stomach whenever I received news of a senseless crime and a sacrificed human existence took over control from the pounding noise inside my head. I began to conjure mental images of Dr. Dogen, and scores of questions—about her life and death, her career and family, her friends and enemies—followed each other into my mind before I could form the words with my mouth.

"When did it happen, Mike? And how—"

"Sometime in the last fifteen to twenty hours—I'll fill you in when you get here. We got the call just after midnight. Stabbed six times. Collapsed a lung, must have hit a couple of major organs. The killer left her for dead, soaked in blood, but she actually held on for a bit. We got her as a 'likely to die.' And she did, before we got anywhere near the hospital."

Likely to die. An unfortunate name for a category of cases handled by Manhattan's elite homicide squad. Victims whose condition is so extreme when police officers reach the crime scene that no matter what herculean efforts are undertaken by medics and clerics, the next stop for these bodies is undoubtedly the morgue.

Stop wasting time, I chided myself. You'll know more than you ever wanted to know about all of this after a few hours with Chapman and Wallace.

"I can be there in less than forty-five minutes."

I got out of bed and closed the window, raising the Duette shade to look out from my apartment on the twentieth floor of an Upper East Side high-rise across the city as it began to come awake on this gray and grisly day. I have always enjoyed the crisp chill of autumn, leading as it does into the winter holiday season and the snowy blankets of January and February. My favorite months are April and May, when the city parks blossom with the green buds of springtime and the promise of warmer days of summer. So as I scanned the horizon and saw only a bleak and cheerless palette, I figured that Gemma Dogen might also have scoffed at the great poets and agreed with my personal view that March, in fact, is the cruelest month.

2

"Sorry, ma'am, there's no parking in front of the hospital."

The uniformed cop was waving me away from the curb as I pulled in shortly before 7 A.M., so I rolled down the window of my brand new Grand Cherokee to explain my purpose and knock ten minutes off my arrival time by avoiding the multistory underground parking lot which was two blocks farther south.

Before I could speak, a gruff voice barked out at the young recruit and my head snapped around to see Chief McGraw slamming the door of his unmarked car. "Let her be, officer. Unless you want to find yourself walking a beat on Staten Island. Pull it in behind my driver, Alex, and stick your plate in the windshield. I assume we're headed for the same place."

Dammit. Danny McGraw was no happier to see me heading for a murder scene than I was to see him. Once police brass were on the location, they liked to tighten their control of the circumstances and not yield to direction from prosecutors. He'd probably berate Chapman for getting to me so early, preferring that we not learn about cases like this one until he had a complete opportunity to brief the Commissioner. I fished my laminated NYPD vehicle identification placard out of my tote and wedged it above the steering wheel facing out, announcing my presence as official police business. The numbered tags were harder to get than winning lottery tickets, and most of my fellow bureau chiefs considered them the best perk of our job.

I stepped out of the Jeep into a puddle of filthy slush and hustled to catch up with McGraw so that I could follow him through security and up to meet the detectives. The square badgers—cop slang for unarmed guards who stood watch at hospitals and department stores, movie theaters, and ball games—looked more alert than usual this morning, and were themselves flanked by real police at each information booth and elevator bank. Everyone we passed recognized the Chief of Detectives and greeted him formally as we strode quickly down the enormous central corridor of the medical center, through four sets of swinging double doors, until we were led by a detective I had never met before into the hallway marked Minuit Medical College.

McGraw was moving at twice his usual speed, which I guessed—from his repeated glances at the two-and-a-half-inch heels I was wearing—was an effort to leave me behind in his wake, so he'd have a few minutes alone with his lead detectives before I got my nose into things. But his three-pack-a-day cigarette habit was no match for the aerobics of my regular ballet lessons, and the Chief was so short of breath when we reached the med school elevators that I was tempted to suggest he stop off at cardiology on our way up to the neurosurgery department. Like a lot of his colleagues, McGraw didn't remember that Ginger Rogers did all the same things Fred Astaire did in those great old movies—except that she did them going backward *and* wearing heels the height of mine.

When the doors opened, the three of us got on and I pressed SIX. I tried to chat up the young detective and give his boss a chance to recover, but he was stone-faced and uninterested in offering any information while McGraw was in earshot. It was a relief to reach the floor and see the familiar faces of the Homicide Squad's B team, one of the four units into which its workers were divided, gathered in the lounge. Shirt sleeves rolled up, fresh steno pads with notes scribbled on them in every hand, coffee cups scattered on each table surface, and bodies storing adrenaline to pump them through the days and nights that would inevitably follow—barring some lucky break in the case that might solve it sooner.

My arrival prompted a range of reactions from the guys. A few friendly salutations by name from those who were pals of mine or had worked other cases with me, a couple of grunts accompanied by "Hello, Counselor" from those who were indifferent to my participation, and two who ignored me altogether.

McGraw's robot whispered something into his ear and the pair continued on past the lounge to a door halfway down the hall, after the Chief signaled me to wait for him out here. George Zotos, a detective whose work I had respected for years, chuckled as he walked over to talk with me. "Chapman's gonna have trouble sitting down when McGraw gets through with him. Last thing he wants here at this hour is a D.A.—and a dame, no less. The Commissioner's been at a conference in Puerto Rico and is flying back 'cause of this. Chief's got to meet him at Kennedy at noon with every fact in hand, and preferably with a killer ID'd. Sit down, have some coffee, and I'll go get Mike for you. He'll bring you up to speed."

He offered me his own brew, light with three sugars. I screwed up my nose at the sweet smell and asked if there were any containers of black around. George pointed to the cardboard box with half a dozen unopened cups in it and I found one with a *B* penciled on the lid, which was lukewarm but strong enough to get me started.

By the time McGraw let Chapman out of the room to find me, I had slugged down two of the cups, thumbed through the morning tabloids that had been left on a couch in the corner, and rehashed the basketball game with several of the men. I learned that the room the Chief had been taken to was the office of the deceased, where she had been slaughtered and left for dead, although she had not been found until many hours later. There were no obvious suspects and no easy leads, no trail of bloody footsteps heading to the laboratory of a mad scientist with a homicidal streak. This team was settling in for the long, tedious professional job that each of them loved, with assists to follow from the forensic crews in the medical examiner's office and the criminalists who would pore over every fiber and substance placed in their steady hands.

"Whew, Blondie," we could all hear Chapman exclaim as he started back up the hallway to the lounge, "the sight of you first thing in the morning turned that man into a beast. There's no accounting for taste, huh?"

Chapman was in his element. While I would spend parts of every day wallowing in the emotional aspects of this woman's loss and wondering who would miss and mourn for her, Mike was ready for the chase. He liked working the murders because he didn't have a breathing victim to worry about—while aiding the recovery process of such a victim was the feature I valued most about dealing with survivors of sexual assault. It was so much more rewarding than homicide cases, where all we could hope to do was avenge the death of the deceased by caging up a killer who would spend his empty days testing the weaknesses of the system. Without any means of restoring the human life that had been lost, there could be no such thing as justice.

I watched Mike walk toward us, pleased that whatever McGraw had said to him had not wiped that trademark grin off his face. His shock of black hair was uncharacteristically messy, a sign that what he had seen during the night had disturbed him. I knew, even though he wasn't aware of it himself, that he ran his fingers through his hair constantly when something upset him more than usual. His navy blazer and jeans, the dress style he had adopted while at Fordham College fifteen years earlier, were the equivalent of a uniform for Chapman and set him apart from most of the brown- and gray-suited members of the elite Homicide Squad.

"Let's sit over in that corner so I can tell you what I got here," he gestured to me, hoping for a bit of privacy within the open area of the lounge. "D'you hear any news this morning? This break on the air yet?"

"I had WINS on the radio on my way over here. Not a thing. The garbage strike and union negotiations are still the lead story. Followed by the price tag on Princess Di's latest gift from that Saudi prince."

"That'll give us a few hours. You get video?"

"Sure. Bannion will be here himself to do it." I had called the head of our technical unit at home to make certain we'd get the best job done. "He promised to be here by eight."

"Here's what we got. Gemma Dogen—female, Caucasian." Mike was flipping his steno pad to the front page, but didn't need to look at his notes for the basics. "Fifty-eight years old, but I gotta tell you," Chapman editorializing now, "that was a good-looking old lady—"

"Fifty-eight isn't exactly old, Mikey."

"Well, she was no cupcake, kid. When I think sex crime, I think a young, attractive woman who gets—"

"That's one of your problems: you think with your own personal, private parts. And they're probably no bigger than your brain." Rape cases, especially when the assailant is a stranger, rarely have anything to do with sexual acts as we know them in consensual settings. It's a hideously violent crime in which sex is the weapon chosen by the offender to control, degrade, and humiliate his victim. Mike knew all of that as well as I did.

"Anyway, she was a very fit, very strong fifty-eight-year-old who put up a good struggle. Medical doctor. Divorced, no kids."

"Who's the ex and where is he?"

"As soon as somebody tells me, I'll let you know. I've only been on this a few hours more than you and we didn't get a lot of help in the middle of the night. Most of her colleagues and the staff have just started coming into the building during the past hour so I expect to get some more answers soon."

I nodded as Mike went on talking. "From the scene in her office, the personal side looks pretty sterile. No family photos, no dog or cat snapshots, no handmade needlepoint pillows with cute proverbs and initials. Just rows of textbooks, dozens of file drawers with X rays and medical records, about thirty plastic models of the brain—and what used to be a fairly attractive Oriental rug that's now bathed in blood."

"Who found her?"

"Night watchman was going around just before twelve, last check of the floor. He'd been through that corridor twice earlier and heard nothing. This time, he said there was a moaning sound. He's got a master key, opened Dr. Dogen's door, and called 911, right after he threw up—fortunately for the guys from Crime Scene, in the hallway."

"She was still alive?"

"Using that term very loosely, kid. Body was like Swiss cheese—lost most of her blood. I'd bet she was unconscious when the killer left her. Could have been lying there for hours, then got a last spurt of oxygen good for a few gasps, which is what the guard heard. Doctors came running up from the ER and tried to hook her up to life support and get her into surgery to inflate the lung and size up the internal damage but she was too far gone for that. Nothing could have saved her. 'Likely to die' was a gross understatement of Dr. Dogen's condition."

"ME give you a time the stabbing occurred?"

"What do you think this is, the movies? After the autopsy, and after I interview the coworkers and friends and neighbors who tell me when they last saw Gemma and spoke with her, and after I tell the pathologist that I've narrowed the killer's window of opportunity down to fifteen minutes on the day the good doctor disappeared, he'll look me in the eye with great sincerity and give me exactly the time I just spoon-fed to him."

A single professional woman, no children, no pets, no one to depend on her for contact. I tried to push any personal comparisons out of my mind and concentrate on the facts Mike was feeding me, but I kept bringing up the image of my own corpse, lying behind a locked door on the eighth-floor corridor of the District Attorney's Office, with people passing by it all day and nobody checking on whether anyone was inside. Was it possible?

"You think she could have been in that room all day and not a soul knew about it or looked for her? That's really gruesome."

"Alex, she had a schedule just like the one you try to keep. She's lucky her right hand and left hand showed up in the operating room on the same day. She taught at the medical school, did surgery next door in the hospital, lectured all over the world, consulted in major cases wherever she was called in, and in her spare time had the government fly her over to war zones like Bosnia and Rwanda for trauma work, like for charity—and that's just the stuff I can scan from the date book on top of her desk for the month of March."

"What was her schedule yesterday?"

"I had the dean of the medical school check it out for us when I woke him up. Dogen had been out of town over the weekend and had been expected back in the city sometime on Monday. But she wasn't due at the hospital until eight o'clock Tuesday morning—yesterday—when she had been invited to participate in a surgical procedure by a colleague. Everybody on the team had scrubbed and was in the OR, the patient was anesthetized and had his head shaved and was waiting—and they got this amphitheater where all the med students can watch—"

"I know, it's a very prestigious teaching hospital."

"Well, she just never showed up. The surgeon, Bob Spector, sent one of the nurses out to call. Got the answering machine, which was still playing the message that Dogen was out of town. Spector just picked out a couple of the young residents or attendings from the peanut gallery to work with him, bitched about Gemma and her overambitious schedule, and went right on drilling a hole through the middle of some guy's cerebellum."

"That will teach me to call Laura more regularly and let her know my whereabouts," I mumbled aloud. Too often I put myself "in the field," while I raced from the Police Academy to a squad room to the rape crisis counseling unit at a hospital, squeezing in lunch with a girlfriend along the way. There were days when Laura, my secretary, had a hard time keeping up with me and figuring out where I was.

"What are you daydreaming about, Blondie? If you're missing too long the judge just tells somebody to check the dressing room in the lingerie department at Saks—probably find you strangled by whoever didn't get to the sale items as fast as you did. Whoops—turn around and wave good-bye to McGraw."

The Chief was making his way back to the elevator, pausing long enough to call out to Chapman, "Show Miss Cooper around, Mike, then let her get on down to her office to get to work. I'm sure she's got things to do today."

"Let's go. Did you catch the question last night?"

Mike was referring to the Final Jeopardy question on the quiz show to which both of us shared an addiction. "No, I was on my way to the Garden for the game."

"Gotcha, then. Category was transportation. How much would you have bet?"

"Twenty bucks." Our habit was passing ten dollars back and forth every few days, since we had different strengths and weaknesses, but this didn't sound like too esoteric—or religious—a topic.

"Okay, the answer is, the U.S. airport that handles the greatest volume of cargo in the country every day of the year."

Just my luck, a trick question. It couldn't be O'Hare because that would be too obvious, and it specified cargo, not passengers. I was running all the major cities through my mind as we walked down the hall toward Dogen's office.

"Time's up. Got a guess?"

"Miami?" I asked tentatively, thinking of all the kilos of drugs that passed through there on a daily basis but knowing that the show's creators weren't apt to be banking on contraband.

"Wrong, Miss Cooper. Would you believe Memphis? It's where all the Federal Express planes go and get rerouted to whatever their final destination is. Interesting, huh? Pay up, kid."

"Why? Did you get it right?"

"Nope. But that isn't the issue in *our* bet, is it?"

Mike knocked on the heavy wooden door with its elegant gold stenciled lettering that spelled out Dogen's full name and title. Mercer Wallace swung it open and I reeled at the sight of the light blue carpet drenched in so much human blood. It was incredible that she could have had a single drop left in her veins, much less the strength to have tried to drag herself out of harm's way as she obviously had. It was moments before I could look up, and it would be days before I could get that shade of deep scarlet out of my mind's eye.

3

Mercer reached his hand out to steer me around the stained portion of the floor and across Gemma Dogen's office to the area near her desk. Raymond Peterson, the lieutenant in charge of the Homicide Squad and a thirty-year veteran of the force, was talking into his cell phone, his back to me as he stared out the window, which overlooked the East River and the shoreline of Queens. One of the guys from the Crime Scene Unit was still hunched over the open file drawers, rubber-gloved hands poring through folders to consider which surfaces he might dust for latent prints.

The usually laconic Peterson was obviously agitated as he shouted into the telephone, "Bullshit. I don't care how many guys you have to pull off that security detail or authorize for overtime. We need 'em here to go through the garbage. Yeah, that's exactly what I mean. Garbage. Whoever did this had to be covered with the deceased's blood when he left this room. Not a pail goes outta here until it's searched for clothing, weapons—"

Chapman was shaking his head at Mercer and me. "Every container in this hospital has waste items covered with blood in it. It's a medical center, not a nursery school. We're never going to break the case that way."

"Gotta do it, man," Mercer responded. "Probably be a huge loss of time and manpower, but you just can't ignore it."

"Good morning, Loo," I said to Peterson, calling him by the nickname used to address police lieutenants throughout the department. "Thanks for letting me in on this one."

He punched the end button on his phone, then turned and smiled in my direction. "Glad to have you here, Alex. These clowns think you might be able to help us shed some light on it."

I was grateful for Peterson's acceptance. He and Chief McGraw were from the same era in their NYPD training—a time when females were not allowed to be either homicide detectives or prosecutors. They had both entered the Academy in 1965 when murder was considered men's work only. Paul Battaglia had changed the face of our business a decade later when he opened the ranks to young women who were graduating from law schools in great numbers. The New York County District Attorney's Office had grown to six hundred lawyers in the 1990s. Now half of the assistant D.A.s who handled every crime from petit larceny to first degree murder were women.

"I gave Alex the broad strokes, boss. You got anything you want to ask her while we got her here?"

"I'll have a lot more for you after the autopsy, Alex. Sexual assault seems to be the motive. Doesn't look like the place was ransacked for valuable property. Wallet's still in the desk drawer. Right now we're all assuming she was raped. The guy gagged her with a piece of cloth to keep her quiet—we got that over at the lab. Skirt, panty hose, underwear were removed. You think how long she lay around in here will make any difference in whether they find any, uh, well, things, that might link a killer to her?"

"You mean like DNA evidence?" I asked.

Chapman interrupted. "He means that the fact he decided to become a cop and not a priest still doesn't make it any easier for him to talk about body functions and sexual organs. He's Irish Catholic, Cooper, first and foremost. What are the chances that there's gonna be semen in the doctor's vagina and will it be useful to us? That's the kind of stuff he really wants to know."

"Too many variables at this point. If the killer ejaculated, and if he did that in her vaginal vault or on her body, then I'd expect to find seminal fluid," I started. "Unless your killer wore a condom. Believe it or not, now there are even rapists who carry condoms with them."

Chapman shook his head in disbelief as I went on. "I'm sure the medical team that attempted to save her was more interested in trying to revive her than in evidence collection, so there's no way to know whether anyone even did an internal exam yet. The ME will do it during the autopsy anyway. Was she facedown or faceup?"

"Facedown when the guard found her," Mercer told me.

"Well, if she was in here for hours, facedown is better."

"Why's that?" Peterson asked.

"Gravity, Loo. The semen is less likely to run out of her body that way. And the sooner she died after the assault, the smaller the chance her own body fluids would have participated in the deterioration of the sperm. So there may be something of value.

"Next problem," I went on, "is that somebody has to give

us a clue about when the last time she had intercourse was. You could have intact semen from a lover or gentleman friend deposited a day or two ago. If your killer was dysfunctional or didn't ejaculate, you may have a motive for him to get enraged and stab his victim, but the semen will be from an earlier encounter that was entirely consensual. Red herring. Mike, when you talk to the ME, make sure they do a pubic hair combing. That's a possible for DNA, too."

"Here's what we'll do," the lieutenant said. "There's no point batting this around until we've got more specifics. Not just about this stuff, but the whole situation. The Chief's setting this investigation up as a task force. He's gonna give me detectives from a few other commands to work with the Squad; Mercer and some more guys from Special Victims because of the sexual assault angle."

"Where's our base gonna be?" Mercer asked.

"We'll handle it out of an office in the 17th Precinct. Chapman, you'll be going to the autopsy and dealing with the medical examiner, right?"

Mike nodded and lifted his pad again to take some notes.

"I also want you to sit down with someone from hospital administration. Get a complete breakdown and description of every one of these buildings—how they're connected, what the access is, where every door and lock and guard is supposed to be, and where they actually are. I want a list of every employee in the medical center—doctors, nurses, students, technicians, messengers, bedpan cleaners. Every patient, ambulatory or not. Every name from that nuthouse psychiatric hospital next door—and I don't want to hear any crap about 'privileged information.' They cooperate or they'll all be in straitjackets by the time I get done with them."

Mercer also had his pen poised ready for his assignment.

"Wallace, you start with the personal side. Find the ex, interview her neighbors and colleagues, get a picture of her

habits and hangouts. Zotos will do this part of it with you. We
need a location check—every other crime that's occurred on
premises here—and then move on to every other hospital in
this city."

"Done, boss."

"After that, check with medical centers in Philly and Washington and Boston—see if anything like this has happened
anyplace else. I'll get somebody to supervise the garbage
detail, and I'll set up the tips hotline this afternoon. Alex, have
your people check all your records for anything with a similar
M.O. or connected to a medical setting."

"We'll start on it right away. I'd also like to have a look at
Dr. Dogen's apartment if I can. I don't mean for evidence—
Mercer can do that. But when he's finished, I'd like to go back
with him once. It always helps me to get to know the victim,
to get a sense of her life." In murder cases, unlike rapes, there
was no survivor for me to work with, no way to get inside the
spirit that was destroyed by death. And if there was no family
member to entrust that being, that life, to me for the purpose of the investigation there was no other way to come to
know it.

"No problem, boss. I'll have the apartment processed
today, then we can go back with Cooper whenever she'd like."

"Okay, Mercer. But be sure and have it sealed up—I don't
want any relatives or friends taking anything out of there until
we know the lay of the land."

"What do you say we all meet at the end of the day and see
what we got?" Chapman asked of Peterson.

"Exactly. Be back at the 17th Precinct station house at
seven o'clock. I'm sure the Chief will want a briefing on the
situation, so come prepared. You, too, Alex."

I thanked him again and followed Mike around the perime-
ter of the soiled carpet toward the door. As I looked down to
avoid stepping on Gemma's deadly trail, my eye caught on a

thick blotch of deep red color that almost looked like an intentional design set against the pale blue dhurrie. It was even and clear, quite a contrast to the ragged discoloration that marked the rest of the deceased's path from the point at which the assault had started.

"What do you think that is, Mercer?" I asked over my shoulder since he was still behind me.

"What is?"

"That mark on the floor, in the blood?"

"Don't go seeing ghosts on me, Coop. It's just blood."

Mike had turned to look down, too, and both were bending over the spot I had focused on. "It looks like a cattle brand. Maybe some object—a belt buckle or a clasp of some kind got imprinted or pressed into it. Crime Scene photoed it."

It didn't seem a bit like that in my view. "It looks like she was writing something, like it was part of a word."

Chapman was all over me. "She didn't have the strength to breathe, Blondie, much less write. She was checkin' out, not doing a grocery list."

I ignored him and traced the shape in the air for Mercer. "It looks like the letter *F*, you know, a capital *F*—or maybe an *R*, but with squared corners—and then a tail going off this way, wiggling," I said, drawing an invisible line from the bottom corner, downward and to the left. "Doesn't it?"

"We'll have your video guys take some shots of it, too, Alex, but I'm sure it's wishful thinking."

"Get me a Polaroid of it, Mercer."

He nodded his head but was already whistling the old Temptations tune "Just My Imagination" as he made another notation on his pad.

Mike held the door open for us and closed it behind Mercer and me, telling the uniformed cop beside it not to let anyone in without authorization, as he mimicked me on our way down the hall. "I can hear the summation already—that's what you start prepping for as soon as you get a case, isn't it?—with one of your dramatic lines about the hand from the grave, pointing a finger at the killer. Good try, Cooper. The jury may laugh but the press corps will love it."

4

It was eight-thirty when I parked the Cherokee on the narrow street in front of the entrance to the District Attorney's Office and dug into my pocketbook to remove the identification tag that would get me through the metal detector inside the main door. I picked up my third cup of coffee from the vendor who wheeled his cart of bagels and pastries to the corner of Centre Street every morning and walked inside past the security guard who was too engrossed in a skin magazine to notice my arrival.

I liked to get to my desk at least an hour before nine o'clock, when the huge office comes alive with lawyers, cops, witnesses, jurors, and miscreants of every description, in addition to the noise of thousands of telephones ringing constantly throughout the day. In the quiet of the early morning,

I can read and respond to motions in my pending matters, screen and analyze the case reports forwarded to me by assistants in the unit, and return some of the calls that inevitably pile up by the end of each working session.

There was no one else on my corridor yet, the executive wing of the Trial Division, so I flipped on the hallway lights, unlocked my door, and passed by my secretary Laura's desk to hang my coat in the tiny closet in the corner of the room. It felt as though it was fifty degrees in my office, so I slipped off my shoes, climbed on top of Laura's computer table with a screwdriver to reach the thermostat that some sadistic city engineer had locked into a metal grid out of human reach, and readjusted the heat to a comfortable level so I could settle in at my desk and get to work. My colleagues and I were entrusted with the safety and well-being of the millions of inhabitants and daily visitors to Manhattan but not with the temperature control of our decaying little cubicles in the Criminal Courts Building.

I dialed my deputy's extension to leave a message on her voice mail. "Hi, Sarah. Call me as soon as you get in. Caught a murder with Chapman at Mid-Manhattan and we're going to have to do a search on all our cases involving health care professionals, hospitals, and mental institutions. I'm probably going to need some help with my schedule, too."

Next call was to my paralegals, who shared an office on the adjacent corridor. They were both smart young women who had graduated from college the preceding spring and were apprenticing with me for a year before going on to law school. "There'll be a meeting in my office at ten. New case with lots to do. Forget about going to that lecture at Police Headquarters today—I'm going to need you here."

I speed-dialed the number of my friend Joan Stafford who was undoubtedly in the middle of her daily workout with a personal trainer, and got her machine. "It's Alex. Scratch the dinner and theater plans for tonight and see if Ann Jordan wants my ticket. I've got to work. Apologize to the girls and I'll speak to you tomorrow." Joan had bought tickets for a group of friends to the new Mamet play that had opened two weeks earlier, but I would not be able to join them.

Rose Malone, the District Attorney's executive assistant, was already at her desk when I called to ask for him. "What time is Paul due in?"

"He's addressing the City Council at nine but I do expect him here before noon. Shall I add you to the list?"

"Please, Rose. I picked up a homicide this morning and he really ought to know about it."

"He does, Alexandra. He just called me from the car and mentioned that the Commissioner's Office had alerted him. I don't know if you're aware of it but Mrs. Battaglia's on the board at Mid-Manhattan."

Just once I'd like to tell Paul Battaglia something that he didn't already know. The man had more sources than McDonald's has hamburgers.

"I'll be at my desk, Rose, so just call when he wants me."

I flipped through my appointment calendar and made a list of the meetings and witness interviews that Sarah could cover for me, circling in red the handful that I would have to keep for myself. The computer screen lighted up when I logged on and I quickly typed a response to the boilerplate motion my adversary had submitted in a marital rape case in his halfhearted effort to suppress the admissions his client had made to the cops. Laura could format and print it when she got in, and I would proofread and sign it and have it in front of the judge well before his three o'clock deadline for my papers.

By the time I had finished writing, Sarah Brenner turned the corner into my office, both arms full of legal pads and case folders. "This is just a start," she announced to me, shaking her head. "Let me grab some coffee and come back—the raptor had me up half the night. She's teething."

Somehow this meticulous young lawyer with enormous charm and a delightful disposition worked every bit as diligently as I did but managed to do it all while also being the devoted mother of a demanding toddler nicknamed for her uncanny ability to cling to Sarah and wail, usually in the middle of the night when she was trying to sleep. Now she was pregnant with her second, and still had more energy and enthusiasm for our work than half of the lawyers I had ever been shoulder-to-shoulder with during the most intensive investigations.

Sarah came back from the vending machine and sat in the chair on the far side of my desk. "Want to keep her for a few nights? Bring out your maternal instincts and all that?"

"I've got my own raptor. Chapman. Woke me up this morning to give me a case. I'd like to keep it, if the boss lets me, but I won't do it if it's too much for you."

"Don't be ridiculous. I'm not due for another five months. I'm perfectly healthy, and I'd much rather be here than at home," Sarah hesitated. "I've been waiting for something to engage your interest again. You need a tough case to get you moving. I'll handle all of your overflow. Promise. What's this one about?"

I explained what I had heard and seen at Mid-Manhattan and what Lieutenant Peterson had assigned everyone to do.

"Just be sure it's solved before I go into labor. I don't want any home delivery job, like *Rosemary's Baby*, but it's chilling to think of some madman loose in a hospital. Wait until you start to review the cases we've had. I mean, they're all in different facilities, and over periods of time, but it's certainly eye-opening."

I had investigated and tried some of them myself during the years that I had run the Sex Crimes Unit, but we had never tracked them as a single category. Sarah and I started anecdotally from memory, calling up to each other the cases we remembered from recent interviews and precinct referrals. When the paralegals Maxine and Elizabeth joined us at ten, we gave them the task of doing a hand search through our screening sheets, the record of every victim and suspect who had made a complaint about or been the subject of a sexual assault investigation in Manhattan going back almost a decade.

"Pull each one of them in which there is any mention, other than the victim's examination, of the words 'hospital,' 'doctor,' 'nurse,' 'technician,' 'psychiatric patient,' or anything else that seems to be related to a medical setting. Xerox copies for Sarah and me. I want everything you can find before I leave here at the end of the day."

Laura had also arrived shortly after ten and was given the same assignment for her computer files. They didn't go as far back as our screening sheets but would be a faster check than the tedious exploration of those handwritten documents that Sarah and I had collected since we took over the unit—the most thorough record of sexual deviancy compiled anywhere in the world.

"Anything else I can help with this morning?" Sarah asked.

"No, thanks. I've got Margie Burrows coming down any minute. I'm going to reinterview one of her witnesses. She missed a few of the essential points first time around."

Nothing unusual about that. Burrows had asked to be appointed to our unit and we had given her a couple of cases to work on, under our supervision, to check her skills. She had the requisite compassion and manner for working with rape victims—a trait some prosecutors come up short on—but hadn't yet developed the critical eye to probe for inconsistencies. It was a delicate balance that some questioners like Sarah Brenner seemed to be born with and others would never be able to learn.

Sarah left as Margie announced herself to Laura. I invited

her in and pulled up a third seat for the complaining witness, Clarita Salerios.

I had reviewed Margie's notes, and knew that Salerios was a forty-seven-year-old woman who worked as a clerk in the shipping office of a large company. She was divorced, with grown children who lived in the Dominican Republic. Recently she had become severely depressed because of the death of her ex-husband, with whom she had tried to reconcile. One of her girlfriends had referred her to a *santero*—sixty-six-year-old Angel Cassano, who had been arrested for attempting to rape her several weeks earlier.

I introduced myself to Clarita and explained that although Margie had already interviewed her at length, there were some facts that remained unclear to me. Like, why a *santero*?

"Is no problem, Miss Alex. I tell you whatever you wanna know. I guess you call him a witch doctor."

It would certainly hold my attention for a few hours and keep my mind from wandering back to Gemma Dogen. Of the thousands of matters I had worked on in the last ten years, none had involved a witch doctor.

Clarita explained that she had gone to the defendant several months ago to help her through her ex's death. Angel—such an appropriate name for the job description—began by taking her to the cemetery where Señor Salerios was buried, in Queens, and performing some rituals there. Because he was partially blind, Clarita accepted Angel's request to help escort him back to his apartment in the barrio. On the fourth or fifth trip, he invited her upstairs for an additional ritual.

By mid-February, Clarita and Angel skipped the cemetery visit and she went directly to his apartment. The ritual changed a bit. Angel suggested that the trusting woman take off all her clothes and lie on a blanket he placed on the floor in his room.

"Did you think that was strange, Clarita?"

"No problem, Miss Alex. Is mostly blind, the old guy."

I nodded my understanding, remembering how many times I had urged cops and colleagues not to be judgmental of rape victims.

He put her in some kind of trance, she explained, and while she was meditating, he kneeled beside her and began to touch her.

"Where, exactly, did he do that, Clarita?"

"In my bagina."

"I see. Go on."

After a little while, she asked Angel to stop and he did.

"Wasn't it unusual for a *santero* to do that?"

"I ask him why he do it. He tell me the spirits told him to do it to me."

"Did you believe that, Clarita?"

She laughed. "Not no spirit of Nestor Salerios, I tell you that myself. I know that for sure. He used to beat me if another guy even looked at me, Miss Alex. He's a jealous man, even if he dead now."

I glanced down at the arrest report in the case, which the police officer had prepared when Cassano was apprehended. It noted that he had a strong odor of alcohol on his breath.

"Tell me, Clarita, what was Angel drinking that day, at the apartment?" Margie had made no mention of that fact, but that was probably because Clarita had neglected to bring it up.

"Let me think," she said, looking up at the ceiling as though trying to decide what to tell me. "Rum. I pretty sure it was rum."

"And did he make you drink it, too?'

"Yeah, he did. He tell me the spirits like it. But I just sip it a little bit. No much."

Love Potion Number Nine. The only thing missing was the

gypsy with the gold-capped tooth, but she'd probably be in it by Clarita's next visit.

Clarita paid him for the session—I bit my tongue and didn't ask if she tipped him for the extra ritual he'd thrown in at the end—and left.

The more surprising part of the story is that she called him again to go back two days later. Yes, she admitted, it had crossed her mind that perhaps what he wanted most was some kind of sexual relationship with her and perhaps he wasn't such a holy man as she had thought. That's the point in many of these stories at which I am reminded of those children's puzzles that present a drawing of a neatly ordered room in which one object is inverted or out of place and the caption underneath reads, "What's wrong with this picture?" In this instance, Clarita had already been sexually abused by Cassano, knew that what he had done was improper and inappropriate, and had been fortunate enough to extricate herself from his advances and walk away a few dollars poorer but without further molestation. Go back for more? Her loneliness, confusion, and vulnerability screamed out at me as they must have also signaled themselves to the blind *santero*.

On her next visit, after some rum and a few invocations of the spirit, Clarita again fell into a trance, undressed, and lay on the floor. This time the spell was broken when Angel got on top of her body and tried to penetrate her vagina with his penis.

"I've got to stop you here and go back over a few things," I interrupted. Things that aren't in Margie's note.

"This 'trance' you describe, were you conscious? Were you awake and aware of what was going on?" I needed to make sure she had not passed out or been drugged or intoxicated.

"Oh, sure, Miss Alex. This time I keep all my eyes opened."

"And this time, Clarita, did Angel begin by touching you with his fingers?"

"No, ma'am. I'm no stupid. I woulda got up and slapped him, he did that."

"So the first thing that happened, he just laid himself down on top of you, to have sex?"

Again, Clarita sought the answer in the ceiling of my office. She looked back at me as she spoke. "Is right."

Angel either had to have removed his pants, lowered them, or opened his zipper and exposed his penis before actually mounting her—but any of those actions would have given his target the time to save herself from his approach.

"Can you tell me exactly when it was that he took off his pants in order to have sex with you?"

"You're right, Miss Alex," Clarita said, pointing a finger in my general direction with a look of consternation on her face. "That's a berry, berry important question, I think. When did the man take off his pants? I have to think about that some more before I could tell you."

"We'll come back to that. It's okay. I know this is the part that's hardest for you." I eased her through the end of the story, where the defendant's actions finally escalated from merely taking advantage of Clarita to criminal conduct. Once she decided she was not ready to receive the spirits, she pushed Cassano off her body and got to her feet. But when she ran for the door, still naked, the blind witch doctor followed with a machete that he picked up from the kitchen counter. With that, he forced her back into the room and demanded that she give him oral sex. She was only able to escape when she offered to go to the nearby liquor store to buy another bottle of rum and instead called 911 to summon the police.

I thanked her for her cooperation and patience, directed her to the water fountain for a break, and went back over the case with Margie Burrows, clarifying which parts of the incident were chargeable as crimes and which were not.

Laura opened my door to tell me that Rose Malone had called. The District Attorney had arrived and wanted to see me as soon as possible, before his luncheon date with the head of the editorial board of *The New York Times*. I sent Margie on her way with instructions for the grand jury presentation she would make later in the day, grabbed my pad with the notes I had assembled about the Gemma Dogen case, and headed over to Battaglia's office.

Rose was standing at one of the file cabinets that ringed her office, paging through folders stuffed into the drawers like too many clowns in a Volkswagen. "I'm trying to find the last few op-ed pieces the *Times* published on 'quality of life' crimes in the city. Paul's trying to convince them to run a series on our success rate with neighborhood cleanups of marijuana dealers and prostitutes."

She smiled at me over the sheaf of yellowing papers she was examining and that was my first sign that the D.A. was in a good mood. Rose was my personal early warning system.

"He'll be right out with you, Alex. He's just on the phone with his wife."

I busied myself reviewing the few facts I had learned during my stop at the hospital, knowing that Battaglia was a stickler for detail and bound to want more information than I had here.

His voice boomed out at Rose from within his huge office. "Have you got Cooper yet?"

I answered the question by turning the corner and showing myself to him as he waved me in with the two fingers of his left hand that secured the ever-present cigar.

"If you know what's good for my domestic tranquillity, you'll tell your pals in Homicide to solve this one fast. My wife's running the Mid-Manhattan fundraiser—the spring gala—and the tickets were supposed to go on sale in two weeks. The caterer from the goddamn Plaza called her at eight-thirty this morning when he heard the news asking for a check today to guarantee five hundred *saumon en croûte* dinners in case the committee loses supporters over this. So much for the late good doctor. Is it yours?"

"I'd like it to be, Paul. It's a rape-homicide and I've—"

He cut me off, not needing to hear things he already knew. "I take it you've been up at the crime scene already?"

"Lieutenant Peterson let Chapman bring me in on it. I stopped by for an update and then came down here to start checking M.O.s and parolees for similarities. I don't think there's a hospital in Manhattan where we haven't had some kind of criminal problem in the past, so there's a lot to look at."

Battaglia puffed on the cigar, lifted one foot against the edge of his desk, and pushed back, letting his chair rest on its rear two legs. He stared directly at my face, eyeballing me to make me answer his questions without evasion.

"It's a perfect assignment for you, Alexandra, if you're up to it. Even though you got it through the back door. Nobody knows more about sex crimes than you, and I doubt the media glare, which I expect will be pretty intense, will bother you much."

He left off the phrase "after the last time" but I met his gaze and returned it, telling him that I was looking forward to getting to work with the Squad.

"You'll report straight to me on this one. And if Chapman gets any of his creative ideas, like dressing you up in a nurse's uniform and having you work the midnight shift to try to gather intelligence, you'd make me very happy if you resist the urge."

I laughed and assured Battaglia that I wouldn't dream of doing anything like that, while making a mental note to suggest to the team that we consider admitting Maureen Forester, my favorite decoy detective, to the neurological floor of Mid-Manhattan Hospital as a patient—for observation.

5

The rest of the day passed quickly as I fielded the usual range of problems and inquiries from the young lawyers who worked with me in the unit. Sarah and I had spent the lunch hour in a conference room, eating salad and sipping Diet Coke, while we made lists of defendants and suspects who might warrant a close look during the Dogen murder investigation. Laura shielded me from all the nonessential phone calls, and I spent the last part of the day sorting through messages and returning those that could not wait until the next morning.

At six-thirty I shut off the lights, went down the hallway to tell the Chief of the Trial Division, Rod Squires, that I was on my way to the task force meeting, and left the building with my folder of case summaries to walk to the Jeep. I had missed most of the rush hour traffic so I sailed up First Avenue with no trouble, using the time to call my best friend, Nina Baum, and leave a voice mail recording on her office system at her law firm in Los Angeles, as I did almost every day.

I parked near the station house on East Fifty-first Street and entered the building, explaining the purpose of my visit and showing my identification to the cop at the desk, who nodded in response and pointed me in the direction of the staircase. I climbed the flight and as I pushed against the bar on the heavy metal door, it swung open onto the green-tiled hallway of the second floor. The locker rooms for the uniformed cops were to my right, the anticrime office straight ahead, but most of the working space on the floor was consumed by the detective squad room off to my left.

Walking into the headquarters of a breaking major homicide investigation was, as always, a chance to see the cream of the NYPD at its best. The energy level was electric as Peterson's hand-chosen task force gathered and prepared for the briefing that would begin after the arrival of the big bosses within the hour. I glanced around the room to see who would be working the case with me, subconsciously rating them not only as investigators but as trial witnesses and testifiers. Whatever skills they brought to this part of the process would be compromised or enhanced by the quality of their paperwork and their ability to account for details like preserving the chain of custody and the proper methods of gathering minute traces of evidence, carefully accumulating clues, or sloppily overlooking significant leads.

The squad area was like a rabbit warren as I viewed it from within the doorway. More than twenty detectives were clustered around the twelve desks that filled one side of the room. On each desk stood a standard manual typewriter, a couple of telephones, a wire basket—empty now but about to begin to fill with reams of pink-papered police reports called Detective

Division 5s. The computer age, I noticed, had made little impact on the day-to-day life of these officers. The two desks closest to the entrance were each manned by a glum-looking plainclothes cop, and it was obvious to me that they were two of the team of 17th Precinct squad members whose home had been taken over by the task force and who were shut out of the Dogen case—their natural turf—while relegated to handling all the usual business and public relations for the neighborhood. They looked on at the elite corps of interlopers like Cinderella must have looked at her stepsisters as they dressed for the ball.

To my right was a large holding pen—a jail cell furnished with only a long wooden bench, used to detain arrestees for the hours between an apprehension and the time the prisoner is taken down to Central Booking to begin the arraignment process. I was accustomed to seeing two or three men stretched out on the bench or the tile floor behind the locked bars when I arrived for a lineup or interrogation. I had never seen what I noticed tonight. There were eight men in and around the cell, which was wide open—some sitting, some reclining, one on the outside with his back against the bars, one pacing in and out of the entryway. They seemed from their filthy, mismatched clothes and unkempt appearance to be rejects from a homeless shelter. Nobody was watching them, and they didn't appear to be in any particular distress.

At the desk in the far corner I could see the only other woman in the room. She was Anna Bartoldi, a mainstay of the Homicide Squad whom Peterson had no doubt assigned to supervise the detailed record keeping of what was bound to be a complicated investigation. Anna's photographic memory, combined with her writing skills, would help the lieutenant track the hundreds of documents that would begin to be generated by the officers, whether working on the case or not, who would make note of statements given by witnesses or phoned in by well-meaning citizens, which would become the building blocks of evidence against the killer. Anna held a receiver to one ear and was writing in an oversized log that covered the desktops so I assumed she had already been running the tips hotline that had been announced just an hour earlier on the local news stations.

In the corridor behind Anna's chair was the door to the office of the squad's commander. Whoever he was, he had been displaced for the foreseeable future by Peterson, who would be under pressure to make an arrest in such a high-profile matter as speedily as possible.

Mercer Wallace, the biggest, blackest man in the room, was the first to notice my arrival as I let the door swing shut behind me and took off my coat and scarf. "Don't look so surprised, Cooper," he called to me, waving me in and bending his head toward the motley collection of strays in the holding pen. "Welcome to our Salvation Army outpost. C'mon aboard."

I knew most of the cops on the team, and chatted with those who had not been at the hospital this morning as I worked my way through the group to reach the desk at which Mercer had seated himself.

Wallace continued when I reached his post. "Peterson's inside waiting for McGraw to get here. The Commissioner and McGraw did a stand-up on the evening news broadcast. The usual crap—urging the public to stay calm, asking for help. Mayor offered a ten-thousand-dollar reward for information leading to the conviction of the killer. Hotline started to ring immediately, everybody looking to give up their nearest and dearest for the money."

I looked over Anna's shoulder and saw that she was up to the forty-seventh entry in the tips book. Years ago she had given me the odds that only one in sixty calls usually had any relevance to the investigation, so it didn't surprise me when she leaned her head back, rolled her eyes at me for dramatic effect, and went back to recording the notes that were most probably an exercise in futility. It would be the job of a couple of members of the team to follow through on every one of the messages no matter how far-fetched they seemed, because sandwiched in among them might be the real thing—a call from someone who knew the killer and was willing to sell his soul for the financial reward.

"Hey, Blondie, get your cash on the table. We're up right after the commercial break." Chapman's voice boomed into the squad room as he emerged from the hallway adjacent to the lieutenant's office, chewing a mouthful from the slice of pizza he held in one hand. "TV's back here in the detectives' locker room. Move it!"

Mercer pushed away from his desk and prodded me in the back. "Let's go, Alex. My money's on you. Besides, that's where the food is, so we might as well humor him."

I followed Mercer around the corner and down the corridor to its end. Rows of battered dark green lockers lined the walls of a twenty- by fifteen-foot room. The furnishings featured a Mr. Coffee machine, a vintage 1940s-style Amana refrigerator, a television set, and a large rectangular table that was covered with soda cans, three pizza boxes, a carton that at one time had held two dozen Dunkin' Donuts in a variety of flavors, and half-empty packages of nachos, pretzels, and assorted brands of cigarettes. The sole artwork displayed on the only wall without lockers was a centerfold from some old issue of *Penthouse,* with a head shot of Janet Reno superimposed on the voluptuous body of the nineteen-year-old manicurist who had posed for the layout. I remembered that Reno had visited the precinct in late '96 for a photo op when she delivered some of the Crime Bill money to the Police Commissioner and I chuckled at the fond memento that her visit had inspired.

"Category tonight is Famous Leaders, Coop. I'm going for fifty. Gonna start this investigation on an optimistic note."

Chapman took the bill from his wallet and placed it on the table while reaching for another slice. He shoved the box across to me and I opened the lid for Mercer, noting that it was ice cold and covered with grease spots. "Damn, that stuff's been sitting here since four o'clock this afternoon, girl. Pass. My fifty's on the filly, Chapman."

"Hold it, Mercer. This is his field," I cautioned as he reached for his money. Chapman had majored in history at Fordham and it was one of the topics he could beat me at easily.

"You used to have balls, Cooper. What happened? Famous leaders—you read the newspaper every day—maybe it's current, not old, news. If it's some relative of Mercer's heading a Tutsi tribe on the Dark Continent or the Baltic president of an abracadabra-stan that didn't exist until three weeks ago, you'll drop me in a heartbeat. Get it up, here's Trebek."

"I'm good for it. I left my wallet in the other room."

Alex Trebek had just revealed the Final Jeopardy answer to his three contestants. I saw the name Medina Sidonia on the screen and was clueless.

Chapman was poker-faced, waiting for me to guess first. With all of the vocal authority I could muster, I gave him the question: "Who was the head of the Brooklyn faction of the Gambino family before John Gotti?"

"Bad answer," he shot back at me, washing his pizza down with a jelly doughnut. "Señor Sidonia—a Spanish nobleman, by the way, and not a goombah, Miss Cooper—was the commander in chief of the Spanish Armada, leading the doomed sailors up the coast with the backup assistance of the land army of Alessandro Farnese, the Duke of Parma—"

"I guess I'm buying dinner," I threw back over my shoulder as I walked away from Mercer and Mike, impressed anew with

Mike's almost encyclopedic knowledge of military history. "Sorry to take you down with me, Wallace. I owe you on that one. I'm going back out to talk to Anna."

I emerged from the locker room to see Chief McGraw standing in the open doorway of Peterson's office. The lieutenant had an old wooden easel next to his desk, on which was propped a large sketch pad opened to the first sheet on which someone had neatly lettered "Mid-Manhattan Hospital." McGraw was suggesting that they go into the back for the briefing, so he could see how the story was playing on New York 1, a local TV station that repeated the news headlines every half-hour.

Mercer had stopped short behind me, whispering in my ear: "McGraw has probably only seen himself on the tube six or seven times since the press conference an hour ago, but he never seems to get enough, does he?"

As the two of them came out, Peterson signaled to us to go back inside the locker room, handing the easel to Mercer, while he walked to the edge of the squad room and called out the names of the three other men he wanted in attendance for the briefing. Since McGraw was ignoring my presence, I walked on in ahead to make sure that Mike wasn't standing in front of the tube doing his imitation of the Chief. He was watching the newscast, which was running with a print of the next morning's tabloid headlines over the familiar image of the entrance to the hospital: MAYHEM AT MID-MANHATTAN. Reporters were clustered around the mayor as he decried the fate of Gemma Dogen and affirmed his confidence in the city's medical centers.

"Wait 'til superdick finds out he didn't get any air time," Chapman chuckled. "He hates getting bumped by the mayor."

"Maybe you'll want to tell him yourself. He's about five steps behind us," I cautioned.

Mercer followed after me and set up the easel. He flipped

over the top sheet and revealed the first in a series of sketches that one of the police artists had already prepared with a lay-out of the hospital buildings in order to familiarize the bosses with the territory. Though the rough diagram didn't show it, we all knew the complex had a larger population than half of the towns and villages in the entire country. There were dozens of entrances and exits to streets, garages, and other structures; there were miles of corridors lined with offices, laboratories, storage rooms, and surgical theaters; and thousands worked in, visited, or used its facilities every day of the year.

Lieutenant Peterson led McGraw into the crowded area in the back of the locker room, followed by three detectives from the task force. They were the ones who had spent the day starting the groundwork at the hospital, patiently speaking to witness after witness to see whether anyone had seen or heard anything unusual during the preceding day or night. Peterson shoved his glasses on top of his head, told us all to take our seats around the table, and directed Mercer to begin with what he had learned about the deceased. Chief McGraw stood off to the side, arms folded and cigarette dangling from the corner of his tightly pursed lips, positioned so he could see each of us as well as the TV screen, which had been muted but continued to replay the frenzied scene in front of the medical center.

Laura had sent me off with a standard D.A. Office's homi-cide Redweld, the rust-colored accordion folder that would expand and then multiply quickly throughout the course of this kind of investigation. I removed the legal pads she had placed inside—several blank and two filled with the notes Sarah and I had assembled during the day for this meeting—while each of the cops opened the pocket-sized steno pads that would be their lifelines to the case. We would all be tak-ing notes as Mercer began to speak.

"Gemma Dogen. As you know, gentlemen, the doctor was fifty-eight years old, white, a fitness nut, and a real loner. She's a Brit, born and raised in a small town on the Kent coast called Broadstairs. Got all her degrees in England and moved here about ten years ago with an invitation to join the neurosurgery department, and eventually took it over. Quite a plum for a woman doc. Add to that the distinction of an endowed chair at the medical college. Well respected as an academic, not only a practitioner. Divorced before coming over here. No kids. The husband, Geoffrey Dogen, is out of the picture. Also a physician; met Gemma in medical school. Remarried in '91, and his young bride has him trekking in the Himalayas this very week. They live in London and from some of the letters I found in Dogen's apartment, still have a pretty nice relationship. He's due back next week, so we'll need to talk to him and see what he knows about her personal life, but he's certainly not a suspect."

The Chief wasn't engaged yet. His eyes were still fixed on the tube and as usual he seemed oblivious to the fact that the cigarette in his mouth had burned so far down that it was about to be extinguished by his saliva. Then he would automatically reach into his pack and light up the next one, as we had all seen him do thousands of times.

Wallace continued. "Dogen lived on Beekman Place, walking distance from the hospital. Doorman building, high rent, large one-bedroom with a terrace overlooking the river. George Zotos is still over there now. There's tons of papers to go through. Lady was like a real pack rat with her files, so it's hard to tell if there'll be anything useful or not. But it's the same as her office—not a lot of signs of a personal life. Most of the photos are old family shots from her childhood or pictures of herself getting degrees and awards."

McGraw's mouth opened to exchange cigarettes. "Find any neighbors or doormen with gossip?"

"Guy on the door confirms the erratic schedule. Back and forth to the hospital, lots of airport trips, jogging along the river early in the morning and often around sundown. Very few visitors. Occasionally, some sleep-over parties with a guy—with different guys, actually—but no names that he could remember. And so far, next door neighbors were no help at all. One couple just moved in two months ago, the ones on the other side weren't home all day, and the building canvass is still going on."

Mercer flipped his pad to the next page. "We started the location check, loo—looking for other crimes in the medical center itself, but I'm not going to have computer results on all that 'til some time tomorrow. Alex probably knows more about those things than I do at this point.

"On the professional side, we've got all her colleagues lined up for interviews the rest of this week. Neurosurgery's a really small department—we'll get through most of them by the weekend. The short version we're getting is, she was no Mother Teresa but didn't seem to have any obvious enemies, either. A tough taskmaster, but she'd have to be—it's a specialty where a nanofraction of a millimeter is the difference between a patient's life and death.

"My other piece was checking for similar cases in major cities on the East Coast. Washington Metro had two docs shot and killed in parking lots leaving their offices, a month apart. Both males, both seemed to be robberies, looking for drugs and prescription pads. Bullets match. No suspects. One of Philly's private hospitals had a patient—get this, a quadriplegic—raped by a junkie who broke in during the night to steal hypodermic needles, but he was caught by a nurse on rounds before he dismounted. The Boston cops didn't know of anything, but I expect a call back in a day or two. That's all I've got for you, Chief."

McGraw grunted and Peterson nodded to Chapman to move to the easel. Mercer joined me at the table while Mike rose to speak.

He picked up the black marker that hung on a string from the top of the sketch pad, humming the theme music from the *Twilight Zone* TV show and launching into his best imitation of Rod Serling. "Good evening. You are about to enter a new dimension, Chief McGraw—a place where the sick and tired come for balm, the wounded to be made whole, the lame to walk again. What do we find instead? The Mid-Manhattan Zone." Serling became Chapman again. "A space invaded by every frigging lunatic who's been let go from Bellevue and Creedmoor and Manhattan State and all the other psych wards you could think of, living in the hallways and bathrooms and basements of this hospital like they're paying guests at the Pierre."

Wallace whispered to me, "He's got the Chief's attention now, Cooper. Hold on to your seat."

McGraw shifted his focus onto Mike and lit up another Camel.

"Sorry, Chief, but it's really a disgrace. By the time we get done with this case, none of us is ever gonna close our eyes in a hospital again. The place is the size of a small city, without a single real cop in its borders, and it's a frigging security nightmare of the first frigging order."

"All right, Mike," Peterson interrupted. "Clean it up." I knew he hated it when his guys cursed in front of women.

"Don't worry about Cooper, Loo. Her friends from Wellesley tell me she spent junior year abroad—at the Marine training camp on Parris Island. Don't blush for their benefit, Blondie—you got a bad mouth."

No point even protesting. Truth, as they tell us in law school, is an absolute defense. Chapman was clowning like Charlie Brown, and the Coasters were right—some day he'd get caught.

"Okay, back to the crime scene. Like the lieutenant suggested, I spent a couple of hours touring the place with the director of the hospital, William Dietrich. Every one of us in this room has been to that complex, every one of us in this room has visited a patient or had an appointment or interviewed a witness in one of those buildings. I'm telling you I saw things there today that would scare the living daylights out of you and make you long for the days when doctors made house calls.

"Let's start with the setup. You all know the basics of this sketch. The main entrance on Forty-eighth Street is the easiest access to Mid-Manhattan. That's eight sets of double doors right off the street, into the so-called private part of the hospital. It's a state-of-the-art facility that holds one thousand five hundred and sixty-four beds stretching up over twenty-six flights. I can give you a breakdown of all the floors into medical and surgical departments when you're ready for that kind of detail. That entrance hall is a bit smaller than the main lobby at Penn Station, and about as attractively populated."

"What kind of security, Mike?" the lieutenant asked.

"Security? That's really using the term loosely, boss. Square badges. You might as well have my mother sitting at the information desk handing out passes while she watches her soaps. We're talking unlicensed, untrained, and unqualified for any kind of serious caretaking."

He went on. "There aren't very many of them, either, considering the volume of the traffic passing in and out every day and night. And most of them, when you watch like I did today, stop the old ladies and benign-looking visitors they can safely harass, and let the ones who look like they would cause trouble walk on through without a challenge.

"That's just the front. There are doors to the street on every side of the main building. They're only supposed to be used as exits, so they're locked from the outside. But if you happen to be standing nearby when someone walks out, you can just help yourself right inside and there's no one there to stop you. Then there's another bank of doors off the rear, facing the parking area. It's designed to be just for employees, but there's not much to get in the way of any passerby who saw an opening and took it."

McGraw pushed Chapman along. "What about the medical college, where she was killed?"

"Minuit Medical College, built in 1956 and endowed by the heirs of Peter Minuit, director general of New Netherlands and the man who stole Manhattan from the Indians for twenty-four bucks." Chapman started drawing arrows from the main building to the sketch of the modern tower that housed the medical school.

"A masterpiece of modern architecture, Chief, and not only is it connected to Mid-Manhattan by a number of hallways and elevators on every floor but also, unbeknownst to me before today, by the series of underground tunnels built in the days when your cronies thought that bomb shelters would save us all in a nuclear disaster. The medical school is a child of the fifties—it was supposed to be a central headquarters in case of an atomic bomb blast in the city—and there's underpasses and mole holes that could probably stretch to China if you laid 'em end to end."

"What's in them?" Peterson queried Mike.

"Wrong, Loo. Who's in them, not what. You see those skels out in the pens in the squad room? Those tunnels and rattraps are lived in by hundreds of homeless people. We walked through there this morning—you got sad old men just curled up along the wall asleep, you got junkies with crack vials littered all over the place, you got a girls' dorm with bag ladies who are dressed like they used to be Rockettes sitting around talking to themselves. In one stretch of roadway, I saw three guys I locked up in '94 during a drug sweep and I think the old fat man wearing a silver lamé jumpsuit who was urinating in a corner when we walked by might actually have been Elvis—I'm not sure."

"Chapman," the Chief asked, "any sign they get up into the hospital buildings?"

"Every sign. Half of them are dressed in doctor's scrubs or lab coats—obviously stolen from the floors. They've got trays with remains of patient's meals and empty bottles of prescription pills. They use bed pans for pillows and rubber gloves for warmth. I wasn't kidding, you open your eyes at night, in that private room your insurance company is dishing out a thousand dollars for, and you gotta see most of these creatures roaming around the hallways. It would either cure you or kill you, no question about it."

Mike flipped the chart to the next sheet, bringing his marker from the top corner to the middle of the page.

"And don't forget the third piece of this puzzle, guys. We haven't yet mentioned the friendly folks at Stuyvesant Psychiatric Center, located just to the south of Mid-Manhattan and, of course, you guessed it—linked to both other buildings on every level above ground and below."

Wallace whispered to me again, trying to suppress a smile. "He's about to do Nicholson now—he's going into the *Cuckoo's Nest* mode. McGraw'll go bat-shit."

Mike was off and running with his next imitation, leading us on his morning tour through all nine hundred and forty-six beds in the psych hospital. He described the patients and their varying degrees of confinement, from the locked wards that held the prisoners declared incompetent while awaiting trial, through the straitjacketed screamers, to the quiet malingerers and psychotic lifers who, by virtue of their familiarity and long-term residence, had more freedom to walk around most of the day.

Peterson tried to make him be serious again. "Don't tell me these patients aren't supervised?"

"The most severely ill certainly are, but there are some regulars who seem to have the run of the place."

"Meaning in and out of the building, into the rest of the Center?"

"Nothing to stop them, loo. Just put on their slippers and shuffle off down the hall."

"Past the square badges?"

"Loo, I'm telling you, if one of them walked up to the security guards I talked to today and said, 'Hi, my name is Jeffrey Dahmer and I'm hungry,' these morons would give him a pass and direct him to the adolescent clinic."

McGraw was incredulous. "Jesus, this place was a felony waiting to happen. It's amazing this is the first."

"Not so fast, Chief. Cooper's got a few surprises for you, just to open the field a little wider. If you don't think *I* have enough suspects to keep us busy, Nurse Ratchett'll give you something else to worry about. I think we've got our best shot of finding our killer among the walking wounded of the underground, but Alex has a few stories that suggest we keep our options open."

6

"You know how I hate to start off by agreeing with Chapman, but most days it really does look like the inmates are running the asylum," I commented as I turned to my padful of case notes, "and with a good number of problems contributed by some of the staff, too."

"Chief," Peterson said by way of explanation to McGraw, who was not used to prosecutors playing a role in a police briefing, "I asked Alex to round up all the sexual assault cases she's had in any of our hospitals during the last couple of years. My guys wouldn't know about anything that wasn't a homicide, so I thought it might be useful 'cause of the way Dogen got it in this case."

"Sarah and I pulled everything we could think of, but it's just a sampling. Any of your loved ones thinking about elective surgery in the near future, try the Animal Medical Center or a visiting nurse service—these big hospitals could kill you. I'll start close to home.

"Here at Mid-Manhattan we've got a few open investigations. The 17th Squad just locked up a janitor who's only worked in the place for three months. He likes to slip into a white lab coat, look for rooms with women patients who don't speak English—they don't seem to question his presence, probably because they can't. The women assume he's a doctor, so when he pulls back the covers and starts to do a vaginal exam they submit to it. His name's Arthur Chelenko— arrested and fired two weeks ago. Only then did Personnel get a record check. He was fired from Bronx Samaritan last year for doing exactly the same thing. Just lied on his résumé—no one checked it out—and he's back here in business again."

"In jail?"

"No. He made bail—he's out pending indictment and trial."

McCabe, Losenti, and Ramirez—the three detectives who'd get stuck with doing the legwork—were taking down all the information and I passed them copies of Chelenko's rap sheet, with his address and pedigree information.

"Any history of violence?" Wallace asked.

"Not according to his sheet. But, of course, we've got to factor in the grudge motive, or the possibility of a frenzied response if his intention was a sexual assault and Dogen struggled with him.

"Then there's Roger Mistral. Anesthesiologist. Got a heads up from the D.A.'s office in Bergen County, New Jersey, when they heard about the murder on the morning news. They convicted Dr. Mistral of rape last month—found him in an empty operating room having intercourse with a patient he'd resedated with a horse tranquilizer after she came out of surgery for a foot injury."

"What does that have to do with Mid-Manhattan?"

"Maybe nothing. We're checking his records, too, though. Would you believe that the state licensing people here in New York, the Office of Professional Discipline, issued a ruling right after the jury verdict that his conviction won't be final until he's sentenced in May? Well, they did. So he's still allowed to be doing per diem work anywhere on this side of the Hudson River for another six weeks."

McGraw asked if we knew his whereabouts for the past forty-eight hours. "Can he account for his time since Monday night, when Dogen was back in town?"

"Nobody's talked to him yet," I ventured in response. "His wife kicked him out after the Jersey trial so we don't have a current address on him. Rumor has it that he sleeps on an examining table in one of the X-ray rooms in whatever hospital he's spending his time in 'cause he's too cheap to spring for a hotel. Somebody from the team will have to talk to him when he shows up for duty tomorrow. We're checking all the local staff."

"Talk to him?" Chapman broke in. "I'd like to beat the crap out of him. The only difference between what he did to an anesthetized patient and necrophilia is that the body was still warm. What the hell is that kind of thing all about?"

"Come to my lecture for the Lenox Hill Debs tomorrow night, I'll try to explain it. Now, Sarah Brenner has an active one. She's got a complaint about an attending ob-gyn. He's a world-renowned fertility expert with an office on Fifth Avenue. He's got privileges at Mid-Manhattan, as well as three other East Side hospitals, so he's in and out of here all the time. No record—name's Lars Ericson. Victim claims he raped her when she came into town from New Hampshire last month."

"Has he been collared yet?"

"Not—"

McGraw barked at me. "What are you waiting for?"

"Well, Chief, the victim suffers from multiple personality

disorder—she's thirty or forty different women, depending on what day of the week you talk to her. It seems that two or three of her personalities wanted to have sex with Dr. Ericson, but at least one of the others didn't want to consent. Sarah's trying to figure out which one made the complaint."

Wallace passed behind me to grab a soda out of the refrigerator, whispering as he bent over, "Welcome to the wacky world of sex crimes. This should be an eye-opener for the Chief."

McGraw wasn't amused.

"Then we have our stalker: Mohammed Melin. Remember De Niro in *Taxi Driver*? Well, this guy makes him look easy. Melin drives a yellow. Owns a medallion. Seems he had some kind of prostate infection, so he showed up in the emergency room here late one night. A young resident treated him—she's a very good doctor, and she's lovely as well. Examined him, prescribed some medication, and simply rubbed a little salve onto his penis—fifteen minutes of tender loving care and she hasn't been able to get rid of him ever since that encounter."

"Actually, Chief, that's how it started with Coop and me," Chapman interjected. "One stroke and I've been following her like a slave for ten years. Love really *is* a many-splendored thing."

I ignored him and went on with my litany. "Now Mohammed waits outside the hospital in his cab whenever he's in the area. Elena Kingsland—she's the doctor—finishes a shift, walks out of the hospital exhausted in the middle of the night. She steps off the curb to hail a cab and there's Mohammed. No charges against him yet, if you can imagine it—just sitting in his taxi on a public street, not doing anything to anybody according to the Penal Law. Twice he's been caught in the hospital, roaming around trying to find Kingsland at 3 or 4 A.M. Those arrests for trespass have been misdemeanors, so he's been walked in and out of the system both times. We've been trying to work him up for something more serious. Finally found a welfare fraud and we now have a warrant for his arrest on that case, but he hasn't been around in at least three weeks."

That was all I had on the list for Mid-Manhattan Hospital. Wallace watched me put down the first pad and reach for the next one in the pile, where I had gone on to note incidents in other facilities.

"Hey, Alex, don't forget that one I'm sitting on in Stuyvesant. We'll have an answer on that in a few weeks."

"Tell them about it, Mercer. I didn't even include it in the roundup. Sorry, my fault."

"There's a twenty-six-year-old woman in the psych wing. She was emotionally disturbed as a teenager. Tried to kill herself with an overdose when she was seventeen. Been in a coma ever since. Almost ten years and the most she can do is move her eyelids from time to time. They've had her on life support, in long-term care, at Stuyvesant for all that time."

I remember being struck by the horror of that story four months ago when Mercer first came to me with the case. It still hurt to hear him describe the unthinkable.

"Well, she's about four weeks away from giving birth. The fact that she hasn't been conscious for a decade didn't stop somebody from climbing on top of her bones and raping her. The security's real tight on her wing, so if it's not her old man— her parents and sisters are her only visitors after all these years—it's obviously some sick bastard who works there."

McGraw and the others who had not known about the case were shaking their heads in amazement.

"Suspects?" Lieutenant Peterson asked.

"Everyone from the broom pushers who swab her cubicle to the head shrink on the service," Mercer responded.

"Cooper got us a court order so we could draw blood and do DNA on the fetus. Then we'll be getting the same thing from every one of the guys who had access to her. We'll nail him."

I continued on my institutional odyssey around Manhattan in which not a single private nor public hospital seemed to have been spared the indignity of some kind of sexual assault on the premises within the past three years. Occasionally, the assailants were health-care professionals themselves; frequently, they were technical workers who were assigned to the departments essential to the operation of these little villages—maintenance, food services, janitorial staff, aides, and messengers. Sometimes they were patients, free to move about from one area of the hospital to almost any other, and often they were interlopers who wandered into these enormous structures with no business being inside at all.

"Obviously, we've got to look at everybody—from the professional staff to the underground population." I had already learned the hard way that it was better to cast a very wide net at the start of an investigation in order not to overlook any potential suspects.

By the time we had gone around the room and each of the detectives had described his actions for the day, it was close to ten o'clock. McGraw told Wallace to turn up the volume on the television and switch it to Fox 5 News to catch the headline stories. One of the guys who had retired from the squad was now covering the crime beat for the station, and from the posture of attention McGraw suddenly assumed it was obvious he had leaked something to his former protégé in order to get his face on the tube.

Mike shook his head and suppressed a snide remark as all our business stopped so McGraw could admire himself on the screen, telling the public that his detectives had a lot of great leads and expected to have someone in custody by the weekend. The guys in the room didn't appear to be surprised by his phony optimism, just annoyed. The moment the camera lens shifted to the Mayor's face, McGraw rejoined our group.

"Who's got the autopsy?"

"The Chief's doing it himself in the morning," Chapman answered. "I'm observing."

Good news for me. I had enormous respect for the Chief Medical Examiner, Chet Kirschner, and an easy relationship with him. I was likely to have preliminary results of the procedure by tomorrow afternoon.

"Motives," McGraw went on. "Who's thinkin' what?"

"Could be a straight-out sexual assault," Jerry McCabe offered. "Pick from any one of your categories of guys walking around these empty halls at night. Late Monday, around midnight, say, he comes across a woman alone in her office. She's strong. Thinks she can fight him off. Can't overcome the knife. Bingo."

"Just as easy for it to be a burglary, and Dogen surprised *him* in the middle of it," countered Wallace. "Even though the wallet's still there, doesn't mean there isn't something missing and we're not yet aware of what it is."

Wallace was one of the most thorough detectives I had ever worked with. His methodical mind would be certain to go over every object in the doctor's office, looking for any paper, file, or book that had been moved or rifled through. He went on. "Maybe he was in there, starting to look for something to steal, when she showed up in the office. He panicked and what started as a robbery became a sexual assault."

"Yeah, but which came first, the rape or the stabbing?"

McGraw was too stubborn to throw that question directly at me and too stupid to know that I wouldn't be able to answer it, either. Most people liked to think that logically the forced sex act had occurred before Gemma Dogen's firm, trim body had been shredded into ribbons of bloodied skin. But there is no logic in this world of murderers and madmen. I had seen just as many cases in which the attacker had become aroused by the frenzied act of killing and then committed the sexual assault as an afterthought.

Chapman said, "Let's wait and see what Kirschner finds. We're all just guessing at this point."

McGraw was still looking for a motive. "Say it's not one of these lunatics, for the sake of argument. Keep your eyes open for somebody who had a reason to do this. When you talk to her colleagues, see who benefits from getting her out of the way. Who replaces her as head of the department. Get hold of her will and see who gets the money. Don't overlook the usual stuff here just 'cause it's in a hospital."

The men around the table were closing up their pads and getting ready to stand up for a stretch. They had heard what they had come in here for, and were ready to blow off McGraw in favor of food and a night's rest. Despite what he had said on the news about closing this case quickly, they knew the greater likelihood was that there were going to be endless round-the-clock shifts of interviews and interrogations for weeks to come unless or until one of them got very lucky.

I walked toward Lieutenant Peterson as I remembered to ask him about the eight men who had been in the holding pen when I entered the squad room. "What are they in here for, Loo?"

"Jeez, Alex, those are some of the guys we found living in the hospital corridors. This was just on the first sweep of the Mid-Manhattan building today. I'm not talking about the tunnels or the psych wing or the grounds. A couple of 'em were in empty patient rooms, and one was sleeping on a gurney in a hallway near a storage area. Ramirez'll have to tell you exactly where they were. He's got it all charted out. I got a couple of men talking to each one of 'em now."

"Are they sus—"

"I don't know if they're suspects, or witnesses, or simply poor old souls without a roof over their heads, so don't ask me. They were just somewhere they ain't supposed to be, living in a hospital, so now they're in the middle of a homicide investigation and I don't know what to do with them myself."

We were both thinking the same thing. Each one of them was a potential lead in our case and the moment we let them out the door of the precinct we were not likely to find them again. I was treading on sensitive territory. If they were being kept here, in a holding pen, then any questioning of the men by detectives would be viewed by the courts as custodial interrogation. The police conduct would be considered coercive. The judge eventually assigned would criticize the length of time each man had been detained without legal counsel and examine the conditions under which he had been confined.

It was obvious Peterson's team could not ignore these Mid-Manhattan freeloaders, but we had to think of the legal ramifications. And we had to do it now. The value of any information we got from these individuals would be compromised by the manner in which we obtained it.

I tried again. "What are you going to do with the men after they're interviewed?"

McGraw snapped at me as he picked up a telephone to dial out, almost inhaling his cigarette butt in his haste to open his mouth and respond. "They're our *guests*, Miss Cooper. Understand that? I've extended the hospitality of the precinct to them—for tonight and for as long as they want it. So before you write me up and snitch on me to your boss, take a good look around out there."

Peterson shrugged his shoulders as McGraw dropped the receiver and motioned for me to follow him to the archway that led into the main squad room. His booming voice continued to ring out. "The door to the pen is wide open. See it? These gentlemen are free to sleep on the bench or the floor.

We've been feeding them better than they've eaten in years. Haven't we, Scrubs?"

A grizzled old man with no hair and dried scabs all over his forearms looked up at McGraw from his perch on the edge of a detective's desk.

"That one's called Scrubs. Says he can't remember his real name. Had nowhere to go when he was discharged from Stuyvesant Psych four and a half years ago, so he just made the hospital his home. His shopping cart is down by the precinct garage, full of green uniforms and God knows what else. He steals—make that 'borrows'—surgical scrubs from the linen supply closets and sells them to other homeless guys without clothes.

"You hungry, Scrubs?"

"No, sir."

"Any of my boys feed you today?"

"Yessir, Mr. Chief. Had me two sweet rolls and a pastrami sandwich. And five Coca-Colas."

"Tell the lady what else you did today."

"Watched television. Right in that room where you is. Saw cartoons, saw wrestling, saw a picture of the lady doctor what got killed over at my place."

"You know her?"

"Never seen her 'cept on television."

"Where do you want to go tonight, Scrubs?"

I had the distinct feeling the poor old guy had been asked this question earlier in the day, before he was made to perform for me.

"Happy to stay right here with you, long as you'll keep me."

McGraw turned to eyeball me. "Tell *that* to Paul Battaglia, will ya? I don't want anybody thinking I'm rough riding over these nutjobs. I'm taking very good care of them until I know what we got here. Those are my orders."

I figured I'd better save the $64,000 question for Peterson.

As McGraw stormed away from me, I looked over at the lieutenant and quietly asked, "What if any of them told you he wanted to walk out of here tonight. Are they free to leave?"

Chapman brushed past me as one of the men handling the phones yelled out his name. "Let her take a couple of them back to her place for the night, Loo. She's got a real soft spot for the old guys, don't you, Coop? She won't cook for them, but I guarantee they'll be back here tomorrow with fine-looking new threads on, every one of them."

"You know I can't let any of 'em walk out the door, Alex. They obviously don't like to stay in shelters, and none has a single family contact to give us. We'll never see them again. We printed each guy—"

"You *what*?"

"Alex, they consented to it."

"This kind of 'consent' won't hold up for ten seconds when we get to court. You know better than that. Heaven forbid any one of these men has anything to do with Dogen's murder, we'll lose all the evidence you get out of this."

"Actually, on a couple of the name checks we ran in the computer there are outstanding warrants for at least three of them. Minor stuff—jumping the turnstile, petit larceny, criminal trespass. Nothing to suggest violence but just enough to let us keep them in our care until we take them down to the courthouse to arraign them on the charges."

More complications. "So do you know if they've got lawyers on the pending cases?"

"Easy, Alex. We didn't run the name checks 'til after we asked all the questions. I know you don't like the way we're running this aspect of it, but we really don't have any choice under the circumstances."

I wasn't going to resolve this tonight, but it would be first on my list to take up with Rod Squires in the morning. As Chief of the Trial Division, he had taken on McGraw more frequently, with more success, than any dozen of my colleagues combined.

I packed my notepads back into the Redweld, walked over and sat on the chair next to Mercer's desk while we both waited for Chapman to get off the phone.

"What do you feel like eating?" I asked, since I was picking up the dinner tab.

"I got a real craving for Chinese food tonight."

"Shun Lee Palace?"

"Attagirl, Cooper. That's the best."

Chapman replaced the receiver, said his goodnights, and joined us as we stood to walk out.

"Could be the break we need. That was a psychic who called in. She saw the story about Gemma Dogen on the early news and has been getting vibrations all evening. Told me that if I could give her a few more details, she might divine the killer's identity for us by morning.

"Don't screw up your puss at me like that, Blondie. How do you know it won't work?"

"What did you tell her?"

"I told her to join the three of us for dinner and we'd discuss it with her."

"Mike, I really don't feel like ending my night with—"

"Relax, Cooper, don't lose your sense of humor the first day. Where're we going? I didn't tell her the name of the restaurant and I didn't tell her what time we'd be there. I just told her that if she was a *real* psychic, she'd show up. C'mon, Mercer, let's get out of here."

7

The restaurant on Fifty-fifth Street was nearly empty when the three of us walked in at eleven o'clock. Patrick Chu bowed his head in greeting and led us back past the bar and single row of tables to the large dining room area. Deep cobalt blue walls, hung with shadowboxes framing porcelain antique plates and scent bottles, created an atmosphere of luxe and style uncommon in Manhattan's Chinese eateries.

"Good to see you, Madame Prosecutor," Patrick said, smiling as he handed us each a menu.

"That's better than last time," Chapman remarked to Wallace. "Coop and I came in here a few weeks after the end of the Lascar case, when her face had been plastered all over the papers. I hear Patrick, the maître d', telling the owner that the 'famous prostitute' had just come in."

"My English much better now, Mister Mike. Never make that mistake again."

"Lucky you survived it once, Patrick. Prostitute—prosecutor—no big deal in my book. I don't know which one ought to be more insulted by the mix-up."

We ordered our drinks and told Patrick the menus weren't necessary. "Hot-and-sour soup, spring rolls, shrimp dumplings. A Peking duck, and a crispy sea bass," said Chapman without missing a beat. "If I'm still hungry after that, we'll add to that. Did I miss anything?"

"I don't know about you, Alex, but I guess that's what I wanted for dinner," Mercer said with a wink. "What's the plan, Mike?"

"I'll be at the morgue first thing in the morning. Why don't you pick Alex up at her office and bring her there around lunchtime? I'm sure Kirschner will go over his results with us then. I'm helping with the hospital personnel interviews in the afternoon, and maybe that's a good time for you two to check out Dogen's apartment."

I raised my idea of setting Maureen up to go in undercover as a patient. Both Chapman and Wallace jumped on it, but we all agreed that once we cleared it with Peterson it would be foolish to let anyone on the Mid-Manhattan staff know about our mole.

Maureen Forester and I had worked on dozens of cases together. She was the daughter of one of the NYPD's first black detectives, and her petite frame and pretty face belied the strength, speed, and tough spirit that made her such a fine cop. Battaglia had petitioned the Chief of Detectives four years ago to move her to his own unit—the District Attorney's Office squad—so that she could work with us on sensitive investigations. Frequently, I was the beneficiary of her talent, and always of her loyal friendship.

"How will we get her in?" Wallace asked.

"David Mitchell." My close friend and neighbor was one of the most prominent psychiatrists in the city. "I'll call him in the morning. Migraines, double vision, memory lapses—he's got the weight to get her in for a neurological observation the same day he asks for it."

"Does Mo know yet?"

"I thought you'd call her, Mercer. I can't imagine she'd ever object. Probably be thrilled to get away from the kids for a week and have some room service and breakfast in bed. Her husband will take it better coming from you than from me, don't you think?"

"Consider it done. You know that none of us'll be able to visit with her, don't you? We've all been made as investigators on this one."

"Of course. And if Charles doesn't like the idea, we'll get a detective to be her designated spouse and some friends like Sarah to hang out with her for a while. I think we should wire her up and install a hidden camera in the room just so someone from the tech unit can monitor it while she's sleeping. There's too many things creeping around there at night to leave her unobserved."

The dank and chilly March evening, combined with my fatigue, made it a perfect soup night. I sprinkled some noodles over the steaming bowl that the waiter sat in front of me and told him to follow my Dewar's with a Tsingtao. The warmth of the thick broth soothed me even as its piquant taste revived me.

I spaced out of the conversation going on between the two detectives. Who in the world would be missing Gemma Dogen tonight, I wondered? I reminded myself of my own good fortune in the friends and family relationships I was able to count on to sustain me through the emotional intensity of my work. And I raised my glass in a silent toast to Mike and Mercer, who had become as close to me as any of my lifelong companions.

I had met Mike Chapman almost ten years earlier, in my rookie stint as a prosecutor in Paul Battaglia's office. My background of privilege and comfort had secured me a first-rate education at Wellesley College and the University of Virginia School of Law. But my parents had instilled in me as well a devotion to public service, which had attracted me to my job as an assistant district attorney. Serendipity—and Paul Battaglia's unerring instincts—landed me in the newly created specialty of sex crimes prosecutions after my initial rotation through the Trial Division, in which general felony cases were investigated. The satisfaction of this work, the rich rewards of guiding victims through the process with better results than the criminal justice system had ever been able to offer, kept me in the office years longer than I had planned to stay.

Chapman's background was a sharp contrast to mine. His father was a second-generation Irish immigrant who had met his wife on a visit to the family birthplace in Cork and brought her back to the States. Brian Chapman had been a cop in the NYPD for twenty-six years and dropped dead from a massive coronary two days after he turned in his shield and gun. Mike and his three older sisters had been raised in Yorkville, a working-class neighborhood in Manhattan still known more for its corner pubs and German butchers than for the chic restaurants and Korean nail salons of the Lenox Hill area that bordered it to the south.

Mike was in his junior year at Fordham, courtesy of student loans he had taken out to supplement his jobs waiting tables, when his father died. He completed his degree and went right to the Police Academy, unabashedly following in the footsteps of the man he had idolized. Brian Chapman had spent his entire career in uniform, walking a beat in Spanish Harlem where he had known every shopkeeper, schoolchild, and gang member by name, face, and alias. Mike had distinguished himself as a rookie cop with arrests in a drug-related massacre of a Colombian family in Washington Heights on Christmas Day of his first year on the job. He broke the case using informants his father had developed on the street and was pulled out of line for an early promotion eight months later after rescuing a pregnant teenager who had jumped into the rough water from the shoreline beneath the George Washington Bridge.

Mike, at thirty-five, seemed hopelessly single, living in a tiny fifth-floor walk-up studio apartment he called "the coffin." He and Mercer Wallace had worked together in the Homicide Squad, before Wallace transferred to Special Victims, where he was the lead man on most of the serious rape investigations in Manhattan.

Mercer, now thirty-nine, was almost five years older than I. His mother had died in childbirth and he was raised by his father in a middle-class neighborhood in Queens. Spencer Wallace worked as a mechanic for Delta at La Guardia Airport and liked to remind his son that it nearly broke his heart when Mercer turned down a football scholarship to the University of Michigan in order to become a cop.

In whatever command or precinct he had worked, Mercer Wallace was known for his meticulous and detailed approach to investigations. His brief marriage to a woman who had owned a small clothing business in his old neighborhood ended in divorce. He claimed she never understood nor believed the demands of his job, which kept him away from home such erratic hours of the day and night. A second marriage to a detective he had worked with at headquarters ended just as unsuccessfully for reasons she never articulated to him.

And this big, sweet guy was always looking for someone to give him his distance, his freedom, but also his three squares a day.

My parents were both alive, enjoying good health and a comfortable retirement on an island in the Caribbean. It was strange for me to enter this world of a medical center as crime scene because I had always been so at ease among healers in white lab coats and medical professionals who saved lives.

Benjamin Cooper, my father, was a cardiologist who had invented a plastic valve that had revolutionized open-heart surgery. It was used in nearly every such operation in this country for more than fifteen years after he and his partner created it, and I was vividly aware of the lifestyle that little piece of pliable tubing made possible for me.

No aroma from any kitchen impressed itself upon me in my childhood as it does for so many children. My clearest olfactory memory is the strong odor of ether that permeated my father's handsome face and graceful hands from long days spent in the operating theater and was passed along to me when he bent down to kiss me goodnight after he came through the door late in the evening. It was before the use of sodium pentothal as an anesthetic, and I welcomed the unpleasant smell because it signaled the return home of my busy and adoring father.

Conversation at the dinner table, on those nights Ben made it home in time to eat with us, was always about medical subjects. My mother's nursing degree made her equally conversant in the field and my brothers and I were exposed to the day's surgical procedures throughout most of our meals. I had often accompanied my father to his office in the hospital on weekends and so was accustomed to the sights and smells, antiseptic and medicinal, of every wing of the medical center.

"Watch this guy move that machete," Mike urged.

I stopped daydreaming and rejoined Chapman and Wallace

in conversation, as the waiter hacked at the carcass of the duck with amazing speed and accuracy, wrapping and twisting the slivers of fowl in paper-thin pancakes stuffed with scallions and hoisin sauce.

"That's one I never had yet, Mercer, have you? I mean, I've had lots of killings by Latino machetes, but I've never had a Peking duck carver. This guy's like lightning." Mike was biting into his first serving before ours even hit the plate.

"What's new with your love life, Miss Cooper, anything I should know about?" Mercer asked.

"I think I've been waiting for the spring thaw."

"I'm giving her another few months before I sign her up with the Sisters of Charity. Don't you think she'd make a great nun, Mercer? All those little parochial school boys would remind you of me or McGraw, Blondie, and you could go around all day whacking 'em on the ass with rulers. Wouldn't have to moan about getting your roots done, and there'd be no feeling sorry for yourself when the phone doesn't ring on Saturday night. Oscar de la Renta could design a special habit for you, Mercer'd get Smokey Robinson to craft some tunes—"

"Stop laughing, Mercer. Don't humor him. Let's switch it to *your* love life, shall we? What's with you and Francine?"

Wallace had been dating one of my colleagues, Francine Johnson, who was assigned to the Special Narcotics Division of the office.

"It's still alive, Cooper, still alive. If I don't mess this one up, you can be a bridesmaid, okay?"

Mike was eager to divert the conversation away from the topic before it turned to his own social life. "What do you know about neurosurgery? We're going to need to find out exactly what Dogen's practice consisted of and what her duties were, so we know what we're looking for when these docs start to talk to us. Both in the hospital and in the medical school 'cause they're really two separate roles she had."

"Who are you scheduled to see after the autopsy?" I asked.

"William Dietrich, the director of the hospital who toured me around today, is setting up the first interviews. I've got most of what I need from him. Then I'll sit down with Spector, the guy who invited Gemma to assist in the surgery."

"Neurosurgeons really consider themselves the elite of the profession," I offered. "It's a prized specialty, brain surgery, and one of the highest-paying fields in medicine, too."

"After Spector, I got a couple of other professors lined up, and a mix of students and practitioners. Dietrich wants me to see the two guys who subbed for Dogen in the OR when she didn't show up. Whaddaya think, Coop, it's like 42nd Street, no? Ruby Keeler as the understudy who steps in for the star and makes it big on Broadway.

"This time—" he flipped open his steno pad to check the names on his list with his left hand, while his chopsticks kept working the sea bass with his right. "Yeah, it's a combination. A Paki and a WASP, the kind with two last names. The Paki—Banswar Desai—I know that guy is destined to wind up in my HIP program. I ought to tell him not to bust his ass working too hard in this classy joint. Every doctor on my list has a turban, I swear."

"When are you going to learn that it's really obnoxious to talk that way?" Mike's ethnic slurs were a constant irritant in our conversations.

"Easy, Coop. I'm an equal opportunity offender. The other guy is Coleman Harper—don't you hate those fancy names? I've probably insulted him already—he's undoubtedly a third or a fourth or a fifth, named after granddad's maternal great-grandmother."

"My favorite's that orthopedic surgeon who had the office next to Dogen," said Mercer, "the young guy with the slicked-back hair and the phoniest grin I've ever seen. Bonded teeth, of course. D'you see him? I swear he thinks he's Ben Casey. I think the only thing he's worried about is whether they can get the bloodstains out of Dogen's office so he can move into it. It's one doorway closer to the dean's office, and he's awfully keen on moving up."

I was full, long before the fish arrived and fading quickly. Patrick had taken the imprint from my American Express card. I told him to give the guys whatever they wanted and add on twenty percent for service.

"I'll see both of you tomorrow," I said, pushing away from the table.

"Don't you want a nightcap?"

"No, thanks. I'm ready to fold."

"Can't leave without a fortune cookie. Hey, Patrick, give Miss Cooper a good one, will you?"

"Only have good fortunes at Shun Lee, Mr. Mike. No bad news."

I ripped off the cellophane wrapper, split the crisp cookie in half, and pulled out the small white strip to learn my fate. "Thanks, Mike, I needed this news: 'Things will get much worse before they get better. Be patient.'" Not my long suit.

"Want me to walk you out?" Mercer asked.

"I'm fine. I'm parked right in front, and I'll go directly home, into the garage."

"I'll see you in your office by noon. *Ciao.*"

I told the night attendant I wouldn't need my car the next morning, unbolted the door leading into the apartment building from the garage, and climbed the stairs to the lobby. One of the doormen handed me my dry cleaning and the stack of mail, which contained too many magazines to fit in the box. I shifted the Redweld to support the pile of paper, tried to hold the hangers in my left hand so they didn't pinch my fingers in their heavy load, and pressed the twentieth floor. As I opened the two locks and pushed the door in, I spotted a sheet of David Mitchell's note paper on the floor of my entryway.

When I had unloaded the bundles, I picked up the missive and read it: "Going to Bermuda for the weekend to escape the weather. Can you look after Prozac or shall I use the kennel? I'll call your office in the morning. David."

That's an easy deal. I'll babysit his affectionate weimaraner, Zac, while he's off—with his latest squeeze, no doubt—relaxing and catching some rays on the beach. In exchange I can ask him to find a hospital bed at Mid-Manhattan for the newly ailing Maureen Forester.

I stepped out of my shoes in the living room as I scanned the mail. Fashion, decorating, and garden journals were the weightiest of the bunch, as spring approached; four mailorder catalogues filled with schlocky gadgets and gimmicks, destined for immediate dumping in the garbage pail; bills from all kinds of local merchants and take-out places, which I set aside on the credenza; and I carried Nina's postcard into the bedroom with me while I shimmied out of my panty hose and threw them in the hamper.

As I read about her weekend in Malibu, written on a card with a Winslow Homer seascape, I longed for a heart-to-heart talk with my closest friend. We had been roommates in college, and although separated by three time zones and two hectic lives, we tried to keep in contact by daily messages and mailings of the art postcards we both collected. We filled them with running commentaries of our thoughts and experiences. There were years when she complained, in mock earnest, that my life was so much more interesting than hers. We had penned lively descriptions of our beaus and our romances, and she had eased me through the months of mourning when my fiancé had been killed in a freakish car accident the year I graduated from law school.

Lately, the news of her weekends with Jerry and their son

at the beach house, coupled with her high-powered legal job at Virgo Studios, had made my winter seem even duller and lonelier than it was. But tonight, back in the center of the excitement of a breaking case, I was anxious for Nina to know that all was well.

I stripped and hung up my suit as I played back the three messages on the machine. First was my father from his home on St. Bart's. An old partner had phoned to tell him about the tragedy at Mid-Manhattan and he was offering his assistance if I needed it. Next was Nina responding to my rush-hour call and asking me for all the details of the case. Last was Joan Stafford reminding me that I was expected at her dinner party at eight o'clock Saturday evening— "No far-fetched excuses like murder, if you don't mind."

I tried to relax and escape from the day's gloom by picking up the copy of Trollope that was next to my bed. I had started *The Eustace Diamonds* over the weekend and knew it would take only ten or twelve pages of tasteful nineteenth-century crime to cause my lids to droop and convince me to turn out the lights.

I thought I had pushed all consciousness of Gemma Dogen out of my weary brain but I couldn't stop myself from thinking about whether her death was keeping anyone else awake tonight—out of a need for mourning, out of a sense of loss, or out of guilt.

8

Don Imus may not be everyone's idea of a wake-up call but he worked like a charm on me.

The alarm went off at seven and the radio came on automatically. Imus was doing the news and led with the story of Mid-Manhattan, referencing everything from the murder to the teeming underground life in the medical center's bowels. "Sounds like the Bates Motel has nothing on *this* joint," he said, launching into his imitation of one of the Stuyvesant Psych patients giving a tour of the place. I hated to turn off the radio and walk out the door when I finished dressing, fearful that he and his crew, who had carried more insightful daily commentary on the Simpson trial than the entire national news corps, would divine the killer's identity before the cops did.

I wrapped myself in my black shearling coat and prepared

for the brisk, thirteen-degree temperature as I walked from the building to Third Avenue to hail a cab to the office. The driver knew the route to the Criminal Courts Building in Lower Manhattan, so I sat back and looked over the headlines in the *Times*.

Gemma Dogen's death had claimed her a front-page position, not the usual Metro section. Some of that might be attributed to her prestige, but more had to do with the geographic location of the brutal act. *Times* readers were generally at a fair remove, physically and emotionally, from the housing projects and street gang turf that were so often killing grounds, the expected backdrop for violence and homicide. But knock off somebody in a milieu that "we" frequent—a major city hospital, Central Park, or the Metropolitan Opera House—and the death always took on a different dimension. Page one, above the fold.

I read the story carefully to see how accurately the facts had been reported and whether anyone from within the NYPD had leaked information. So far the plugs were still in place and no one had made the mistake of naming likely suspects, including our eight precinct "guests," nor of pointing a finger prematurely.

By the time I read the editorials, the book review, and the Thursday Living Section feature on an upcoming auction of antique samplers, my taciturn driver had pulled in front of 100 Centre Street and opened the plastic safety partition to collect his fourteen dollars and thirty cents.

"The usual?" my guy at the coffee cart asked as I approached.

"Make it a double, please. Two black coffees, large."

Most of the support staff would clock in after nine, but a dribbling of young lawyers and paralegals were making their way toward the building from a variety of directions as different subway and bus routes let them out on streets all over the courthouse area.

Johanna Epstein followed me onto the elevator. She hadn't been in my unit very long but was aggressively picking up cases and preparing them for trial. "Do you have time to go over an indictment with me today? The case I picked up last weekend, do you remember the facts?"

"The burglary on East Ninth Street—your girl's a crackhead?"

"That's the one."

"Go in to the jury okay?" The woman's apartment had been broken into by another junkie who knew that his victim might be reluctant to deal with the police because of her own substance abuse. She had surprised him, and surprised Johanna, with her candor and her cooperation. Yesterday, she had been scheduled to testify before the grand jury in our effort to obtain an indictment.

"Yeah, she was fine. I just have a few questions about how many counts of rape to charge. I mean, he kept assaulting her, then he'd get up and walk into the kitchen to get a beer, then he'd come back and go at her again. Are those all separate crimes or is it just one 'rape'?"

"Bring up your paperwork around eleven. I'll look it over and listen to the facts more carefully so we can make a decision. It's pointless to overcharge him, but if there are distinct sexual acts, punctuated by other events, you'll definitely have some multiple counts."

She got off the elevator on six as I continued up to the eighth floor, where my office had been since I took over the Sex Crimes Prosecution Unit. It was across the main hallway from Battaglia's suite and on the corridor with other executives of the Trial Division who supervised the thousands of street crime cases police officers brought to our doorstep every single day and night of the year.

I turned on the light in my secretary's cubicle, the anteroom to my office, and unlocked my door. My space was neater than usual as I glanced around, which pleased me. I knew how cluttered it would soon become with the reams of paperwork, police reports, diagrams, notes, and news clips that were the staples of a major investigation. I liked to start out with a spot of visible green blotter under the piles of case reports so that I didn't lose control of any matter that required action or attention.

My first call was to David Mitchell's office.

He had read the morning papers and knew that I was assigned to the Mid-Manhattan case. "I would never have left the note about Zac last night if I had known you would be this busy. I'm sorry to have bothered you."

"Are you kidding? It will be a pleasure to have her to come home to, David. Plus, she may even coax me out for a jog over the weekend. You know I like her company. If I'm not home when you leave, just let her in with your key."

"Great. I'll walk her tomorrow morning, then take her back to your place."

"Have time for a favor before you go?"

"Always. What do you need?"

I outlined what was going on in the medical center and explained that we wanted Maureen to be inside as an observer—unknown to administration or staff.

"Shouldn't be too much of a problem as long as they have available beds. And as long as you'll back me when the AMA tries to lift my license for—"

"No problem. The Police Commissioner has to approve the whole thing, so you'll be acting at his direction once we tell him about it. And I know there are beds. Two of the homeless guys were sleeping in private rooms the past four days. For a change, no complaints about the food, either."

"Okay, here's what I suggest. Have Maureen call me so we can discuss some of her symptoms. Then I'll call a neurologist I've done some work—"

"No, David. Dogen was a neurosurgeon. We want Mo on the neurosurgical floor."

"Don't worry, it *is* the same floor at Mid-Manhattan. The first referral would be quite naturally to a neurologist."

"I don't know the difference. Why don't you start with that?"

"Of course. Neurologists are the physicians who study and treat the structure and diseases of the nervous system. A neurosurgeon wouldn't be involved at this stage unless you're ready to wheel Maureen into the operating room."

"Do they work with each other, the neurologists and neurosurgeons?"

"Yes, but the neurologists can't perform operations, they can't do the surgery themselves."

"Dogen did mostly brain surgery."

"So I see from her obituary. Remember, Alex, that the brain, the spine, and even the eye are part of the central nervous system. That's why there's so much overlap among some of these specialties—psychiatry, ophthalmology, and orthopedics. We'll give Mrs. Forester enough pains, tics, and twitches to keep the whole crew looking her over until I get back to town on Monday. Will that help?"

"Thanks, David. Mercer's calling to get Mo on board and I'll connect her to you as soon as she agrees.

"So now that I'm done with business may I ask who's your traveling companion?"

"I'll introduce you when we get back. Renee Simmons— she's a sex therapist. I think you'll really like her."

I had the feeling that our Sunday evening *60 Minutes* viewing session and cocktail hour was about to expand to a threesome. "Was she the slim brunette with the perfect smile and great legs who was waiting for you at the bar at Lumi last Tuesday?" I had been on my way out the door of one of my favorite Italian restaurants one night last week when David had whipped past me on his way to claim a late reservation.

"That's the one. Between her business and yours, you can probably mop up a few of the dysfunctionals around town."

"I look forward to it. I'm sure I'll speak with you again before the end of the day."

By the time I hung up the phone and threw out the empty coffee cups, Marisa Bourgis and Catherine Dashfer had walked into the office. Both were longtime members of the unit as well as my pals. Like Sarah, they were a few years younger than I. Each was married and the mother of a toddler, and all three balanced their personal and professional lives with admirable form and boundless reserves of humor.

"So much for our plans for lunch at Forlini's today," Marisa said, pointing to the headline in the paper on top of my desk.

"It may be the only virtue of a high-profile case, but it's a big one. Immediate weight loss, guaranteed." Meals on the fly, liquid diets of coffee and soda, rattled nerves, and more running around than anybody needs in a day—stretching into weeks or months. "Perhaps a mental health shopping day at the end of all this, ladies, when I am hoping to be back to my law school size six. Takers?"

"That's a deal. Need help with anything in the meantime? Marisa and I can help Sarah with your overflow while you get started on the murder."

"Great offer. I'll go through my book this morning. There may be a couple of interviews you could do for me next week. Of course, if we don't pick up any leads by the time the weekend is over, it'll all be in the hands of the task force, not mine."

Laura Wilkie, my secretary of many years, peered into the room, said good morning, and told us that Phil Weinberg needed to see me before he went up to court. Urgent.

Marisa, Catherine, and I exchanged smirks as Weinberg "the whiner," our alias for him, skulked into my office. Nothing was easy with Phil. Although he was a good lawyer and compassionate advocate, he needed more hand-holding to get through a trial than most victims ever did.

Phil was less than pleased to see that I had company. He knew we'd be talking about him the minute he left the room but he reluctantly told me the problem.

"You won't believe what happened with one of the jurors yesterday afternoon."

"Try me." There was no end to the curious stories my colleagues could tell about Manhattan veniremen and -women.

"I'm in the middle of the direct case in the Tuggs trial."

Sarah and I had spent the better part of Monday and Tuesday taking turns watching Phil in the courtroom. We did it at most proceedings with the junior members of the unit, so that we could give detailed critiques and advice about technique and style to improve the performance of these promising litigators.

I knew the facts of the case well. It was an acquaintance rape in which the victim had accepted an invitation to the defendant's home after meeting him at a party. The twenty-three-year-old photographer was a compelling witness on her own behalf, adamant about her nonsexual reasons for choosing to go to visit Ivan Tuggs.

But this category of case still remained inherently difficult to try, despite the fact that our unit had prosecuted hundreds of them within the last ten years. It wasn't the fault of the law but rather the general societal attitude about this kind of crime, which often made unenlightened jurors reluctant to take the issue seriously.

The basic problem faced by women who are raped by acquaintances is that the classic defense relies on painting them as either liars or lunatics. The crime never occurred and therefore the woman is fabricating the entire story. Or "something happened" between the two parties but she's just too weird to believe.

For the prosecutor, then, more than half of the battle is in the successful selection of a jury. Intelligent citizens, who are blessed with common sense and a lot of the liberal instincts acquired by daily exposure to urban social life, handle these matters pretty well. But unsophisticated women, who tend to be far more critical than men are of the conduct of other women, are usually better candidates for judging stranger rape cases than for assessing most dating situations. That had been my own experience too many times to count and I had tried to pass on that wisdom to my troops.

"You saw the jury, right, Alex?"

"Yes, why?"

"Well, what did you think?"

"More women than I like for this kind of case, but you told me that your panel was uneven."

"I swear, Alex, it was a sea of women in that jury pool. There was nothing I could do about it."

Stop whining, Phil. "What's the problem?"

"Everything was going fine 'til the end of the day. It was so cold in Part 82 that the jurors asked the judge to turn up the heat, just before the first cop on the scene took the stand. An hour later, it was so overheated that we were all sweating. Juror number three stood up, right in front of everybody, gave out a big ''scuse me,' and pulled off her sweatshirt.

"What's she got underneath? A T-shirt the size of a billboard, spread around her 44D chest, emblazoned with big fuchsia letters: FREE MIKE TYSON."

It was hard to stifle my laugh, but Marisa and Catherine were ahead of me.

"It's not funny, guys, really. Tyson was tried in, what, '91? That means this woman hasn't bought a lousy T-shirt in more than half a dozen years and had no choice but to wear this one, or else she sincerely believes in her cause. And if that's the case, I think we're screwed."

"What did the judge say?" Marisa asked.

"Well, nothing. We just kind of exchanged glances, but—"

"You mean you didn't ask her to examine the juror in chambers? Get your ass up there immediately, Phil. I heard the part of your voir dire when you questioned them about whether they believed the nature of the relationship between the parties made this a 'personal matter' and not a crime. You got all the right answers.

"You're in front of a really good judge for issues like these. Tell her you want a sidebar and that you'd like her to ask number three some questions before you get under way today."

"Don't you think *I* should be the one to ask them?"

"No way. We'll give them to you now, and you write them out for the judge. The last thing you want the juror to think is that *you're* singling her out to pick on her. If she survives this challenge and stays in the box, let her believe it was the judge who didn't like her taste in casual wear, not you. We don't want her taking it out on your case."

Catherine offered to go up and give Phil a hand with his application so I could get on with what I had to do.

Laura buzzed me on the intercom. "Mo just called while you were dealing with Phil. Count her in. She's already feeling achy and dizzy, just from talking to Mercer."

I picked up a legal pad, checked my watch, and told Laura that I was on my way to the grand jury rooms on the ninth floor to officially begin the investigation into Gemma Dogen's death. New York County seated eight grand juries a day to hear the scores of cases that required their decisions every month. Four of them convened at 10 A.M. No felony could proceed to trial in New York State without the action of the grand jury.

But before I even had to worry about how and when we would be able to identify a suspect to indict for the crime, I had a more pressing need to be before the twenty-three people who constituted the grand jury. It is only through their power that a prosecutor has the legal authority to issue subpoenas to request evidence in a criminal investigation. Although more than half of the states in this country have abolished the system in recent years, it remains very much in place in the State of New York. No D.A. here has the power to demand the production of documents or the presence of witnesses in his or her office. Police reports and pathologist's findings would be forwarded to me with a couple of phone calls. But medical records, telephone logs, security guard sign-in sheets, and the other paper links to potential evidence in a case like Dogen's all had to be obtained with the permission of the grand jury.

Most citizens' have no reason to know the purpose or function of this body, called "grand" to distinguish it from the "petit" jury of twelve that sits on criminal cases. Derived from British common-law practice, it was created to serve as a rein on prosecutors whose investigations were politically motivated or unjustified. And its rules are entirely different from those of the trial jury. It is a secret proceeding, to which no members of the public can gain admission; the defendant is entitled to testify, although he rarely does; the defense has no right to call witnesses; and those that the prosecution calls are not cross-examined. The duty of the grand jurors, after listening to the state's evidence, is to vote a true bill of indictment when enough evidence exists to warrant a trial.

The waiting room was full of assistant district attorneys and their witnesses. The former were mostly bright-eyed and eager, busily picking up their caseloads of human misery on the first step toward a preparation for trial. It is what young lawyers came to offices like Battaglia's to do, and they were generally happiest when juggling a lot of balls in the air at any one time. I watched them write out their charges in triplicate on forms that would be submitted by the warden to the member of each jury who had been designated to serve as the foreman. They stood shoulder to shoulder at an oversized counter in the front of the room as they worked against each other and the clock, to seek indictments on their cases.

Witnesses were a more somber accumulation—people who had been mugged or stabbed, relieved of their wallets or their cars, conned by strangers or kin, and who were anxious about both their victimization and their anticipated hours of frustration dealing with the court system.

Only two of my dozen colleagues scowled openly when I walked past them to the warden, who controlled the sequence of cases that were presented during the session. My presence in the waiting room, and my new assignment to a high-profile case, meant that I had come up to ask to be taken out of order and jumped over the line of grand larcenies and drug busts whose crews had been assembled for more than an hour.

"Relax, Gene. I'll only be a minute. No witnesses. I've just got to open the investigation so we can start serving some subpoenas. I won't hold you up."

"Debbie's got a five-year-old in her office down the hall. Father's girlfriend scalded her with boiling water when she wouldn't stop crying. She's really a mess—"

"That goes first, obviously. I'll just slip in after she's finished."

When the warden gave the signal that the jurors had a quorum, I phoned Debbie's extension and suggested she bring the child down to testify. The badly scarred kid, her hair missing and her skull scorched on the left side of her head, clutched the hand of the prosecutor as she walked the gauntlet of lawyers, cops, and civilians. They paused together at the heavy wooden doorway of the jury room as Debbie looked the child in the eye to reassure her and ask if she were ready.

An affirmative nod was the reply and the door opened for Debbie to lead her by hand to the witness chair in the front of the room. The court stenographer brought up the rear. I had done it hundreds of times over the last decade—with women,

men, adolescents, and children. I had seen the mouths of the twenty-three jurors drop open in gapes of horror, repelled by the damage one human being had inflicted on another. I recognized the traditional importance of the body and respected its power. But in addition, I understood how a manipulative district attorney could use the inherent imbalance of the process to his or her own end, so I also credited the more modern maxim that most prosecutors could indict a ham sandwich if they chose to do so.

The child was out after six minutes, having told her tale. Her father testified next, followed by the two police officers who had responded to the scene and made the arrest. A clean presentation—bare-bones, as we teach it—just the essential elements of the criminal act laid out by the assistant district attorney for the jurors. No need to try the case to them, as there is neither judge nor defense attorney nor defendant himself in attendance.

Debbie and the steno rejoined us in the waiting room so that the jurors could begin the process of deliberating and voting. The buzzer, which signaled their decision, rang within seconds. No one who saw the child doubted that a true bill had been returned—the defendant was indicted for attempted murder.

The warden waved me into the room. I walked to the front and placed my pad and Penal Law on the table provided.

"Good morning, ladies and gentlemen. My name is Alexandra Cooper. I'm an assistant district attorney and I'm here to open an investigation into the death of Gemma Dogen."

So far, no bells went off. I was facing the jurors, who were arrayed in amphitheatrical fashion opposite my position. Two rows of ten sat in a double-tiered semicircle, capped by three seats at the top from which the foreman, his assistant, and the secretary ran the proceedings. As usual, they were still holding newspapers in their laps and chewing on the bagels and muffins they had smuggled in past the posted signs that cautioned that no food was allowed.

"I am not going to present any evidence to you today, but I will be back throughout your term on the same matter. I'd like to give you a code name by which I will refer to the case whenever I appear before you. I think that will help you remember it since you'll be hearing so many different presentations. The code will be 'Mid-Manhattan Hospital.'"

Not as clever as some of our reminders but it had the virtue of clarity. Jurors began to sit up and look more attentive. Several whispered to their neighbors, obviously explaining that this must be the stabbing of that woman doctor they had heard about on the news and read in their papers. Brown bags with breakfast remains were crumpled and stowed under seats. Two men in the front row leaned forward and gave me a careful once-over, as though it might make a difference when I finally returned later in the month to offer them up a murderer.

"I would like to add a special reminder today. As some of you may be aware, there are accounts of Dr. Dogen's death in the newspapers and on television. When you come upon those stories, I must direct you *not* to read or listen to them."

Fat chance, I thought to myself as I said the words aloud. Now that they're sitting on the case, most of them will be surfing the channels looking for coverage they would never have bothered with before.

"The only evidence you will be asked to consider in this case is the testimony of witnesses who appear here before you or documents that are properly qualified and submitted to you in this room. News accounts and opinions of your family and friends are not evidence. And of course, you must not discuss this case among yourselves.

"I'm going to leave some subpoenas here for the signature of the foreman, and I will be in again sometime next week. Thank you very much." Unless the detectives had some lucky breaks in a day or two, it was unlikely that I would begin to present testimonial evidence until the time a suspect was targeted.

I was out of the room quickly and turned the jury back to my colleagues. "You coming to the party for Broderick tonight?" Gene asked as I swept by on my way back to my office. Another classmate was leaving the office for private practice.

"Yeah. I've got a lecture to do at seven-thirty, but I'll swing by when I'm done, assuming this case doesn't heat up."

Laura met me at the foot of the staircase on the eighth floor and told me that Battaglia wanted me immediately.

I turned toward his wing instead of my own, and was admitted by the security officer on the desk.

"Hey, Rose, great suit. I love that color on you."

"Good morning, Alex. Thanks. Just wait a few minutes 'til he gets off the phone, then go right on in."

Rose was turned to her side, pounding away at the word processor. I glanced over the mounds of correspondence on her desk, trying not to "do a Covington." Rod Squires had often ridiculed one of the guys who used to work in the office, Davy Covington, who had taken the surreptitious reading of Battaglia's mail to an art form. He used to stand opposite Rose, pretend to engage her in pleasant conversation, and scan the District Attorney's letters upside down. Battaglia had caught him at his own game more than once. When Davy gossiped about a local congressman's fraud investigation before the matter was even officially brought to the office, the District Attorney gave him some very warm references for another job about fifteen hundred miles away. The temptation to peek was overwhelming, but the penalty made it much easier to resist.

I picked up the day's *Law Journal* and skimmed the headline decision. The Court of Appeals's reasoning on a ruling about a police officer's search of an abandoned suitcase in

Port Authority looked interesting and I made a note on my pad for Laura to clip the opinion for my files.

The familiar odor of a Monte Cristo No. 2 wafted out to announce that Battaglia was on his way to summon me into his office. It was one of the features that Rod and I most appreciated when the D.A. made his unexpected forays onto our end of the corridor. The inevitable cigar smoke and smell always preceded him by a few seconds, time enough for Rod to get his feet off the desk or for me to slip back into my shoes.

"Anything new, Alex? C'mon inside."

He had an amazing facility for doing four things at once. Not a word that I said would be missed or forgotten, while at the same time he would be scrutinizing a handful of the letters that Rose had just printed out for his approval and prioritizing the calls on two of his six telephone lines, which were blinking on hold as he led me in.

"You need to take those calls, Paul? I can wait."

"Nah, the senator can call back later. He's pressing me on that victims' rights legislation, and I just like to keep him guessing. The other one will just take a minute. Sit."

Battaglia pressed the clear lucite button and resumed the conversation. "I've got her in here now. What do you need to know?" Pause. "Hold on."

He looked up at me. "What do you know about Dogen's husband and family?" Three similar questions followed, all innocuous.

I gave him the information I had, and wondered which newspaper he was favoring with it. He was a master at this, never giving out anything inappropriate, but serving up to a rotating group of reliables a couple of bites that would soon be available through ordinary channels. I listened as he controlled the conversation with ease and assurance. Something his caller said to flatter him caused him to break into a wide smile. I smiled, too, looking at his lean face, strong aquiline nose, and thick graying hair. The man was a genius at his dealings with the press.

"That ought to hold them for a while. Now, any leads I don't know about?"

I told him what had gone on throughout the evening and what my plans were for the day.

"Y' know, nobody at the medical center is very happy with all the articles being printed about the security problems."

"Well, Paul, you've got to admit—"

"Just try and keep a lid on these stories, Alex. People desperately in need of surgery and treatment are checking out like it was a leper colony. It's not just Mid-Manhattan—I'm getting calls from Columbia-Presbyterian and Mount Sinai. You'd think they were writing about Grand Central Station or the Bowery Mission, not a medical center.

"And another thing, Pat McKinney was in right before you. Says Chief McGraw called him to gripe about something you did last night at the precinct."

It figures that one asshole would find the other. And McKinney, one of my supervisors who welcomed any opportunity to embarrass me, ran right in here like a washerwoman to badmouth me to the D.A. I squirmed but held my tongue, knowing how much Battaglia hated infighting among his staff.

"All I can say, Alex, is that you must have been doing something right. McGraw's a real pain in the neck. He crossed me twelve years ago, when he was commanding Manhattan South. He's never been able to work with women—quite a Neanderthal. So don't let him get to you."

He stood up and walked in the direction of the door, marking an end to my audience. The cigar was clenched in his teeth and he was smiling even more broadly as he saw me out: "If he gives you a hard time, send my regards. Tell him I said he should zip up his pants and get out of your way."

*   *   *

I picked up the messages that were stuffed into the clip on Laura's desk, flipping through them until I found the one I wanted. David Mitchell had called back to confirm that he had made a referral of Maureen Forester to a neurologist affiliated with Mid-Manhattan Hospital. On the basis of her complaints to Mitchell and the results of his preliminary exam, he had recommended that she be admitted to the hospital Friday morning at 10 A.M. Dr. Mitchell had insisted, of course, that no invasive tests or procedures be performed until his return to New York at the beginning of next week. Just observation and lots of rest.

I called Sarah to tell her the news and ask her if she could spend Friday afternoon "visiting" with Mo. Then I phoned Bergdorf's personal shopping department and ordered a mocha-colored vicuña robe, to be delivered to the neurological floor the next day— "You're our devil in disguise—stay well, with love from your pals—Mike, Mercer, and Al."

Gina Brickner waited until I hung up the phone before she came in with her legal pads and a cassette recorder. She looked miserable.

"Laura told me you're leaving at noon, but you gotta hear this tape before you go. I got an indictment on that Columbia University frat party rape last month. The 911 tape was just delivered this morning, with the printout.

"Jessie Pointer, the victim, told me she'd only had one or two beers that night. Said she was cold sober by the time she got back to her girlfriend's dorm room to make the call. I played the tape—Alex, she's so damn drunk that she's hiccuping all the way through it."

"Unbelievable."

"It gets worse. Every time the 911 operator asks for a

response address, Jessie can't answer the question. She can't remember the name of the dorm. Then the dispatcher wants the telephone callback number in case the address she finally came up with was wrong. Jessie gives her six digits, and then the two of them keep arguing over whether phone numbers have six or seven figures. I can't believe how intox'd she sounds."

"Get her back in here tomorrow. Read her the riot act. Make her listen to the tape. Tell her she's got one chance—and only one chance—to correct her story. And she'll have to admit to the jury, at the trial, that she wasn't honest with you or with the cops about her condition.

"I'll never understand why some of these women lie about the circumstances leading up to the attack but then expect us to believe that everything else they testify to is true. This isn't a goddamn game—it's peoples' lives at stake. We're here to help them, and they think we're stupid enough not to know how to find out what really went on. If she wants us to salvage the rape case, every other detail she tells you has to be confirmed."

Nothing infuriated me more than the real victims who compromised their own cases by trying to shade the events. The few who did it made everyone more skeptical of the scores of legitimate victims who followed in their footsteps.

By the time I had finished returning the calls and reassigning interviews, Mercer had arrived to pick me up.

"Beep if you need me, Laura. We'll be at the morgue."

9

Mercer worked his department car around the yellow bobcats and backhoes at the construction site on First Avenue, a block south of the entrance to the blue and gray building that housed the office of the medical examiner. He parked at a meter after letting me out to climb over a curbside mound of frozen ice to get onto the sidewalk.

"Look at that fool," Mercer said, pointing across the street at Chapman. "Man's never owned a winter coat."

Mike was coming from the deli across the street, seemingly oblivious to the bitter cold in his blazer and open-collared denim shirt.

I waved in his direction and he hoisted a large shopping bag, pointing to it as he called out to us, "Lunch." Mercer looked at me and shook his head. Neither one of us was as at home in the morgue as Chapman. It was commonplace for members of his squad to be present for the autopsy procedure, while those of us who worked on sexual assault cases were fortunate enough to deal with survivors—wounded but living and breathing.

"Forget the front door," Chapman shouted, as I started up the stairs to the building's entrance. "C'mon. Kirschner's still in the basement."

I had never entered on the Thirtieth Street side so I followed Mike and Mercer around the corner and down the block to the parking bay where ambulance and emergency service trucks disgorged their bodies. A police officer checked our identification as he admitted us through the wide doors and we started down the sloping ramp toward the autopsy rooms.

Mike saw my eyes fix on the painted green walls as we walked; they were pockmarked at about waist level where large chips were missing. It was especially noticeable when we reached the bend at the bottom of the incline and turned to the right to go down another twenty feet.

"I know, I know. You're ready to give the place a paint job and redecorate. Forget it. That's the way it's always gonna be, Blondie. They unload the body onto a gurney at the top, then somebody gives it a shove down the ramp. It bounces off the side a few times, hits the corner, and caroms around and down to the bottom. Believe me, the patient doesn't feel a thing. You don't need a candy striper to walk the stretcher down the hall."

"Sensitive motherfucker, isn't he?" Wallace murmured.

Mike led us into a small conference room at the far end of the corridor. It held an eight-foot-long table, a dozen chairs, a chalkboard, and wall-mounted clips all around the circumference to display X rays and photographs.

Before Mercer and I could take off our coats and sit down, Dr. Chet Kirschner joined us in the room.

We had worked together on a number of occasions

throughout the five years since he had been appointed to the post of Chief Medical Examiner by the Mayor and I always welcomed his calm and dignified mien as much as I valued his professional judgment. Chet was tall and razor thin, with dark hair, a quiet voice, and an engaging smile that was rarely exercised during the discussions of his daily procedures.

We exchanged greetings and placed ourselves around the table while Mike went on unpacking his bag full of sandwiches and sodas.

"What I'm going to tell you is very preliminary, Alexandra. It will take some time to get lab results on the toxicology and the serological samples, so let's just start—off the record—with the general picture."

"Of course."

"I got all four turkeys on rye, Russian dressing, okay?"

"Not right now, Mike," I answered. The sterile surroundings, the faint aroma of formaldehyde, and the grim task ahead of us combined to suppress all thoughts of food or hunger.

Mercer and Chet also passed. Mike unwrapped his overstuffed sandwich and popped the top on his root beer while Dr. Kirschner took out a set of Polaroid photos of Gemma Dogen's blood-soaked body and spread them on the table.

He looked up at Mike, who was crunching potato chips between bites of the sandwich and grinned wryly as he said, "*bon appétit.*"

"There is no mystery about *how* the doctor died. As you're all aware, there were multiple stab wounds—seventeen, to be exact. Several hit vital organs, including the wound that was probably the fatal one, which collapsed one of her lungs completely. The other lung was punctured as well.

"The repeated blows, most of which were quite deep, caused massive internal bleeding. It was intra-abdominal and intrathoracic. There were a few superficial cuts on the anterior surface of the body, but most were thrusts that didn't miss.

"She was stabbed in the back as well as the front. Clearly a frenzied attack—far more strikes than were necessary to cause her death. Any one of a number of these would have done the job handily."

"Defensive wounds?" Mercer asked.

I picked up a handful of the Polaroids to follow Kirschner's commentary. I had seen Gemma Dogen's face responding to camera flashes at the celebratory events caught in the photographs on her office shelves. Now I studied the same features—colorless, expressionless, lifeless—as they rested on the head support atop the autopsy table.

"None at all. But if you look closely at the Polaroids of her wrists, you'll see some faint markings. They'll show up much more clearly on the actual photographs we took."

I found the two close-ups of Dogen's lower arms and noticed the linear red discolorations.

"She was obviously restrained at some point, and I would presume that happened—along with the gag, which was left in place—*before* the stabbing began. I would doubt that she had any opportunity to resist the knife attack.

"The restraints might have been the same kind of material as the cloth the killer used to gag her. Twisted into narrow strips and wound around her wrists, they would have caused the marks that you see here but not have broken the skin."

Chapman swigged a mouthful from his soda can. "D'you have a chance to look over that strip from the gag, Doc?"

"It's in the lab now for analysis, but I saw it when they brought the body in. You'll get a definitive answer later, but it looked to me like ordinary hospital-issue bed linen, cut into long pieces. Could have come from any patient room, supply closet, delivery service, or even the laundry."

"Make a note for me please, Mercer. I assume the lieutenant has someone checking the laundry staff on the list with all the other employees, but I never even thought of all the types of deliverymen who are in and out of there every day."

"They're on it, Coop. Laundry, food, medical supplies, flowers, gift baskets, balloons—it's endless. We're talking at least several thousand transients."

Chapman had wiped his hands and was standing over my shoulder, pointing out puncture wounds as I continued to sort through the snapshots. He asked Kirschner, "So if you had to reconstruct the events with what you know now, how do you figure it happened?"

"I can only speculate at this point, Mike. You know that. I assume whoever did this, whether it started as a burglary, or a prowler looking for a victim, came prepared. He had the weapon, he had the strips of cloth, and he probably had a purpose.

"I'd have to guess that Dogen was surprised by the attacker and overcome immediately. That woman was in fantastic condition. The muscles in her thighs and calves could have been from someone half her age. The fact that there aren't any defensive wounds on her hands suggests she never had the opportunity to struggle."

"Any idea about what time the assault could have taken place?"

"Tougher than usual. Obviously, we know exactly what time she died, since it was after she was found by the watchman. Any doctor would tell you that she couldn't have survived these wounds. I'm sure she was unconscious while the killer was still striking at her, and I'd also bet that when he left her *he* had assumed she was dead. It's one of those medical oddities that she hung on for as long as she did, whether it was thirty minutes or thirty hours.

"The collapsed lung gave out quickly and completely. The other one must have acted like a slow leak. Mike told me that you all thought at the scene that she may have come to for a brief moment and used up the remaining oxygen supply in an effort to move herself. It's possible."

"With enough energy to drag her body across the room to the door?"

"My clinical answer to that would have to be no. But every day we see impossible things happen when the body is in extremis. Yes, Gemma Dogen might have summoned the strength for one last shot at saving herself. There's no medical explanation for it. Absolutely none."

"Chet, did Mike tell you about the, well, sort of squiggle on the floor where the body was found? I mean, in the blood."

Mike was still behind me as I spoke and tousled my hair to indicate his dismissal of my idea.

"Cooper thinks the deceased was trying to talk to us."

Kirschner's eyes met mine as he nodded slightly, willing to consider the prospect. "I assume you've got crime scene photos to show what you're thinking about, right?"

"Yeah. We should have a couple of sets by this evening, Doc. I'll shoot 'em down to you."

"May I?" Kirschner reached across to pick up some of the autopsy Polaroids. He held them up close to his face looking for the detail he needed to refresh his memory. "Obviously, I'll be able to show you this better when our own body shots are printed later today, but the blood pattern on her right index finger is consistent with your theory.

"Keep in mind, there was an awful lot of blood here, even on her hands and arms. I'll get to that in a minute, when we talk about why she was untied. But there *is* a different sort of coating on that finger, either from dragging herself through some of the pooled blood or—I guess it just never occurred to me—by intentionally putting her finger in the blood, like to draw something. I'd like to see your pictures before I jump to any conclusions that suggest she was writing.

"I'm surprised you're such a doubter, Chapman. Wasn't it you who had the case with me a couple of months ago? The guy who was shot six times in the back on a subway platform, but ran up two flights of stairs and onto the street 'til he found a phone booth to make a call. Then he collapsed and died."

"Yeah, 'Lucky Louie' Barsky, the loan shark. Last gasp for a phoner to his mother, to tell her she could live off whatever she could find in the shoe box marked '12D Black Croco Loafer' on the third shelf of his bedroom closet. Lucky for him he survived to make the call. Unlucky for Mom, I was there with a search warrant before she could find a stepladder. His ex-girlfriend had ratted on him and knew where the dough was stashed. I guess miracles do happen, Doc."

Mercer brought us back to Dogen's killing. "So you think she was untied *after* the stabbing?"

"No bindings were found at the scene, isn't that right? Only the gag. So after she was disabled—whether that was with the first couple of thrusts or after all of them—it would seem that he untied her then and moved her to the floor."

Mike was seated at the table again, shaking his head back and forth. "So he rapes her while she's unconscious and bleeding like a stuck pig from some, if not all, of these wounds?" He leaned back in his chair, then it dropped forward with a crashing noise under his weight as he pounded both of his fists on the table. "Can you believe that some perverted sicko gets sexually aroused by the sight of a bloody corpse? I'll never understand your end of this business, Mercer, I swear it. How does a guy get it up after he's mutilated and savaged a woman's body? I swear, there should be a death penalty all its own for this kind of crime, and I'd be the executioner. Dammit."

Kirschner's even voice picked up the narrative. "What I'm about to say doesn't make this crime any better, Mike, but perhaps your killer wasn't as stimulated as he thought he might be. It's pretty clear to me, the way Mike described the position of Dogen's body, the removal of her underwear, and the lifting of her skirt to expose her genitals, that some kind of sexual assault was contemplated or attempted.

"But it wasn't completed. No sign of seminal fluid, neither on the body nor within the vaginal vault. No sperm. I did swabbings of the vaginal and anal orifices, and you'll get lab results on those, but I think we'll come up with a negative."

Mercer grimaced. "You thinking like I am?" he directed the question to me.

I was crestfallen, too. For the past few years, Mercer and I had come to rely on DNA evidence and its stunning genetic fingerprinting techniques to resolve a growing number of rape cases. Even when the victim survived the attack, as most do, and picked out her assailant in photo arrays and lineups, the reliability of DNA testing to confirm her identification had dramatically increased the success rate of prosecutions all over the country.

"I guess I was counting on evidence we're not going to have," I said, the dejection apparent in my tone. "I just assumed that we'd get seminal fluid and develop a print ready for comparison when we find our suspect."

"That's a luxury I don't think we're going to have in this case, Alex."

"Any chance the guy used a condom, Doc? That's why you're not finding any semen?"

"Unlikely, Mike. I mean, it's entirely possible. But most of the time condoms leave substances in the victim's body that we would detect at autopsy or in the lab. Whether it's the lubricant or the spermicides, there's—"

"Well, I mean, can you tell if she was even penetrated?"

"There's no trauma, either vaginally or anally. Now, that doesn't tell us much in and of itself about vaginal penetration."

Mike didn't have the experience with sexual assault cases that Mercer and I did, so I went on with the facts to which Kirschner had alluded. "More than two-thirds of adult women who are raped don't sustain any kind of physical injury or trauma, Mike. Someone who's sexually active isn't likely to exhibit internal damage. The vaginal vault is pretty elastic, and if she was unconscious when the rapist penetrated, there'd be even less likelihood of meeting resistance."

Kirschner was a step ahead of me. "What I find even more unusual, though, is that there was not a shred of any other trace evidence suggesting an attempt at a sexual encounter. If he had actually tried to penetrate, I would have expected to find some of *his* pubic hair in our combing of hers."

A standard part of evidence collection in rape cases, as well as at autopsies, is a combing of the victim's pubic hair. Frequently, the rapist's own hair becomes entangled and left on the victim, and becomes another means of forensically linking a perpetrator to his prey.

"When you've got a rape, the crime scene *is* the victim's body. It's the only crime for which that's true. I'm convinced there is too little evidence here to believe our attacker committed a sexual assault."

"So now all we gotta figure is what stopped him," Mercer said. "Anything from getting scared off by noise in the hallway to losing his erection. Maybe Mike's right in this case. If his intention was to rape Dogen, but he had to use more force than he had planned to subdue her, he might have been disgusted or simply unable to maintain an erection."

"Don't forget," I added, "with a lot of the psychiatric types living in and under the medical center, you're starting out with some candidates who are sexually dysfunctional even though their intention may have been to complete an assault. Are we back at square one, guys?"

"I hate to disappoint you, Alexandra, but I don't think the solution to this crime is going to come from *my* work or *my* laboratory. Chapman knew as much about how Gemma Dogen died before he got here this morning as he does now. He just didn't know where each of those knife wounds landed, internally, until we opened her up. I'm sorry I can't give you any more help right now but your killer didn't leave the kind of incriminating evidence we had all hoped for.

"If you find him before too much time goes by," Kirschner said, turning to the two detectives, "his body and his clothing are likely to tell more of the story than Dogen's. Whether or not she was able to scratch or bite or hit him, I have no idea. But he certainly must have left that room looking like he'd come from an abattoir. He'd have had more blood on him than anyone except a surgeon leaving the operating theater."

Chet reminded us to forward the crime scene photos to him as soon as we had them, collected his Polaroids, and excused himself, noting that he had half an hour until he began his next procedure at three o'clock.

Mike, Mercer, and I gathered our belongings and walked out of the room. "I'm taking a pass on those sandwiches, Cooper. Want a cup of coffee across the street before we go on?" Mercer asked.

I had absolutely no appetite, either. "Sure, maybe it'll take the chill off." We walked back up the ramp and out onto the sidewalk.

"You taking Coop over to see Dogen's apartment?"

"Yeah."

"I'll be at Mid-Manhattan doing interviews. Coming by the station house later, kid?"

"What can I do to be useful? I'm still stunned by Chet's findings. I was just counting on something that the lab could give us to move forward with by the weekend. I've got to give a speech at Julia Richman High School tonight."

Mercer stepped off the curb to cross First Avenue. I turned back and flashed a grin at Chapman. "Why'd you ask? Do you need me, Mikey?"

"In your dreams, Blondie. In your dreams."

10

Burgundy-suited doormen flanked the entrance to Gemma Dogen's apartment building on Beekman Place, a short walk from the medical center complex. Wallace palmed his gold detective shield to the older of the two, on our left, who acknowledged his recognition by swinging back the large glass doors.

Wallace pointed me to the right, through the lobby and past an enormous display of forsythia and pussy willows that seemed to be rushing the season. We got on the elevator and Mercer pressed twelve.

"Damn," he said as the doors opened onto a dim hallway made more oppressive by a heavy pattern of taupe flocked wallpaper. "I brought a camera in case you wanted any photos. Left it in the trunk. It's the third door on the left—12C.

Here are the keys, large one for the bottom lock. Let yourself in and I'll be back up in five."

I fingered the key chain as the doors pinched shut behind me. I hesitated while toying with the miniature replica of London's Tower Bridge from which the two keys dangled, thinking I might be more comfortable entering Gemma's home with Mercer than alone.

Grow up, I told myself. There are no ghosts inside and Mercer will be here within minutes.

I slipped the shorter key into the top lock, then turned the long Medeco one into the cylinder below. The knob seemed to stick for a minute before it cracked open, and I was startled at that exact moment by a noise behind me. I stepped on the threshold and looked over my shoulder to see only the swinging door at the service end of the hallway moving back and forth.

There were no voices and no other noise on the corridor and yet I could have sworn I saw someone's face peeking out from behind the small porthole window there toward me. It was a creepy feeling, as though I were being watched, and I reassured myself that nosy neighbors were likely to be concerned about the strangers who were parading in and out of the dead woman's home.

The entryway light switch was on the wall next to the front closet, so I flipped it up as I closed the door behind me.

My eyes swept around the large space. It was a postwar building with rooms of a generous size, spoiled by concrete ceilings that resembled a huge, upside-down vat of cottage cheese but saved by a floor-length wall of windows that looked over the expanse of the East River. Today the clouds hung dense and low and I could barely see beyond the Fifty-ninth Street Bridge and the traffic gliding toward La Guardia Airport.

Gemma Dogen's taste was simple and stark. I moved through the living room, which appeared to have been furnished during a single stop at a low-cost, contemporary Scandinavian store. Every piece had sharp angles and lines; all fabrics were neutral in shade and slightly rough to the feel. I wished her the deep, rich colors and thick, soft materials of my own home, which enveloped and soothed me when I was ready to relax, kick my shoes off, and leave my professional world behind me at the end of a tough day.

I placed my coat over the back of one of the chairs at the dining table and turned into the short hallway that led to her bedroom. Antique British travel posters of Brighton, the Cotswolds, and Cambridge lined both sides of the wall leading into another sterile-looking chamber with its queen-sized bed.

If the photographs with which she surrounded herself were any evidence of her priorities, Gemma Dogen certainly liked her role in the academic community. She beamed from platforms and podia when she was dressed in her professorial garb. Flags flanking the stage settings showed her equally at home in England and in America and I silently applauded a woman of her accomplishment who had been such a brilliant success in a specialty dominated for so long by men.

The alarm clock next to her bed was still displaying the correct time. I pressed the little button on top to see at what hour Gemma scheduled her days to begin. It flashed a reading of 5:30 A.M. and I admired even more the discipline that drove her out that early, especially these March mornings, to run along the riverside path before going to work. The harsh buzz of the front door bell brought me out of my reverie and I headed back to let Mercer in.

"Who else you expecting?" he asked, ridiculing the fact that I had looked through the peephole before turning the knob.

"You know my mother's rules, Mercer." I supposed I'd been doing that peephole thing instinctively since I moved to

Manhattan more than a decade earlier. "And someone was lurking around out there when I let myself in. Did you see anybody?"

"Not a soul, Miss Cooper. Carry on, girl."

"Did you see the alarm clock?"

"Not that I remember. Anything significant?"

"Just worth checking out the time of her usual schedule. It was last set for 5:30 A.M.—we should note it in case it helps backtrack if we get any closer to knowing the time of the assault."

"Done." Mercer opened his pad and scratched in some notes. "Now, your video guy took some film in here, and we had Crime Scene go over it, too. George Zotos has been pouring through a lot of the files. Seems like she didn't entertain here much. Used this living room more like an office. That whole wall unit to the left is full of books, but the one on the right is all files and stuff from the med school.

"We've been over a lot of it. Take your time, I'll be here with you. Let me know if you want a picture of anything."

I started back to the kitchen. Like mine, its shelves and cupboards were pretty bare. The standard upscale equipment—Cuisinart, Calphalon pots and pans, Henckel knives, and an imported espresso machine—all looked pitifully underutilized. This was the Gemma Dogen I could relate to.

"We've been through there, Coop. Zotos inventoried the fridge but then threw everything out. Skim milk, carrots, head of lettuce. You're welcome to look, but it won't tell you much."

I walked back into the bedroom and sat in the armchair that was adjacent to Gemma's bedside table. The bed was neatly made up and the spread was pulled tight without a crease. Either she had arisen at her usual time and straightened up after her jog or she had never gotten home during the night to go to sleep.

I picked up the book from the bedside table—a slim volume on spinal cord injuries, just published by Johns Hopkins University Press, which seemed as depressing as the task ahead of us. I looked at the pages that Gemma had dog-eared and underlined but they meant nothing to me and I replaced it under the lamp.

Closet doors were on runners, which I slid back to look at the way she presented herself to her world. On one side were dark suits with no trim or detail, utilitarian but not of any style. The other end was mostly casual gear—an assortment of khaki slacks, simple cotton shirts, and jackets. Running shoes and sneakers of every variety and condition covered the closet floor. Several pairs of solid English walking pumps must have carried her through her professional appointments. Sensible, my mother called them, but unexciting. A few white lab coats, cleaned and starched, hung between the business and the play clothes. My hand reached for the sleeve of a navy wool suit. I wondered if anyone had claimed Gemma's body from the morgue and thought of taking an outfit for her burial.

I went back into the living room. Mercer stood up from the chair at Dogen's desk, where he had been looking through some of the manila files that lay on top, and offered the seat to me.

"Here's the mail that was left for her today. Doorman gave it to me on my way back up. Bills for Con Ed and cable TV, statement from Chase Bank, and a postcard from her ex on his trip to the Himalayas. Read it—looks like he expected to see her in England in a couple of weeks. Medical symposium at the University of London. Take that with us to give to Peterson, okay?"

"Fine." I looked it over, pleased that she had such a civilized relationship with Geoffrey that he actually expressed pleasure at the idea of seeing her soon. Most of my friends didn't enjoy that status with their exes, a thought that had me smiling until I caught myself with the sad realization that Geoffrey might not yet even know Gemma's monstrous fate.

Mercer moved over to study the bookshelf wall. With his usual eye for detail, he started listing titles and descriptions as I opened desk drawers to flip through agendas and calendars.

"This lady was serious, Cooper. Very little here that isn't medical or strictly business. Small collection of classics, kind of stuff you like. George Eliot, Thomas Hardy. Then you move to the CDs. Lots of German opera, plenty of Bach. Can you imagine a music collection without a single piece of jazz or even one Motown disc? Too whitebread for me, girl."

"I don't think I noticed, Mercer. Is there a computer in her office?" I was surprised not to find one in the apartment.

"Yeah, they're working on downloading that, too. She didn't keep one here, which is why it wouldn't have been unusual to see her in the med school office so late. When we were there yesterday morning, practically everyone we spoke to said Dogen liked to do her writing late at night, when it was really quiet over there. Unfortunately, anyone who knew her knew that."

I slid the chair over to the wall opposite the one Mercer was facing. The lower half of the cabinets were file drawers, each hung with legal-size Pendaflex folders. Some were divided by color and all were split up by year. Beyond that, I could make no particular sense of the order or subject matter. Like Mercer, I held onto my legal pad and tried to make notes about what categories the documents covered.

"For such a logical lady, some of this makes no sense. I can't imagine her system for finding stuff. She's got scores of folders on 'Professional Ethics'—"

"Yeah, that was one of her areas of expertise, Coop. She gave a lot of lectures about it."

"Well, wedged in between that and a couple of folders on 'Regenerative Tissue' is her file on 'Met Games.'"

"She was quite a jock, apparently."

"Yeah, but Laura Wilkie could have straightened out her life a bit. Organized everything. You go in looking to renew your baseball season tickets and it's somewhere in the middle of brain tissue. Two file drawers later you get to all the stuff about running equipment. Uh, uh—Laura wouldn't stand for it. She'd have all the brain material in one place and the sports files in another."

I was getting bleary-eyed from looking through file labels and listings. I had wanted to get a sense of Gemma Dogen and, beyond that, none of these documents would have any meaning unless they surfaced later as a piece of the investigation.

Mercer was photographing the items on the desktop as I stood up and stretched my back. "I'll just take a few shots so we can keep the context of how we found things."

"Whoever speaks to the next of kin, we'll have to let them know what's here. Pictures will be useful."

"You can come back any time. Rent's paid up through April, so Peterson doesn't want any of this touched until we know who her heirs are. And know whether she was an intended victim or an accidental one."

The early darkness of a March day had descended over the city while Mercer and I had intruded on the personal effects of Gemma Dogen. It was after six o'clock and I needed to be at the small supper reception the Lenox Hill Debs Board was holding in the principal's office at the high school hosting my lecture.

Mercer's flash went off several times as he aimed at a few areas of Dogen's living room. The light reflected the shining surface of a small golden object and I approached to see what had glimmered so brightly in the otherwise drab room.

"Take it easy, Cooper. It's not jewelry."

Mercer lifted a foot-long black stand from the third shelf of the case and read the bronze plate that was affixed to its edge. In italic script was printed the inscription: *To Gemma Dogen, in honor of her induction into the Order of the Golden Scalpel. June 1, 1985. Fellows of the Royal Infirmary. London, England.*

A solid gold surgeon's scalpel with a steel blade rested on the ebony box. I lifted it to admire its beauty. "Can you imagine what a superb physician she must have been to get this kind of award when she was only in her forties?" I was conjuring up a clubhouse full of older English doctors, bespectacled and bewigged, presenting the talented young woman with this solid gold token of their respect. "It looks pretty lethal but it's a magnificent thing, isn't it?"

"Would have been a hell of a lot nicer for her if she'd kept it in her office. Maybe she'd have had a fighting chance."

It wasn't a weapon, as we both knew. It was the tool of a woman who had saved lives and done it thousands of times.

I laid it back on the shelf and told Mercer that I was ready to leave. We put on our coats, turned off the lights, and I locked the door behind me while Mercer rang for the elevator.

It was six-thirty when I said goodnight to Mercer. He dropped me in front of Julia Richman High School and I hurried up the steps to find the chairwoman of the evening's event.

Sexual assault had been a taboo subject in the sixties and seventies when I was growing up. Rape was a crime that didn't happen, so the myths went, to "nice girls"—to our sisters, our mothers, our daughters, our friends. Victims "asked for it," and once they got it none of them were supposed to talk about it. If they didn't deal with it openly, maybe it would go away.

All of the legislative reform that had been accomplished in this field had come in the last two decades. But the laws had been easier to change than the public's attitudes.

So most of my colleagues and I spent a considerable amount of time trying to educate about the issues to which our working days were devoted. The people we tried to reach—in religious organizations, high schools, colleges and universities, professional clubs, civic groups—all of them might one day wind up as jurors in these cases. That's when they bring with them to the jury box every preconceived notion and misconception about this category of crime.

There were very few invitations I turned down if audiences were willing to let themselves be informed about the facts—the differences and similarities between stranger and acquaintance rape, which sexual predators are incapable of being rehabilitated, legitimate offender treatment programs and which assailants they can help, the phenomenon of false reporting, and the ability of the criminal justice system to do better for survivors of sexual assault by dedicating more resources to the issue. Sarah Brenner and I knocked ourselves out at early morning breakfast meetings and evening sessions like this one. The more we helped ourselves, the more we helped those women, children, and men who would someday be victimized and need to count on the response of twelve of their peers to render a fair verdict.

Handwritten yellow posters announcing my appearance were stuck on the bulletin board inside the school entrance, with a large black arrow pointing the way to the auditorium. I followed the designated path, stopping at the open door a few feet before the large hall and stepping inside.

A heavyset woman with a tangle of blond hair pushed into a bun atop her head strode toward me with an outstretched hand. "Hello, you must be Alexandra Cooper. I'm Liddy McSwain. I'm in charge of the speaker's program for this year. We're really delighted you could be here, especially with all this murder business going on. We saw your name in the paper this morning and I was certain we'd have to call this off."

She guided me into the room where a dozen or so of her committee members were munching on finger sandwiches. I introduced myself to some of them and decided to feed myself before I got too lightheaded to go on stage. The crustless slivers of seven-grain bread were divided onto three trays: watercress, egg salad, and tomato. I cursed at myself for having passed up Chapman's overstuffed turkey sandwich so many hours ago in favor of these debutante miniatures and put a handful of the little morsels on a paper plate.

I moved around the room politely answering questions about the District Attorney's Office and assuring handshakers that I would convey their warmest regards to Paul Battaglia. More and more middle-aged women kept drifting into the reception. There were obvious distinctions between the older half of the crowd and the younger. The over-fifties carried Vuittons on their arms and wore flat Ferragamos on their feet. The natural blond hairstyles, more up than down, were enhanced by Clairol, clearly a two-step process. The newer inductees favored Dooney and Burke—on the shoulder, not the arm—and the Ferragamo with a slightly higher one-inch heel. The blond seemed mostly natural, with a few streaks thrown in for variety. There was not a lot of diversity evident in the crowd and I was mentally censoring my notes to substitute the words "private parts" for my usual references to "penis and vagina."

Ten minutes before I was scheduled to go on stage, I freshened up in the ladies' room and we moved into the large auditorium. More than two hundred women had taken seats around the room and I shuffled my note cards to make certain that I had outlined all of the points I wanted to cover during the hour I had been asked to speak.

Mrs. McSwain had crafted a pleasant opening for her group and a generous recitation of the credentials from my curriculum vitae. I climbed the four steps to the stage, crossed to the lectern, and began my remarks.

I talked about the history of Battaglia's Sex Crimes Prosecution Unit, which was the first of its kind in the United States. I wanted to impact them with the enormity of the problem of sexual assault in our country, so I was armed with some shocking statistics. Not even twenty-five years ago—that is, in our lifetimes—in this very city the laws were so archaic that in a single year although more than a thousand men were arrested and charged with rape, only eighteen of them were convicted of the crime. A few gasps from the girls down in front. I shook off my thoughts of Gemma Dogen and concentrated on my purpose.

I explained how the laws had changed: eliminating the corroboration requirement that demanded witnesses beyond the victim herself, adding rape shield statutes to prevent defense attorneys from inquiring about a woman's sexual history, ridding us of the dreadful insistence that victims must resist their attackers even when the latter are armed and threatening deadly physical force. All these accomplishments had come about in just the last two decades.

The hour went quickly for me as I illustrated legal issues with anecdotal material from actual cases. It became clear as the question and answer period began that these women were well aware, unlike the generations before them, that rape was a crime that affected their lives. No one in that room, I was willing to bet, had not been touched—directly or indirectly— by some aspect of sexual assault. Almost everyone I met these days would disclose the experience of a friend or relative, child or adult, who had survived some kind of abuse that was connected to my painful specialty.

As I pointed at raised hands for the first few questions, members of Liddy McSwain's committee walked up and down the auditorium aisles collecting index cards that had been on the sign-in table at the entrance. Audience members filled in their queries on the four-by-six cards, which were forwarded and handed up to me in a pile.

"That's a good one," I said, reading from the card on top. The question is, 'How important is the use of DNA technology in your work?'" The enthusiasm with which I answered belied my disappointment in the lack of its existence in Gemma Dogen's case. "It's the most significant tool we have in this business now. We use it, when seminal fluid is deposited on or in the victim's body, to make a positive identification or to confirm one that she has made visually. That really takes the weight off the victim at a trial—it's not just a matter of 'her word' in proving the case.

"It's just as critical that we use it to exclude suspects. If a defense attorney tells me his client was in Ohio on the day of the rape, I simply ask him to provide us with a vial of blood. If the suspect is not our man—that is, if there's no DNA match—there's no arrest. And it also lets us be more creative. Four times now in the last few months we've used it to convict rapists who could never have been identified otherwise because the women were blind or blindfolded by the attacker. Ten years ago we were calling it the tool of the future. Well, *this* is the future and it's helping to resolve issues in a growing number of cases."

I skipped over two cards that asked about how prosecuting these jobs affected my personal safety and my private life. Sorry, girls, not the kind of thing I discuss publicly.

"This question is about sentences for rapists. It's a bit complicated to answer because of the different degrees of crimes involved, and since so many offenders have previous convictions they're often eligible for longer incarceration." But I set out to give a five-minute exposition on the range of sentences as they related to each kind of assault.

Liddy McSwain was coming to the rescue. She stood on the side of the stage and announced that we only had time for three more questions.

I took another one, which asked about the new system of handling domestic violence cases that the NYPD had inaugurated a couple of weeks earlier. Then an easy one, to describe the medical services available in our city hospitals for pediatric and adolescent cases of child abuse.

The question on the next card made me bite my lip, look up to the rear of the room, and scan for a couple of faces I might recognize.

The familiar writing on the card read: "The Final Jeopardy answer is: it's black and twelve inches long. What is—?" Chapman and Wallace were flanking the rear door of the room. Mercer's head was bent down, shaking with laughter, while Chapman looked dead on at me, pointing his finger across his chest toward Wallace.

I was almost tired enough to lose it in front of these lovely women. "I'm sorry, ladies, most of the rest of the questions are about the tragic death of Doctor Dogen at Mid-Manhattan and the course of that investigation. It wouldn't be appropriate for me to comment on any matter that's pending but I can assure you that the city's best detectives are working on it right this minute. Thanks for coming out in this bad weather tonight. I really appreciate your interest in these issues."

As I stepped down onto the auditorium floor, several audience members hovered around me. A few made gracious remarks about the speech, one wanted to know whether I could put her in contact with the Crime Victims Assistance Program at St. Luke's so she could volunteer some counseling, and—as always—three wanted to talk about "something" that had happened to them at some time in their pasts.

I listened briefly to each in turn, told them that we should have these discussions in a more private setting, and gave them my business card to arrange a time to call on Monday to make appointments. It never failed that after a speaking engagement at least one woman disclosed an incident of victimization for which she now had the strength to seek help—whether it was her own experience, her college daughter's, or her best friend's. Rape remains a dreadfully underreported crime.

My coat was on a chair in the last row. Mercer had picked it up and held it for me as I walked toward them. "No need to apologize, gentlemen. How would I have been able to recognize you two if you *hadn't* been rude and juvenile? I might have thought it was someone else. But in Chapman's case, it's a more reliable means of identification than DNA. Whatever invitation you're here to offer tonight, I decline. I'm busy." I kept walking and pushed open the solid wooden door. "Don't call me, as they say, I'll—"

I could hear Chapman's stage whisper follow me out. "Don't worry about it, Mercer. If she's serious, I've got Patrick McKinney's beeper number. He'd never say no to doing the Q and A on Dogen's killer. Give him a call."

My head whipped around at the mention that the murderer was in custody and I stopped immediately.

"I apologize, Blondie. You're right, that really wasn't the question tonight. Is that what you're upset about? Oh—and, yes, we have a suspect. Looks good. The lieutenant sent us to pick you up 'cause he's determined to do everything by the book. Screw Chief McGraw."

"Someone from the hospital—staff?" I asked as we walked out to the front steps, now coated with a thin layer of sleet.

"Nah. One of the tunnel men. Covered with blood up to his knees. Like Chet said, this guy must have been in a slaughterhouse."

"We've had him in the 17th for a couple of hours."

"Talking?"

"I'd call it babbling at this point. You'll see for yourself."

I got in the backseat of Wallace's car for the short ride down Lexington Avenue to look the beast in the eye.

11

"Can you believe," Mercer asked of Chapman as he pulled up in front of the station house, "McGraw hasn't leaked this yet?"

He was referring to the fact that no reporters or cameramen were circling the building like sharks, smelling the fresh blood of a suspect in a hot case.

We got out and went into the lobby, past the uniformed sergeant on the desk, and upstairs to the squad room. This time even the precinct detectives and cops looked interested in all the activity. Every one of them would be used for some chore in nailing the pieces of the puzzle together during the next twenty-four hours.

"Hey, Chapman, you on this dirtbag?"

"Paulie Morelli. Damn, I haven't seen you since your partner nailed the Zodiac killer. Did that arrest catapult your ass out of Bed-Stuy or what?"

We were on our way up a flight as Morelli was trying to descend. "Yep. Right here to the 17th Squad. A little slow if you're used to catching homicides."

"Yeah," Chapman said, leading us up, "but if you like your women with teeth, Paulie, the Upper East Side's the place to be. Helping us out with Dogen?"

"I'm on my way to look for stand-ins for the lineup."

"Lineup?" I asked. "Somebody better slow this train down and let me know what's going on."

"That's what you're here for, Blondie."

Mike steered me through the squad room. Unlike the night before, every man was actively engaged in an aspect of the case work. A few were handling the phones while others were interviewing witnesses. Alongside almost every desk, being questioned, was a civilian—some in nurse's or doctor's uniforms, others in outfits labeled with the name of the delivery service that employed them, and still a few in the ill-fitting, mismatched, unwashed apparel of the homeless population.

As we walked toward Peterson's command module, I noticed that the holding pen door was still wide open. But tonight it held only a single visitor.

I glanced in. Sitting alone on a bench was a black man I guessed to be about sixty years old. He was slumped against the far wall, his legs outstretched in front of him. Also in the pen with him were two large shopping carts whose contents remained a mystery to me from this distance. I could see that he was wearing a plaid flannel jacket with long sleeves over a T-shirt. When my focus dropped to his lower torso, I noticed the pale green surgical pants with the drawstring waist. My eyes were riveted on the dark red stains that blotched the calves on both legs of his trousers. Gemma Dogen's blood.

Lieutenant Peterson was standing at the desk, phone to his

ear, finishing a conversation as I entered his room. He winked at me as he spoke. "No, Chief. I won't let that ballbreaker tell me what to do. Nope. Just thought it was smart to have her here for legal advice—search warrant, lineup, Q and A. Nope, we're running the show, I'll make it clear. I hear you.

"Welcome back, Alex. Looks like we got a break. C'mon into the locker room and we'll bring you up to speed on the day's events." Mercer and Mike had gone directly into the briefing area, where some new faces had been added to last night's crew.

Peterson made all the introductions and I took one of the seats at the table.

"Okay, here's what we got. The B team spent the day at Mid-Manhattan. McGraw let me bring in the A team as well and use the 17th Squad for canvassing below the buildings in the bomb shelter tunnels. My guys had the administration and medical staff interviews set up in some of the conference rooms at the medical college. Must have had thirty or forty people from neurology and the Minuit faculty lined up for their initial questioning, just comin' and goin' all afternoon. Background on them, what their relationship was with Dogen, anything they saw or heard the night before her body was found—the usual.

"Nobody's expectin' any solutions on the first round. Nice and easy, getting the lay of the land.

"About six-thirty, Detective Losenti here gets a call from two of the doctors we'd already spoken with earlier in the day—they're both right inside, Alex. I thought you might want to talk to them yourself. The two of them left the neurological floor together to go down to the radiology department on the second floor. Had to look at some X rays in a case they're both consulting on. Walk into the supply closet opposite the X-ray room and this guy—the one you see in the pen—is curled up on the floor taking a nap. They roust him to get him out when they notice his pants legs are covered with blood. One of 'em stayed in the room while the other one called Losenti, whose beeper number was on the flyer we handed out asking people to call if they saw or heard anything. He was still in the hospital complex so he went right over to radiology."

I looked around the room at the faces of the detectives. It was 9:30 at night and everyone had been going since dawn, but the optimism of breaking the case so quickly boosted everyone's spirits and brought them back together as a team.

"What does he say?"

"He's either playing dumb now or we got a real psycho on our hands. A few of the guys have tried to talk to him and got nowhere. I want Chapman and Wallace to take him into one of the interview rooms and see if they can make any progress with him. It's gonna take hours. He mumbles, says the only name he has is Pops, and the stuff on his pants is red paint. Stepped in a bucket of red paint. Then out of the blue he apologizes for 'what happened to the lady.'"

"Is it possible?"

"It's blood, Alex. Human blood. I ain't tested it yet but I've seen enough of it to last me six lifetimes. That's why I wanted *you* here. Figure out what we can take with or without a warrant, how you want this handled so we don't jeopardize any evidence we seize. I'm not interested in McGraw's suggestions. He can spend his time doing all the media spin he wants, we'll finish off this investigation my way.

"Used to be an expression, forty years ago, back when he and I were in the Academy together and things were different in New York. Used to say about a boss who'd never worked his cases like a real detective that he couldn't find a Jew on the Grand Concourse. No offense, Alex."

"Forget it, Loo," Chapman said, "Sherlock Holmes couldn't find a Jew on the Grand Concourse anymore." An area of the Bronx that once had been home to thousands of upwardly mobile Eastern European immigrants was entirely Hispanic today.

"What's the lineup for? I mean, who can ID this guy doing what?"

"Almost everyone we've talked to saw someone on a hallway or in an elevator or a stairwell Tuesday evening or night. I don't know if we're talking about one person in the medical center or a dozen different prowlers or a lot of wishful thinking. But we're gonna let some of these hotshots take a gander at Pops and see if he looks familiar."

"I don't think a lineup makes any sense at this point, guys. We don't have any witnesses who claim to have heard anything in Dogen's office or seen someone leaving it, do we? Let's not waste our time with it."

"Alex, we got a lot of people—housekeeping, nurse's aides, medical students—who were on and off those hallways all night. I'd like to see if anybody can put this guy in the general vicinity. You can keep working on whatever you want. This can't hurt."

"Sure it can, Loo. Suppose he's our guy, and nobody's ever seen him before. It's premature at this point.

"The most critical thing is to get those pants off him and get them to the lab *immediately*. Let's get that blood tested and make sure it matches Dogen's. Have you got Crime Scene here to photo him?"

"Yeah, Sherman's waiting."

"Fine. Get a few shots of him as he is. Make sure they shoot his legs, too, to show he isn't injured anywhere. Go over his hands and arms to see if she was able to scratch him—"

"Done that. Negative."

"Well, Chet didn't think he gave her the chance. You got something to put on him when we take his pants?"

"We've got more surgical outfits here than Scrubs has. Yeah, we'll give him a clean pair."

Chapman asked the lieutenant what had been found in the shopping carts that were inside the pen.

"One of them happens to be Pops's *home,* Mr. Chapman. Now, I certainly don't want to search his home without a warrant, do I? So we've just parked it right there in my driveway for the time being. It's a two-car garage, you might have noticed. The other one belongs to Pops's good friend, who's being questioned now by Ramirez."

"And your eight 'guests' from last night, they're gone?"

"Don't be ridiculous, young lady. Ralph," Peterson looked at Losenti, "who are my friends visiting today?"

"We've moved them over to the Anti-Crime Office, loo. Watching the basketball game tonight. Just fed them a tasty assortment of ribs from Wylie's. Why would they want to leave?"

Peterson laid out his plan. Chapman and Wallace were to take Pops into the room used for lineups to begin their interrogation. That way if he and I wanted to observe any of it, we could view them through the two-way mirror that allowed us to see into the room, although the men on the other side couldn't see out.

"We won't have fillers to run the lineup for at least an hour, but there's a lot of other things to be done. Alex, what would *you* like to get to work on?"

"First, I want to call Battaglia, just to give him a heads-up before he hears it on the late news. I think I'd like to speak with Sarah Brenner and get her up here with me to work on this. I'll need a second hand to get busy on warrants once this gets moving, and she's the one I'd most like to have on board. Then I might as well get started reinterviewing the doctors who found Pops and the guys who are going to view the lineup.

"Oh, Mike, do me a favor and call Maureen. Tell her no matter what she hears on the news, she's still going in tomorrow for us. It's all set up, we might as well see what intelligence we get out of it, and know exactly what's happening in there."

"Fine. Use the phone in my office to make your calls and I'll try to find you another room for the interviews."

"Coop, does Steve's Pizza deliver this far south?" Wallace asked.

"What's wrong with the joint around the corner?" Peterson interrupted.

Chapman settled it. "It's gonna be a long night, Loo. You don't want any of us to have agita, do you? Steve's is the absolute best and the guy would deliver to Jersey for Cooper. It's only on Seventy-first Street—he'll have it here in twenty minutes. Know the number?"

I could dial it in my sleep. I called out the number and heard Chapman order six large pies, extrathin crust, everything on them, and hold the anchovies off two slices for Miss Cooper. "And put it on her tab, okay?"

It would be foolish of me to think I was telling Battaglia something he hadn't already heard, especially because of his wife's position on the board at Mid-Manhattan. It didn't disappoint me, then, when he told me he thought I'd be calling this evening.

"How do you think it looks?"

"I don't even have my foot in the door yet, Paul, but there's an awful lot of blood on this guy's clothes. Peterson tells me they also looked his body over to make sure it wasn't from a wound of his own and he's completely clean. I think we'll be here a few hours. I won't call 'til morning, but you know where to find me."

Sarah had already put the baby to bed when I reached her. She and James were finishing a quiet dinner together. "I'll take a cab right up there to meet you."

"Are you *sure* you should be doing this? I don't want to skip over you and give someone else the chance but I don't want you to do this if it wipes you out or endangers the pregnancy."

"You know I wouldn't. I'd love to work with you on this. I'll stay a few hours tonight and we'll see where it goes. I'll just need an extra chair to stick my feet up on every now and then. See you in half an hour."

"I'm ready, Loo," I said, walking out into the squad room to meet up with Peterson.

Wallace was leaning against the door of the holding pen. I could hear him talking to Pops and asking if he'd be good enough to come along and tell his story one more time. As they walked single file down toward the lineup room, I told the lieutenant that I wanted to see the notes on the interviews with the two physicians before I spoke with them.

"Chapman, get off the phone and bring Cooper here your paperwork."

Mike was using a desk in the far corner of the room. He hung up, grabbed his folder, and came back to Peterson's office accompanied by a well-dressed man of about fifty-five.

"Mr. Dietrich, I'd like you to meet Lieutenant Peterson, my boss, and Alexandra Cooper—well, she's sort of my boss, too," Mike added, laughingly. "She's the assistant D.A. on the case. This is William Dietrich, the director of Mid-Manhattan."

"How do you do? I'd like to thank you for everything you've done so far, lieutenant. We're all just stunned by Dr. Dogen's murder. I, uh, I was wondering if there's anything you can tell me at this point—"

Peterson cut him off. "We know how your people feel, Mr. Dietrich. As soon as there's anything we can go public with, you'll be the first to know."

Dietrich's artificial skin bronzer and touched-up black hair added to his aura of unctuousness. He was the number one man at the hospital complex and in the desperate position of trying to control the public image of a medical center in complete chaos.

The lieutenant walked back to his desk to get another cigarette, and Dietrich tried the personal approach with me.

"I've checked you out today, Alexandra—you don't mind if I call you that, do you?"

"Not at all, Mr. Dietrich."

"You've got quite a good reputation, I mean, for this kind of atrocity."

Checked me out with whom, I wondered. Now he moved to the hands-on approach, standing beside me and lifting my elbow with his fingers to gently guide me away from the direction of Peterson's room for a private talk.

"I'm a great admirer of your father's, Miss Cooper. He's really a legend in the medical profession. He's enjoying his retirement, I take it?"

Don't even think about using my family as a way to get to me, you schmuck. "Very much, Mr. Dietrich, thanks."

"Be sure to give him my regards. I'd love to get him back up to New York to lecture to our students and do some consulting with our cardiology department."

"Well," I said, gripping my folder with both hands, "you come up with an interesting aortic regurgitation to study and I'll have him on the next plane. Now, Mr. Dietrich, if you'll excuse—"

"It's Bill, Alex. Just call me Bill."

"I'm going to ask you to step back outside while Detective Chapman and I get to work."

"I'm counting on you to keep me informed, Alexandra. I think you know better than anyone here what it's like in a great hospital like ours. There are too many lives at stake for me to be hearing about these things on the eleven o'clock news with the rest of New York."

"We'll do the best we can, Mr. Dietrich," I said as I pulled away from him and returned to Peterson's office.

Mike closed the door and I sat at the desk to look over his notes. "Dietrich came here with his boys—the two witnesses. Tried to lawyer up but the guy who represents the hospital was on his third martini before dinner. Told him to just go ahead and cooperate with the police.

"The two you want to talk with are across the hall. Losenti made the mistake of interviewing them together. I've got them separated so we can speak with them one at a time."

"Who've we got?"

"John DuPre. Male, black, forty-two years old. Married, two kids. He's a neurologist. Howard University, Tulane med school, residency down South. Opened a private practice in Manhattan two years ago and he's been affiliated here ever since. The other one is Coleman Harper. Male, white, forty-four. Divorced with no children. Also a neurologist. Vanderbilt undergrad and med school. Practiced for a while. Now he's here as a 'fellow.'"

"What does that mean?"

"You'll have to ask him. I didn't get that far. He's one of the guys Spector—the neurosurgeon—pulled out of the gallery to assist on the operation when Dogen didn't show up. And the patient's doing just fine."

"Who do you want to start with?"

"I'll go get DuPre."

Chapman returned a couple of minutes later with Dr. John DuPre. I stood up to greet him and he extended a hand as I looked him over. He was eight years older and a few inches taller than I, with short-cropped hair, a mustache, wire-rimmed glasses, and a trim physique. He was dressed in a sports jacket and navy slacks and had the same earnest expression on his face that most people sucked into a murder investigation present to their interrogators during the early rounds of questioning.

"I know it's been a long day for you, Dr. DuPre. Detective Chapman and I would like to have you go over your story once more if you don't mind."

"If it will help, I don't mind at all. Seems like I've been doing it all evening.

"I arrived at the medical college in the middle of the afternoon. My private office, where I see most of my patients, is on Central Park West. I came over to Minuit to use the medical library. That's on the sixth floor, where, uh, where Gemma's office is. Or was.

"The library was pretty busy—it usually is in the late afternoons. I got into a discussion with several of my colleagues about a case that Dr. Spector is working on."

"Bob Spector? The neurosurgeon who had asked Dogen to assist the morning she was killed?"

"Exactly. Spector's doing some very important research on Huntington's disease. Do y'all know what that is?"

DuPre cocked his head and looked up at us, his soft southern drawl framing the question.

"Only that it's a hereditary illness, no known treatment."

"That's right, Miss Cooper. It's a disturbance of the central nervous system and it's characterized by progressive intellectual deterioration and involuntary motor movements. Spector's devoted a lot of attention to the disease, and, well, he's the big cheese around here so—"

"Dogen was the chief though, wasn't she?" Chapman asked.

"Yes, but rumor had it that she was moving back to England at the end of this academic semester. So quite frankly," DuPre said, pulling one side of his mouth up into a smile, "a lot of us have figured that Spector's ass is the one to kiss. Forgive my bluntness, Miss Cooper. A lot of us have been trying to hitch our wagons to Bob Spector. I think he'll be our next chief."

"What kind of relationship did you have with Gemma Dogen?"

"The ice maiden? A very distant one. Mind y'all, we got along fine when we had to. But I didn't know her very well and—I know you'll hear this from other people—she really didn't have very much use for me."

"Because?"

"No idea, no idea at all. I don't want to play the race card, as y'all say. Could just as easily have been that she was a snob—didn't think it worth her time to talk to me because I wasn't a surgeon. She kept to herself quite a bit. Every now and then I'd catch up and run with her in the morning—we both jogged on the walkway along the river—but I think she was happiest when she was alone."

"Were you one of the doctors who assisted Spector in place of Gemma Dogen the morning she was killed?"

"No, no. I don't know anything about that, detective. I wasn't even in the hospital Wednesday morning. As a neurologist, I can't do surgical procedures, y'see. I can treat patients with brain disease, but not in the operating room."

"What prompted you to go down to the radiology department when you did, doctor?"

"It wasn't my idea, actually. The credit goes to Dr. Harper, Coleman Harper. Spector had some X rays done of a patient with Huntington's that he's been following for several years. We were talking about the project and Coleman suggested that he and I go down to look, to compare them to the set taken last year.

"We got down to the second floor. Quite surprised to find the door to the room unlocked. But, then, you know the problem we have here with security. It's not unique to us, mind you.

I've seen it at all the large medical centers. I even remember hearing about a murder like this one at Bellevue before I ever came up here to New York."

"What happened, I mean, *exactly* what happened when you went into the room?"

"The gentleman you've got in custody, he was just curled up on the floor sound asleep. Coleman had flipped the light switch on and there he was. You couldn't help but notice the stains on his pants. I knew it was blood. I told Coleman to go out and call someone immediately, that I'd wait to make sure the guy didn't go anywhere."

"Did you wake him?"

"Not 'til Coleman got back. I mean, I couldn't see any weapon, but I couldn't be sure he wasn't sitting on top of it. We just sort of nudged him with our feet. Opened his eyes and started mumbling. Just kept saying, 'Sorry. Sorry.' I have absolutely *no* idea whether he was talking about bein' sorry about bein' somewhere he wasn't supposed to be, or for what he did to Gemma."

"Then?"

"Then the detective we beeped was over there in less than ten minutes. Took the gentleman away with him."

Chapman asked DuPre a few more questions while I recorded some details on my pad. We thanked him and asked him to stick with us a bit longer while we spoke to other witnesses, reminding him not to discuss his statement with anyone else.

Peterson ushered him out of the room and Chapman went to get Coleman Harper.

Dr. Harper was still in a white lab coat when he walked into the office more than three hours after he had been brought from the hospital to the station house to retell the story of the discovery he and DuPre had made. He was a little shorter than DuPre—about my height—with flecks of premature gray in his dark brown hair. He was stocky and solidly built, and his left leg jiggled nervously as he sat in the chair opposite me at the desk.

We shook hands as I explained to him why I needed to question him and told him to relax.

"It's really weird, Miss Cooper. I've never been involved in anything like this before. Where do I start?"

"Don't worry. Most witnesses we meet have never been through anything like this. Mike and I have some questions to ask you."

Chapman started with the usual background information. He got Harper talking about himself and his credentials.

"I first affiliated with Mid-Manhattan about ten years ago. But I left, it was a year or so after Dr. Dogen arrived here, so I wasn't around for much of her tenure. I moved back down to Nashville, where my wife's family lived, to continue my neurological practice there.

"Then, when my marriage broke up, I just thought it was time to try to come back to a great teaching hospital and do some of the things I've always wanted to do. I've been here since last September."

"And you're here on a fellowship?" I asked, looking at Chapman's briefing notes.

"Well, yes. It's a bit of a trade-off, actually, but once my wife left me I decided to try and do things that would make *me* happy for a change. i've always been interested in neurosurgery. So I took a healthy pay cut for this position—I'm a little older than most of the men and women in the program—but the upside is now I can assist in the operating room. I may actually go ahead and try to get into a neurosurgical program here. Something I should have done a long time ago."

I exchanged glances with Chapman and looked down at

Harper's twitching leg. I assumed Mike was thinking like I was and was thankful he didn't make a crack about how steady Harper's hands must be for brain surgery. A friendly interview with the local constabulary and the doctor was completely aflutter. It was the kind of effect Mike and I had on lots of people.

"So you were in the OR when Dr. Dogen was a no-show yesterday morning, am I right?"

"Yes, yes, I was. Dr. Spector was doing a procedure on a stroke victim. The patient had suffered a stroke on the right side of his brain, actually. I try to watch Spector whenever I can. He's really a genius."

"And he picked you out of the crowd to assist?"

"Yes, well, so to speak. There were only a dozen or so of us present and only a smaller handful who'd even worked with him on this kind of thing before. It's quite an honor."

"With a good result for the patient, we understand."

"Not quite out of the woods yet but looking pretty safe at this point."

"Are you involved in this Huntington's disease program with Spector as well?"

"Not officially. But I'm certainly counting on his support to get into the neurosurgical program. And, of course, my years of experience as a neurologist have given me an opportunity to study the disorder. You could certainly say I'm following his work closely."

"So how did you come to be with Dr. DuPre this evening?"

"I had gone to the library to find a volume I needed. When I got there, a bunch of my colleagues were talking about Spector's new X rays of a patient he's been studying and DuPre suggested we go take a look. The X rays were mounted down in radiology. I wanted to wait and finish my research but—"

"Excuse me," I interrupted, "but whose idea was it?"

"John DuPre. He told me he couldn't wait for me because he had to get home for dinner and asked me to go along with him right then."

Great. Half an hour into the case and I've already got conflicting facts, just on the minor stuff. DuPre says it was Harper's idea to go to radiology, Harper says DuPre pushed him to do it.

Inconsistencies, Rod Squires used to lecture me in our training sessions, the hallmarks of truth. A pain in the ass, if you asked me. It's natural for different people to see the same events from different perspectives, we were encouraged to believe, but it sure could foul up a good case.

"Okay, so Dr. DuPre and you went to the second floor—then what happened?"

Harper's version dovetailed with DuPre's from that point on. "I mean, once I saw the blood I thought immediately of Gemma. Has he admitted anything yet?"

"Let me ask *you,* Dr. Harper, did you hear him say anything about Dr. Dogen or the assault?"

"No, he barely spoke in my presence. But I ran down the hall to use the telephone. He wasn't making much sense between the time I got back to him and the time your detective got there. Man seems unstable to me."

"Did you know Dr. Dogen well?"

"Depends on what you mean by that. She wasn't an easy—"

Lieutenant Peterson opened the door. "Excuse me, Alex. Sarah's here, and I think we're almost ready to go with some stand-ins. And keep away from the windows in the squad room. Somebody's flapping his mouth to the press. You got a couple of camera crews setting up in front of the building and if they could get a shot of you up here I'm sure they'd love it."

"Thanks, Dr. Harper. Sorry to interrupt you. Would you mind waiting across the hall again? We'll try to get back to you as soon as we finish up some of this other business."

"Have a slice of pizza, Doc," Chapman said as he got to his feet and gave Coleman Harper a slap on the back. "We got some homeless guys watching the ball game inside who could use a good checkup. Maybe you and Dr. DuPre could make yourselves useful."

12

"What do you want me to do?" Sarah asked, already set up at a desk with her laptop computer.

"Try cranking out a couple of warrants for those two shopping carts. One of them belongs to Pops, the other one to a friend of his. See if Ramirez and Losenti can help you with the probable cause—they know a lot more about the facts than I do at this point. Peterson wants to run some lineups, and I may need help interviewing a couple of the witnesses if they make IDs. Pace yourself, please, will you?"

I left her in the squad room and walked down the hallway to the lineup cubicle. Wallace and Chapman were trying to arrange Pops and the five fillers in positions for the viewing. Jerry McCabe was handing each of them a clean, V-necked surgical blouse so all of their clothing would be similar.

Pops had been relieved of the bloody pants and was sitting in the fourth chair from the door holding a placard with his number printed on it and talking to himself.

"No good, Jerry," I said as I scanned the pack. "The two closest to me look much too young."

"Yeah, well, *you* try finding stand-ins at this hour of the night. They're not exactly throwing themselves at me."

"Send one of the uniformed guys down to that all-night drugstore on the corner of Lex. Get some talcum powder. I'd just like to gray them up a bit so they look a little more like Pops, okay?"

Mercer was telling the array what they had to do to earn their five dollars for the night. Hold their numbers in front of their chests, on their feet when he told them to be, approach the mirror and stand before it for as long as directed, facing front before turning to display each profile, then come back and sit in their seats. A half-hour's work as a lineup extra would keep these guys in Thunderbird wine for the night.

I walked out to check on Sarah. She was pounding away at her laptop computer and looked up to tell me that Pops's clothing was on its way to the lab for analysis.

Anna Bartoldi was still manning the hotline phone in the corner of the squad room. She got up from her desk and passed me on her way out to the soda machine. "Dinner?"

I waved Sarah along and the three of us crossed the hallway to pick up a soda from the vending machine and munch on a slice of lukewarm pizza. "Calls still coming in?" I asked Anna.

"I'm up over three hundred fifty. So far, four women have turned in their husbands and six suspect their boyfriends. It'll slow up for me tomorrow once word gets out we got a candidate."

I put down the pizza and took the soda can with me when I heard Mercer's voice booming out my name. When I got back to the lineup room, he was sprinkling Johnson's baby powder on the heads of the younger fillers and I viewed them through the window to compare them to their more mature companions. "Much better, Mercer. Let's not waste any more time."

Peterson's men had assembled four people to look at the array. One was a third-year student at Minuit who had worked in the sixth-floor library—down the hall from Dogen's office—until one in the morning on the night she was killed. Two others were the cleaning staff who covered that shift, and the last was a nurse's aide who sneaked into the medical school on her breaks so she could use the phones at the reception desk to call and talk to her boyfriend at odd times throughout the night.

I stood in the back of the darkened viewing room while Wallace and McCabe led each of the witnesses through in turn. None of the group looked familiar to the medical student or the nurse's aide. But both of the women who cleaned the professors' offices each night recognized the man who called himself Pops.

I left the room and told Mike to bring the two housekeepers in to me, one at a time, in Peterson's office.

I took out a fresh pad and headed it with the date and time: 11:45 P.M. Pedigree information on each had already been documented by the detectives who had canvassed the hospital, so I reviewed the Xerox of the notes that told me that Ludmila Grascowicz and Graciela Martinez were both assigned to clean the fifth- and sixth-floor offices in the Minuit Medical Center.

Both women were immigrants—Ludmila from Poland and Graciela from the Dominican Republic. The former had been at Mid-Manhattan for three years and the latter for six months. Ludmila had requested a change of assignment to day duty after the murder of Gemma Dogen and Graciela had resigned altogether. Both of them knew Dogen by sight since she was often around in the midnight-to-eight shift that they had worked. Neither had much to do with her because they had strict instructions never to enter Dogen's office during the night. She didn't like to be disturbed when she was doing her research and writing so her chambers were always cleaned by the day staff and only if her door had been left open. The doctor didn't like intrusions and she didn't like anyone touching her files.

Ludmila's accent was as thick as her waist and her ankles. Her chest was heaving as she tried to answer my questions, making the sign of the cross after every response. Yes, during the last few weeks she had often seen the man who was holding the number 4 in the lineup. He had tried to talk to her several times but she was unable to understand his speech. She came on duty at eleven-thirty Monday evening and had encountered the man in the stairwell between the fifth and sixth floors. No, there was nothing unusual about his appearance or his clothing. But, then, she usually averted her eyes when she approached him since she had repeatedly complained to security about his presence after hours in the medical college. One last sign of the cross, and an extra blessing for Dr. Dogen, and Ludmila had no more to add.

Graciela's jumpiness made Ludmila seem almost calm by contrast. She shared responsibility for cleaning the same two floors. Although she and Ludmila rarely communicated with each other, they had joined forces to complain about Pops's nocturnal wanderings. The water cup that someone had given the young woman to fortify her for her conversation with me was spilling its supply over the edge onto the desk where I was taking notes because her hand was shaking so badly. Graciela was certain she had seen this man on the sixth floor after midnight in the early hours of Tuesday morning coming out of the men's room. She didn't call security because they never listened to her when she tried to make herself heard. But she went immediately to the library to clean there since she knew it was likely that at least one of the students would be burning the midnight oil.

I thanked the women for their cooperation and passed them on to the lieutenant to arrange for their rides home.

Sarah came into Peterson's office to see what we would do next. The warrants were completed and she would make certain they would be signed in the morning as soon as the judge took the bench in the arraignment part.

We walked back to the lineup room and looked through the two-way mirror. Mercer had rearranged the area after the stand-ins had been discharged and was again sitting at the table with Pops, talking with him in a quiet, steady manner in an effort to gain his confidence and trust. Sarah and I had watched him do it hundreds of times.

"It's odd, isn't it?" Sarah remarked. "They always look so benign when you get these guys into a station house or a courtroom. All the way here in the cab I was hating this man—rethinking my beliefs about capital punishment. A murder like this and I think I'm capable of giving the lethal injection myself."

"I thought the same thing the moment I got here and saw him drenched in Gemma Dogen's blood. How do you *do* that to another human being and just walk away?"

"Then you see the guy half an hour later and he looks absolutely pathetic, doesn't he?"

We were standing with our arms crossed, peering in at the duo. "He doesn't even look strong enough to have taken on someone as fit as Dogen. I guess, like Chet Kirschner figures, that's the advantage he had in surprising her."

"Do we know who he is yet?"

"Mercer's trying to get that now. Losenti printed him when they brought him in. Figured they got him for criminal trespass if they couldn't hold him on anything else. They'll run the prints through the computer and hopefully have an answer by morning."

Sarah stifled a yawn.

"Let's make some decisions about what's next and let me get you home."

We walked back to Peterson's office and asked him to bring Mercer and Mike in to give us a sense of where we stood.

Mercer came in shaking his head. "He's falling asleep on me. I don't think there's any point in going on tonight. It's almost one o'clock. Let's put him to bed, find out who he is, and I'll start on him fresh in the morning."

"You girls oughtta go home," Peterson added. "Pops is a keeper. He's under on the trespass. What do we give out about the murder?"

Sarah and I looked at each other. At the moment, we had nothing at all except the potential for a circumstantial case. "Let McGraw tell them we've got no charges on anybody. Still an open case. There'll be a feeding frenzy if we say much else."

Mike came in and closed the door behind him. "You got anything?" the lieutenant asked.

"Yeah," he said. "Almost an arrest for public lewdness. Your hospital homeless are in the Anti-Crime Office watching old movies on the television. The short guy in the gray sweats, turns out he's T. T. Thompson. The T.T. stands for 'Tippy-Toes'—has fourteen collars for burglary. He's in there looking at *To Catch a Thief* with the rest of them. All of a sudden he stands up, drops his pants, and starts giving himself a lube job. I don't know if he's playing with himself because Grace Kelly looks so great or because the movie's about a cat burglar who gets better stuff than T.T. ever dreamed existed. I practically had to smack him to get him to stop."

"How about anything more useful to *us,* Mikey?"

"Well, the second shopping cart belongs to another tunnel dweller who's in there. Agosto Marín. He's known as 'Can

Man.' Seems he wheels the cart around the outside of Mid-Manhattan all day picking soda cans out of recycling bins and garbage pails. Sells 'em to get the money to buy crack. Says you'll find all he has to his name are several hundred cans—you don't need a warrant to look.

"At the moment, Can Man is sober. And he's swearing to me that Pops was with him in the tunnel from a little bit after midnight until the two of them went above ground Wednesday morning. He knows it was that night because by the time they came up at daybreak, it was snowing. And it *did* snow Wednesday morning, remember?"

"What the hell have we got here, huh?" Mercer asked of no one in particular.

"We've got a blood-soaked suspect who won't tell us who he is. Opportunity? You bet. 'Cause he lives in the hospital, illegally. Motive? Depends on what we decide the motive is," Mike answered. "If it was a sexual assault attempt that failed, I'd say just by looking at him he'd have trouble getting it up."

"Wait a minute." I interrupted Mike's narrative. "You're telling me you know by *looking* at someone whether or not he can get it up? I've got friends who would pay dearly for your services, Mr. Chapman. Let's leave that point for later debate. This could have been an aborted attempt at a rape *or* a robbery. We still don't know if anything's missing from her office."

He went on. "We've got two people who put Pops on or near the sixth floor within the probable time range of the murder. And we got an aluminum can-collecting junkie who's gonna be his alibi. We got no weapon. No DNA. Unlikely to find prints, according to the Crime Scene guys—but, then, you could pick up surgical gloves anyplace you look in that hospital."

"I'm getting nowhere with him tonight. Let's knock it off and pick up again tomorrow," Mercer said.

The excitement of a solution to this brutal killing had

lifted all our spirits several hours back and now we were about to crash from the combination of our exhaustion and the stalled progress of the investigation. Detectives were signing out and saying goodnight as they ferried the assorted witnesses—civilians and physicians—to their homes. We packed up our case folders and note pads, figuring our schedules for the next day. Mercer offered to take Sarah, and Mike said he'd drop me at my apartment.

We walked downstairs and the precinct commander directed us out the back door and down an alley that led out to Lexington Avenue to avoid the camera crews staking out the front of the station house. We turned in a separate direction from Mercer and waved good-bye as Mike led me to his car.

"What's your gut say on this one, Mike?"

"Confused at the moment. I want this guy bad and the blood puts him over the top. Then I look at him and I gotta think, maybe there was a second guy, an accomplice. That would certainly help explain why she didn't have a chance."

"Yeah. Maybe we're just tired at this point. It'll look better tomorrow."

"I called my mother. For your sake, so you know you didn't miss anything, I mean. She said the Final Jeopardy question tonight was about physics—something about the quantum theory."

"Forget it. I plead ignorance. It'd be my luck to get on the show and lose 'cause the big question would be about calculus or the New Testament or some of those topics I couldn't bet a nickel on, you know? Physics is one of them."

"Me, too." Mike was cruising up Third Avenue toward the block my apartment was on, ignoring the string of red lights and making the drive in under ten minutes.

"She was a real beauty, wasn't she? Such a class act."

I looked quizzically at Mike. "Gemma Dogen?"

"No, sorry. I was just thinking about Grace Kelly, from the

movie tonight. She looked fabulous in this one with Cary Grant. But I remember the moment I fell in love with her, when I saw her in *Dial M for Murder*. Plain and simple, dressed in those dowdy clothes, with that grainy black-and- white film."

"Great flick." We both had a weakness for classic movies.

"I think she looked even more beautiful when she wasn't all dolled up, like in the scene at the end of *Dial M*. She's been in jail for the murder, then they decide to test her story and they let her go home. Remember? Man, she looked so vulnerable, you just had to love her."

"I never realized you liked your women so vulnerable, Mike," I said, intending the line as a joke.

He pulled in the driveway in front of my building and waited for one of the doormen to open my car door. "Not everybody can handle the self-sufficient types like you, Blondie. It's nice to be needed every once in a while."

Take your best shot, Chapman, I thought to myself as the car pulled away and I walked inside. What would I have to do to look to the rest of the world as vulnerable as I felt?

I emptied the mailbox of its usual impersonal tidings and took the slow elevator ride to my empty apartment. I didn't bother to hang up my coat but simply threw it on the ottoman in the living room.

The change from the precinct's soda vending machine weighed on the threads in my jacket pocket, so I reached in and stacked the quarters on my dresser before hanging the suit in my closet. I had forgotten to return Gemma's apartment keys to Mercer and laid the chain, with its souvenir of London's Tower Bridge, on my bedside table next to the thick volume of Trollope. No one would be needing them tonight.

At least by this time tomorrow I'd have the company of a cold-nosed weimaraner to console me.

13

I was up at 6:45 on Friday morning and out of the shower by seven when Chapman called. "Shut off your radio and turn on the tube. I haven't checked the *Today* show yet but Jim Ryan's leading with the story on the local news. He's got great sources. Says we're holding a blood-stained psycho in the med center murder case."

I clicked the remote to activate the set but Ryan was already on to the story of the subway shooting in the Bronx IRT station. "Damn. I just missed it."

"If you're coming to the station house before you go to your office this morning, I'll give you a lift, okay?"

"Fine. I'll be ready in twenty minutes. Pick me up around the corner, in front of P. J. Bernstein's." I finished blow-drying my hair and tried to bring myself to life with some mascara and a touch of blusher. I was sick of the somber colors of the winter wools I had worn throughout this dreary week and decided to lighten the palette and perhaps, thereby, my mood. I sifted through my clothes for a favorite Escada suit—lipstick red with black trim on the collar and around the kick pleat.

The deli owner greeted me warmly when I walked into Bernstein's and ordered two dozen bagels, rolls, doughnuts, and enough coffee cups to earn me a moderately pleasant welcome to the squad room.

Mike's car was curbside when I emerged with my small load. He drove downtown to the 17th Precinct station house, gnawing at a piece of coffee cake held in one hand and steering with the other. I picked up the *Post* from the car seat and found Mickey Diamond's byline on page 3: DOC DIES DEFYING RAPIST—SUSPECT HELD IN QUESTIONING.

There were no reporters outside the building when Mike and I arrived. We walked in together, past the sergeant on duty at the front desk and the uniformed cops in the muster room who were about to turn out for a day on foot patrol, 8 A.M. to 4 P.M.

Lieutenant Peterson was already at the desk that had become his command center since Wednesday morning. He lived fifty miles outside of the city but had spent the night—or the three hours' sleep he had allowed himself—on a cot in the Homicide Squad office farther uptown.

"Good morning, Alexandra. Morning, Mike. Had some progress overnight. Albany came up with a hit on the fingerprints and we got an ID on Pops."

Peterson handed Mike the printout of the New York State Identification System rap sheet. Chapman read from it aloud. "'Austin Charles Bailey. Date of birth, October 12, 1934.' Makes him sixty-three. Looks like he's got about twenty priors. Burglary, grand larceny, possession of stolen property, burglary again." He flipped the pages, his eyes scanning the list faster than he could call out the charges.

"Last one, twelve years ago. Murder. Not guilty by reason of insanity."

Peterson had already checked out the rest. "Yeah, institutionalized in the state loony bin for the criminally insane in Rockland County. Only problem is, he walked off the campus two and a half years ago and nobody reported him missing."

"Who'd he kill?"

"His old lady. He'd been in and out of mental hospitals most of 'em were drinking. She hit him with a sixteen-ounce bottle of Colt .45—a broken one. That accounts for the scar that runs across his cheek and down his neck. He went loco and—"

Chapman broke in. "Let me guess. He stabbed her with, what? A kitchen knife?"

"Serrated steak knife."

"Not once or twice, right, loo?"

"About twenty-two points of entry. Not to mention some extra slashes on the face just for good measure."

"Typical domestic," I murmured. It fit the pattern of most familial homicides. Not only the fatal wounds but the savage disfigurement of the victim in addition, usually saved for someone the killer knows well enough to hate.

Many batterers were never violent outside the home against strangers, saving their venom for the people closest to them while presenting a different face to the world. But for scores of others, the first killing broke down the boundaries and expanded the focus of the rage.

"Still feeling sorry for the old guy, Coop?"

I was already shifting gears, mentally and emotionally. The challenge was no longer figuring out who had killed Gemma Dogen. Now I needed to think in legal terms, to build the careful and logical blocks toward cementing a circumstantial case that would withstand procedural challenges in a court of law.

"Is he talking this morning?"

"I haven't let anybody near him yet. Mercer's got the best rapport with him so far. I'll send him back in as soon as he arrives."

"Mike, why don't you take him some breakfast and see if you can make nice to him while we're waiting for Mercer."

My beeper went off as Mike opened the shopping bags of food and coffee to distribute to the guys in the squad room. I unhooked the little black device from my waistband and checked the number that appeared on the screen.

"Schaeffer," I said. Chapman paused at the door and waited for me to return the call to Bill Schaeffer, the serologist who ran the laboratory at the Medical Examiner's Office.

He answered his own phone. "Didn't want to disturb you during the night but thought you'd want to know first thing. That *is* human blood on the pants you sent down to me last night. Sure you all knew that but I figured you'd want it confirmed."

Things were falling into place. I thanked Doctor Schaeffer and nodded at Chapman, mouthing the word "blood" as I gave him a thumbs-up.

"What else can you tell me?"

"I'll have preliminary DNA results for you in the next day or so. We're working on it. Can you get me a sample of the suspect's blood, too? Just on the chance he nicked himself anywhere and it's on the deceased's clothing."

"Great. Sure thing. Sarah can write up a court order to get a sample from the defendant this morning. You want to send someone up here to draw his blood?

"And thanks for the call, Bill. I'll speak to you over the weekend." Setting up the gels and running the probes for DNA results, the genetic fingerprinting that could determine to a virtual certainty the source of the blood on Pops's pants, was a process that could take as long as two or three months. A new technique, known as the PCR testing of DNA, would give Schaeffer an early reading, which could be confirmed by later tests, in as short a time as forty-eight hours.

"Nothing much in these but I've made copies of all of 'em for you," Peterson said, handing me the police reports he'd been reviewing. Each one summarized an interview with a hospital employee or official concerning their whereabouts and activities in the hours before and after the stabbing.

I glanced at the contents but my thoughts were in the room with Austin Bailey. I fast forwarded to worries about how tough an adversary the judge would appoint to represent him. I knew that every step we took from this moment on would be scrutinized under the harsh and unforgiving eye of the trial and appellate courts.

"Mercy, mercy," Wallace said, looking at his watch as he walked into the squad room and saw Peterson motioning him over to where we stood. "I didn't realize you were holding a sunrise service today or I would have been on board hours ago."

"Get in here. We need you to go to work on Pops right away. We're going to have to get him downtown to be arraigned by the end of the day or some kneejerk's likely to void the arrest," Peterson said. "I want you to see who you're dealing with."

The courts in New York have a very strict rule about the length of time during which a defendant may be held without the opportunity to appear before a judge for a bail hearing. The latest trend was the complete dismissal of the charges when police and prosecutors dragged their feet getting the suspect into the courtroom.

Peterson briefed Wallace on Bailey's sheet and background. "Sounds like he ain't goin' anywhere except back to his padded cell. Lemme see what he'll give me this morning."

Wallace picked up two cups of coffee and balanced a bagel on top of each. He walked to the still open door of the holding pen and greeted Austin Bailey, who was stretched out the length of the wooden bench. The prisoner—we'd all assumed his status as a "guest" had been downgraded to a custodial relationship during the night—sat up and appeared to smile as he talked to Mercer.

After the detective handed Pops his breakfast, he led him back down the hallway to the interrogation room.

Wallace emerged briefly to come back to Peterson's office, pick up a pad, and suggest to us that we watch some of the conversation through the two-way mirror. "Don't want to lose this good thing, baby," Mercer said aloud, to no one in particular. Then he nodded at me. "Think Eddie Floyd, Coop," he urged, smiling and whistling the chorus of the R&B singer's only big hit, "Knock on Wood," as he turned around to head back to talk with Bailey.

"Anybody Mirandize him since last night?" I asked, referring to the Supreme Court ruling that had crept into the criminal justice lexicon as a verb, a noun, and a landmark decision.

"Don't worry, that's what I'll start with. I'll read him his rights but I don't think it'll much matter. I'm not sure we're talking on the same wave length."

Mercer returned to start his session with Pops. I walked over to the adjacent room and peered through the glass. Both men sat at the Formica-topped table in the bare room. Mercer was clean-shaven and well dressed, sitting erect and talking with Bailey, who was taking bites of his food and sips of his coffee. The older man was slumped over the table, his few front teeth nipping at the soft doughnut while he slurped from the cup without lifting it to his mouth.

Detective Wallace was warming up his subject, chatting about himself and his father, trying to find some level on which to connect with the broken figure he was hoping to engage in a coherent conversation.

I walked into the hallway, chastising myself for mingling

the pity I felt when I looked at Pops with the outrage I had internalized because of Gemma Dogen's murder.

Chapman came toward me and we reentered the room with the viewing window. Mercer had thrown away the paper cups and was eyeballing Austin Bailey across the table. He was explaining the right to remain silent to his target, using language and paraphrases that a second-grade child would have been able to understand.

I wondered if Mike was thinking, as I was, about the futility of this questioning. A killer with this kind of psychiatric history would necessitate a competency hearing and I was already cross-examining the shrinks who would testify for the defense that Arthur Bailey was unable to stand trial.

As we watched Wallace try to hold his subject's attention, Bailey reached for the old black rotary phone on the end of the table. He was ignoring Mercer and picked up the receiver to dial a series of numbers.

"Hello, Ma? Yeah. Charlie's back—"

Mercer's long arm gently wrested the phone from Pops's grip and replaced it on the hook.

"I wish he'd just let the guy talk," I said under my breath to Chapman. "Now he's going to claim he wasn't allowed to make his phone call."

"Coop, you know where that phone goes? It's a friggin' intercom. You can't dial out—it only goes to extensions in the station house. He's not talking to his mother, he's talking to Harvey the rabbit, for Chrissakes. I don't even know why we're wasting our time with this nonsense. Let's just take him down to Criminal Court and get on with it," Mike said, walking out of the airless room.

I followed him back to Peterson's office. We were trying to figure out what to do next when Wallace joined us.

"He says he'll talk to you, Cooper. Might as well come in and see what you think. I wouldn't bother with your video unit. This is either an act worthy of the Ringling Brothers or he's really deranged. I think this is one scene you wouldn't want to show a jury on videotape."

I shrugged my shoulders and retraced my steps, this time going into the interrogation room with Mercer.

Pops looked up at me when I closed the door behind us and offered a grin in my direction. "Ruthless and toothless, ma'am," Bailey said by way of introduction. "That's what the doctors always say about me." Dead on.

Wallace told him who I was and why I was there as I pulled one of the chairs alongside Mercer's position.

"I want to talk with you about some things that happened at the hospital, Mr. Bailey. D'you understand me?"

"I'm sorry about the hospital, ma'am. I'm sorry. Sorry, sorry, sorry."

How much more frightening, it seemed to me, Gemma Dogen's struggle must have been against a madman with whom she had been unable to reason when she was pleading for her life.

"That's what I want to talk about. I want you to tell me what you're so sorry about so I can tell the judge."

It would be imperative for me to prove to a judge, and then to a jury, that Bailey had been given his rights in a manner he comprehended if there were any statements he was about to make that I wanted to introduce into evidence.

"Did Detective Wallace tell you that you don't have to talk to me, Mr. Bailey?"

"I *do* want to talk to you, lady. I haven't talked to a nice girl since my wife passed on."

"You see, you don't have to answer any—"

"She talked to the knife, didn't she? That doctor talked to the knife."

A chill passed through me like a bolt of lightning. Was he talking about Gemma?

"What do you mean?"

"Didn't talk to me. Didn't talk to nobody. She talked to the knife all right."

Now I had to bring him back to a logical conversation. I had to finish some kind of Miranda warning but not lose his willingness to talk about the killing.

Suddenly Pops's facial expression changed, his mouth drew tightly closed and his hands clasped against both ears as though responding to a loud noise. I leaned forward toward him as Mercer reached for one of his arms and pulled it away from the side of his head. Pops rocked back and forth in his chair, wailing for us to get him some Kleenex. Mercer nodded at me and I got to my feet, running down the hallway to grab some tissues from my purse. I returned with a handful of them and placed them in front of the prisoner, who smiled and began to shred them into tiny bits, ball them up, and press them in each ear.

He kept rocking as he stuffed the Kleenex, which hung in little strips past his lobes. "Charlie's talking to me. See?" he said, looking at Mercer. "I told you that's who tells me what to do. Nothin' you can blame on me 'cause everythin' I ever done is what Charlie makes me do."

"Tell her who Charlie is, Pops."

"He's my brother, lady. Born the same day I was only he never left the hospital. Kept him there all these years, but he always talks to Mama and me. Every day. Tells me what to do."

I looked at Mercer and tried to find an outlet for my temper. My elbow rested on the table, head in my hand, as I struggled with a plan for how to proceed.

Could he be malingering and doing it as well as this? Or was I simply wasting my time talking to someone who would never make any sense, never be found competent in a court of law?

"Why don't you tell me what Charlie told you to do to the

doctor? Why don't we talk about that for a while? Charlie told me to ask you about that."

Pops smiled at me again when I spoke Charlie's name. "Yeah, but I can't hear him now. All's I can tell you is how I'm sorry that the doctor isn't feeling good today."

The three of us chased each other's words around in circles for the next twenty minutes. We didn't move Bailey from his senseless ramblings, and when he tired of us altogether he crossed his arms on the table and rested his head against them.

Wallace stood and motioned me out of the room. Chapman and Peterson had been watching through the window and started back to the lieutenant's office when they saw us leave. I was frustrated and annoyed and certain that nothing Bailey said would be of any use to us in building the case against him.

"Going nowhere."

"This is not a scene to memorialize on tape, that's for sure."

Mercer took off his jacket, rolled up his shirt sleeves, and announced that he'd go in and keep the conversation up until we made a decision about booking Pops and making the arrest official.

"Let me make some calls to my office. See how Battaglia wants me to go on from here. Make sure Public Relations is ready for the blitz from the press. Give me half an hour on the phone."

The lieutenant got up from behind the desk. "Use this one. I'll be out in the squad room.

"You ready for a little more pressure, Alexandra?"

"Shoot."

"Capital Defenders Office called. Steve Rubinstein. Heard on the news you have someone in custody and they want to represent him. Want to send someone up here to talk to him, make you cut off the questioning."

"Tell 'em to call his brother, Charlie," Chapman said.

New York had reinstated the death penalty in 1996 and the intentional killing of a woman during an attempted rape would make the murderer a prime candidate for a lethal cocktail after his conviction. Battaglia had opposed the legislation and I guessed he would be relieved that Pops's psychiatric condition might take him out of the running for such a result.

I took the slip of paper with Rubinstein's number on it from Peterson and added his name to the list of calls I needed to make.

I sat at the desk and dialed Battaglia's number. Rose answered, told me he was in the car on his way to deliver a speech to the Citizens Crime Commission. She patched me through.

"Good work, Alex. Congratulate Peterson for me."

"I need your advice on this one, Paul. At the moment, everything we've got is circumstantial. Forget statements. Nothing he says makes very much sense.

"It could be another day or so until we get the DNA match on the blood. I'm hoping that by then we'll turn up some hard evidence, like something he took from Dogen's office, or maybe even the weapon. I mean, they're going through all the garbage receptacles and all the alleyways around the hospital. I'm reluctant to stand before a judge and ask to hold the guy with what we've got on the case at this point," I said, outlining Bailey's history to the District Attorney as I finished up my presentation.

"He's never been discharged from Rockland State?" Battaglia asked, referring to one of the psychiatric facilities of the New York prison system.

"No. He absconded."

"Let's do an end run, Alex. Skip the arrest and arraignment until you have all the evidence you want. Get him over to the psych ward at Bellevue and tell Rockland you want them to do a hearing on the escape charge. That way, he's held in the prison section of the hospital, which buys you a little time to put the case together while he's under police guard. We won't lock him up for Dogen's killing 'til you tell me you're ready."

"You'll back me on it, boss?" I asked, knowing that my nemesis, Deputy Chief of the Trial Division Pat McKinney, would be second-guessing every decision I made on the case.

"Absolutely. No point in sticking our necks out 'til we have the results you need. Screw the Capital Defenders. He hasn't asked for a lawyer yet and we haven't charged him with murder. I'll handle the media on this myself."

I hung up and dialed Mid-Manhattan Hospital. Maureen Forester had been admitted earlier this morning. The operator gave me her extension number and connected me to the room.

"How do you feel?"

"So far, so good. Even better since I heard you got your man. And thanks for the robe."

"Well, I understand there's a solarium at the end of your hallway where all the ambulatory patients wander in and out. I figured if you're the best-dressed girl in the crowd, you might attract some companions who'll gossip with you."

"I take it you still want me to stay in here for a couple of days, then?"

"Yeah. We don't know what we've got yet. Mike thinks Pops may have had an accomplice when he attacked Dogen. Some of his cronies may have heard or seen something after the murder. We'd just like to play it safe if you don't mind."

"Mind? This is a piece of cake. My first audition is at eleven-thirty. They're bringing some interns by to have me describe my symptoms."

"Show-and-tell?"

"No show, thank you very much. Just a history for the moment."

"Well, Sarah will be up to visit later. I'll be in touch. Mercer and Mike send their love. 'Bye."

I made some more calls, then opened Peterson's door and checked what was going on in the squad room. Almost all of the men had gone back to the hospital to continue to canvass for evidence or witnesses. Wallace was still in the room with Bailey but making no progress.

The lieutenant was reviewing the memo books of two of his men. "Battaglia's got a great idea to keep us from jumping the gun on arraigning Bailey." I explained the plan to lodge him in the prison psych ward on his old case and avoid a premature statement on the strengths of our case until the evidence was analyzed and asked Peterson to tell Chapman, Wallace, and the rest of the team.

"I feel pretty useless here, Loo. It makes more sense for me to go down to my office and get some work done, don't you think? If you need me for anything else, just call and I'll come on back."

I gathered all of my paperwork and left the precinct, again by the rear exit. I grabbed a cab on Lexington Avenue and continued to read police reports as it plodded downtown through the busy traffic of a midday Friday. I arrived at the office as most of the assistants were breaking for lunch. Laura handed me my messages, offering to bring me something to eat on her way back from a round of errands. I placed my order for some tuna salad and a Diet Coke and settled in to return calls and check on the lawyers in the unit.

The afternoon dragged for me. No word from anyone at the Squad, and Sarah was at the hospital keeping Maureen company. The usual trail of complainants in new cases dropped off as it always seemed to on Fridays after the lunch hour. And for those of my colleagues not on trial, it was a get-away time. If I wasn't looking for them, they certainly weren't looking for me.

It was after four-thirty when Laura told me that Jordan Goodrich, my best friend from my first days at law school, was on the line.

"Susan just called me. She knows you're in the middle of a big case but wonders if you feel like joining us for a simple dinner at home with the kids tonight?"

"Thanks, but I don't think so. I'm whipped. I'm just going to make it an early night at home. Me and my Lean Cuisine."

"How about a drink first?"

"I'd love it."

For the ten years that we had been out of school, Jordan and I had a tradition of meeting every couple of Fridays to catch up on each other's lives. From a modest background and a small-town Georgia family, Jordan had worked his way through college and outsmarted most of our law school class-mates to a position on the Law Review and a brilliant career. He and Susan had been my closest friends in Charlottesville and there were few experiences of my adult life that we had not weathered or celebrated together.

I checked with Peterson before leaving the office to meet Jordan at our regular haunt, Bemelmans bar at the Carlyle. The lieutenant told me that Wallace and Ramirez would be taking Austin Bailey down to the Bellevue prison ward in a couple of hours and that Chapman and the rest of the team were still at the hospital. Chief McGraw planned to announce to the press crews that there had been a break in the Dogen case but not yet an arrest. That way they'd get Pops out of the precinct after the camera crews disappeared. I said I'd keep the beeper on 'til I reached home, where I'd be for the rest of the evening.

Jordan was waiting in a corner booth at the Carlyle, below the whimsical mural of the animals skating in Central Park. The piano player was in the middle of a Bachrach medley when I arrived and somehow wound up in an elaborate rendition of "I'll Never Fall in Love Again" as I walked over to Jordan's table.

"Timing is everything," I said, laughing at the musical selection.

George, who had waited on us for as many Fridays as the two of us had been coming there, appeared with my Dewar's before I could unbutton and remove my coat. Jordan was halfway through his first Stoli martini as I kissed him on the cheek and settled onto the leather banquette beside him.

I had barely gotten past the usual questions about Susan and the children when my beeper went off. I looked at the numbers and saw that it was Bill Schaeffer again, calling from the lab.

"Great. Let me just call him back. Maybe I will join you guys for dinner. This'll give me a second wind—it's the news about the blood match I've been waiting for."

I had to go through the hotel lounge to get to the pay phone, weaving around small tables topped with drinks and baskets of homemade potato chips and surrounded by well-dressed patrons from the nearby art and antiques galleries.

I dropped a quarter in the slot and dialed Schaeffer's number. "Bill, it's Alex. Got something for me already?"

"Yeah, but you won't like it. It's *not* her blood."

"It's what?" I said. I was incredulous. "It *has* to be Dogen's blood."

"Well, it isn't. I know they told you Bailey had no injuries but it's entirely consistent with his blood type, Alex. I don't have DNA results on him yet but I'm certain this is going to turn out to be his own blood. I don't think the man you're holding is the killer."

Calm down, I told myself as I tried to absorb the impact of Schaeffer's information.

I dialed the 17th and told Peterson the news. "I'm coming

back over. Get me an EMS crew there immediately. I want somebody to examine Austin Bailey in my presence, *now*. We've wasted twenty-four hours on a false lead. Tell McGraw he should start leaking the fact that we *don't* have a suspect, for a change. And you'd better let Maureen know what's going on before we do anything else. Somebody may still be on the loose in that hospital."

Jordan had ordered another round to congratulate me on the good news I had gone out to receive. "Save it for next time," I snapped at him, grabbing at my things. "Sorry to run on you, but I've just been blindsided by a murderer."

I left him with his mouth hanging open, a setup of drinks on the table, and the bar tab. My head throbbed.

14

It was close to seven o'clock Friday evening as I pounded up the staircase in the station house. The excitement that had animated the task force team members in the morning had dissipated. An aura of dejection was palpable.

Jerry McCabe was talking on the phone behind a desk against the window. He put his hand over the mouthpiece and called out to me, "They're in the room at the end of the hall with Bailey, Alex. Go ahead on in."

I left my coat and books in Peterson's office and went down to the locker room. The lieutenant and Wallace were standing with their backs to me, a couple of other men were leaning against the wall, and Pops was sitting on the table stripped down to a filthy green pair of boxer shorts.

A medic from the Emergency Medical Service was kneeling in front of Austin Bailey examining his left leg from the thigh down the calf to the sole of his foot.

"Not a scratch," he announced to the lieutenant as he stood up and pushed away from the table.

Peterson introduced me to Juan Guerra, who had just finished a head-to-toe inspection of Austin Bailey. The prisoner was still atop the table, his chin resting against his bare chest, mumbling to himself as this small band of unhappy cops looked at him like a specimen in a public zoo.

"Mercer, you got a copy of the Polaroid of Pops's pants showing the bloodstains?" I asked.

As Wallace removed a batch of photos from his jacket pocket, Bailey looked up at me and grinned. "I told you it's paint, lady."

I passed the Polaroid to Guerra, pointing out to him the large areas of discoloration on the lower part of the left pants leg and explaining that there had been a substantial amount of blood on the right side and in his shoes as well.

He nodded his head as he viewed the picture and spoke a single word: "Varicosities."

A chorus of "What?" echoed in the locker room.

"I'm ready to throw the switch on the electric chair myself 'cause of this bloodbath and you're telling me this guy's got varicose veins?" Wallace asked.

"See it all the time, especially with a lot of the homeless population who haven't had any regular medical care." Guerra kneeled in front of Bailey again and calmly asked him to extend both his legs. He picked up the older man's feet one at a time and ran his hand over the skin, circling the area around the prominent bone that protruded from the inner aspect of each ankle. "He's certainly got varicose veins. And when they burst, he could bleed to death right on the spot if you don't control the puncture."

Pops was looking back and forth as everyone talked about him, scratching his midriff with one hand and nervously running his fingers over the desk with the other.

I squatted and looked at Bailey's ankles with the medic.

"I know my grandmother had 'em, Juan," said Peterson, "but what the hell are varicose veins, anyway?"

"Keep a watch, Lieutenant," the young EMS worker told him, "they're usually hereditary. Dilated or twisted veins, most often in the legs and thighs, develop a weakness.

"The valves in the vein that circulate. he blood back up to the heart, they can't do the job. Could be old injuries from drug use or just—"

Wallace pointed at the lines of old needle marks on Bailey's arms and thighs. "Damn, he's got more tracks than the B and O Railroad."

"But there's not a new mark there that I can see. Not a scratch, not a scar, not a blemish, except for those dried-up old areas," I said.

Guerra continued. "Miss Cooper, I've seen 'em spurt like an oil well. Heart keeps pumping, the vein opens up, and the blood's got nowhere to go. Last week, my partner and I responded to a call on Thirty-sixth Street. Old guy's shoes just filled up with blood and flooded over.

"I put my finger right on the vein—that big one next to the ankle bone—applied pressure for a minute, and stopped it right up. Go to look at it half an hour later and there's nothin' to see. Comes out of a hole the size of a pinprick. You either stop it pretty quick or the patient can bleed to death."

"Well, why the hell didn't he just tell us it was his *own* blood?" Mercer asked of no one in particular.

Pops reached for my hand as I pulled away from the table. "Told you it was a bucket of paint. Told you I was sorry about hurting that lady."

It was clear that Bailey didn't know which end was up and

probably wasn't even aware of what was staining his own clothes.

"Let the guy get dressed," I said, leaving the room. "When you deliver him to Bellevue, make sure they give him a complete physical. He might as well get something for himself out of all this aggravation."

The squad room was quiet. Peterson and the others followed me inside while the pair of medics packed up their bags to leave.

I fished through my pocketbook to dig out my Filofax and look up Chet Kirschner's home telephone. The Chief Medical Examiner listened to me repeat Juan Guerra's story about a burst varicose vein and assured me that it was a logical explanation to account for the blood that had made Pops Bailey such an outstanding suspect.

When I hung up, I could hear Peterson talking to Bill Dietrich. He wanted the hospital administration to know as soon as possible that the murder had not been solved and the probability remained that staff and patients were still at risk.

"Anybody checking on Maureen?" I asked.

"Charles agreed to go along with the plan so he's spending the evening with her." Maureen's husband had retired from the Police Department to run the investigations division of a major corporation. "Everything was smooth today. The men who went into her room to hook up her television service were actually our tech guys. They installed a microcamera and recorder behind a duct in the ceiling linked up to a monitor in their truck. They're parked right behind Minuit Medical College. So she can get a good night's sleep, Alex—she's covered."

"You want to tell me what we do now?"

"I vote we knock off for the night," Wallace said. "We come in fresh tomorrow morning and begin right back over at the hospital. Underground and aboveground.

"Start looking real close at Gemma Dogen. Once we

focused on Pops, we were all thinking this was a random thing, he just hit on whoever was around. Now we got everyone telling us how aloof she was and how strong her dislikes were, gotta go back to thinking somebody was trying to get rid of *her* in particular."

"I can't believe we lost twenty-four hours on this red herring."

"Where's Chapman?" Peterson asked, looking at his watch, already more than twelve hours into his working day.

Mercer and I exchanged looks, bringing a smile to my face for the first time since Schaeffer beeped me with the blood results. Mike was undoubtedly taking a fifteen-minute break in a bar somewhere between Mid-Manhattan and the station house, enjoying a beer while he matched wits with Alex Trebek.

"I'm getting out of here before he shows up, otherwise I'll get stuck for the rest of the evening.

"I'll be around home all weekend, Loo. Call if you need me for anything, will you?" I said, picking up my case folder and readying myself for the short trip to my apartment.

"Sure thing. Get some rest. I have a feeling we'll be coasting the ups and downs of this thing 'til we get back on track. Need a ride?"

"The sergeant on the desk will stick me in a patrol car. I'm just over the precinct line. G'night, Mercer. 'Night, Loo. Speak to you guys tomorrow."

I sat in the rear seat of an RMP with two young uniformed officers who dropped me in front of my building. The doorman told me I had packages in the back room so I waited until he returned with a bundle of mail and magazines and a load of clothes from the dry cleaner.

When I opened the door to my apartment, Prozac was splayed in the middle of the entryway on my needlepoint rug. Her stubby tail was wagging before she lifted her head and I was delighted to have her company for the weekend.

David Mitchell's housekeeper had brought Zac into my

apartment with a note she left on the table next to the lamp, underneath the dog's leash. "I fed her dinner before I left at six o'clock. She just needs another walk before you go to bed."

I put my things away, changed into leggings and an over-sized man-tailored shirt, and splashed some Calèche behind my ears and on my pulse points. I'd been off my favored Chanel since my last romance had soured.

I walked into the kitchen to study the freezer contents. The bottom shelves held a few containers of ice cream—assorted flavors with the common denominator of chocolate as an ingredient, several stacks of Lean Cuisine above the desserts, and a plastic holder full of cubes from the automatic ice maker. More than enough supplies for a perfect evening at home.

I decided on a 143-calorie lasagna dinner, removed its cellophane wrap, and popped it into the microwave. While it started on its six-minute route from rock solid to well done, I filled a Baccarat glass with cubes. It always made me feel better to use crystal and china when I dined alone, as if I were having a real meal.

The Scotch decanter was in the den, and Zac followed my footsteps as I poured a drink. I set one place at the table, with a matching linen napkin and placemat, facing out my window toward the spectacular view of midtown. When I turned on the CD player and heard Smokey telling his girl how he lost her when his heart went out to play, I assisted the backup singers with some "Oooh, baby, baby"s 'til the buzzer told me my entrée was ready.

The *Times* was too unwieldy for the dinner table, the tabloids were too full of crime stories to let me escape the events of the day, and the misfortunes of Trollope's Lady Eustace were too convoluted to accompany my modest repast and were better left until bedtime. I plucked the April issue of

In Style from the unread magazine stack in the den and hoped that the elegant spring fashions would uplift my spirits.

After dinner, I lounged in the den and called some of my friends. I didn't expect to find many at home at this hour on a Friday night so I tried Nina Baum, figuring that the three-hour time difference to the Coast might make her available for a chat. The answering machine took my message, asking her to call back over the weekend.

At ten o'clock, when I could barely hold my eyes open, I pulled my ski jacket out of the closet and hooked Zac's leash on to take her for a walk. I headed out the north end of the driveway and turned left. The wind had died down and the night air was comfortable, so I led her to Third Avenue, across Lexington, and squared the block on to Park.

I stopped in the bodega just off the corner of Lex to buy orange juice and some Colombian cinnamon beans for the morning.

The sidewalks were fairly empty, except for some other dog owners and a couple of joggers and bladers. Zac and I walked the last block, past town houses and a private school that was darkened and empty. I waited for the light to change on Third Avenue and stepped off the curb as the rectangular sign invited me to WALK.

A little man with a muffler wrapped around his neck and a Boston terrier heeling at his side was approaching from the middle of the next street. Zac pulled on the leash, straining to reach the sidewalk, while I was still on the blacktop of the roadway. "Easy, girl," I said, trying to pull her back.

Over my right shoulder I could hear the sound of a car braking as though to make a sharp turn. My attention had been on the dog but my head whipped to the side to see what was happening. The car was coming toward me as it took the corner at a ridiculous speed, two wheels seeming to lift off the ground, racing directly at me.

Zac lurched forward to sniff at the terrier and I let go of her leash, throwing myself against the last car parked at the curb before the corner.

The terrier's master grabbed Zac by the collar and called out to me from the sidewalk. "Are you all right? Did he hit you?"

I caught my breath and ran to embrace Zac, kneeling beside her as I held on to make sure she hadn't been hurt. My hands were shaking uncontrollably.

"Don't worry, Miss," the man, who most resembled the nearsighted Mister Magoo, went on. "The dog wasn't in any danger. It was only *you*. Are you okay?"

"I'm fine." I answered, standing up and brushing myself off. "Whoever was driving must have been out of control, drinking or—"

"Whoever was driving looked like he was out to get you, if you ask me. Seemed deliberately to be heading for you." He tugged at his dog to try to separate him from Zac, chuckling as he asked, "Want me to call the police? You got any enemies?"

"Too many to tell you about. Why? Did you notice the plate on the car?" I tried to tell myself that it was ridiculous to think someone had been aiming for me with that car; at the same time it struck me as a distinct possibility.

"No. Fool turned his headlights off as he went through the light. Couldn't see anything except that it was large and dark colored."

I thanked him for his concern and stroked Zac's smooth cocoa coat, holding her close against me—on the side away from the street—as we walked the short distance to my apartment.

I took my weekend charge upstairs with me and I undressed, carrying a nightcap into the bedroom in an effort to calm my nerves before trying to sleep. I wanted to believe the speeding car had just been an accidental swipe yet couldn't help but wonder who wanted me dead.

15

Sunlight streamed through my bedroom window for the first time in days. Last night's episode seemed like a bad dream. Surely my imagination had overtaken reality.

Zac and I walked around the block the opposite way from the night before, avoiding the avenue where the speeding car had given me such a fright. I kept her back from the street traffic and walked toward the direction from which cars were coming so I could see them as they approached.

Upstairs again, I changed into my leotard and tights, then went down to the garage to retrieve the Jeep and drive it to the West Side. I parked in front of the building that housed my ballet teacher's studio.

Five or six of the regulars had already assembled and were doing stretches on the smooth wooden floor. William came in and we took our places at the barres that ringed three walls of the room.

The music was Tchaikovsky's Symphony No. 6 in B Minor. William seemed to adore the *Pathétique*, and he held his shoulders back and his head majestically erect as he led us in a first position plié and relevé from the center of the room.

As always, it felt wonderful to lose myself in the music, straining to concentrate on the steps he called out to us over the crescendos of the rich orchestral arrangement. My mother had introduced me to ballet class when I was four years old and it still remained my favorite sort of exercise.

William danced with the American Ballet Theater for years before retiring to teach. The discipline and demands of the art form allowed me to escape whatever unpleasant matter I was working on for the hour that I remained under his spell.

He walked down the line of dancers, each of us holding our left hands on the lower barre, and studied our positions. "Tuck in your tummy, tuck in your tail, Judith," he admonished the slender young woman behind me. "Shoulders back, Alex. Let's see a nice line with those long legs, young lady." I arched my foot and extended my toe as far as the soft white leather slipper would take me.

William paced us through second, fourth, and fifth positions, then we swept into a turn to repeat the same movements, holding on with our right hands. I glanced in the mirror as I shifted sides, picking out the professionals from among this troupe of frustrated ballerinas and fairy-tale princes. As a child, I used to get to the studio for the first class every Saturday morning with the girls my own age, then stay on through most of the sessions of the day watching the older ones perform the more complicated routines and mimicking their steps. I dreamed of the day that I could be Odette and Odile, Giselle or Coppelia, never expecting to make my stage in front of a jury box.

William directed us to the center of the floor, where we practiced pirouettes and fouettés until sweat dripped down the small of my back and ringlets formed at the base of my ponytail. I didn't want the hour to end and be ejected from this fantasy world back to real life and time. But when the *adagio lamentoso* concluded, William bowed to the class and we returned the gesture, applauding lightly toward him in the tradition of students of the old-style masters.

I showered in the changing room and dressed in my weekend uniform of leggings and long shirt. Next stop was a parking garage on the East Side, as I hurried to Louis' Salon on Fifty-seventh Street for a haircut and a few streaks to lighten the blond hair I had inherited through my mother's Finnish genes. I hitched my beeper onto my waistband as I sat in Elsa's chair while she wrapped the strands in tinfoil. "With any luck, this thing won't go off 'til my head's out of the sink," I said, patting the little black box that had become my lifeline to the police department.

"You'd give them quite a scare in the Homicide Squad if I let you out of here looking like this."

I listened to Elsa's recommendations of the latest movies and Broadway plays, which she somehow managed to see before I even knew they had opened. Like a conveyer belt, she passed me along to Louis, who cut an inch off my newly blonded locks while doing a skillful cross-examination about my love life. Ever the Frenchman, he despaired of my lack of a steady beau and was always trying to suggest ways for me to meet a man. Once he finished snipping, Nana styled me an elegant coif when I told her I was invited to a dinner party at a friend's house for the evening.

Half the day was already shot. I drove home and deposited the Jeep back in the basement. The light on my answering machine was blinking when I got upstairs. Nina had returned my call and asked what was new on the case. Maureen was bored and just wanted to say hello. Chapman called to give me an update but had nothing serious to report.

I phoned Mid-Manhattan and asked for Mrs. Forester's room. "Just a petit larceny so far," she said after I told her about my morning. "I walked down to the solarium. Girl, it is *the* place to be. Everybody's whispering about what *their* doctor thought of Gemma Dogen—who liked her and who didn't. I'm keeping lists for you."

"What larceny are you talking about?" I asked.

"Don't sound so concerned. While I was in the solarium, one of the aides came to pick up the lunch tray. She stood there behind the curtain, which was drawn around the bed, eating my leftovers. Half a piece of toast, the most tasteless cup of vanilla pudding you could imagine, and a slice of turkey. She didn't realize she was on candid camera. Then she opened the drawer on the nightstand and looked through my cosmetic case. Guess she didn't like my lipstick color 'cause she looked it over good before she put it back in the bag. How many times a day you think *that* goes on in these places, huh?"

"Lonely yet, Mo?"

"Not complaining. No beds to make, no dishes to do. Company's coming later. Have fun tonight and give me a call."

I beeped Chapman and went in the kitchen to have some yogurt while I waited for him to get back to me.

"I'm over at the hospital," he said when he returned the call. "We're reinterviewing most of the med school staff, trying to get more of a handle on Dogen this time. I think you should sit down with Dr. Spector yourself. He probably knew her better than anybody.

"I saw him for a few minutes this morning when he was checking on a patient postsurgically. He says he can see us Monday afternoon at two. Can you do it?"

"Of course."

"Only other news is one of the guys from the 17th found

some folders in a trash bin in the parking lot. Wallace thinks they came from Dogen's office. They've got some blood stains on 'em, but then almost everything in the garbage here does."

"What kind of folders?"

"Empty ones. Three or four. They seem to be sports-related stuff, not anything medical. Labels say things like Mets, Braves, Cubs. I knew she was a runner, but I guess she was a baseball freak, too.

"And the ex-husband's due back in London on Monday, so we should be able to get some personal scoops on her from him."

"Okay. I'll be out doing errands in the neighborhood this afternoon. You taking tomorrow off I hope?"

"Yup. Got a hot one tonight with that reporter from the Italian magazine who did a feature on the squad last month. Thought I'd take her to your place—Primola. Between Giuliano and Adolfo, they can charm her into forgetting I'm Irish."

I tried to sound like I meant it when I told him to have a good time.

I scooped up an armful of clothes to take to the dry cleaners and three skirts for the tailor to shorten. Next door to that was the lingerie shop, where I stopped in to buy a dozen pairs of panty hose. The salesgirl talked me into some new lacy underwear—powder blue—to start the spring season, and I walked to the cash machine in the bank on the corner to replenish the supply I'd been doling out all day.

By the time I reached the nail salon, it was after three. I was overdue for a manicure and endured the loud gossip back and forth across the crowded space knowing I didn't want to be the only woman at Joan's dinner table without clipped cuticles and an even coat of polish.

I went home, fed Zac her late-afternoon meal, and walked her once more. Too restless to nap, I relaxed on my bed with the

Saturday *Times,* struggling over the bottom left corner of the puzzle until I could work all the letters around the missing word to fill in the name Galle for the clue—German astronomer who discovered Neptune—that I was unable to come up with.

Joan's Saturday-night dinner parties were fancy affairs and I was looking forward to a festive evening with her friends. It was always an occasion to dress elegantly and wear some of the jewelry my mother had collected over the years but let me keep in New York ever since she had moved to the Caribbean. I primped with great pleasure and called for a car to pick me up at a quarter to eight.

The housekeeper opened the door and took my coat as well as my drink order. Vases in the foyer and living room erupted with French tulips and pale coral roses. Joan was in the library regaling the first of her guests with a story about the production of one of her plays several years ago in an off-Broadway theater. She had made a remarkable transition from writing drama that was staged here and abroad to authoring novels, the latest of which had gone into its fourth printing.

Jim Hagéville, the man Joan had fallen madly in love with when she met him during the winter, was the first to see me. He was a foreign affairs expert who wrote an internationally syndicated column, and both of them had been commuting on the shuttle for the first three months of the romance. Part of the reason for the dinner was to introduce him to some of Joan's other friends.

We exchanged kisses and Joan brought me into the circle, telling the people I hadn't met who I was, while I greeted the others I knew. Cocktails were served for an hour and I made small talk with the guests, shifting conversation away from the investigation when anyone asked about it.

Shortly after nine, Joan moved us into the dining area to find our seats at the three circular tables. "Don't say I've never done anything for you, kid," she said, looking like the cat who'd swallowed the canary. "That adorable guy who was talking to you inside about the *New Yorker* profile of your boss? He's your dinner partner. Drew Renaud."

Joan was repinning my antique brooch at a different angle on my dress as we stood at the door of the room. "Where'd you put his wife, Joanie? I saw the guy, but I also saw the wedding band," I said, laughing at her machinations.

"He's a widower, Alex."

I bit down on my lip. "Whoops. Sorry. Glad I found out from you or I really would have stepped in it. Now, don't tell me you're playing matchmaker here. I'm going to kill you. You know I can't stand being set—"

"Oh, stop it. It's just a dinner party. He's an old friend of Jim's from Princeton. Partner at Milbank, Tweed. His wife had a brain tumor and died two years ago when she was thirty-seven. It's a terrible story, and Drew's just been coming out of it the past couple of months. So lighten up. Don't be such a grouch, Alex. And stop blushing.

"Besides, you've got friends all over the room—it's not a blind date. He's been dying to meet you. Says you were on a panel together last year at the Bar Association but you were dating— ahem—some*thing*, I mean, some*one* else at the time. Turn your damn beeper off and let yourself go for the evening, will you?"

"I can't believe you did this to me with no warning, Joanie," I said, laughing at my own agitation, trying to get a glimpse of my hair and makeup in the mirror on the wall over her shoulder and reapplying my lipstick.

"That's a smarter response, darling. I've put him right in between us and by tomorrow I'll expect garlands in tribute and gratitude. You look great so just go take your seat."

The guests were circling the tables to find their place cards. Drew was standing behind his chair waiting to help seat his hostess and me as we took our places on either side of him.

He picked up the thread of conversation that had started in the library quite easily and guided me back to our meeting the previous summer. I sipped my wine and ate the superb pâté de foie gras that Joan's chef had prepared, finding myself charmed by the warmth and wit of my dinner companion.

When the medallions of veal were served, accompanied by an incredible Margaux, I was conscious that I had started to flirt with Drew but uncertain about whether the cause was the wine or a genuine interest. I liked the way it felt again and I liked the sense of intoxication the whole evening had fostered.

We talked about acquaintances we had in common, the vacation he had taken the previous summer on my beloved Vineyard, Joan's incomparable skills as both hostess and friend, and the books we were reading. We rambled on about dogs and movies and restaurants and basketball and nowhere did I get a sense—so frequently transmitted when I met men socially—that he confused my professional interest in crimes of sexual violence with my personal life. I had all but forgotten that Hugh Gainer was sitting on my other side, I had become so completely engaged in my conversation with Drew.

"You've been to the Palais Soubise, haven't you, Alex?" Joan was asking. She had an astounding memory for all kinds of anecdotal information. "I really think it's the most exquisite façade in Paris. Louis XIV built it for the Princesse de Soubise, you know. Whenever the Prince was on the road, the *princesse* wore one emerald earring to court. That told Louis that the coast was clear, *et voilà*! Not a bad price to pay for the grandest home in town, don't you think? Anyway, Hugh, you must be sure to see it when you're over there. It's divine.

"Coffee and brandy in the living room?"

We all rose from our seats and Drew brushed against me as he went past. My hand was on top of the chair back, pushing it under the table. He rested his own on top of mine and asked, "Want some cognac or—?"

"I'd love some."

"You didn't let me finish, Alex," he said, talking softly into my ear. "Or would you rather come to my place for a nightcap?"

"I—uh—I don't think I can do that. I sort of have to go home because—um—there's a—well—" I was stammering as I found myself in the unusual situation of having to get back to the apartment to take a dog for a walk.

"I'm sorry. You don't need to explain," Drew offered coolly. I could tell that he assumed I was playing some kind of game with him, that I had someone waiting at home for me while I egged him on all evening.

I spoke over him as I shook my head, "No, no. I mean, it's a dog." He looked up and laughed. "It's my neighbor's dog," I went on, "I'm just not used to having to keep such regular hours and have some living thing depend on me."

"My rival's a *dog*? I can deal with that. How about a brandy at your place, then, and someone to keep you company on your midnight dog walk?"

"An offer I can't refuse. Let's find the hostess."

Joan was making the round of her guests as they sipped at demitasse cups while Jim passed cigars to those men who still smoked.

Drew and I thanked her for the evening. She hugged me goodnight as he went to fetch our coats. "For once, I'll forgive you for leaving early. Did I mislead you?"

"Not so far. I'll call you tomorrow?"

"Brunch at Mortimer's with me and Jim?"

"I don't think so. I've got tons of paperwork to review on the investigation and indictments to proofread in seven other cases. I'm going to work at home, but it'll take the better part of the day. Me and the usual suspects."

"Alex, don't be a sex crimes prosecutor tonight, will you please? Be a girl."

"Go back to your guests, Joan." Drew helped me on with

my coat and we went down to the street to get a cab to my apartment.

Prozac was pleased to have our company when we came in and followed closely on my heels as I turned on a few more lights in the hallway and den. I poured us each a brandy as Drew walked around the living room, picking up picture frames that sat on most of the tabletops and asking who the people were in each of the scenes. When I flipped on the CD player, the velvet voice of Sam Cooke sang to us, soothing me with "You Send Me" and the thought that his big thrill started as infatuation, too.

We settled onto the wide sofa with our snifters, Zac nestling below me as I kicked off my shoes and made myself comfortable. I chattered with Drew about my girlfriends, his childhood, my career, his partners, and all the time I wanted him only to reach over to me and kiss me into silence.

When it happened—somewhere between the tales of my first college romance and his last fly-fishing trip to Scotland— I opened my mouth and tasted his tongue, drawing him deeper as I reached up to stroke the soft brown hair that curled up at the nape of his neck.

Drew leaned back, lifting me with him and pulling me against his body as he embraced me and whispered "Alexandra" over and over again, his mouth pressed against the crown of my head. I took the knot out of his tie, unfastening the top buttons of his shirt to kiss his throat and chest. He raised my face, holding it between his hands so he could look at me, meeting my eyes with his smile and approval. I shook free, searching out his mouth again with my tongue.

It seemed this gentle foreplay went on for hours, but it was only three or four songs later when Drew planted a more playful kiss on my nose and suggested we take Zac for a walk before he left for home.

All this and sensible, too, I thought to myself as I got up

from the sofa, pulled down my skirt, stepped back into my shoes, and ran my fingers through my messed-up hair.

The whole thing felt so good that I didn't mind putting brakes on the sexual progression. My face was flushed and my body tingling with the fresh excitement of arousal, a feeling I hadn't experienced for far too many months. I wanted to savor it and make it last and I wanted Drew to want me as badly as I wanted him. I was already fantasizing making love to him and I knew it was going to be without the false stimulants of alcohol and wine.

I hooked Zac's collar onto her leash and we put on our coats and descended in the elevator. We walked a couple of blocks, Drew holding the dog's leash with one hand and me with the other. Perhaps it was that March was nearing an end, or because of the warmth of my company, that I didn't seem to mind the night chill and didn't want the stroll to end.

We returned to the front of my building and Drew kissed me another time, holding me against one of the large pillars that framed the entrance to the driveway. "I'll call you tomorrow. I've got to take a trip to San Francisco this week to close a deal. Save me some space on your calendar, will you?"

"Days or weeks?" I asked, not ready to turn to go inside.

"Am I too greedy to think months?" he said as I laughed at his enthusiasm. "Does a case like this one consume you entirely or will I be able to find you when I call?"

It was his first reference to the murder investigation all evening and the sudden insertion of Gemma Dogen into my thoughts eliminated every trace of giddiness instantly.

"I don't think you'll have any trouble finding me if you try, Drew." We pulled apart and he turned to walk away.

I watched as he went out to the street to hail a cab, then took my four-legged companion upstairs to go to sleep.

*   *   *

Lounging in bed on Sunday morning with the *Times* was a rare treat for me. Zac had an early outing, then I came back inside with the paper, got under the covers, and devoured every section of the news and features before I got up to shower and dress for the day.

Joan called at eleven. "Can you talk?"

"As in, is Drew still here?"

"Well, that thought did cross my mind."

"He's gone, but I do owe you for this one, Joan. Yes, I had a wonderful evening. Yes, the dinner was fantastic. And yes, I am going to see him again. Can you hold a minute? The call-waiting thing is clicking."

I pushed the button on the telephone console and Chapman came on. "I got news for you, Blondie—"

"I'll call you right back, Mike. Let me get off the line."

"Okay, but I'm not at home. I'll give you the number."

He reeled off the digits, then told me to ask for extension 638.

I held my curiosity in check while I told Joan I had to blow her off to talk business.

I dialed and heard a switchboard operator answer. "Saint Regis Hotel, how may I direct your call?"

I gave her the extension number and waited until a sultry accented voice picked up and said, "Hello."

"Mike Chapman, please."

"Certainly," she said, and after several seconds Mike spoke into the receiver.

"Her expense account or yours?" I asked.

"Last time *I* paid for a hotel room, the bathroom was down the hall and my date was gone before I could find the switch to turn on the space heater. There's a minibar in this place you could live out of longer than I could stay alive in your kitchen."

"This the reporter from Milan covering the police beat?"

"On-the-job, Blondie. On-the-job. This is all business—no need to be jealous.

"But Peterson beeped me this morning and I thought you oughtta know right away. One of the old hairbags in the precinct, working in the record room, came across a 61."

Sixty-ones were the complaint reports filled out by uniformed police officers when civilians reported crimes in New York City.

He continued. "Complaining witness was Gemma Dogen. Call came into the precinct a little over a month ago, at the end of February. It's listed as an aggravated harassment."

Telephone calls that annoyed or alarmed the recipient.

"What does the report say? Who took it?"

"Easy. I don't have it in front of me. I can just paraphrase it for you. Dogen was getting a series of threatening messages on her home machine. Male caller. Didn't recognize the voice but thought it was disguised. Veiled threats—"

"Exactly what kind of threats?"

"Peterson says she never said they were life threatening. Foul language, mostly, telling her to get out of town if she knew what was good for her. The lieutenant wants me to interview the cop who took the call and see what he remembers. That's all I know at this point."

"Well, what about the follow-up? Didn't anyone refer it to the detectives to interview Dogen?"

"Yeah. Two empty DD5s." Detective Division reports. "First one, guy tried to call her every day for a week and she was out of the country. Her office never returned the calls. Second one was two weeks before the murder. Detective wanted to set up an interview and Dogen refused. Told him the calls had stopped and she didn't want to pursue it. Said the problem had resolved itself."

"Whoa. Can you imagine if they're related? We've got to find out who she was having trouble with, on and off the job."

"I'm driving out to Queens. The cop who did the 61s is assigned to the pound," Mike said, referring to the huge facility where the department stored recovered cars that had been stolen or had been forfeited during searches for contraband.

"I thought you said the complaint came into the 17th Precinct?"

"That's where the guy used to work 'til your deputy got hold of him."

"Sarah?"

"Yeah, she had him flopped ten days ago. Guess she didn't want to bother you with this one.

"Dental hygienist brought a guy home with her from a party. Had sex with him in the backseat of his car, parked on First Avenue. Then claimed he got wild in her apartment and raped her. Phones the station house from her living room the next morning to say he's asleep in her bed, could they send a cop to get him out 'cause she's scared of what he might do now."

"Don't tell—"

"Yeah, this genius says, 'Lady, we don't *do* wake-up calls.' Girl pitched a complaint, Sarah asks the sergeant about it, and next day the guy's filling out endless reams of paperwork on stolen Tauruses and Novas. No human contact advised for a couple of weeks. Sensitivity training to follow."

I could hear Miss Milan giggling in the background.

"Maybe you ought to sign up for classes with him, Mike."

"Anyway, throw this one into the mix. You order the phone records on Dogen?"

"Yes, I had the grand jury issue subpoenas and Laura typed them all up and got them out on Friday. That should give us all her phone information. If you give me the dates of these incoming calls, I'll do a dump first thing in the morning."

Telephone "dumps" would actually reveal the source of an incoming call to a number if we could narrow down the date and time. They were hugely expensive procedures for the phone company—at least five hundred dollars a shot for only three days' worth of numbers—so they weren't authorized in most cases. Like almost everything else in a high-profile matter, however, the stakes were raised and the rules were broken.

"You got it. It's still gonna take more than a week to get the answers, isn't it?"

"That's the problem. But at least we'll get started."

"I'm off to the outer boroughs. Call you later."

We hung up and I went into my second bedroom, which had been converted into an office when I had moved to the apartment years earlier. The papers from my case file were spread all over the desktop and I found the folder with Dogen's name on it. Sitting down, I opened it to add the facts about her complaint of the previous month.

I slipped out one of the photos that had been taken at the crime scene and looked at the gruesome image it depicted. The old ivory-handled magnifying glass I bought at the Chilmark flea market to use as a paperweight was holding a stack of bills. I lifted it to look closely at Gemma's corpse, angling it to see whether any secrets would yield themselves to my eye.

I started a new pad of notes, under the heading "Blood," followed by a question mark. Had she been trying to draw a figure or design that could identify her killer? Was it a letter that would have been the start of a word or a name? In a column, I listed letters of the alphabet, lower and upper case, that could possibly have been formed if she had retained the strength to finish the symbol. Tomorrow, as we tried to move on away from Austin Bailey and isolate a string of suspects, I would bring my photo and my list to see whether any of the bloody squiggles on the carpet could be matched.

Who were the demons that peopled the life of this good doctor, I wondered as I looked at her butchered body. What was it that her files held, and not her wallet, that made the files the object of a search?

I kept at the paperwork most of the afternoon, forgoing my usual Motown accompaniment for the background of Schumann's calming Sonata for Piano.

Drew called from his office at five. He was working on Sunday, too. "I don't know how productive *your* day has been but mine was a lost cause. I kept thinking about last night and haven't been able to come up with a good reason for leaving when I did. Meet me for dinner? I have to come back to the office tonight to get these documents ready to go to the printer but I'd love to be with you for a little while."

"I accept."

"Pick a place in your neighborhood—casual but good. I'm in jeans."

"Butterfield 81, just off Third? Great steaks and salads."

"Perfect. I'll call for a table and meet you there at seven."

I fed Zac and took her out for some exercise, then walked up ten blocks to the restaurant. Drew was waiting for me in a booth and I sat down across from him as he pushed the menus out of the way to grab hold of my hands and pull them to his lips.

We talked and ordered, talked and ate, talked and lingered over cups of decaf coffee.

"I'm leaving for the West Coast tomorrow night. Any chance you'd fly out next weekend and spend it there with me? Get a hotel room with a view of the bay and—"

"I'd love to do it, Drew, but it's really impossible at this stage in the case. If the cops are no further ahead than they are now, we'll still be interviewing all week and weekend. And if there's a break in the investigation—I mean, a good one— then it shifts completely to *my* responsibility. There's no way I can leave town at this point."

"Then I'll just have to speed things up with my client and

get back here as soon as possible. I don't think the view's going to matter very much, is it?"

I shook my head and smiled.

"C'mon. Let's grab a cab and I'll drop you. Or shall I come up?"

"Tomorrow's a 'school day.'" I said. I knew that I didn't want our first night together interrupted by the buzz of the alarm clock.

We left the restaurant arm in arm, exchanged kisses during the short drive back to the apartment, and I let myself out of the cab reluctantly to send Drew back downtown to his office.

The doorman held open the door. "I didn't see you go out earlier, Miss Cooper. You must have left while I was on my dinner break. I just sent the guy with the deli delivery up to you on the service elevator. I tried to ring you, but I got interrupted 'cause 24C's got a leak on her terrace. Emergency."

"I didn't order anything. I've been out for two hours. Wrong apartment."

Many of the young kids bringing food in from local take-out restaurants were immigrants and few of them spoke good English. Like most of my neighbors, my doorbell often rang at odd hours with meals someone had ordered to the floor above or below. Mr. Hooper on nineteen wound up with Miss Cooper's pizza more times than he cared to, and, as Cooper, I was regularly confused with Kupler on twenty-three.

I was daydreaming as I removed my keys from my jacket pocket and opened the door. Zac was sitting upright as though she had been waiting for my arrival. Her left paw covered a sheet of paper, which must have been slipped under the door.

I picked up the plain white page, which had huge red letters scrawled across it in a childlike hand, and stared at the words. "CAREFUL. IT'S NOT ALL BLACK AND WHITE. DEADLY MISTAKE."

My heart raced as I bolted the door behind me. Zac stayed

at my heels as I ran to the phone and dialed Lieutenant Peterson's number at the small office within the squad room. It rang in dead air. No one was around to pick it up. My watch showed ten-thirty as I went to the intercom and called down to Victor on the front door.

"That guy you let up here, the deliveryman? Have you seen him go out?"

"Yeah, he came out of the back elevator while you was on your way up, I guess. Still had a bag in his hand. Said he had the wrong building—off by a block. I shoulda checked that, Miss Cooper, sorry."

I slammed down the phone and sat on the sofa. No point spoiling Chapman's foreign affair at this hour or bothering Battaglia until morning. The reason I paid the ridiculously high rent I did each month was for the security of a luxury building. Someone was obviously trying to put a scare into me. He was succeeding.

16

Court officers on their hands and knees were backing out of the row of sickly looking shrubs that lined the front of the Criminal Courts Building when I got out of the cab at eight-thirty on Monday morning. It was a well-kept secret that one of the best places in Manhattan to find a loaded gun was behind those pathetic bushes, some civil servant's ludicrous notion of urban landscaping.

Directly inside the main doors of the building were groups of metal detectors set up to screen everyone who passed through. Each day hundreds of present and future felons arrived in the halls of justice to appear for the calendar call of their cases. Many of them were too dense to realize, at least on the first visit, that they would have to be searched and scanned. Occasionally, throughout the day and night, you could watch men and women mount the stairs, then turn back and step behind the scrawny growth to deposit guns, knives, and assorted homemade weapons.

Those who entered via the front but failed to anticipate they might be leaving the building through the back door—in a green bus with caged windows, courtesy of the Department of Correction—regularly deposited their debris behind the greenery. Two or three court officers who swept the area several times a day retrieved the overflow.

"Find anything good?" I called out to Jimmy O'Mara as he stood up and dropped some items into a leather bag.

"Two automatics and a box cutter. Slow night, Alex."

I ran into Sarah at the bagel cart. We bought our coffee and went upstairs together to open the office. Chapman had beat me to it and was sitting in my chair, feet up on the desk, laughing hysterically into the phone. He slammed down the receiver when we entered and stood up, his voice booming in his best imitation of a television announcer.

"No more calls, ladies and gentlemen, we have a winner!"

"What are you talking about?"

"The hospital follies have reached a new height and Detective Forester may have snagged the big one."

I winced at the idea that Maureen had been in any danger while I was enjoying my evening with Drew. Sarah and I spoke over each other as we asked what happened to Mo.

"Nothing, nothing, nothing. She's fine. Had the husband and kids with her all day. Right before it's time for lights out, the nurse comes in with an order to give Maureen an enema before bedtime. From her doctor.

"Mo knows it's not possible 'cause her doctor's out of town until today. The R.N. was insistent, so she and Maureen battled back and forth for twenty minutes while the broad goes to get her supervisor.

"Meantime, half an hour later Maureen's phone rings.

Man introduces himself as Dr. Haven. Says he's covering for the night and her doctor left orders for a soapsuds enema. Mo pretends to go along with him. Says she just had it. Then the guy starts asking her all kinds of weird questions, telling her to describe how it felt—I mean, he wanted detail."

Sarah shook her head and eased herself into one of the chairs.

"While Mo has him on the phone, she signals the guys on the monitor to trap the call. Little does this idiot know he's talking to the one patient who's wired up. She jerks the guy around for eight minutes, he thanks her for the information and hangs up." New technology allows us to literally trap the source of incoming telephone calls and recover the originating number.

"Let me guess. Someone on the staff at Mid-Manhattan?"

"Don't be silly. The call came from the private line, home office, of Arthur J. Simonsen. 710 Park Avenue."

"Sorry, doesn't ring a bell."

"Mr. Simonsen is the president and CEO of PILLS—Pharmaceutical Industry Life Line Support. Biggest distributor of capsules and tablets in the country."

I groaned at the thought of what the tabloids would do when they got hold of this story.

"Not a first, ladies. Peterson reached Bill Dietrich a little after eleven last night to tell him the facts. Apparently, the same scam's been going on here, at Lenox Hill, and at Mount Sinai. At least half a dozen hospitals. Dietrich knew all about it but the administrators had been trying to keep it quiet.

"Because of the business they're in, Simonsen's company gets the patient logs from each of the medical centers, which also tell who the attending physician is. Then he goes through the lists, apparently, and looks for names of women in private rooms. He calls the nurses' station in the early evening, when the doctors have all made their rounds and left. Says he just got a call from the attending who admitted the patient or examined her—and orders the enema and a rectal thermometer.

"He gives himself about an hour until he calls the patient, assuming the procedure's been done. What he wants is to make the patient describe it back to him in exquisite detail, while he listens and, well—who the hell knows *what* he's doing on the other end of the phone.

"I'm not sure I'm ready to take the next step and find out exactly what the thrill of this little prank is. I'm leaving that to Mickey Diamond."

Diamond, the veteran courthouse reporter for the *New York Post,* thrived on the bizarre and berserk. "He'll be breaking his neck to get this on page one, for his wall of shame," I added. Mickey's office was papered with the yellowed remains of headlines trumpeting the city's most outrageous crimes. Sarah and I were cover girls in his world, since our cases drove his stories from the middle of the crime section to the front of the sheet.

"Don't worry, Mickey beat you here by fifteen minutes. Got the info from headquarters this morning. He's going with ENEMA MAN IN HOSPITAL HOAX."

"And the patient? How's Maureen in all this?"

"She's great, naturally. Nobody laid a glove on her and she broke the whole thing with one phone call. Simonsen admitted everything. They've got him under a suicide watch at Central Booking. They're going to use the witnesses from the other hospitals, along with his confession, so Mo doesn't have to be identified at this point.

"She's happy as a clam. Waiting for your pal David Mitchell to come back, eating bonbons in her fancy robe and reading murder mysteries faster than we can bring 'em in to her. Give her a call. I know she wants to hear your voice."

Mike shifted his remarks to Sarah. "What are you looking so glum about this morning?"

She rubbed her hands over her stomach and laughed. "Just thinking. I was going to quit working three weeks before the baby was born so I didn't go into labor on my way to the office on a subway car. You know, then we'd have to name the kid Vito or Jesús after my fellow straphangers who deliver him and wrap him in a slightly used *Daily News* from the day before. But with all these things going on in hospitals, a subway birth may be the way to go."

"Hey, you know Warren Murtagh's rules." One of my friends, the longtime chief of a trial bureau, had created a set of canons that seemed to apply to a wide range of office events. "Murtagh's Rule Number Nine: 'All nuts congregate in the same time, place and case.' So far, we're on a roll."

I was still standing. "Figure this one out." I removed the sheet of paper from my pocketbook and handed it over to Mike.

His demeanor changed abruptly as he sat upright in my chair and dropped the paper onto the desk in front of him. "Where did this come from? Why didn't you call me?"

Sarah reached for a corner of the page. "Let's get you in to Battaglia, pronto. He's not going to like this."

"Get me a plastic folder—that kind you use to hold your trial exhibits. Might as well take it over to look for prints."

"Yeah, but first you've got to do eliminations on your favorite weimaraner. Some guy slipped it under the door. Zac's paws were on it—probably some drool, too. I don't know what you'll get off it even though *I* was careful with it."

"What's wrong with you? Didn't you hear anything at the door, see anybody—?"

"I wasn't home, Mike. I'd gone out for dinner and the doorman just let some delivery guy type on upstairs. It was there when I got home."

"I'm just as curious about the dinner date as I am about the note," Sarah said.

"Look, whoever left it is just trying to throw a scare into me. The doorman didn't even know I wasn't home and the guy didn't wait around to see."

"Yeah, and you're not going to have Zac there all the time to scare him off if he had tried. How do you know what he was doing at your door? *This* time you just happened to have a dog who was likely to bark at an intruder, am I right?"

He probably was. I called Battaglia's office and Rose answered. I told her that I needed to see the District Attorney about something urgent that had come up, and she told me to come right over.

"Let's go. Might as well all hear what he has to say."

The three of us left our coffees on my desk, crossed the corridor, and were buzzed into Battaglia's suite by the security officer on duty. Rose looked happy to see us and told us to go right into the boss's office. He was on the phone and waved us over to the conference table in the middle of the room while he finished his conversation.

"Another three-quarters of a million dollars in that grant proposal and we can knock those garment district thieves out of the ballpark. I've got to finish my speech before I go out of town at the end of the week. The Congressional committee meets in mid-April and I'm the floor show. The usual pitch— figures don't lie but liars figure. Tell the Senator I'll be there."

Battaglia joined us at the table, nodding to Sarah and me and shaking Chapman's hand. "Cigar, Mike? Ladies?"

"No, thanks, Mr. Battaglia," Chapman said.

"You did a great job with that drug massacre on Forty-third Street. Nice collar—quick and clean. Congratulations."

"It helps when they're stupid, Mr. B. Makes my job a lot easier. Shoots four people to death at twenty to eight in a flop-house in the middle of the theater district, then tells the get-away driver to step on it. I think only thirty or forty witnesses had time to get the plate number. It didn't hurt. Wish this Mid-Manhattan nightmare'd give us a break."

"What's new?"

We filled the District Attorney in on everything that had

happened since I had phoned him about Bailey's exclusion and showed him the letter that had been delivered to my home. I even mentioned the episode with the car that I thought had tried to sideswipe me while I was walking Prozac, but I tried to downplay it as best I could.

"Do I have to worry that—"

"Absolutely not, Paul. I just wanted you to know about it and see if you had any other ideas."

"My best idea is that you solve the damn thing quickly. I'm leaving Thursday for London. There's an interdisciplinary conference on ethics. Guidelines for the new millennium or some such crap. I promised to participate six months ago, but it doesn't come at a very convenient time now with Congress trying to take back the money they promised me last fall."

Chapman teased him. "Hey, Mr. B., while you're over there, mind interviewing a few witnesses? I'll show you the ropes before you go, give you a few pointers on technique."

Battaglia rose and returned to his desk, signaling the end of our meeting. "Might take you up on it. Beats sitting around a stuffy boardroom listening to some European sociologists talking about how their biggest crime problem is hooliganism after soccer games. Watch out for yourself, Cooper, understand?"

By the time we were over the threshold, he was on the phone to City Hall telling the Mayor that his position on narcotics sweeps was untenable and had to be reworked.

We walked back under the glare of dozens of the District Attorneys of bygone days whose unsmiling portraits lined Battaglia's hallway. I had spent so many hours waiting to see him over the last ten years that I could name each of the long-forgotten lawmen and their periods in office. Put that in the category of "nice to know" as my father used to say, referring to the useless trivia with which Mike and I cluttered our minds.

"Game plan?" I asked as we trailed back to my office. Chapman sat at my desk listing all the people he thought we needed to see and talk to while I gazed over his head at the pigeons perched atop the baroque gargoyles of the building across the street.

"Sarah holds down the fort here at the office. We start with Bob Spector. Then Spector wants us to go to New York Hospital to interview a doctor there. Name's Gig Babson. Spector says Babson was one of Gemma's closest friends. We gotta run down this rumor about her leaving the hospital—when and why. That should keep us going through the afternoon."

My ordinary business traffic began to appear in the doorway.

Stacy Williams stood by Laura's desk with a voucher in her hand. She needed my signature to authorize the expense of a plane ticket to bring a rape victim in from Kansas City for trial.

"Where you been, Stace?" Chapman asked. A paralegal who worked for one of the guys in the unit, Stacy had been dating one of Mike's friends from the Homicide Squad for almost six months.

"It's over, Mike. I broke up with Pete a couple of weeks ago. He lied to me, you know. All that time, he told me he'd been separated from his wife."

I looked over the flight arrangements and signed the form. Sarah was into her maternal role. "Stacy, don't you remember Pat McKinney's orientation speech? When a cop tells you he's separated, it means that at the moment he's talking to you he's at one end of the Long Island Expressway and his wife is eighty miles away at the other end in their house with the four kids. That's the PD's definition of marital separation."

One look at Stacy's adorable face and figure as she turned to walk away and I doubted she'd be pining for him very long. "Here's the voucher. Be sure and let me know when the trial starts, Stacy."

"Not exactly a rocket scientist, Coop," Chapman said. "Three words printed on the front of the baseball cap that Pete wears every day and she couldn't figure out he was married? I guess she thought MASSAPEQUA LITTLE LEAGUE was his favorite charity."

"Leave the girl alone, Mikey." Sarah got up to go back to her office and organize her day. "Let me know what happens, Alex, okay?"

Mike called Lieutenant Peterson to get a detective to my office to pick up the papered threat for lab analysis. We called Bob Bannion to arrange a viewing of the video of the crime scene so that we could spend an hour examining it in close up, to get ideas about what parts of Dogen's files and shelves had been rifled through.

Sitting in a carrel in the video unit, Chapman and I replayed the scene over and over, zooming in and out of targeted areas in an attempt to determine what had been the goal of the trespasser. Did the files we could see—and we'd obviously have to examine them in person—resemble the files the detectives had found in the garbage? If the killer had taken the files that had been found in the garbage from Dogen's office, where exactly had he found them? On top of her desk or inside one of the many file drawers?

"Any help?" Bob asked.

"I'm sure it will be when we figure out what we're looking for. That hasn't happened yet."

Janine Borman, one of the misdemeanor assistants in the Trial Division, was waiting for me when we got back downstairs to my office.

"The judge in AP5 gave me half an hour to come up with some law or he'll grant the defense request for a dismissal. I don't have time to do the research. Figured you might have had this situation before."

Great excuse—no time for research. Read that one as

doesn't know how to do the research, I thought to myself. "What's the problem?"

"I've got a sexual abuse case. Happened in the subway—no CW. All I've got is the statement of the transit cop." CW is our shorthand for "complaining witness." As usually happens with minor crimes that occur in the subway system, local victims rarely wait around long enough to talk to the police. They know from long experience that the odds of anyone being apprehended are slim—and punished, even slimmer. Someone rubbing his private parts against their rear end in a crowded train is part of the price most women pay to get to their jobs every day in the Big Apple. The only advantage of the cold season is the extra padding of a winter coat against the offender.

"And the issue?"

Janine looked uncomfortable with the language that made up the fabric of my daily work. She hemmed and hawed as she glanced over at Chapman explaining the facts to me. "Well, this—um—this defendant, Anthony Gavropoulos, he was, like, on the other platform, across from the cop.

"The cop says he saw the defendant move in behind the woman who was standing all by herself. He claims Gavropoulos, well, that he could see him expose himself—"

"His penis?" I asked.

"Yeah. And that he had—um—an erection and was, like rubbing against the woman."

"*Like* rubbing against the woman or rubbing against the woman, Janine? One is a crime, the other isn't."

"I'm sorry, it's just—"

"Look, if you're going to handle these cases, you're going to have to deal with the language and the body parts. No euphemisms, no embarrassment. It's a business."

She gathered her composure and started over. "The offer is

a plea to the charge. Misdemeanor sexual abuse. And a condition of the sentence is that the defendant go to a sex offender program."

"Fine. So?"

"Defense attorney says his client won't take the plea. Says his defense is going to be that the cop is lying. Gavropoulos says, well, he claims he's too small. That the cop couldn't have seen him from across the tracks even if he had an erection. Have you had any other case like this?"

Chapman cut her off, jabbing his finger in the air to make his point. "You don't need any law, you don't need any research. Here's what you do. Go down to court, tell the lawyer to step out of the picture. Get lost. We don't need him. And you tell Mr. Gavropoulos to take this like a man. 'Anthony, be proud. Take the damn plea,' you tell him. I'd rather have a conviction than admit I've got one that's too small to be seen."

Janine's jaw dropped, believing as she did for a moment that Chapman's advice was to be followed.

"He's just kidding, Janine." I walked her out of the office into the hallway and told her how to handle the judge by giving her some case citations on point before sending her on her way back to the courtroom.

Chapman was holding my coat for me when I went back into the room. "C'mon, Blondie, let me take you away from all this. Let's go pick up Mercer and get to work on a real case. Remember what your Granny Jenny told me that time your mother had the surprise party for you a couple of years ago?"

I knew exactly what he was going to say. It was my Jewish grandmother's favorite lament, having come to this country from Russia as a young adult, priding herself on having put her sons through college and professional schools.

She had looked at Mike when he was introduced as one of

my colleagues and said, as she often did, "Seven years of the best education my son could afford for her and Paul Battaglia makes her an expert on penises and vaginas. *Oy*. Only in America."

17

"Love or money?"

"Fifty-fifty. It's a toss-up."

"I think it's one more than the other."

"How're you counting lust? How're you counting just out and out rage? Sex-related homicides? As love? That is *no* good."

"Doesn't matter. I think it's money way more often than it's love."

"Take all your domestics. It's not 'love' like you might think of it. But it's love gone bad."

"Yeah? Well those domestics are about money just as often as they are about any kind of emotional miswiring."

I came out of the ladies' room in the Mid-Manhattan Hospital cafeteria to rejoin one of the Chapman–Wallace dialogues on murder.

"What's your tally, Coop?"

"Don't know. Probably money."

"Mercer, most of what we got is Paco shoots Flaco over red tops and blue tops." The typical homicide squad investigation these days centered over arguments about crack vials from drug wars in all their rainbow glory of plastic stoppers—scarlet, navy, lavender, yellow, and so on.

"Sometimes, Flaco stabs Paco 'cause his woman cheated on him," Mike went on. "But he usually only gets pissed off about it if she's a moneymaking part of the operation. Certainly not 'cause he loves her. These guys love their pit bulls and their pythons and their cockatoos. Not their broads."

"So what hit Gemma Dogen? Love or money?" Mercer asked, knowing that neither Mike nor I had an answer. "C'mon, let's go see what Spector says."

The three of us wound our way through the maze of double doors and elevators from the cafeteria in the hospital complex to the quiet sixth-floor wing of Minuit Medical College. Mike gave his name to the receptionist at the main desk.

"Is Dr. Spector expecting you?"

"Yes, ma'am. We're homicide detectives and Miss Cooper's from the D.A.'s office."

He hadn't said that we were typhoid fever carriers but our job titles elicited about the same kind of response. She frowned once at us, rolled her chair away from our direction, and then avoided all further eye contact as she rang Spector's office to tell him that "those" people were here.

"Last door on your right, before the library."

We proceeded down the corridor, past the darkened office that had been Gemma's.

Spector stood in the doorway to welcome us, his easy smile and open manner exuding the confidence that his reputation suggested he owned. At five foot six inches, he was shorter than each of us, and his reddish brown hair was beginning to recede.

Still, he appeared to be younger than fifty-two, which is what Mercer's notes had given as his age.

Like Gemma's, Spector's office was crammed with an assortment of professional items and devices, photographs and awards. But unlike hers, his was also alive with signs of personal connection—children's faces beamed out of Plexi- glas frames and humorous tributes from students were painted on posters as well as on plastic vertebrae.

"So you're the people who are trying to restore some order to our little household, are you?"

"You wouldn't think so, from the way the receptionist greeted us just now," Mike answered.

"As you might guess, things haven't gotten anywhere near back to normal yet, if you can ever describe a complex like this as 'normal.' The press hasn't been very kind to us. Makes us sound like we're not running a very tight operation.

"And you, young lady," he said, gesturing toward me. "Well, once you bring a lawyer into the mix, a lot of the doc- tors just panic. The stereotypical distrust between the two professions is like a bad joke. I've tried to reassure my staff that you don't do malpractice work, you're just a prosecutor."

"We thought you could help us understand Dr. Dogen a lit- tle better," I began. "It's been very difficult to find out much about her. She seemed so very private."

"That she was. I can give you some of the occupational information, and Dr. Babson, whom you're going to see later, knows more about the personal side.

"Gemma came to Mid-Manhattan before I did, about ten years ago. A real coup for a woman—for anyone, really—to get an invitation to join this department, then to go on and head it. She was a brilliant intellect, very innovative in the field."

He talked animatedly for twenty minutes about the care with which Dogen had built up the neurosurgical faculty at Minuit and the pride she took in recruiting students for the grueling work of her specialty.

When Mike had heard enough of the lavish praise, he interrupted the narrative. "Enough about Florence Nightingale, Doc. Who'd want her out of the way?"

Spector started at the abrupt question and sat back with one arm stroking the back of his head. "Shall I put myself at the top of the list or is that being too immodest?"

"Wherever you'd like."

"I'm sure you've heard the rumors already. Gemma was planning to go back to England and chances are very good that I'll be the one to succeed her as chief. That's if Bill Dietrich and his boys don't try and bring someone in from the outside, over my head."

"How certain was it that she was going?" Mercer asked.

"None of us knew for sure. She played it as close to the vest as everything else she did. I know that on her last trip to Bosnia she stopped in London on her way home. Heard from friends at the university there that they'd welcome her back with open arms. Great credentials. And, of course," he said, nodding in my direction, "the 'woman' thing."

"Did she have any kind of deadline here for that decision?"

"A lot of things at the medical college are going to be decided in the next couple of weeks. April fifteenth, really. That's when the faculty appointments and contracts have to be tied up for the next fall and that's when we make the final decision about which students are accepted into the neurosurgical program.

"You'll have to ask Dietrich, of course. His office is in charge of all those administrative decisions."

"Yeah, we've been talking—"

"And be sure to take some of what he tells you with a grain

of salt. He had a real weakness for Gemma even though their affair broke up months ago."

The three of us were well trained enough to let that bombshell hit us without comment or reaction.

Mike tucked it away in his head and brought the conversation back around to Spector. "So suppose *you* became chief of the department next month. How does that change life for you, Doc?"

"If you're looking at me as a suspect, Mr. Chapman, the answer is, in very minor ways."

"Salary?"

"No change. Oh, it might raise a few honoraria when I go out on the road, but here in the hospital it's simply the prestige of the title. No extra dollars."

"But you'd be happy to have the job."

"I'd be a fool not to want it, of course. Look, the truth is, most people in our field regard it as *my* department. Dogen was becoming more and more removed, taking herself out of the mainstream here, traveling abroad to third-world countries all the time. When people talk about Mid-Manhattan, with or without your saintly Gemma, they're talking about Bob Spector's department. That's just a fact."

"How many neurologists have you got—"

"Correction, Mr. Chapman. Neurosurgeons, not neurologists." Spector snapped the answer at Mike like it was a more serious distinction than whether Gemma Dogen was alive or dead.

"I'm sorry, Doc, I've been using the two words interchangeably. Would you just remind me of the difference between them?"

Spector laughed his response. "The difference? About half a million dollars a year, that's all.

"We're the ones with the saws and the drills, Chapman. We operate, they don't."

"And why is it you think Gemma was leaving Mid-Manhattan?"

"I don't think, Miss Cooper, I know. Most of us in this field make our living removing tumors from the brain and doing surgical procedures on disks. Some of us supplement that, intellectually, by doing research on diseases and disorders, like the study I'm running here on Huntington's.

"Gemma started out like the rest of us, but she became interested in trauma, in brain injury. Started here in New York for her because of all the gunshot wounds and car accidents. She'd never seen shooting victims in London. The Brits may go for grouse and pheasant but they've only recently begun to have the handgun problem we have here. Their guns have traditionally been in the hands of the upper-class hunters, thank goodness. I'm sure you law enforcement types know that.

"Anyway, once she became fascinated with trauma you couldn't keep her out of a war zone. Hear about a village decimated somewhere in some unpronounceable country that didn't exist a decade ago and she'd be on a plane the next day."

"Couldn't she stay at Mid-Manhattan and still do that work? Sounds pretty noble. Seems like they'd benefit from the prestige," Mercer said.

"Trauma doesn't pay the bills, gentlemen. Most of the folks in car accidents and most of the innocent people caught in the crossfire don't have medical insurance. It may sound crass but I can bring in a lot more money for the hospital than Gemma's do-gooding ever would.

"Trauma is, shall we say, more like an afterthought for most neurosurgeons. And besides, the best neuro-trauma expert in the world is right here in New York. Jam Ghajar's his name. Leading man in the field and a real comer. Much younger than Gemma and much more outgoing. I'd guess that was too crowded a field for her. It added to her homesickness."

The line between Spector's confidence and his cockiness was an extremely thin one.

Chapman tried to ease back into the talk about Dogen's social life. "What else did you know about her relationship with Bill Dietrich, doctor?"

"That I wasn't supposed to know about it, that's the first thing. I had met Geoffrey—that's her ex—quite a number of times over the years—conventions and meetings here and there. I'd say he was lucky to get out when he did. Second wife's a much warmer girl. Lets her guard down, and her hair.

"Gemma never did much for me, sexually. Always thought getting in bed with her would be like—sorry, Miss Cooper—like putting your private parts in a vise.

"But lots of men around here didn't seem to mind that prospect. Dietrich can tell you better than I who some of them were. I think he actually wanted to marry her at one point. Talk about a salary boost. That would have given him a nice cushion. Could have indulged his taste in antique cars."

"You started off this meeting with an absolutely glowing review of Gemma Dogen, doctor. Then you sort of trash her. It is true, isn't it, that you had asked her to assist you in surgery the morning her body was found?" I asked.

"There's no question she had superb skills," Spector said. "It was a very secure feeling to have her by my side in an OR and I invited her often. But once we left that operating theater, she had become like fingernails on a chalkboard to me. Hypercritical of a lot of the students, not to mention her colleagues.

"She did great things for this hospital and this school but I really think it was time for her to move on. No secret about it, I'd have been thrilled to see her leave—by the Concorde, though, not in a pine coffin."

Spector was done with us. He rose to his feet, told us that he had a meeting to attend in the library, and ushered us to the door.

Mike waited for the elevator doors to close before he spoke. "I'd rather screw a snake. Bill Dietrich? With his Man-Tan skin and his Grecian Formula hair, he should be dating someone who owns a laundromat. She'd have to be washing the sheets twice a day with all the stuff that'd rub off him. What was she doing with that guy?"

"Hard to imagine. So what do you think of Spector?"

"Well, he laid his cards out on the table. I thought he was pretty straightforward, and I suppose that cuts both ways."

We rehashed his comments as we drove uptown to New York Hospital. The guard at the main entrance on York Avenue directed us to Dr. Babson's office at the rear of the fourth floor.

A petite woman of about fifty, with shoulder-length brown hair and soft hazel eyes, opened her own door when I knocked.

"I'm Gig Babson. It's Katherine, really. Please come in."

Having presumed Gig to be a man, I was pleasantly surprised, and even more delighted at the prospect of getting a woman's perspective on Gemma. I glanced at the diplomas on the wall—Vassar College '69 and Harvard Medical School '73—while Mercer introduced each of us to the doctor.

Babson went through the background of her relationship with Dogen. "We only met three years ago, working on something together, actually. We were part of the trauma team handling the Baby Vanessa case. Perhaps you remember it?"

Of course we did. The story had touched everyone in New York. A private jet had crash-landed at La Guardia Airport, killing all eight adults aboard. Four-year-old Vanessa had been thrown from the wreckage and survived without a burn but remained in a coma for sixteen weeks. Relatives had wanted to take her off life support, despairing of any meaningful recovery of brain function.

But a team of neurosurgeons—none whose names I could recall—had performed medical miracles. The child came out

of the coma and within months regained all her mental facul-
ties and was released from the hospital. The photograph of
the smiling child, standing on the steps of Mid-Manhattan in
front of the medical team that had given her a new life, was an
image most of us would always be able to call to mind.

"Gemma was brilliant at her work. It was she who saved
Vanessa's life. She discovered the bruising on the frontal cor-
tex that had caused a massive clot. When the rest of us hesitated about the risks of the surgery, Gemma got in there and
removed the hemorrhage—steady, daring, and absolutely
flawless in her work. That child would have been a vegetable
without Gemma's involvement."

"Give us the other side, if you will, doctor. Why," I asked,
"why would anyone want to hurt her?"

"Do you really think Gemma was chosen as a target? I
mean, not just some thief or homeless person stumbling upon
her during the night? That's just so hard to believe.

"You know we all thought she was crazy to stay in her
office at night, the hours she did. It's not that we ever dreamed
she'd be unsafe *in* the hospital, but I certainly worried about
her comings and goings. There was no changing her, though.
She didn't need very much sleep. It was part of her routine to
be at that office in the middle of the night, not getting home
'til three in the morning. A couple of hours' rest, then up for a
predawn jog. If you knew Gemma, you'd know when to find
her at Minuit."

"What did you know about her plans to leave New York?"

"Only that she was making them. Nothing firm, but she'd
had it at Mid-Manhattan."

"Not enough trauma work?"

Babson looked at me with a questioning expression on her
face. "In New York? Are you kidding?"

"Well, Dr. Spector says that she—"

"Forget what *he* says. There's only one person she confided in about that topic. That's Geoffrey Dogen, her ex-husband. She wouldn't even tell me the details."

"Why is that?"

"Didn't want me in the middle of it. Tried to protect me from the political infighting with the administration. I'm a few years younger than Gemma and she didn't want my career derailed like she felt hers was becoming."

We all looked puzzled. What was the infighting about if it wasn't the issue that Spector had described?

"Why the derailment?"

"You know she was a whistle-blower, don't you? I assume Bill Dietrich has told you about that."

"Actually," I said with more candor than Chapman or Wallace would have displayed at that point, "no one has mentioned any kind of whistle-blowing to us. We all assumed that this crime was the random act of a stranger, Dr. Babson. Do you know who'd been harassing Gemma?"

"Harassed? She'd never said anything about that to me. But if she did resign, it was going to be with a major statement to the medical community. That much I can assure you. No going quietly into the good night."

"Well, what was the whistle-blowing about?"

"Not sure, exactly. Some kind of ethical dilemma for her. It had something to do with Minuit, with the medical school, rather than the main hospital. She wanted to hold everyone to the standards she set for herself. That's an extraordinary burden—some might say unreasonable.

"There was a med student from the West Coast who applied for a neurosurgical residency with Gemma. Someone alerted her to the fact that he had lied on his application—phonied up his résumé or something like that. She booted him from the program even though a couple of her colleagues wanted him in. That kind of thing always ate at her.

"They were all trying to shut her up over there whenever

something like that occurred. None of them wanted her airing their dirty linen in public. Scares away patients and so on. But once she got up on her high horse, it was impossible to get her off."

The shrill noise of a beeper pierced the room. All four of us clutched at our waistbands, then looked at each other and laughed.

"What did we do before these things were invented?" Babson asked. It was hers that had signaled and she picked up the phone to see why she had been paged.

"Can we finish this up for now?" she asked. "I've got to get down to the emergency room. Second Avenue bus just went out of control and jumped the sidewalk. They're bringing some of the pedestrians who were hit over here and want me to stand by in case I'm needed."

"I'd like to talk with you again, Dr. Babson, after we've seen Bill Dietrich."

"Of course. Just give me a call whenever I can be useful."

Babson was leading us to the door. "Can you tell us anything about her involvement with Dietrich? Personally, I mean?" I asked on our way out.

"I'm just glad she ended it. I never trusted him, really. Just something sleazy about him, not vicious. But she was lonely, I think, and flattered by his attention. He pursued her quite avidly for a while. She didn't talk about him much anymore. And they always seemed to be on opposite sides in her recent battles. He's a real user. I can't imagine what she ever saw in him, so I didn't encourage her to bring up his name."

I rang for the elevator as Babson pushed open the exit door to walk down the back stairs to the ER. Mercer had one more question. "Ever go to a ball game with Dr. Dogen?"

"Excuse me?"

"Was she a sports fan? Baseball? Football?"

"Gemma was a superb athlete. She loved physical challenges. Running, kayaking, skiing. Kind of thing I don't really make time for, though. I've never been to a ball game with her, no. And I don't remember Gemma ever talking about one. The only reason I ever go is for the sake of the hot dogs at Yankee Stadium, once a year. I couldn't tell you a thing about that part of her life. Sorry."

Babson was off down the staircase before the elevator doors opened to take us to the lobby. It was after five when we walked out of the hospital.

"Where to?"

"What would you think of a nice, home-cooked meal for a change?" Mercer asked.

"I'm out, guys."

"No, no. Let's pick up something from the supermarket. Mike and I'll cook it. All you have to do is load the dishes in the dishwasher."

"Deal."

We were only a few blocks from my apartment. I waited in the car while they went into the grocery store and came out ten minutes later with shopping bags full of food.

"Okay. We're doing a Caesar salad, my mother's recipe for chicken breasts with Dijon mustard sauce, and sautéed string beans."

"With garlic," Mike added. "That a problem for your love life?" he asked.

"He's out of town, Mikey. Let's go."

We parked on Third Avenue and walked to the apartment. In place of Zac's leash on the table in my entryway was a bouquet of flowers and a note from David's housekeeper, who had reclaimed my weekend companion for her master.

Mike and Mercer set up shop in the kitchen while I changed into leggings and checked my answering machine. There was a message from Drew, who had tried me at the office with no success, a call from my mother reminding me not to forget my sister-in-law's birthday, and a rambling message from Nina while stuck in a traffic jam on the Santa Monica Freeway.

I watched my two chefs cut and chop and squeeze their ingredients into a meal. Mike's blazer and Mercer's suit jacket were laid on the living room sofa, ties in pockets. Their shirt sleeves were rolled up and Martha Reeves was singing to them. "We're all prepped," Mercer said. "Let's have our dinner after the evening news, okay?"

We went into the den and I served drinks as we waited for the six-thirty broadcast. Mike called Lieutenant Peterson to tell him the results of our two interviews and to learn what had gone on with the rest of the team. Detectives continued to plod through the corridors of the underground bomb shelter, talking to vagrants and searching for leads.

He hung up the phone and looked at Mercer and me. "Peterson wants to know what your thoughts are at this point. I told him we haven't even talked about it yet."

"It's been gnawing at me all afternoon. What do *I* think? I'm convinced we've had it all wrong from the start. From the very first moment you guys got to the crime scene."

Mercer leaned forward, drink in hand, and nodded his head slowly up and down. He knew where I was headed.

"I think you saw exactly what the killer wanted you to see. A sexual assault. A victim who died trying to fight off a rapist. A chance attack by a madman who happened to come across a woman all alone in her office in the middle of the night, random and opportunistic. And I think it's all bullshit."

Mike muted the television and stared at me.

"Gemma Dogen's death was a murder, plain and simple," I said. "Whoever did it staged it to look like a rape, to take us off course, have us looking for somebody who had no connection to Dogen. Like Pops. Like Can Man. The place is full of them.

"Kill her. Take off her panties, lift up her skirt. Make 'em think sex crime. I don't think anybody tried to rape her. That's probably the last thing whoever killed her wanted any part of—a sexual encounter with Dr. Dogen."

"Maybe I wanted you to work on the case with us so bad I didn't even consider staging as a possibility that morning," Mike responded.

"Isn't it logical? The killer leaves the body positioned to look like a rape—or a good attempt at one. But there's no semen, no trace evidence in the wounds, not even a strand of an assailant's pubic hair on her body. Sure, he could have been interrupted or scared off, but my bet is he didn't even want to try to rape her.

"The more we know about Dogen," I told them, "the more I've got to think that somebody wanted her dead and had the good sense to plan this to throw us off track."

"They're wasting their time squirreling around in the basement with the whackjobs. It's gonna be somebody really *sane*, like the guys we've been talking to in business suits and white lab coats," Mike said.

"Like Spector told you," Mercer said, "these doctors are already paranoid 'cause you're on the case."

"That's asinine. They'd be hard pressed to find someone who respects the medical community as much as I do. The two men I've loved most in this world," I responded, thinking of my father and of Adam, my late fiancé, "have been doctors— the most caring and devoted people I've ever known."

"Besides," Mike added. "Nobody's saying the killer's a doctor. But the odds are pretty good that it's someone who knew Dogen. Knew her habits, her hours. Knew that everyone would think her strong enough to fight back against a rapist and fit enough to try it even though he was armed."

"I think tomorrow's another day for us at Mid-Manhattan," Mercer suggested. "Who's reaching out for the husband? Any idea?"

"Yeah, the lieutenant said he called London this afternoon and broke it to him. Very cooperative, appropriately upset. Told Peterson it was like losing his oldest friend."

"I hope they're gonna try to bring him over here to talk to us. There must be some light he can shed on her for us."

We argued our way in a friendly fashion through most of the news stories, disagreeing with each other about which of the witnesses we liked or disliked and what the order of our interviews should be throughout the week.

Mike shushed us up when he saw the lead-in for *Jeopardy!*

Mercer called Maureen to check on her spirits at the top of the show since neither Mike nor I took the first round seriously. He passed the phone to each of us and she told me about her day.

She'd had a visit from John DuPre on his neurological rounds. "He's one of the guys who found Pops in the X-ray department, isn't he? I was tempted to give in and let him do a physical on me. Don't you think he's fine, Alex? Quite a looker."

"I'll let you know tomorrow. Mike wants us to reinterview him. We promised your husband there'd be no hands-on medical practice, Mo. Behave yourself."

"What's a girl to do? The only news from the solarium today was from my next-door neighbor. Says her internist told her Gemma had a thing for younger men."

"How young? And did she name names?"

"Well, the woman telling the story is eighty-two so anything in her book is young. Sorry, no names."

"Sarah's coming up to see you tomorrow. Meanwhile, I'm being wined and dined by the other two musketeers."

"I'm jealous. Call me later."

By the time Trebek got to the highlight of the show, the legally blind linguist from Tampa was leading both other contestants by four thousand dollars. "Today's Final Jeopardy category," he announced, "is Art. We'll be right back after a commercial break."

Mike yelled at the television screen. "How the hell can they ask a blind man a question about art? That's a disgrace—it's discrimination, it's—"

"It's basically because you're ignorant in that area, Detective Chapman," I said, winking at Mercer and imitating the tone of a cross-examining attorney, "is it not?"

"Five dollars, Coop. That's my bet."

"Sorry once again, Chapman. House has a ten-dollar minimum. I'm willing to go to fifty on it with you. Get my money back."

Mercer was the referee as usual. "Ten dollars is the bet."

Trebek looked at the tense trio before him and revealed the answer. "Seventeenth-century Dutch portraitist famous for his miniature paintings of wealthy burghers, whose best-known work is *The Peace at Münster*."

While the theme music marked the time, Mike ranted at the ridiculous notion that any of the contestants would know the answer to such an obscure query.

"No, I'm sorry, Mr. Kaiser," Trebek told the first contestant. "Frans Hals is a good guess, but you're a century off."

"You want me to tell you before *he* does so you know I'm for real?" I asked Chapman as the second contestant misfired with a try at Rembrandt.

"See, Mercer? This is the kind of bullshit they teach at a Seven Sisters school. That's why they're all so arrogant when they get out of those places. Who is it, Blondie?"

"Who is Gerard Terborch?" I said, complying with the basic rule by, putting my answer in the form of a question.

Trebek was consoling the blind man, who didn't have a clue and had left his Braille answer card completely blank.

"I can't believe how useless the stuff you learned in college is. It's amazing you can hold down a job."

"I didn't learn it there," I said as Mercer waited for Trebek to confirm my answer before he turned off the television, pressed the CD changer to start *Rod Stewart in Concert,* and led us back to the kitchen.

"I know, I know. Your old man probably has one, right? That little painting of the guy with the bald head and the pipe in his mouth used to hang near the coat closet in the old house before they moved, right? *My* mother's got Norman Rockwells she ripped off the cover of the *Saturday Evening Post* in 1952 still pinned to the wall in every room of the house, Mercer.

"No point in my paying up, Coop. You could sell that little sucker—that Terborch—and support the three of us for the rest of our lives if you were a real sport. Let's eat."

We carried the food to the dining-room table. I lit the candles and sat between my two friends, happy for the diversion the evening provided from the problems of the case.

I pushed the anchovies to the side of the plate and lifted the first forkful to my mouth. I had forgotten about Gemma Dogen for almost half an hour until Stewart's gravelly voice came on to remind me that the first cut is always the deepest. Cuts, blood, crime scene. I had forgotten to compare my list of initials to the stains on the office carpet.

18

There was a message from Rose Malone on my voice mail when I got into the office at eight on Tuesday morning. "Alex, Mr. Battaglia called from his car. He's got a meeting with the Police Commissioner at nine. Wants to see you as soon as he gets in after that. Wanted me to try and catch you before you go out to do interviews on your case."

C'mon, Rose, give me a hint. Good tidings or bad? Her tone was businesslike and I couldn't make a guess.

I spent the first hour at the word processor writing some disposition letters to witnesses whose cases had been resolved and responding to mail Battaglia had received about proposed changes in stalking legislation. Rod Squires came by to catch up on details of the investigation and tell me about his wife's new job.

His collegial drop-in was to camouflage the message that Patrick McKinney was up to his old backstabbing tricks. Rod had overheard Pat tell Battaglia that some of the detectives, who still thought Pops and Can Man were the likely culprits in Dogen's death, felt I was persecuting the professional staff at Mid-Manhattan and Minuit.

"Dammit. That's probably why the boss wants to see me. If I'm making too many waves at the medical center, the board of directors—including Mrs. B.—will be looking for me to lay off. You think it's time for me to go over to Stuyvesant Psych and get myself fitted for a straitjacket or will you defend me if I take a shot at McKinney?"

"I have you covered, Alex. Just thought you should know that some things never change. Pat's still out to get you."

Rod had watched out for me since my rookie days and I counted on his loyalty and support whenever I was too busy to look over my shoulder for slings and arrows.

Laura wasn't in yet so I answered the calls when the phone started to ring after nine. The third one was from Drew.

"Good morning. And I do mean morning. It's only six on this coast. Am I interrupting anything?"

"Perfect timing. My supervisor just left and the customers haven't started lining up yet."

"Well, I've just opened the curtains. I'm up at the peak of Stockton Street, looking out over the bay, and it's glorious. Wanted to give one more shot at getting you out here this weekend—"

"Can't do it, Drew. I have no idea where this is going, but we're smack in the middle of it."

"Will you hold some time for me over the weekend, then? I'll take the red-eye back on Thursday night. Dinner Friday?"

"Absolutely."

"Pick the place. I'll call you later, Alex."

I flipped the pages in my desk diary to check my schedule. No wonder my mood was improving so dramatically. Not only a new man but the beginning of a new month.

Laura came in with a coffee cake she had baked the night before. "Have some of this," she said, placing a slice in front of me. "I don't know how you go all day without starting off with a good breakfast.

"Patti called. She's been in ECAB"—the Early Case Assessment Bureau through which all new arrests were channeled every day from 8 A.M. to midnight. "She's got a case you ought to know about so she's on her way up here with the cop. And your dentist's office called. Should I confirm your appointment for a cleaning next Monday?"

"Please. I'll take care of Patti."

Chapman arrived minutes later accompanied by Mickey Diamond who was making his daily sweep through the executive wing on his way to the press office. The tall, lean reporter with his silver hair and beat-up brown leather bomber jacket was a morning fixture. I tried to move him along on his way so I could find out what the new case involved before he did, and I was sure he sensed my brush-off and would be back to determine the reason for it.

Patti Rinaldi, another senior member of the unit, rounded the corner just after Mickey left. She was smart and intense, slim and as tall as I am, with lots of dark, curly hair. She and police officer Kerrigan, whom I had never met before, came in while Chapman sat in the corner and perused the tabloids.

"Two new cases came through so far today. The first was a date rape. No problem, I'll put it in to the grand jury tomorrow. Very credible witness. She's a grad student at NYU.

"This one's really weird and I thought you and the boss should know about it. The defendant's name is Fred Werblin. Ever heard of him?"

"No," I said, shaking my head. "Should I?"

Kerrigan was chuckling, clearly anxious to get his two cents in. He had a thick brogue and a friendly smile as he told me his news. "He's a rabbi, Miss Cooper. Can you imagine that? A rabbi who sexually abused these women."

"Easy, Brian," Chapman cautioned. "Miss Cooper's Jewish."

"Oh, well," he said a bit surprised. "I didn't know that, did I? Couldn't tell from the name, now, could I?"

"Ellis Island neutral," Chapman shot back. "Didn't leave the old country that way. Somebody just shortened it up when Grandpa got off the boat, right, Coop?"

"Well, I didn't mean anything by it," Kerrigan said. "It's just that—well, the papers made such a big fuss and all when that priest was convicted up in Rhode Island last week. Molesting those boys. Terrible thing for the Church. It just made me feel better to know it's not only us that has this kind of problem. I didn't mean to offend you now, Miss Cooper."

"No offense taken, officer. Yes," I said, "I *am* Jewish. And one thing I can tell you about sex crimes cases is that they really cover the waterfront. We've had defendants from every ethnic, racial, social, religious, and economic background. Let me hear what you've got."

"It's really a tragedy," Patti began. "Werblin's fifty-five years old, lives in the East Sixties. Doesn't have a congregation, Alex. He's a scholar and writer. He's also a diagnosed manic-depressive."

"Anybody treating him?"

"Says he was being treated at Payne Whitney. He'd been on lithium but took himself off it, which is when these episodes began."

"Episodes? More than one."

"Yeah," Kerrigan offered. "We got three complaints. Different ladies."

"What happened?"

"There's a cleaning service. Name of Happy Elves. Call them and you can have someone come in and clean your apartment or your office.

"Werblin orders a cleaning lady. When he meets her at the door in the morning, he's dressed in a robe. Lady comes in and gets to work straightening up the place. He usually waits 'til they're in the kitchen, then he comes out of the bedroom starkers—nothin' on. He corners 'em in the kitchen, grabs 'em, and starts fondling and kissing 'em all over. Each one was able to break loose and get out. He chased this one down the hallway with a wooden-handled fork, like from a barbecue set."

"All three reported it?"

"Well, Miss Cooper, not right away. Y'see, they're all immigrants. Illegal. Two from Eastern Europe, one from China. The first two didn't say nothin' at all, just refused to go back to the apartment. Bet they were afraid that they'd be deported if they said anything about it. When the last one came forward, the owner of the company asked the others who'd been to the rabbi's apartment if they'd had any bad experience. That's when the first two opened up."

I addressed Patti. "Have you interviewed the women yet?"

"No. Officer Kerrigan's going to set that up for me."

"Good. I'll tell Battaglia about the case when I see him this morning. When you talk to these women, make sure you find out whether you have the whole story."

It was common for witnesses, especially those who had some reason to be apprehensive about becoming involved with the criminal justice system, to minimize their victimization. Illegal aliens feared deportation or punishment and rarely expected access to the protection of our laws. Whatever their status, they were entitled to help and to all the support services we could muster on their behalf.

"Will Patti need interpreters, officer?"

"Yeah, I'll find out from the agency what languages they speak. Can you set it up down here?" he asked.

"Sure." We had a list of dialects—more than fifty—for which we had per diem translators on call. It always assured a more accurate interview if we could conduct it in the language in which the witness was most comfortable.

"Schedule it for the grand jury as soon as possible, Patti. I think we can anticipate a psychiatric defense and I'll work on it with you. Thanks for letting me know about it so quickly. If he's got any priors, ask for some bail. And make sure these women understand we'll take good care of them—they've got nothing to worry about."

My telephone hotline, straight from Battaglia's desk, rang and lit up as Patti and Kerrigan said good-bye.

"Got a few minutes?" Battaglia asked. "C'mon in. Bring your sidekick with you if he's down here."

"He wants you, too, Mikey. Let's go."

Rose was cheerful and happy to see us when we reached her desk. "Next time I'm down here, I'll buy you lunch. You're the only person in the whole office who gets better looking every year," Mike greeted her. "All that cigar smoke must do wonders for your skin."

"Go right in, Alex," she said, modestly waving off Mike's remarks as she always did. Rose had worked around cops for almost twenty years and knew exactly how much credence to give their compliments. But at least her warm reception suggested that I wasn't facing the firing squad.

"Sit down, you two," Battaglia said, biting on an unlit stub, as he waved us to the red leather seats facing his desk. "Just met with your boss, Chapman. I'm trying to beef up the size of my squad here. He can be tough."

"Should I ask which side won?"

Battaglia's lips pulled back around the cigar into a wide

grin. "He's not *that* tough. I got six more detectives coming on board a month from now.

"While I was there, I asked him if we could borrow you for a few days. Guess I better ask you first."

"Whatever you need, Mr. B."

"My wife got a call at seven o'clock this morning. Director of the board of Mid-Manhattan, who tells her that Geoffrey Dogen called him. Geoffreys's the ex, right? Very gung ho to help. He consults at the University of London. Had the brochure for this conference I'm supposed to go to this week and wanted to know if I'd meet with him if he shows up there. He can't fly over here right away because he's been in the Himalayas for almost three weeks and has some surgery scheduled."

Battaglia hadn't wasted a moment. He'd been plotting something since the board director's wake-up call to his wife and it was aimed clearly at us.

"You two can save me a lot of aggravation if you go in my place. Alex can sit at the meetings and b.s. with the best of them about crime in the twenty-first century and you can get the answers to the questions you wanted me to ask Geoffrey Dogen. I can stay here—keep on the senator's back and make him miserable."

"You serious?"

"Commissioner agreed to pick up your airfare. Room and board is all taken care of by the conference committee. It's only a forty-eight-hour trip, but if you can make it work for your case, you should go."

"I'm packed," Chapman said enthusiastically.

"Alex'll love it," Battaglia went on. "They're holding it at one of those Stately Homes, about an hour out of London. Cliveden. Heard of it?"

"Lady Astor?" I knew the American heiress Nancy Astor

had become the first woman in Parliament to be seated in the House of Commons at the end of World War I, and that a decade later the "Cliveden Set" was notorious for its pro-Nazi sentiments.

Chapman had a different recollection. "John Profumo, Christine Keeler, skinny-dipping and Russian spies?"

Battaglia responded to Chapman's reference. "I thought you were too young to know about that?"

"Profumo was Secretary of State for War. I'm a history buff, Mr. B. Some people use mnemonic devices to remember things. Me, throw a little scandal in and I'll never forget it."

"I think this is going to work out fine. My wife will be thrilled. Gets the board off her back and gives her time to finish the painting she's working on." Amy Battaglia was a talented artist whose works were in several American museums.

Battaglia shuffled through the topmost pile of papers on his desk and came up with the program for the meeting, which he passed over to me.

"You've met Commander Creavey, haven't you?" he asked.

"Yes, Paul, we've both worked with him." Commander John Creavey was Director of Intelligence at New Scotland Yard. A large, bearlike man with a bushy mustache, wire-rimmed glasses, a cockney accent, and an encyclopedic knowledge of the Jack the Ripper murders, Creavey had spent two weeks studying the methods of the NYPD's Homicide Squad a year ago.

"Well, he's leading the British contingent at the conference. The meeting will be chaired by Lord Windlethorne, an Oxford law professor. I don't know him. He's presenting a long paper, but the rest of it is just a series of panels and debates."

"Creavey's an absolutely brilliant investigator, Paul. Might even be a help to us brainstorming on this."

"You're on the six-fifteen American Airlines flight tomorrow evening. See if you can keep Chapman out of those pubs, Alex. Make this trip worthwhile for the case. Rose will confirm all the arrangements for you."

Mike left the room to discuss the travel plans with Rose while I stayed behind to tell Battaglia about yesterday's interviews on the Dogen murder and Patti's new case.

I told Laura to go through my book and move around any appointments that were scheduled for the end of the week. "Those interviews I've got penciled in for Thursday and Friday need to be pushed back a few days. Neither one of them is pressing. Tell Gayle I'll certainly be at her sentencing tomorrow morning. And would you call my friend Natalie—give her my ballet tickets for Thursday night? Tell her Kathleen Moore and Gil Boggs are dancing in *Manon*. She'll grab 'em.

"If a man named Drew Renaud calls, interrupt whatever I'm doing. It's urgent that I speak with him."

The last thing I had expected was an expedition out of the country. The Bronx, Brooklyn, and sometimes a ride up the Hudson to Albany were as exciting as business trips usually got in a local prosecutor's office. Mike and I were flying out Wednesday night for the two-day conference and would return home on Saturday afternoon. Between Drew's schedule and my own, it was obvious that ours was going to be a long, slow courtship.

Laura passed a call through to Mike. It was David Mitchell calling from Maureen's hospital room to let us know he was back and to see if we had any information for him.

"See if you can schmooze with anyone in the Medical College, Doc. One of Dogen's pals claims she was on the warpath about some problems they were having—either about credentials or letting some underqualified students into the program. Called her a whistle-blower, which nobody at Mid-Manhattan had mentioned to us. Maybe they'll tell *you* something they wouldn't tell us."

David assured us he'd give it a try and signed off for him-self and Mo.

Mike stayed on the phone to set up our reinterview sessions at Minuit Medical College. Bill Dietrich had agreed to let us use his office and, after we questioned him, to set up meetings with the physicians, nurses, fellows, and students that we needed to see.

"Holding out on me?" Mickey Diamond asked, standing over Laura's shoulder as she tried to shield my diary from his glance. "My editor liked today's story. Wanna give me a quote?"

"I can't believe you got it already. The ink's barely dry on the complaint. Was it us or headquarters?"

"THE RANDY RABBI. That's what we're going with. Page four in the late edition. I never give up my sources, you know that."

"What is it with tabloids and alliteration? No, I don't have a quote for you. And *don't* make one up for me this time. Got it? I don't care how eloquent you try to make me sound, I do *not* want to be quoted on an open case."

Chapman and I put on our coats.

"Where're you off to?" Diamond persisted. "Gonna round up a few more homeless old men and break their balls, Alex? Or have you got anything new on the case—any real leads?"

"Shoot him, Chapman, would you please? Would you get lost already, Mickey? Don't you have a deadline to meet?"

"Nah. After you guys leave, I'll just hang around Laura's desk and see what I can pump out of her."

It was impossible to insult Mickey Diamond or do any-thing to rattle his mood. He was good-natured and unflap-pable and wallowed in the curiosities of the criminal court.

Mike and I had planned to meet Mercer in Bill Dietrich's office in the administrative wing of the hospital complex. Dietrich was providing lunch in the boardroom so that we could work through the afternoon without a break.

We drove uptown in Chapman's car, slushing along the

city streets as the unseasonably warm and sunny day melted the blackened remains of the last storm. "Dietrich asked if we'd mind if someone from Risk Management sits in on the interviews. I told him it was your call."

"Negative."

"Is that what I think it is, Coop?"

"Yeah. Translation: lawsuit control. Pain in the ass. Since the murder, they must be getting hit right and left with inquiries about civil suits from every patient who's made a beef about something that happened to them in the medical center. Last thing we need is some lawyer for the hospital reporting back on everything anybody wants to tell us. A slight chilling effect on candor, don't you think?"

"Fine with me. I'll tell him no."

We parked in front of the complex and Mike stuck his Police Department parking plate on the dashboard. The square badges at the front desk for the afternoon shift seemed to be awake enough to recognize the two of us by this time and they waved us through without demanding our identification.

Mercer was waiting for us in Dietrich's reception area. His secretary led the three of us down the hallway into the boardroom and I told her to give Dietrich the message that we would prefer to conduct our interviews without his attorneys present. That must have had him backpedaling for a while since he kept us waiting another half an hour before making his appearance.

Chapman eyed the spread of food that had been laid out on the sideboard for us. He grabbed a plate, slathered two pieces of rye bread with mustard, then loaded his sandwich with ham, cheese, and tomatoes, eating his lunch while we waited. Mercer and I picked on plates of salad greens as he told us about the seemingly endless series of patient interviews he had conducted the past two mornings at Stuyvesant Psychiatric Center.

The room was paneled in rich mahogany and furnished with a long, sturdy conference table and twenty green leather chairs. Oil paintings of five or six distinguished-looking gentlemen with white hair and starched collars were displayed on the side walls. A period portrait of Peter Minuit, namesake of the medical college, with his knee breeches and walking stick, dominated the far end of the room. He looked rather smug, perhaps still gloating over the purchase of the island of Manhattan from the Indians for his twenty-four-dollar bag of trinkets.

Bill Dietrich looked even more self-satisfied than Minuit when he finally deigned to join us at one-thirty.

"Sorry to keep you so long," he said, although I didn't believe for a minute that he really was.

"So, what can you tell me about where you stand in all this? Frankly, we were quite relieved when you made such an early apprehension of that fellow with all the blood on him. Has he been ruled out completely?" Every couple of minutes, Dietrich reached his left hand to his temple and smoothed back his already slick hair. Each time he lifted his hand, I expected to see a stain on his palm. His head looked like it had been greased with shoe polish or diesel oil.

Chapman wasn't going to give Dietrich much, not that we had very much to give anyone at this point. "Nobody's been ruled out completely, Mr. Dietrich. That's why we're turning over every rock in the place."

"We're trying to be cooperative, detective. The sooner you do your job and we get you out of here, the happier all of us are going to be."

"Then let's cut right through some of this, okay? Was Gemma Dogen's contract going to be renewed next month, or was this her swan song at Mid-Manhattan?"

Dietrich pfumphed around for a few sentences, repeating the respect with which Dogen was viewed by everyone and outlining her accomplishments. Chapman's irritation was obvious. He stood up, hands in his pockets, turned his back to Dietrich, and started to pace around the table.

"You wanna play hardball, Mr. Dietrich? You wanna close up your offices and your medical school for a couple of days and come on down and answer these questions in front of the grand jury or you wanna do it the easy way, right here in your own backyard?"

Dietrich looked over at me for relief, but I stared at the glossy top of the conference table and let Chapman apply the pressure.

"Well—uh—Gemma was being quite obstinate, actually. She was refusing to tell the administration what her plans were, even up to the day of her death. We knew that she had other offers but she was making it very difficult for us to plan for the next year here."

"What were the issues for her, Mr. Dietrich?"

"Oh, same kind of thing I imagine Dr. Spector told you about. Whether we wanted to go in the direction of expanding the department into a trauma center. She liked doing that work but didn't want the responsibility for all the tedious fund-raising chores that go along with it."

He carried on in that vein, feigning puzzlement about the problems the administration had encountered with Gemma. It sounded almost as though he and Spector had rehearsed the script together.

"Bottom line," Chapman said, interrupting the rambling Dietrich. "Did you want Dr. Dogen to stay here or were the powers that be trying to get rid of her?"

"That wouldn't be my decision, Detective Chapman. I mean, that kind of situation would be resolved by the president of Minuit, who operates separately from—"

His effort to distance himself from Gemma's professional fate spoke volumes about her lack of support within the institution.

"It wouldn't be a very popular move, would it, to the medical community outside of Mid-Manhattan?"

"To release Gemma from her contract here?"

"To fire her? Can her? Bag her?"

"Well, not the words I would have chosen, detective. I think that some of her colleagues were hoping she would select that course herself. Go back to London, which was something she often talked about doing. You make it sound a lot more sinister than it was. She was a fighter, Gemma, but she was a stunning asset to this hospital community. It's a tragic loss for us, really."

Chapman had heard him waste enough of our time. "Then I guess you won't mind turning over some records the grand jury wants to see. Alex, want to show Mr. Dietrich the subpoenas you brought with you?"

"Sure." I opened my folder and withdrew the long white sheets of subpoenas duces tecum that Laura had prepared at my request this morning.

"We'd like to have the records of all the students in the neurosurgical program, Mr. Dietrich. I understand that's a very small number—eight or ten. We'd like to have their applications and transcripts for—"

Both hands were skimming over the top of Dietrich's head. His brow was furrowed and he stammered as he tried to question us in return. "I—uh—I don't understand what you're looking for here. There's nothing in these—"

I continued on. "This one is for the personnel records of the other faculty members. The request, as you can see, is for all of the documentation of their credentials, information about their salary, any complaints made against them, any correspondence of theirs with the institution concerning Gemma Dogen. The list goes on but it's quite clear."

Dietrich was scanning the papers as I handed them across to him. "Obviously, I'm going to have to turn these over to our lawyers. There's a lot of information here that's privileged and I won't be—"

"I expect that your lawyers will want to speak with me, Mr. Dietrich, but there's nothing in these requests that gets into any area that's covered by a medical privilege. These aren't patient records. They only involve internal staff matters and I'm sure your attorneys will tell you that the faster you comply and get these materials down to us, the sooner we get out of your hair." And one place I didn't want to be was in Bill Dietrich's greasy hair.

Beads of sweat had formed on his forehead. Chapman had waited until the professional air was cleared before he turned to the personal side.

He had circled the long table and come up behind Bill Dietrich, leaning over with one hand placed on the tall back of the green leather chair. "I know this is rough for a lot of people at the hospital, Mr. Dietrich, but it must be even worse for you."

The subpoenas were clutched in his hand as he picked his head up and looked around into Chapman's face.

"We know about your relationship with Dr. Dogen. We need to ask you some questions about that, too."

Dietrich's head did a one-eighty as he swung it back to make sure the door was closed behind him. "Look, I don't know what anyone's told you about it but Gemma and I haven't been together for months—six months at least. There's nothing about it that needs to mix into this ugly matter about her death, nothing at all." His face colored and his voice rose.

Mercer Wallace calmly picked up the angle Chapman had opened and asked the next question. "Why don't you tell us exactly what that relationship had been six months ago and what it was these last few weeks?"

Dietrich looked like a caged animal, surrounded by the three of us, unable to walk out the door and explain to the medical school staff that the meeting had broken up because he had refused to answer questions about his personal life.

"It's very simple. A year ago—maybe it was fourteen months—we'd been spending a lot of time together on a project for Minuit. Planning a forum for the World Health Organization on brain trauma guidelines. Gemma was brilliant, beautiful—and I don't think you need to know any more than that we had an affair. Left here together one night, I walked her home and she invited me up for a drink. Do you need illustrations, Mr. Wallace, or can you figure the rest of it out for yourself?"

Mercer asked the usual questions about how often they had seen each other, where they had spent their time together, and how the romance ended.

"Gemma wanted out. Frankly, I would have liked to marry her. She'd played with the idea at first but changed her mind rather quickly. Right after the summer, she came back from a trip to England and told me she didn't want to see me anymore."

"D'you give it up, just like that?"

"Do you mean, did I make a fool of myself, chasing her around the operating room with a butcher knife? Sorry, gentlemen, no."

"Didn't you try to see her again, call her?" I asked.

"Of course I did, in the beginning. But like I've said, she was stubborn. She didn't mind the occasional night together, but absolutely no strings attached. And *no* discussion of hospital business."

Wallace was interested. "When was the last night you spent with her?"

Dietrich hesitated as though he was weighing an answer against our ability to measure it through the word of a doorman or a neighbor. "The week before she was killed. Gemma called, asked if I wanted to have dinner. We left here late and stopped at Billy's, over on First Avenue, for a bite. Then back to her place. Made love, went to sleep. I came home when she got up to jog. End of story. Except that whichever friend of mine put you onto this news," he said, sneeringly, "has probably told you about the money Gemma loaned me."

"Yeah," Chapman lied. "We wondered about it from her bank statements." We hadn't—yet—but this would spare us some surprises by the time we were able to get a look at her account information.

"Don't worry, detective, I'm good for it. The estate will get it back."

"Was it only that one payment?" Chapman bluffed.

"Yes, last July. Forty thousand dollars."

I could read Mike's mind. Forty large. More than most people made in a year. Dogen gave it to him when the courtship was hot and it still wasn't paid back.

"Did she ask for it?" Mike said. He left unspoken the word "recently." He wanted to know if the subject had come up at the tryst two weeks earlier.

"Money wasn't terribly important to Gemma. We'd spent a weekend together in the country, down on the Eastern Shore. Went to an auction of antique cars. I saw a DeLage I fell in love with. Thirty-two, quite rare. She wanted me to have it, I couldn't afford it. At that moment she meant it as a gift, but by the time I'd made the deal she'd moved on from our relationship, shall we say. Told me I could pay her back whenever I had the money. Surely you know by now she wasn't materialistic. She had more than enough money for all she needed or wanted to do."

Dietrich pushed away from the table and got to his feet. "I assume you'll be back with more questions for me but you might as well get on with the staff. I've lined up the people you were interested in and I'd like to get you going with them so they can get back to their patients and assignments. I'll get over to my office and contact our lawyers about these documents."

He stroked the side of his head with his left hand before picking up the stack of subpoenas. Then he removed a metal mass from his pants pocket and splayed a handful of keys in his right hand until he held one of them—probably for his office—between his thumb and forefinger.

Bill Dietrich backed away from us without any other comment and I noticed as he did that a replica of London's Tower Bridge dangled from his fist. It was a duplicate of Dogen's key chain that rested on my bureau, the one I had forgotten to return to Mercer. I wondered if Dietrich, too, still had the keys to Gemma's home.

19

John DuPre was the first in the group to be reinterviewed about the circumstances at Minuit on the evening of Gemma's murder. He entered the room and extended his hand to each of us, and when he grinned at me in greeting I understood why Maureen Forester had found him so attractive. With none of the nonsense about how precious his time was and what a nuisance we were making of ourselves at the hospital, DuPre was gracious and expressed his willingness to do anything to move the investigation along.

We had questioned him at the station house days earlier about his discovery of Pops in the radiology department. I apologized to him and explained our need to reexamine all the events surrounding the time of the murder.

"Why don't you start with your schedule last week?" I

asked him. "Take us through it from Monday to Wednesday, just so we can put it in perspective."

His eyes met mine directly and he spoke with confidence and comfort. "Reminds me of the time our preacher was killed, back in Mississippi," DuPre drawled with a smile on his face. "I was only eight but the State Police questioned every one of us in school like we were John Dillinger. Made quite an impression on me. Almost went into law enforcement instead of medicine. I admire what you're doin'. I know it's like looking for the proverbial needle. I suppose some of my colleagues will take it personally, but I'm happy to help."

DuPre pulled out a pocket-sized diary and opened it to the preceding Monday. "You're welcome to see my office appointment book, but I'm pretty clear that I never got over to this side of town until Thursday afternoon when I needed to use the library."

DuPre told us about his neurological practice and described his regular hours at the Central Park West office, which he had maintained since starting out in Manhattan two years ago. His receptionist and his assistant were there with him each day of the week.

"How about evenings, doc? Where's home?"

"Strivers' Row, detective. One hundred thirty-ninth Street, north side," DuPre answered, referring to the elegant group of row houses built in Harlem in the 1890s. "My wife's a designer, Miss Cooper. McKim, Mead and White did the homes on *our* side of the block, and we've been busy restoring this one since we moved in. I'm doin' a lot of the woodwork myself, every night after we finish dinner with the kids. Y'all ought to come see it sometime."

That answer gave us three pieces of news. DuPre was making good money—or needed it—to fund a home at that address. It also placed him a few miles away from the medical center on the night of the murder, if that's where he actually had been. And it provided the worst kind of alibi for us to break, if there was any reason at all to suspect him—a wife and two kids.

Wallace shifted the young doctor away from the domestic scene and back to the deceased. "What was that expression you used to describe Dr. Dogen last week? Ice maiden?"

"Maybe I'm just used to southern charm, Mr. Wallace. I told you I didn't know her well enough to take it to heart, hear? It's just that she was awfully stiff and remote with me. Simply couldn't get through to her no matter how I tried."

"We've just given Mr. Dietrich a subpoena for some of the personnel records here at Mid-Manhattan, Dr. DuPre. We'll be getting the files in a few days, but I'm wondering if there's anything we might learn about you that you'd prefer to—"

"You're taking yourselves mighty serious, detective, aren't you now? Getting *our* records? The staff? Seems to me you've blown every good lead we've given you. Coleman Harper and I led you right straight to someone a hell of lot more dangerous than any of my colleagues and you messed that all up. Only have to be in here a couple of hours to know we've got a real problem controlling access to the hospital."

Unruffled—and sticking it right back at us. John DuPre was certainly a cool character.

"While you're on that other night, Dr. DuPre," Chapman said, "was it your idea or Dr. Harper's to go down to the X-ray room?" Chapman remembered, as I did, that each man had credited the other with the suggestion.

"It was Coleman, definitely. Didn't I tell you that? I had planned to do my work in the library that afternoon. I was talking with some of Spector's protégés—Coleman would like to consider himself one, I guess—and he asked me to go on downstairs to radiology to have a look at some test pictures with him. No reason for me to be there otherwise."

Mike was probing for background. "What brought you to New York City to practice?"

"A combination of circumstances, Mr. Chapman. My second wife grew up here, has all her family in town. And then, professionally—well, I'd outgrown my business back home. I'd been presenting papers at some conferences, began consulting with physicians around town who'd heard me lecture, and I decided to try the big time."

"Are you on the teaching staff at Minuit?"

"No, no. I've got privileges here at the hospital. Just getting my foot in the door, new boy in town and all that. Can't help you a bit with the politics of this place."

DuPre had no other useful information for us, as hard as Mike and Mercer pushed him on details about the medical center and the neurological service. They had finished their questioning and seemed mildly surprised when the quiet doctor asked them if they'd mind stepping outside while he spoke to me in private.

"I gotta call the lieutenant," Mike said. "We'll be back in ten with another witness."

John DuPre waited for the door to close before speaking. "Two things I wanted to say to you, Miss Cooper. First, about my personnel file. You're going to see that I'm in the middle of an ugly malpractice suit. Mean and frivolous. You're welcome to talk with my lawyers about it but I'd sure as hell like to keep it out of the newspapers."

I let him go on.

"A patient of mine died. Back home in Atlanta, before I came to New York. Has nothing to do with Mid-Manhattan or any of these events, of course. Young man had come to me with complaints—dizziness, weight loss, and so on. I examined him, tested him, sent him home with medication and an appointment for a battery of more workups. Two days later, he was dead.

"I assure you I won't try to hide anything from you. I just don't want you looking at that as part of some damn murder case. You're a lawyer and I expect you to be a lot more understanding than those cops about the legal ramifications of this."

"Did Gemma Dogen know about your lawsuit?"

"I'm quite sure she did. Can't swear to it 'cause she never mentioned it to me. Could be one reason she was so cool to me, but we just won't ever know that, will we?"

"And the other matter?"

DuPre smiled again, his serious news behind him. "If there's anything missing from my file that you need, just give my office a call. They've got duplicates. I went through a rather messy divorce a few years back. Left my first wife for this one. Julia got a bit crazy and set fire to my office back home in Atlanta. I had to get new copies of all my diplomas and certificates from the universities. Not sure what they've got here at the hospital but my secretary has everything if you don't find what you're looking for here."

"Thanks, doctor. No reason you couldn't have said all this in front of the detectives. Doesn't sound like anything we can't deal with quietly, professionally."

"Well, Miss Cooper. Maybe it's my southern experience that makes me so damn skeptical of the police. I'd just rather have my private affairs in your hands than theirs," he said, reaching across the table to clasp his fingers on top of mine. "I'm sure I'll be speaking with you again."

Wallace was waiting outside the conference room with Banswar Desai, one of the two doctors who had been tapped by Spector to stand in for Gemma Dogen the morning after the stabbing when she had failed to appear in the operating room.

Desai was short and squat, his skin several shades darker than John DuPre's and his Pakistani accent coated with a thin veneer courtesy of his British boarding school education. I invited him into the boardroom and whispered to Mercer that he should call Sarah and ask her to do a Lexis/Nexis check on DuPre, to search for news stories in the Georgia papers about the details of his pending lawsuit.

I introduced myself to Dr. Desai and sat him at the table opposite me. Chapman rejoined us before I had gotten very far into the résumé.

Desai was one of the newest members of the reurosurgical team, recruited to Minuit by Gemma Dogen the year before to start his residency there. He was clipped in his responses to us and fiercely defensive about his relationship with Dogen. She had been his mentor and his sponsor and it was clear to me that Desai was sincere in his expression of how devastated he was by Gemma's loss.

Mike focused his attention on the operation Spector had performed when he plucked Desai and Harper out of the gallery to stand in for the absent Dogen. "What'd you think when she didn't show up for surgery? Worried about her?"

"Quite unlike her, of course," Desai replied. "Gemma was a consummate professional, Mr. Chapman. Did I think she'd gone missing? Not at all. I assumed something more pressing in her schedule had come up. Or that she and Spector had another row about something and—"

"Row about what, Dr. Desai?"

"I wasn't privy to that information, detective. I knew there were issues that involved the program at Minuit that put the two of them at odds, but I'm much too junior a member of the department to have been let in on those conversations."

"You were Dogen's friend, though, as well, weren't you?"

"Her friend, Mr. Chapman, certainly. But not her confidant. Our relationship was strictly confined to the hospital and medical school. Gemma drew a firm line between her students and her private life and I'm not aware of anyone who dared attempt to cross it."

"And Dr. Spector, he trusted you enough to call on you to

stand in for Dogen in the OR even though you were quite well identified as her protégé?" I asked.

"Spector's primary interest, Miss Cooper, whether one likes his style or not, is the well-being of his patients. I never got myself involved in the politics of the medical school and it's obvious neither Spector nor Dogen held that against me in any manner.

"Besides, there were only a handful of us in the room who were qualified to assist him when the situation presented itself. It was, shall we say, an honorific moment rather than a critical one. I might have passed him a few instruments and nodded my agreement with his decisions, but Harper and I were basically there to admire Spector's handiwork close up, if you will. Neither Coleman nor I added a great deal to the procedure."

There was something old-fashioned and comfortable about Banswar Desai's manner that put me at ease. I had grown up in a home in which the medical profession was revered and respected. My father's accomplishments had won international adulation. My brothers and I had been surrounded from childhood by my parents' coterie of brilliant and caring physicians and nurses who devoted themselves to the finest traditions of the science and art of healing. Our nightly discussions at the dinner table, joined in with equal gusto by my mother—whose nursing background made her as knowledgeable as any of the doctors who spoke—always centered around the most interesting clinical events of the day.

The memories of my lifelong involvement with the health care community led inevitably to thoughts of my love affair with Adam Nyman and the engagement that had shattered so stunningly with his death just hours before we were to be married. I had daydreamed and wandered from the discussion that Chapman was having with Desai, for which I paid doubly. The haunting image of Adam in his OR fatigues when he kissed me good-bye for the last time pushed itself back into view. In addition, I had lost all track of the direction of the conversation that concerned Gemma Dogen's murder.

"That's all we've got for you today, Dr. Desai. If anything comes to your attention that you think we'd like to know about, please give me a call," Mike said, passing a business card to the young resident.

They walked together to the door and, as Desai left, Chapman waved Coleman Harper into the room.

"Thanks for your patience, Dr. Harper. It seems Detective Chapman and I have kept you waiting a second time," I said, referring to our first meeting at the police precinct the night Harper and DuPre had made their discovery of Pops in his bloodstained pants.

Mike flipped through his notepad until he came to the pages that contained the information he had taken from Harper at our earlier meeting. In answer to Mike's first question, Harper repeated that it was at DuPre's suggestion that the two of them had gone down to the radiology department.

"I don't want to get you all twitchy like you were that night we were at the station house, Doc, but DuPre's pretty insistent that you were the one that wanted him to go downstairs with you."

Harper hesitated, his head stationary but his eyes darting back and forth between our faces as he tried to figure out whether there was any significance to Mike's question.

"Are you suggesting that I knew the old man was in the room before John and I went down there together?"

"You tell me, Doc. Did you?"

"Wh-what for? Of course I hadn't known he was there before we found him—I hadn't been to the radiology department all afternoon. What difference would it have made?"

Not much, it seemed to me, and I figured Mike was simply trying to rattle Harper, who rose to the bait rather quickly and seemed as ill at ease now as he had the night we met him.

"I don't think we ever got the details of your relationship with Gemma Dogen, did we, Dr. Harper?"

"Same as most around here. Respected her work, professionally, but had very little else to do with her."

Chapman flashed a glance at his notes. "You two met on your first go-round here, almost ten years ago, is that right?"

"Yes, yes, it is."

"Work for her?"

"Not exactly. I came up here after medical school. Did my internship and residency here, then started my neurological practice. That's about the time we met. Dr. Dogen had just come over here to teach at Minuit."

"She teach you?"

"Just in the sense that we all rotated through the neurosurgical department."

"Never wanted to go into surgery, Doc? Just wanted the medical end up 'til now?"

"Yes, well, more or less. I mean, I did apply to get into the neurosurgical residency right after my internship but I didn't make the cut that year. I was content with what I was doing and, um, didn't push for it very hard. As you probably know by now, it's a very small program, very elite. Lots of us got passed over—no big deal. I was only in New York another year, working up at Metropolitan Hospital, actually. My wife wanted to go back to Nashville and I was ready to get out and start practicing on my own."

"So what does this fellowship do for you exactly?"

Harper's thick fingers clutched the arms of his chair and he massaged the smooth wood of the antique reproduction boardroom furniture as he explained his current function to us.

"I, uh, I guess I was anxious for a change after ten years. Maybe I just never got out of my system the idea that I could do neurosurgery. Felt I'd given up on it too quickly when I didn't make the program on the first shot. This, um, fellowship lets me get started in the OR while I wait for the results of my applications."

"What applications?"

"Oh, I assumed Dr. Spector must have told you. I'm completing the fellowship and hoping to be accepted to the neurosurgical residency here any day now. That's why I was willing to enter the program and take a pay cut for a year."

"What were you pulling in back home as a neurologist?"

"Pulling in?"

"How many smackers?" Mike went on. "Money, dollars, income."

"Oh, about a hundred and fifty thousand, last few years."

"And this year?"

"Well, of course the fellowship only pays a stipend—about thirty thousand dollars—but when I finish—"

"Damn, you're living up here on thirty thousand? You must want it bad, Doc."

"It's just temporary, Detective Chapman. Obviously, I've got enough savings to get me through," Harper said, laughing nervously. "And it's not that I have time for any kind of a life outside of my work at the moment."

"Pot of gold at the end of the rainbow, huh?"

"That's not what I'm here for. It's the most challenging job in medicine, Chapman. It's a creative field, with newer and better techniques evolving every week. You save lives and you restore functioning that was previously considered hopeless and you—"

Harper's squat body held its position firmly centered in his chair as he defended his goal. "And you make about half a million dollars more than you've been making every year," Mike said.

"Something illegal about that I'm not aware of, detective?"

"Nothing at all. Just trying to figure out why, at your age, you'd give up a successful practice for a shot at maybe getting a chance for another residency. By the time you finish, if you get into Spector's program, you'll be—"

"Close to fifty years old. Yes, I will. Look, that's hardly an impediment to a medical career. I've got a solid professional history behind me, no debts, no family to support at the moment, and a dream I'd like to see out."

"Who got in your way the first time?"

"You mean, almost a decade ago? Oh, I don't know. As Spector will tell you, it's all done by committee. A review of the records of each applicant, interviews, recommendations from the supervisors of the internships. It just didn't happen for me that year. I accepted it, had a good career ever since then, and now want to try it over again."

"Dr. Dogen, was she for you or not?"

"I don't know, quite frankly. I had very little to do with Gemma Dogen." Coleman Harper had moved forward on his seat and was ready to spring up and out of the room as soon as Mike ended the barrage of questions. "I didn't have much of an opportunity to work with her, and I certainly never courted her like some of the young toadies have."

"How about the first time you came through here, Doc?"

"That's ten years back, for goodness' sake. I had her on a couple of rotations. Let's just say we had very different styles. I was glad to get away from her and over to Metropolitan at the time. She was out to make a name for herself as soon as she set foot in New York and I wasn't having any part of it."

"You think the hospital records'll have some of the details of your early days?" I asked quietly from my side of the long table.

Harper shot me a glance, thought for a moment, then shook his head, answering that he didn't think the hospital kept files for more than seven years. "I tried to get them myself, of course. Wanted to use some of the letters of recommendation that I had gathered during my internship and then my years at Metropolitan." He forced a laugh. "You don't get professorial references when you're out on your own in a private practice. And what patients think of you is based more on your fee schedule and which insurance plans you accept than on your skills.

"If they come up with those old records in the near future, be sure and let me know. I'm supposed to get a decision from Spector's committee by the fifteenth of April. I could use some of those kind old words from ten years back."

"Even Gemma Dogen's write-up?"

Harper was standing and shaking Mike's hand on his way to the door. "I wish I had saved copies of everything then, not just to prove a point to you. But I think it would have helped me moving forward at Minuit. Dogen wasn't my biggest cheerleader here, but I don't recall she did anything to make it difficult for me."

"Can you think of any reason why anyone would want to hurt Dogen? To kill her?"

Harper was turning the doorknob. "It's all foreign to us, detective. We're in the business of saving lives. Can't imagine why anyone would do such things to other people, the kind of things *you* see day in and day out. No idea at all."

The interview with Coleman Harper had given us no more and no less than any of the others. There still seemed a certain absurdity to questioning these well-respected physicians about the frenzied massacre of a colleague, but they had to be examined and eliminated like any other field of potential suspects.

Mercer rejoined us and we plodded through the rest of the afternoon with a string of witnesses who recounted for us their relationships with Dogen. We spoke with seven nurses, three other medical school professors who shared the corridor with the deceased, and an array of earnest young students and interns who studied with and scrubbed beside the distinguished deceased.

The portraits presented were split right down the line—those who liked and admired Gemma and whom she had allowed some arm's length collegial contact, and those who feared and distrusted her because of the *froideur* of her personality and the distance she automatically imposed.

The effort to trace her final hours was even more futile. Gemma treasured her solitude and admitted companions only at those moments when it suited her to do so. Jogging, writing, traveling, or doing research, she had seemed happiest when in her own company, untroubled by the chatting and politicking of most of those who tried to enter her orbit.

It was after six o'clock when our stream of subjects trickled out and Dietrich's secretary came in to remind us that she needed to lock the boardroom when we were finished. I told her that we were done for the day and knew from the forced smile that flickered across her face when I thanked her for letting us take over the facility that she wasn't the least bit interested in our reasons for having disrupted her boss's good mood. We packed up our notebooks and pads and headed onto the corridor for the long walk back to the entrance.

"Next? Any fresh ideas?" Mercer asked.

"Too many interviews in one day," I answered. "My head's spinning. I'm going home to sort it all out, go over my notes, and pack for tomorrow."

"Wanna grab a bite with us?"

"I'll pass. Too much to do before I leave and I feel like we're not making any headway on this right now."

"Okay, we'll drop you at home. I checked on Maureen. This morning the Chief said he was only going to let her stay in the hospital until Friday. Thinks the whole thing is a waste of her time and the Department's money. Then this afternoon a messenger delivered a box of chocolates to her room. The package was addressed to her and the gift card said it was from the kids. Some fancy French stuff, nicely wrapped."

I stiffened as Mercer went on. "Problem is, Mo's allergic to chocolate. Anyone who knows her well is aware of that. What do you think it means, guys? Has she been made?"

"For one thing, it means the Chief is dead wrong, so Peterson's fighting to keep her in place. The box is over at the lab. They'll look at it to see whether anything was tampered with."

"Why am I thinking this undercover plan of mine was a stupid one, Mercer?"

"It's fine, Coop. Maureen's perfectly safe."

Mercer left his car across the street from Minuit and came with us as Mike drove uptown, pulling into the driveway of the building to leave me at my door.

"What's the plan?"

"Mercer'll drive us to the airport tomorrow evening. Why don't you just bring your suitcase to the office and we'll pick you up and go from there?"

"Thanks, guys. See you tomorrow."

I got my mail, went upstairs, and let myself into the apartment. I turned on the television in the bedroom so I could listen to the evening news while I started to throw some things on the bed to pack for the trip. When I flipped to *Jeopardy!* to check the final question, I gave up without an effort as Trebek announced that the category would be astronomy.

I was on the phone for more than an hour, starting with a call to Maureen, who seemed chipper and unconcerned by the day's events, perhaps because Charles was still by her bedside. By the time I called my mother, Joan Stafford, David Mitchell, and Nina's answering machine to explain why I was going out of town for a couple of days, it was after eight-thirty. I dialed P. J. Bernstein's and asked them to send up an order of chicken soup before they closed.

My papers were spread out all over the dining-room table. Off to one corner I placed the Polaroid photo that I had asked Mercer to take of the marking made by Gemma's blood on the floor of her office. Had it been intentionally drawn by the dying woman? I wondered, and was it a letter or part of a word? I pulled out a yellow pad and wrote beside it the initials of each of the people we had interviewed so far. I tried to compare the capital letters of their names to the incomplete squiggle that had seemed so clear to me that morning last week. Nothing seemed to match and I abandoned the exercise in favor of reviewing and organizing my interview notes.

After I packed and got into bed shortly before midnight, I called Drew's hotel in San Francisco and left a message on his automated mail system. I told him about my unexpected departure for London the next day and asked him to call whenever he got in so I could hear the warm sound of his voice and make plans to see him when I returned home.

I set my alarm for seven and turned off the lights. I worried about Maureen and whether my idea had exposed her to any real danger. Then I tried to make sleep come by thinking of everything except murder. But the puzzle of Gemma Dogen and the way she died kept intruding as I lay awake late into the night.

20

"Likely to die. Another one."

"What do you mean?" I looked at the clock and saw that it was just a couple of minutes after 6 A.M.

"Sorry to wake you," Chapman added, "but I figured you'd want to know as soon as I heard it. This one's uptown, right outside of Columbia-Presbyterian. Really screws up our investigation."

I was halfway out of the bed already waiting for an explanation. "Because?"

"It's eerie. Could be our guy. Maybe Dogen's death has nothing to do with Mid-Manhattan. Maybe some clown is after women in white uniforms, or striking out at each of the hospitals."

"Stop babbling and tell me what it is."

"The lieutenant just called, after he heard it from night-watch. Up in the 3-4, another medical center surrounded by a war zone. Female resident finishes back-to-back shifts, walks out the door a little after midnight to go to her car. When she reaches it, she sees a tire is flat. Good Samaritan—and I'm using the term loosely—offers to help her change the tire. Bastard probably flattened it himself. Tells her he's just got to go into his sister's building across the street and get some tools. Says she can wait in the vestibule for him, to keep warm.

"They cross the street—three eyewitnesses to that part. Say he's polite, holds her elbow, tells her to watch out for traffic. Inside the lobby—it's a tenement, five-story walk-up—he pulls a knife, apparently. Now, we got no witnesses, nada, nobody. We got a trusting young doctor wearing her white lab coat lying on the floor behind the staircase with eight stab wounds in her chest and abdomen, underwear removed, and skirt pulled up to expose the lower half of her body. But no evidence of a completed sexual assault—no semen, no pubic hair, no proof of a rape.

"So you tell me, is it an attempt that got interrupted or is it just staged so the scumbag could steal her ten bucks and her beeper and let us think we're looking for a rapist? Is it a coincidence or a second strike?"

I had no answers for Mike. I was trying to envision the crime scene and thinking about the loss of another useful life.

"Dead?"

"Better off if she were. Very, very likely to die. Hooked up to life support with perfectly flat brain waves."

"You said there were witnesses?"

"Just the people who saw the guy hanging around the hospital entrance, then talking to the doctor near her car. Male Hispanic, six-two or -three, wiry. Looked dirty, unkempt, possibly homeless, like a thousand other men within a stone's throw of the medical center. Wearing a flannel shirt and green surgical pants. He wasn't a professional rival of hers, I'll tell you that much."

"Well, what do you think?" I knew it was a stupid question as soon as I asked it.

"I think I don't have a friggin' clue what to think. I don't know whether this is just a bad fluke of timing or the work of some lunatic that we rousted out of the tunnels at Mid-Manhattan and sent up to Columbia-Presbyterian with a license to start over again in an even more fertile location.

"I'm back to having no idea whether Gemma Dogen wasn't raped because something interrupted the attempt, and because she struggled, like this kid last night. Or whether you're right and Dogen's killing was just staged to look like a sexual assault."

"How many women do you think are likely to die before we figure it out?"

"Hey, Blondie, we're all likely to die. It's just the time and place of this one that's so wretched. Six other guys from the squad are gonna jump all over this one. It'll take us twice as long to sort the whole thing out and figure whether they're related to each other. I'll call you at the office as soon as I get some more details."

I went into the kitchen and turned on the coffee before I showered, wondering why Drew hadn't called during the night. The clothes I had planned to travel in were laid out the night before, so I dressed in the navy cashmere sweater and matching slacks hoping that my blue-and-red quilted jacket would be warm enough for Britain's early spring.

The doorman helped me with my luggage to a cab, and I convinced myself that the extra hour at the office in the early morning would actually benefit me to organize my desk before the staff began to arrive.

I couldn't believe the phone was ringing at seven fifteen when I unlocked the door.

"Alex? It's Stan."

Westfall. One of the guys in the unit who was fine in the courtroom but difficult to deal with almost all the rest of the time.

"I got a problem. Just tried you at home and when I got the machine, I figured I'd give you a shout at your office." He sounded frantic.

"What could possibly be wrong at this hour of the morning?" I'd already had one dose of dreadful news and doubted that anything Stan had to complain about would be in the same league.

"My witness is gone, Alex. You know I'm on trial in front of Sudolsky, right? Well, I finished the direct case yesterday but she hasn't been crossed yet. She's the woman I brought back here from Pittsburgh to testify and—"

"Who's she been staying with?"

"Well, that's it. You were really busy, you know, with your murder investigation and I didn't want to bother you. So I just went to Pat McKinney and got his permission to put her up in a hotel. I mean, a cheap one. Big Apple, over on West Forty-sixth."

"Great. You put a hooker in a hotel in midtown. With a bodyguard?"

"No. Alex, she swore to me she's not a hooker anymore. I really believed it."

It didn't do any good to roll my eyes. Stan wouldn't have gotten the point had he been standing right in front of me. He was more likely to be struck by lightning than ever meet an *ex*-hooker.

"And what happened? She got booted for bringing tricks into the room during the night while the taxpayers picked up the bill?"

"Well, the manager caught her with a guy coming into the lobby around 2 A.M. Knew she was with us, so he stopped them and kicked out the john but let her go up to the room.

See, um, the manager's the one who called me. Sometime after that she just left."

"Don't panic yet. She's probably out working, picking up a few extra bucks before she goes home to the burbs."

"Manager doesn't think so. She's gone. And what he's pissed about is that she took everything in the room with her. It's not the kind of place that has much in it that isn't nailed down tight. But she walked out with the sheets, pillows, blankets, and towels." Stan was krexing at full pitch. "She even took the Bible."

I laughed at his plight knowing McKinney would have his head. That would be the last witness we lodge at the Big Apple, one of the few Manhattan hotels the office could afford.

"I don't know whether to have the cops look for her or not. The jury'll hate her when they hear it."

"Get out your copy of the Good Book, Stan. Give 'em Proverbs. 'Who can find a virtuous woman?' Don't try to change her stripes. Let her be what she is even if she's still a hooker. If I remember correctly, you had a ton of medical evidence that corroborated the force in that case. Point out her vulnerability and let them see what a dirtball the defendant is."

"How do I find her? The arresting officer won't be down in my office 'til nine-thirty."

"Call Midtown South. Get some of the guys from the pussy posse before they sign out. Give them a description and check to see if they spotted her during their tour." The guys who worked the pros detail didn't go off duty until 8 A.M. "And most of all, stop panicking. You'll have to ask the judge for a few hours' adjournment if she doesn't surface this morning, but that's not the end of the world. I don't know how you get anything done when you're so wired."

"Thanks, Alex. I'll check with you later."

I worked on correspondence until Laura arrived, then dictated several letters to her that I wanted to get out before I returned on Monday. At nine-thirty, she reminded me that I had to go across the street to Judge Torres's part for the sentencing in the case of the serial rapist that Gayle Marino had convicted three weeks earlier.

I slipped into a seat in the front row of the large courtroom while Gayle was addressing the bench. Although the judge was well aware of Johnny Rovaro's criminal history, Marino was carefully restating his record to support the heavy sentence she would be requesting. She reminded Torres that Rovaro had been convicted of a similar crime eight years earlier and even ran the prison clinic for sex offenders while he was upstate. When released on parole Rovaro had returned to his home in Brooklyn; a condition established by the board was his participation in a therapy program run by a treatment center in Greenwich Village.

Three months after his release, the quiet neighborhood just blocks away from the center was the scene of a series of sexual assaults. First, the attack on a young Irish nanny who managed to secure the infant in her charge out of harm's way before being overcome by the assailant. Then a housewife with armloads of groceries who was pushed into her town house as she struggled against the armed attacker. And finally, the ten-year-old child who was followed from school and forced into her building by the same man, who struck her in the face to subdue her during the commission of the crime.

Gayle had tried an outstanding case, supporting her fragile witnesses through their moving testimony and shattering the alibi defense of the rapist's witnesses—family and friends—with fine preparation and thorough cross-examination. Rovaro himself had been shaken by her dogged and persistent questions as she steadily destroyed his patchwork of lies and exposed his temper to the panel of jurors. Now she sat, resting his fate in the hands of one of the toughest judges in the system.

Edwin Torres was ready to speak to Rovaro. He rose from his high-backed leather chair, stepped around behind it, and leaned his elbows against it. He looked first at the defendant's wife and mother, who had been gesturing and cursing throughout Gayle's statement to the court. Torres's dark hair and strong features were outlined against the light paneling of the wooden wall that framed him and he glanced over at Gayle before he began to speak. In his eloquent fashion, the judge characterized the rapist's conduct as he looked Rovaro squarely in the eyes. "The record speaks—or, perhaps, shouts—for itself," referring to the acts proved in Marino's case and summarizing them once again. "But what really carries you beyond the pale of civilization—beyond compassion, beyond humanity—is your attack on the child. You are the devil incarnate, for who but a devil could punch that child in the mouth, breaking her braces against her teeth before sodomizing her?" Torres asked. "For that act of savagery alone, there are societies where you would be impaled on a stake, to dance on tiptoes for hours in the Sahara sun."

Mickey Diamond was furiously taking notes behind me and leaned over to whisper, "Don't you wish it wasn't reversible error for you to say things like that in a summation? I don't even have to make stuff up with him—he's always so quotable."

I smiled as Torres went on, standing by his seat to pronounce the sentence of one hundred years for Rovaro, adding his final, personal seal on the record of the twice-paroled offender. "A collective pox on the parole board that ever sees fit to unleash this demon on our society again. I will rise from my moldy grave to visit it upon them myself."

He winked in my direction and then told the phalanx of court officers who stood behind the cuffed prisoner to put him back in the pens. As Rovaro walked out, his expression never changed, but when he reached the door that led from the courtroom to the cell, he turned and spit at the judge's bench. The captain grabbed the collar of his shirt and pulled him out of the room. I walked into the well to congratulate Gayle on the outcome as one of the court officers came back to us to make sure she was okay.

"Rovaro pees ice water," he told us, shaking his head. "You should feel good about this one."

She did, and I waved to Torres, walking out of the part as Gayle wheeled her shopping cart full of exhibits down the hallway with me. With any luck, Gemma Dogen's killer would be tried before a jurist like him. That is, if the killer were caught.

"You just missed Drew Renaud's call," Laura greeted me several minutes later. "He said he was leaving his hotel room. Didn't want to disturb you in the middle of the night. Said he'll try you a little later so he can get you before you leave for London.

"McKinney wants you, too. Wants to know what you're going to do about the new case up near Columbia-Presbyterian and who's going to sit on things while you're out of town. And he's also a bit riled up about something to do with Phil. Wouldn't say what."

"Got it, Laura, thanks."

Both phone lines lighted up before I could reach my desk and I had the feeling it was going to be one of those wild days, as it always seemed to be when I had to go out of town.

Through the intercom I heard Laura announce that Mercer was on the first line while a reporter from New York One was on the backup. "Kick the reporter over to the press office—I'm not talking to any of them. I'll take Mercer."

"G'morning. I gather Mike called you about the attack up at Columbia? I'm going over to the hospital now to see what I can pick up. Would you ask Laura to pound out a subpoena for Dietrich's bank? I called over there when they opened up this morning. Got someone who told me he's way deep in the hole. Racked up a huge bunch of debts and owes people a lot of money. She wouldn't give me specifics without a grand jury subpoena—"

"Will she take it by fax? I'll have one ready in fifteen minutes."

"Fine. It'll give me something to do while you and Chapman are having tea with the Queen. See you later."

I hung up but saw that the button for the second line was still lighted. Obviously, a persistent reporter whom Laura couldn't shake loose. "Alex, the guy on line two says he's not looking for news, he's got a tip for you. Won't tell me what it is and won't tell it to Brenda's office. Want him?"

"Sure." I switched the line and the high-pitched voice of a young researcher for the local channel piped up to introduce himself to me.

"Miss Cooper? We know you're handling the investigation at Mid-Manhattan. Your people know anything about the break-in last night at Metropolitan Hospital?"

No point bullshitting him if he knew more than I did. I pulled a pad into place and began making notes as I told him I didn't know a thing about it. "What've you got? Any patients hurt?"

"That's what we're looking for. So far, they're denying patient involvement, but we just don't know whether to trust the information or not. Nobody wants it to be another Mid-Manhattan, and I take it you've already heard about Columbia."

"Yes. What's your story on Metropolitan?"

"They're playing it down. Saying the guy never got past the administrative offices on the ground floor. Patients and medical staff were never in any danger. Usual disclaimers."

"Who discovered it?"

"Night cleaning staff. Lady came in and found lights on in

the billing department at 3 A.M. Heard footsteps but couldn't see anybody running out. Door lock had been jimmied."

"I know you're not going to give me your source, but—"

"Not an issue. It's all over the place here. The cleaning lady does one shift at Met, then she does our offices back to back. She was real upset when she got here this morning. All she could talk about was the burglar in the hospital—practically in the president's office, in the middle of the night. She doesn't want to go back to work there—had enough of hospitals after the last two weeks."

"I'll drink to that. Tell her she's not the only one."

"Well, the reason I called was to see if you got word that anything else happened at Metropolitan last night. You know, was this guy on his way in or his way out when our cleaning lady spotted him?"

"Quite frankly, this is the first I've heard of it. I owe you, next time you need a lead I can help with. Give me a number and if there's anything I can tell on this one, I'll give you a call back. Thanks for the info."

I dialed Mercer immediately. "Glad I caught you before you walked out. One more tidbit. Stop at Metropolitan sometime this morning if you can and check out this story." I repeated what the caller had told me and both of us expressed relief at a break-in that had not resulted in physical injury to anyone.

"Let's hope he was just looking for some checks to steal or some cash lying around," said Mercer. "No reason for hospital management to have called us on this one, but I'll see whether they reported it to the precinct and if anything was actually stolen. You'll have a full report later today."

I had three indictments to review before they were filed, a dozen calls that had come in yesterday that had to be returned, and a luncheon meeting in Rod Squires's office with all the bureau chiefs to discuss proposals to change the hours of the late-night arraignment shift.

Faith Griefen stuck her head in and flashed the time-out signal with her hands as I held the phone to my ear waiting to be connected with one of the advocates at the St. Luke's Crime Victims Intervention Program. "Sarah said you're a size A and you always have spares. Got anything in an off-white?"

I nodded my head and held up a finger, suggesting she wait until I finished answering the question about how to recommend that the woman who was getting counseling be advised about the importance of testing for HIV infection after her rape.

"I'm about to do a summation and I snagged my panty hose on the table leg when I stood up to make an objection," Faith said, displaying a two-inch-wide run that started above her hemline and ran into the heel of her shoe. "That old wooden furniture in Part 52 catches me whenever I'm about to reach an important point in a trial. I hate to stand up there for an hour with this grotesque hole down my entire side. Might be somebody on the jury who thinks it's tacky enough they'd vote to acquit."

"I guess juror number twelve's still focused on your legs, huh? They're certainly better than the evidence you've got," I noted, walking to the file cabinet nearest my desk and tugging at the drawer marked "Closed Cases." It pulled open to reveal a neat stack of Hanes Silk Reflections in a variety of colors, several pairs of Escada pumps in different heel heights, basic makeup items, toothpaste and a toothbrush—a little service station for lady lawyers in distress. I fished out a pair of stockings for Faith and reminded her that one of the worst things about starting in the office a decade earlier, as I did, was the very small number of women on the staff. The men had been great friends and fine mentors, but once Battaglia made an effort to recruit more of us to do the trial work there was an entirely different flavor to the camaraderie that was unthinkable under his predecessor. Not only could you now talk about something other than free agents, the Big East, and Demi

Moore's implants, but you could find an emergency supply of panty hose, Tampax, and emery boards without dispatching a paralegal to Bloomingdale's on her lunch hour.

Faith was off to the ladies' room to change her underwear and Rose Malone walked in with a copy of the remarks that Battaglia had planned to use for his opening statement at the panel meeting in England on Thursday afternoon.

"The District Attorney wanted you to have a copy of this. He suggested that you draft something yourself but include the positions he's outlined here on gun control, drug treatment, and the death penalty. He said you should add some of your own comments on sexual assault and family violence, okay?"

"That's fine. I'll work it over right now so Laura can type it up for me. Any other instructions?"

"Mr. B. has called Lord Windlethorne and explained the substitution. They're very gracious and happy to have you. Geoffrey Dogen will drive out to Cliveden on Friday morning, and since your main event will have been completed you and Mike can spend as much time as you need with him. Mr. B'll expect to see you back here first thing Monday morning, of course."

I thanked Rose and told her about the night's events at Columbia-Presbyterian and Metropolitan so that she could bring Battaglia up to date. "He knows where to find me if he's got any questions. See you next week."

Paul's speech was short and to the point. I knew his stand on most issues quite well, and it was easy for me to present his arguments and augment them with the topics that had come to be my specialties. By the time I had crafted my remarks and passed them along to Laura, she told me the group was beginning to assemble in the conference room for Rod's meeting.

Having spent the previous afternoon in the hospital boardroom, the contrast was especially striking. Fourteen of us—Rod,

Pat, six bureau chiefs who led Trial Division teams, special unit heads like me, and assorted directors of training and misdemeanor complaints—were crowded around two Formica tables that were placed end to end to run the length of the room. No glossy wood furniture in the city budget lines—just faux paneling, vinyl seat covers, plastic frames showcasing cheap reproduction photographs. Bring your own sandwich, the memo usually ran, and eat it while disregarding the green pellets on the floor in each corner, which had once poisoned the rodent population of the building although now they seemed to gobble them like candy.

Rod had been my favorite supervisor throughout all my tenure in the office—smart, funny, reasonable. He was easy to approach on any issue, personal or professional, and his judgment was reliable in crises of every kind. I had stopped counting the number of instances in which he had saved my neck by thinking through an issue with me before I responded hotheadedly. His friendship was as valuable to me as his wisdom.

I pulled a chair up to the table and sat against the wall next to John Logan, opening the tab on my lite yogurt while he unwrapped a ham and cheese hero that smelled delicious.

We all kibitzed with each other while Rod and Pat went over the agenda for the meeting, waiting for the last stragglers to settle into the room. "Heard about last night's attack on the resident. How does that cut for you?" Logan asked.

"If you know anybody who wants to confess to both crimes and put me out of my misery, let me know."

"Right. I'm still waiting for an ID on that mob hit at Rockefeller Center. Don't hold your breath. You got any sample voir dires on sexual abuse cases? One of my guys has a misdemeanor about to go to trial—a playground flasher. I told him I'd get some materials from you."

"Sure. Laura's got an entire file on jury questions. She'll dig it up for you on your way out."

Rod was ready to begin. "Let's get to work. There isn't much time this afternoon before we have to see Cooper and Chapman off on their honeymoon in the Cotswolds."

Several heads jerked in my direction to gauge my reaction, reminding me that the rumor mill had been churning as usual. I was used to Rod's bait and was beyond blushing.

"Nice of you to drop by the office for our meeting, Miss Cooper. McKinney told me he wasn't sure you worked here anymore."

"Wishful thinking on his part, Rod." I smiled at Pat, who pretended to be making notations on his legal pad.

"Well, if you're smuggling in any Cohibas for Battaglia, don't forget to bring home a few extras for your old pals."

"You know I wouldn't dream of doing anything illegal. Cohibas or Monte Cristos?"

The cigar smokers seemed evenly divided on their votes and Rod moved on to the discussion about staffing the lobster shift. Traditionally, rookie-level assistants manned the arraignment part that operated between midnight and 8 A.M., but it had been so slow and unproductive these past few months that we were debating its usefulness. Everyone around the table voiced opinions while my concentration drifted from that issue to the things I wanted Mercer to work on while Mike and I were away.

We were about to break up at two-thirty when Rod announced that he had another suspect for us to consider in the Mid-Manhattan investigation. He held up a case opinion that he told us a prosecutor had sent him from Detroit.

"You looked into this doctor named Thangavelu?"

"I'll bite. Who is he?"

"True story. Doctor was charged with cunnilingus while performing a vaginal exam on a patient. Tried and convicted. Michigan's appellate court reversed—read the decision—*People* v. *Thangavelu*. Judges said the prosecutor never proved that what the doctor did was *not* an acceptable part of the woman's medical treatment. You think the jury wasn't able to figure that out by themselves? I'll tell you one thing. You ever get sick in Kalamazoo, Coop, just keep on driving 'til you reach Ohio. Don't get up in those stirrups anywhere in Michigan.

"Better call and make sure that schmuck didn't come to New York and set up shop at Mid-Manhattan."

"Thanks for the tip, Rod, you're always such a help. Somehow, we missed that case when Sarah and I were doing our research. I'll run it down when I get back from England."

By the time I checked back in with Laura and picked up my messages, I had less than an hour to tie up all the loose ends. Sarah came upstairs to go over an additional list of items to be subpoenaed and to assure me that she would cover any developments in either of the cases over the next few days.

I packed the crime scene photos and some of the police reports into a folder, along with a copy of the video that Bob Bannion had made in Gemma's office. Perhaps Inspector Creavey, or even Geoffrey Dogen, would have ideas when they looked at the bloody setting with fresh eyes.

"I think that's Ricky Nelson making a commotion in the hallway," Sarah said, backing over toward the door. Chapman was serenading Laura and Rod's secretary to the tune of "Traveling Man," grinning that splendid smile of his. The small audience was appreciative.

"I told my saintly old mother that Alex Cooper was taking me to London and I swear she almost had the big one on me. Thought it was an April Fool's joke. She pleaded with me to make you stop in Dublin on the way back. Meet the family and all that. What do you say, Blondie?" He was playing to the crowd.

"Why not?"

"The least I could do was promise her that I'd try to convert you. See if I could wean you off the Dewar's and onto some good Irish whiskey. That's my goal, ladies. I'll lift my glass to you right after takeoff.

"C'mon, give me your bags. Mercer's waiting in the car. Wants to beat the rush hour traffic on the Van Wyck." He came in to pick up my suitcase. "What's your bet, Sarah? How many changes of clothes for the Duchess in the next seventy-two hours? How many pairs of shoes? If I get a hernia carrying this crap for her, you know I'm going out on disability. Three-quarters, on-the-job injury."

Chapman took Sarah by the arm and walked her out to the elevator, holding my bag in his other hand. He whispered something in her ear and I saw her expression change as her body bristled and she clasped her hand to her mouth. I thought I had heard Mike say Maureen's name.

"What's wrong?"

"Mind your own business, kid. Nothing's wrong. I just forgot to tell her something about somebody she knows. Let's go." The doors opened and the red arrow flashed the down signal.

I looked from his face to hers but couldn't get through. "Were you talking about Maureen?"

"Don't you think I'd tell you if I were? We're outta here."

I stepped in and the doors slid shut behind us.

21

Mercer was parked next to the fire hydrant on Hogan Place. He popped the trunk so Mike could stick my suitcase inside. I pushed two ratty ties, a half-opened gym bag that appeared to be full of dirty underwear and socks, and a Yankees World Series hat over to one side so I could climb into the rear seat of the standard-issue detective-bureau Crown Vic.

We headed down Lafayette toward the entrance ramp to the Brooklyn Bridge and the choppy sequence of potholed highways that would take us to Kennedy Airport.

"So what are the afternoon updates on last night's cases?"

"Columbia-Pres is still on life support. Not looking good for her and nobody's come forward with anything worthwhile on a suspect. Metropolitan looks like an aborted burglary-in-progress."

"Anything taken?"

"Two schools of thought. Whoever did it was a few feet short of the pharmacy. Could have been planning on drugs and syringes but just never got there. Had a little bit of success in the administrative office. Petty cash drawer was emptied out and personnel files were dumped all over the place."

"Still not clear at this point. It's a mess. Understatement. The guy actually defecated all over the files so it's been difficult for anybody to get, shall we say, a clean read."

"Spare me the particulars."

"Done."

Late-afternoon traffic was heavy as usual. Mercer weaved in and out of the idling cars and we crept slowly along for the last few miles before the freight hangars came into view. The pace picked up as we approached the terminal areas, but I braced myself against the seatback as Mercer slammed on the brakes in front of the Chapel of the Skies. It was a serene little outpost in the center of the airport that I had passed hundreds of times but had never entered.

"Coop and me'll wait in the car. You want to say a few novenas?"

"Man, don't make fun of me." Chapman was terrified of flying but hated to be ridiculed for it.

"Not for the flight. Pilot'll take care of you up there. Just so's maybe you get lucky in England, you know?"

He was moving again and we took the turnoff for the international departures entrance at the American Airlines building.

Mercer waited until he let us out at the curb to drop his bombshell. "The lieutenant called with the lab results on the candies from Maureen's secret admirer."

I glanced over at Mike, who was fidgeting with his ticket, and knew immediately that that's what he'd been whispering about to Sarah as we were leaving the office.

"Chocolate-covered cherries—which were laced with boric

acid. Some sick puppy injected it using a needle that left a hole smaller than a pinprick. Almost invisible."

As I opened my mouth to speak, Mercer grabbed my face between his enormous hands and leaned over to look me directly in the eye, our noses almost touching. "It's okay, Alex. Nothing happened to her, you hear? This is exactly why we wanted her in that hospital in the first place—to draw our killer out."

"But—"

"But nothing. You spoke to Mo yourself last night. You know she's fine. Now, you get out of town and go about your business."

"I just can't—"

"Look at me again, girl—right in these big brown eyes. Are you telling me that you don't trust me with Maureen's well-being, huh?"

I shook my head back and forth.

"Now, go on, Coop. I hate long good-byes."

Mike and I walked into the terminal together while he explained to me that it had been Mercer's idea to tell me about the poisoned candy at the last possible moment. I was fretting because I couldn't be with Mo, but I understood the logic of their decision and knew that she was a consummate professional.

Security was tight and we waited on the long line for the evening flights to Europe until our passports were studied, our luggage scanned, and our seats in the coach section of the 767 assigned.

"C'mon. I'll take you up to the Admiral's Club. We've got half an hour before they board us."

Mike followed me down the corridor and into the elevator for the one-floor lift to the private lounge. I walked to the desk to show the attendant my membership card while Mike moved ahead to use one of the telephones for a last check at his office. The couple in front of me turned and I was surprised to recognize the distinguished-looking gentleman who was pocketing his ticket portfolio as he spotted me.

"Business or pleasure, Alex? Which way are you headed?" Justin Feldman greeted me with a kiss on the cheek.

He was a superb lawyer, with an expertise in securities work, which usually kept him in the more rarefied atmosphere of the federal courts and not our scruffier forum. "It's all business this time. London. Congratulations on that piece I saw in *American Lawyer* last month—ten best securities litigators in the country. Nice press."

"You'll push me off that kind of list someday, as soon as you come over to our side. Meet my associate, Susan LaRossa. She makes it all possible, right?"

Susan was a few years younger than I but I had heard about her talent and courtroom skills from friends in the private sector. She extended a hand and we talked about our mutual acquaintances as we made a tentative date for lunch.

"Where are you two headed?"

"Paris. Quick trip for a client in that banking scandal your boss is digging into. Battaglia's been keeping us all well fed. Susan and I might even get into criminal court for a change on this one."

The airline representative returned my club card and the three of us walked toward the lounge area. "Your name came up yesterday afternoon, in a meeting I had downtown at Milbank. What was it? Oh, of course—"

I was already biting my lip. There really are no secrets in New York. Six degrees of separation wasn't an exaggeration.

"I understand Drew Renaud is mad about you. Just met, isn't that right? Well, his partners say he seems happy and upbeat for the first time since his wife died."

"We don't even know each other, really. I'm sure there's something else that has changed his mood—it's awfully premature to even be—"

"He's a wonderful guy, Alex—smart and solid. I know what brought it up. We were talking about coincidence and the odd circumstance that brought Susan and me into this case that we're working on now. Drew's partner said he'd heard of bizarre happenstances before, but the one about you, Drew, and that murder investigation you're handling really startled him."

I stopped in my tracks and looked at Justin quizzically. "Which 'bizarre' part of it are you talking about?"

"About Drew's wife and the way she died." Justin's smile had disappeared and he looked somber now while Susan avoided my glance and focused her dark brown eyes on a spot on the floor.

"Cancer. She died of a brain tumor, right?" I didn't get any connection and it was becoming obvious to Justin that he had more of the facts than I did. "The doctor who was killed, the case you're handling—sorry I can't recall her name."

"Gemma Dogen."

"Yes, well, we all assumed you knew about it. Carla Renaud died on the operating table. Drew had flown her to London for a procedure that was developed there. Very complicated, done by a crack team of neurosurgeons. Dogen was brought in from Minuit to assist in the surgery. Carla died while Dogen was working on her, in the middle of the operation."

Images raced through my mind as I tried to remember the order of things. Had Drew told Joan Stafford he wanted to meet me *before* or after Gemma had been murdered? Had Gemma's name come up in any of our conversations and had I raised it or had Drew? Why hadn't he mentioned any of this to me? It had to be the most significant and traumatic event of his life.

"Sorry if I've upset you, Alex. We all thought it was great that you two were dating. Just odd that this case should come along right after you started seeing each other."

"Not after, Justin. Dogen was killed several days before I was introduced to Drew."

Why had he wanted to meet me? Was it *me* or was it because I was handling the case? Had he hated Dogen, I wondered? She had apparently failed to save his wife.

"Excuse me, please. Sorry, I'm just distracted. I've got to make a phone call before we board."

"I've obviously upset you, Alex. I'm sorry—"

"It's fine, Justin. Good to meet you, Susan. See you both again."

There was an empty cluster of chairs in the far corner against a window and I made directly for it, picking up the phone on the side table. I dialed Joan's home and punched in the digits of my credit card and PIN number. I got the answering machine. "Pick up, dammit. If you're writing, or you're on your StairMaster, or you're on the other line, pick this up, Joannie. I'm desperate to speak with you before I get on that plane and I'm not kidding."

I waited several seconds and got no reply. If Joan had been anywhere in earshot, she would have responded to me. "Beep me if you find this message in the next fifteen minutes," I begged.

The first boarding announcement was made for our flight. I could see Mike across the large room laughing into the mouthpiece of the phone. I knew we had a long walk to the gate and still had to pass through the metal detector on our way down the hall. I checked my watch, looked at the phone number for Drew's hotel that I had scribbled on the outside of the ticket envelope, and called San Francisco. It was the middle of the day and there was no chance that I would find him in his hotel room. Chapman was standing now, scanning the room for me, and headed toward me as he waved at me to get up to leave.

The operator connected me to Drew's room, let it ring

twelve times, and then got on to ask me if I wanted to leave a message for him. I didn't know what I wanted to say. I wanted *him* to tell me things without my asking. I wanted to know what Joan knew about any of this before I spoke with Drew directly. I wanted to know what kind of grudge he had harbored against Gemma Dogen for the two years since his wife's tragic death. "No. You don't need to leave word. I'll try again later."

I grabbed my tote and met Mike by the front door of the club. "You okay?" he asked. "You look like somebody just hit you over the head with a tire iron."

"C'mon. Let's get down to the gate." I was fuming as we took the elevator downstairs, pushed and were pushed as we tried to cross the entire length of the ticketing counters in the main section of the terminal, and stood in the crowded line of departing travelers to go through the security checkpoint that led down the concourse to our gate.

"What's bothering you?"

I lifted my bag off the screening machine and started to tell Mike about the conversation I had just finished in the club, as we were able to walk side by side for the first time.

"Take it for what it looks like, kid. It's a coincidence."

"Bullshit. You don't believe that any more than I do."

"You're watching too many movies." Chapman was shaking his head and grinning. "Tell me what you're thinking. Your new main squeeze killed the doctor? Then, a day later, he tells your best friend he's dying to meet you. He does. You fall for him. He gets laid—"

"He did *not* get laid."

"You didn't do him? No wonder he didn't kill you yet—he's waiting for one shot at you to see if that's all it's cracked up to be. *Then* he'll kill you to get you off Dogen's case."

"You know how stupid that sounds?"

"Yeah, in fact, I do. That's why I said it out loud and you

didn't. Are you really thinking that this white-shoe lawyer, who's been mourning his wife for two years, has anything to do with stabbing Dogen to death in the middle of the night in her office? And, your obvious charms apart, for what earthly reason would he take up with you—unless it's to kill you to get you off the case because he doesn't want it solved. I know that's the way your mind is working right now and I'm here to tell you that it's crazy. Maybe he doesn't like to talk about his wife. Maybe he doesn't even remember the doctor's name."

"Maybe, maybe, maybe. I want to know the answers. I hate maybes and I hate coincidence."

"You hate any circumstances you can't control. Just calm yourself and put it out of your tired little brain until we get back."

We had almost reached the end of the corridor and I could see the passengers filing through the door of Gate A20. "Go ahead and get on the plane. I want to try Joan one more time. Please."

I stopped at a pay phone, dialed the number, and waited for the connection while I heard the loudspeaker announcement for the last boarding call of our flight. Mike was pointing me out to a woman I guessed was the Special Services agent as the last few stragglers showed their tickets and boarded. She was holding Mike's envelope and he jogged the fifty feet back to the phone bank as I again urged Joan to pick up her line. She still wasn't home, so I told her to call me tomorrow at Cliveden.

Mike picked up my tote from the ground, took a firm hold on my elbow, and guided me up the incline to the gate agent's desk. "She needs your boarding pass."

I handed it over and watched her cross out some numbers and reenter a new designation on the seat assignment. She gave it to the Special Services representative, who asked us to accompany her onto the plane. Instead of turning right and wading through the scores of coach passengers engaged in the battle to squeeze their carry-on luggage into the overhead bins, she pointed us to the left. "You're up ahead in first class, seats 2A and 2B. Hope you enjoy the flight."

"I'm afraid to ask who you bribed to get this done. You didn't show anyone your badge and demand an upgrade, did you?" At least I was smiling again. "Or did some poor stewardess have to put out for this exchange?"

"You're such a skeptic, Blondie. I thought it would be a nice surprise. Remember Charlie Bardong?" Charlie used to be a lieutenant in the District Attorney's Office squad and was now a private investigator. We both knew him well. "His wife runs Special Services at American. I called her this morning and she said if there were any empty seats it wouldn't be a problem. Cheer up, Coop. A few cocktails after takeoff, I'll forget I'm airborne and you can forget about Lew—"

"Drew."

"Whatever his name is. I keep telling you, don't go seeing ghosts where there aren't any. We got enough confusion already."

There were only twelve seats in the first-class section of the 767, half of which were empty. I took the one by the window, emptied some magazines from my tote, put on the slippers from the complimentary travel pack, and settled in with my pillow and blanket at the ready. Mike ordered me a Dewar's and himself a double Jameson's, making good on his plan to transfer my affection to Irish whiskey.

By the time the plane reached our cruising altitude, all I could see was the darkened sky and the occasional lights of another aircraft speeding by below us. We were on our second round of drinks and the assortment of warmed nuts, mulling over our options for the microwaved dinners. The liquor was relaxing me and I was losing the edge of my annoyance about the circumstances of my introduction to Drew. There would be plenty of time to focus on all that after we got home to New York. I was happy to be six miles above the earth, out of the range of beepers and skypagers. I liked my flying isolation booth.

Mike talked to me nonstop during the meal service. He relived old cases and escapades with ex-partners, unsolved murders, and victims whose corpses had never been identified or claimed. By the time the ice-cream sundaes and brandy were served, it was close to ten o'clock and I was snuggled into the reclining chair, somewhere east of Greenland.

"If you could be anybody in the world, who would it be?"

"What?"

"Don't you ever do that? Just take yourself out of your own skin and pretend you could be someone else?" Mike asked. "Tell me three people—dead or alive—that you'd like to have been. Sheer fantasy, no goody-two-shoes stuff. Don't give me Mother Teresa or Albert Schweitzer or Jonas Salk or Clara Barton. Just for fun, who would you change places with if you could?"

My legs were drawn up in the seat, under the blanket, and I cradled the Courvoisier with both hands while I thought of my answers. "First choice—Shakespeare."

"For you? Never would have guessed it. I figured you for great clothes but not cross-dressing."

"I can't imagine any one mind creating all of those remarkable writings—the language, the themes, the images, the range of words and ideas. Maybe I'd rather have been Mrs. S.— simply lie there at night and let him come home and read to me the lines he'd worked on all day. Just be the inspiration for that incredible poetry. I don't think anyone has ever used the language more magnificently."

"You like it all? I mean, you've read all his plays?"

"Not all, but my favorites over and over again. Mostly the tragedies and histories. But, of course, the histories are usually tragedies, too. I adore his tragedies." I picked my head up from the pillow and looked across at Mike. "Something wrong with me, you think? That I like tragedies so much? And murder mysteries, and the kind of job that I have—?"

"You're just coming to that conclusion now?"

"Some days it seems more obvious than others, I guess. Who's your choice?"

"Neil Armstrong. First man to walk on the moon. The idea of being a pioneer in an entirely new world and—"

"Time out." I pressed a finger on the cushioned arm pad and imitated the sound of a TV game show penalty buzzer. "Bad answer. You're terrified of flying—you can't be an astronaut."

"I just want to be the guy who takes the first step on the moon. I didn't say anything about flying B-52s or—"

"Not fair. There's only one way to get to the moon and you would be completely and totally ineligible. Too long a flight, no alcohol. Next idea."

"Okay." He mused before going on. "This one changes from time to time, depending on whose biography I'm reading. Usually, it's the Duke of Wellington. Great military strategist—genius in planning Waterloo. Some days, though, it's Napoleon. Before Waterloo. That's when I get fickle—right around 1815. Sometimes it's even Hannibal, taking those elephants over the Alps. You get the point—a great general, leading his troops into battle. Die with my boots on and all that. Who else for you?"

"No surprise. A ballet dancer." I looked at my watch. "Right now, someone is sitting in *my* seats at American Ballet Theater sighing over Kathleen Moore's performance. It's an art that allows no imperfection—the audience can see every slip and misstep and off-balance move. I'd love to have that grace and elegance. Natalia Makarova—she's the one I'd most like to be. But I'm fickle, too. I could be Ferri or Kent or Moore. Dance like a dream and lose myself in the music.

"You know, even in ballet I like the tragedies best. Should I be worried?"

"Too late for that. D'you ever dance leading roles, I mean, when you were in ballet school?"

"Queen of the Wilis. That's my fate. Never Odile, not Coppelia, no Princess Aurora for me."

"What are the Wilis? Never heard of 'em."

"They're the maidens who died of unrequited love, in *Giselle*. Lines and lines of 'em, in long white tulle skirts, flitting all over the stage. They spend most of the second act dancing you heartbreakers to death. I'll take you to see it sometime. Suits my personality to a tee. And your next?"

"Joe DiMaggio. I sometimes think Babe Ruth or The Mick, but, then, Joe had all the great baseball moments *plus* Marilyn Monroe. He's still such a classy guy. Heroes of the All-American sport, 'til the strike screwed it up. Actually, I was there at the Stadium for Game Six of the Series when the Yankees won it. I would have jumped into the shoes of any one of them—Bernie Williams, Derek Jeter. I'd have sold my soul to the devil to have been Wade Boggs circling the stadium on the rear of that horse after all the years he waited just to get to a Series. What a moment."

"Don't forget Andy Pettitte. Now, *that* is a fox. You turn yourself into Andy Pettitte or Derek Jeter and I could get very interested."

"Last call. Ultimate fantasy. Who'll it be?"

"No contest for me. Tina Turner. *After* Ike, let me make that part of it perfectly clear."

"Now you're talking, Blondie. Great casting."

"Remember the Private Dancer Tour—'85? Tina coming down that staircase suspended from the ceiling in Madison Square Garden? A mane of hair, an endless stretch of legs, a microskirt, and four-inch heels—strutting to the tune of 'What's Love Got to Do with It?' Not holding on to anything for a hundred steps or more on her way down, never missing a beat. I would have killed just to be one of her backups that night. Nina sent me a tape of the concert and I just pop it in the VCR to watch that one number whenever I think I need an anti-depressant. Three minutes and I'm cured. I wanna be Tina."

"You did a damn good imitation of her—for a white girl—the evening of Battaglia's roast. I thought he was gonna lose it when he saw you prancing down the staircase from the private dining room into the lobby at '21.'"

"Jeez, remember that? I thought he had left already. I never dreamed he'd see me."

"You may have a shot at this one, Coop. The only broad in the world with legs as good as Tina's is your old lady. All we gotta do is work on your voice."

"And your third?" I asked, smiling.

"A great director, movies. Probably Hitchcock, Spielberg, Truffaut. That's the kind of creative talent I'd like to have. Bring stories to the screen and give them life—entertain billions of people forever and forever. Sagas, epics, plots with imaginary creatures or escapist themes. Maybe I could be Carlo Ponti."

"He directs? I thought he's a producer."

"Whatever. At the end of the day, he still gets to crawl into bed with Sophia Loren, which wouldn't be a bad part of the deal."

"Predictable. Why did I think there'd be anything unusual about any of your fantasies? These are actually more tasteful than I expected any of them to be."

Mike and I had taken each other's minds off our respective concerns for a little while. We were farther away from home than either of us cared to be during an ongoing investigation and no closer to answers than we had been from the start. Sheep never worked for me, so I closed my eyes and tried to count Wilis until I drifted off to sleep.

22

Once we had cleared immigration at Heathrow, we searched the signs held by gray-uniformed drivers waiting near the doors until we found a printed plaque marked CLIVEDEN. Mike waved to the gentleman holding it in the air, who moved toward us to introduce himself and take the luggage we were carrying. He quickly escorted us out to the roadway where a sleek black Jaguar sedan was parked on the far side of the passenger drop-off area.

Arthur, as he was called, placed the bags in the car's trunk, then opened the rear doors for Mike and me.

"Not too shabby, Coop. I think I'm gonna like it here. Your car, Arthur?" Mike asked, as the driver settled himself behind the wheel.

"Hardly, sir. It's all we have at Cliveden, sir. Jaguars." Pronouncing the name, as the Brits do, with three distinct syllables.

It was daybreak as we started the half-hour ride to the hotel, the only one in Britain that is also a Stately Home. Rush-hour traffic heading into London surrounded us on the A4. But when we turned off the motorway as we neared Buckinghamshire, the fields, woods, and slate roofs of the countryside and villages gave us the sense that we had gone back a century or two in time.

Arthur was giving us a history of the estate as he cruised the Jag around narrow curves on ancient lanes barely wide enough to let another car pass. Cliveden, he told us, was built in 1666 by the Duke of Buckingham. Almost four hundred acres of land—housing the main buildings, composed of bedroom suites, dining rooms, and newly added meeting rooms, plus exquisite formal gardens and natural parklands—perch above the Thames in splendid style. The property remained at the center of Britain's political and social intrigue as its ownership passed through several dukes, one Prince of Wales, and then on to the Astor family before its acquisition by the National Trust in the 1980s.

"Pretty fancy place for a conference center," Chapman said.

Arthur grimaced into the rearview mirror. "We're a hotel, sir. And a very special one at that. Once a year the Home Secretary takes it over for this do. Sometimes the Prime Minister comes and a few nobs from abroad. Hardly worth our while, sir." Arthur looked again, just to reassure himself that we were not in that exalted category. "We'll get a few of our regulars after you go. End of the month we've got a wedding—one of the royals. Then the season gets going with Ascot and Wimbledon and all that."

"If you decide you want to stay on, let me know. I'm sure Battaglia'd find room in the budget," I said to Mike as Arthur slowed the car to turn in through the colossal double gate that marked the entrance. We circled the large sculpted scallop shell ringed by cherubs that stood at the start of the tree-lined drive and rode the last stretch of graveled path up to the majestic main building of Cliveden.

Several footmen appeared at the sound of the car crunching on the stones and coming to a stop—each one dressed in striped trousers, a morning coat, and white gloves. We had pulled in under the porte-cochère and our doors were opened by two of the eager staff.

The third young man, bespectacled and shorter than I by a head, bowed in my direction and shook Mike's hand as he welcomed us to Cliveden and told us his name was Graham. He gave us a brisk introduction to the hotel, explaining that the Cliveden tradition was to treat us all as "house guests" rather than customers. No registration, no signing for meals or services, no keys for the rooms nor locks on the doors.

"Your office phoned ahead with all the arrangements, Mrs. Cooper. We've substituted your name for Mr. Battaglia's where appropriate, and I've alerted all the staff to that change. I'm sure, madam, that you'll be quite comfortable. Let me see," he said, walking back to his antique *bureau plat* inside the doorway, "you'll be in the suite reserved for Mr. Battaglia. The Asquith. We only have thirty-seven rooms, of course, and they're all filled at the moment with the gentlemen who are attending your conference."

Nothing so crass as rooms with numbers here. Each of the suites was named for a titled or celebrated family who had visited Cliveden throughout its history.

Graham told one of the footmen to get our luggage from the car and take it up to the Asquith suite. He gestured in Mike's direction, "And if there is anything at all I can do for *you*, Mr. Cooper—"

"Chapman," Mike snapped. "I decided to keep my maiden name, Graham. It's Chapman."

He picked up his bag without waiting for any help and

started into the building. I was laughing as I followed him into the Great Hall, realizing for the first time that no one had expressly mentioned that the room assignment for Battaglia and spouse should not simply have been reissued to Cooper and spouse.

"What, hurt your feelings, Mikey? Don't like being Mr. Cooper? Or are you scared of being alone with me in the dark?"

"*Mister* Cooper? A guy'd have to have balls of steel to want that job title. Let's check out the room, Blondie."

The footman holding my bags was waiting for us. "The lift is this way, madam. The Asquith suite is on the first floor. Mind your step." He led us across the hallway and under the staircase to a small elevator that rattled its way slowly up to the next landing.

Our suite was at the end of a narrow corridor reached by passing rooms named for Westminster, Curzon, Balfour, and Churchill. When the door opened and Mike noticed the twin beds standing several feet apart, he murmured in my ear, "Only the English. Typical."

The spacious bedroom was tastefully decorated in a pale shade of green with ivory trim and had an adjoining sitting room with a writing desk and chaise as well as a large bathroom. There was a stunning view of the rear of the property with its parterre gardens and trimmed box hedges and miles of riding paths leading down to the Thames.

It was almost nine o'clock by the time we unpacked. But it was still the middle of the night at home and we were both frustrated by our inability to call to speak with Maureen and to check our offices for updates. There were no faxes or messages waiting for us so we had to assume that nothing had developed in either of the cases.

"Want to check out the grounds?" Mike could function on less sleep than anyone I knew.

The luncheon and afternoon conference in which I would be participating started at one o'clock. I didn't want Battaglia to get any bad reports about my presentation so I figured it was smarter to work on my notes. "I'm going to clean up, rest, and change for my speech."

"I'm taking a walk. Been sitting still too long. See you later, Lady Asquith."

I refreshed myself with a hot shower, then, wrapped in an oversized white terry robe with the Cliveden crest embroidered on its lapel, sat on the bed to work. The break revived me, despite the lack of sleep, and I was almost dressed and ready to leave the room by twelve-fifteen when Mike called me from the front desk.

"Are you receiving?"

"I'm just about ready to go down to the lobby."

"Thought I'd shower and change if you were out of the way."

I finished brushing my hair and putting on earrings as Mike came in. I gathered my notes and told him I'd meet him in the dining room for the luncheon. I took myself downstairs and through the expanse of the Great Hall, drawn to John Singer Sargent's famous portrait of Lady Astor, the American-born Nancy Langhorne, who had become the first woman to take a seat in Parliament in 1919. The painting dominated the room and I sat at the desk below it to review the remarks I would be delivering on Battaglia's behalf.

Once done, and noting that it would soon be 7 A.M. in New York, I picked up the telephone and asked the operator to connect me with a number in New York City, billing the charge to my suite. When the switchboard answered at Mid-Manhattan Hospital, I gave the receptionist Maureen's room number.

"What is the name of the patient to whom you wish to speak?"

I gave her Maureen's name, and when I heard no response I spelled the surname for her.

"Let me put you on hold, ma'am."

Several minutes passed until a voice returned to tell me that the patient I was trying to reach had been discharged from the hospital. It was only Thursday and my recollection was that she was not to be released for another twenty-four hours. I was relieved that someone had made the decision to take her out of harm's way.

The time difference was already proving to be a nuisance. I wanted to say hello to Maureen and knew that no one in a hospital could sleep long past six when the clanging of break-fast trays and bedpans roused everyone except the comatose. Now that she was at home I would place that call to her later on. It was a bit too early to hound Joan, still the middle of the night for Nina in Los Angeles, and I was determined not to speak with Drew until I knew what had driven the timing of our meeting at Joan's apartment.

Graham glided toward me as I sat at the desk, thinking to myself and gazing up at the delicate features of Lady Astor, bare shouldered in her white gown trimmed with pink satin ribbons. The pose was a bold one, perhaps struck when she was said to have refused Edward VII's offer to join him in a game of cards with the line, "I am afraid, sire, that I cannot tell a king from a knave."

"Miss Cooper, Mr. Bartlett—that is, the Home Secre-tary—has asked me to tell you that the morning session has ended and your group will be lunching in the Pavilion. That's the building just next door to the boardroom. Shall I tell him you'll be joining them?"

"Yes, thank you, Graham. I'm waiting for Mr. Chapman." He stepped away and within minutes I could see Mike descending the staircase at the far end of the room, stopping every few feet to examine the paintings and armored figures that were part of the Cliveden collection.

"C'mon, let's do the sightseeing later. We've been summoned for lunch."

We returned to the front entrance, followed the path pointed out by Graham's gloved finger, and made our way over to the series of rooms that housed the conference facilities. The Pavilion was a light-filled, cheerful area overlooking the notorious swimming pool—scene of the Profumo scandal—that had been set up with eight rectangular tables for the meeting participants and their guests.

I immediately spotted Commander Creavey's substantial figure as he stood to wave us into the room, where he had held empty seats on both sides for Mike and me to join him. He rose and bellowed to the polite diners after he kissed me on the cheek and embraced Mike with a few sound slaps on the back. "This 'ere is Alexandra Cooper. Top of the line in America. She prosecutes rapists, wife beaters, child abusers—all that type of bloke. I don't advise you to trifle with her while she's here. And this is Commander Michael Chapman. I've promoted him a few notches, but that's because over 'ere—with what 'e knows—'e'd be running the show. Be no need for me.

"Sit and enjoy your lunch. There'll be time to mix with all these fine gents this evening."

Chapman and Creavey jumped right into discussing each other's work and catching up with "on-the-job" events since they had last had the opportunity to talk at a session in New York. I played with my salad as I looked around the room to see whether I recognized any familiar faces. I knew from the list that Battaglia had passed along to me that most of the speakers and panelists were from the United Kingdom and Western Europe and it was quite clear that diversity was not an element in selecting voices to speak about the future of society as we neared the millennium.

The sixty-something, blue-rinse matron with painfully pink skin sitting on my other side began to chat me up, introducing herself as Winifred Bartlett, wife of the Home Secretary.

"And what is it exactly that your husband is going to be speaking about at the conference, dear?" she inquired, pausing between bites of her smoked salmon as she eyed me through cataract-dimmed lenses.

"Actually, *I* am the one who'll be speaking this afternoon. I'm not married. Michael is my colleague, not my husband."

"How refreshing, Alice," came the cheerful response. "Commander Creavey wasn't joking, then? Do you really deal with all those dreadful crimes yourself?"

"Yes, I do. Fascinating work, Mrs. Bartlett, and enormously satisfying."

"We don't have so many of those kind of problems in Britain. Not enough work for you here, dear, I'm afraid."

"Perhaps that used to be the case, but I understand there's been quite an increase in reporting of rapes all over the U.K."

Now she was considering that perhaps she didn't need me as a distraction from her meal. Every ounce of her concentration returned to the plate. "Can't imagine that's so. My husband used to be a Crown Prosecutor. Embezzlement, insurance frauds, the occasional murder. Nothing as unsavory as your work. You should get yourself a husband, Alice, and leave this disgusting business to Creavey and his ilk. It's nasty for a girl. No wonder you're unmarried."

I hadn't been there long enough to answer as I would have liked to and held my tongue as I reminded myself I was standing in Battaglia's shoes for forty-eight hours.

John Creavey caught me back up in the tale he was spinning about how his men had foiled a Colombian drug cartel scam down river at Tilbury until the waiters arrived with the sweet trolley and coffee to end the luncheon recess.

"Nice to have met you, Mrs. Bartlett," I lied.

"Pleasure." So did she.

We followed the well-mannered group as they sauntered from the Pavilion back toward the Churchill Boardroom. Thirty or so stiff-looking men queued near the entry to the conference area and fifteen or twenty of the ladies paired off in the opposite direction. Lord Windlethorne stood at the head of the table and introduced himself as I moved past him to look for my seat. I guessed him to be in his late fifties, lean and angular, with the features and dark coloring of Gregory Peck cum Oxford don.

He welcomed me and pointed to my name plate at the table. I was docked two places away, between Professore Vittorio Vicario of the University of Milan and Monsieur Jean-Jacques Carnet of the Institut de la Paix in Paris. Vicario bowed his head in greeting and Carnet smiled, giving me the once-over and an "*Enchanté*."

"Mr. Chapman," Windlethorne told Mike as he entered after me. "We've only enough seats at the table for the speakers. Behind each one there's a chair, as you can see. Those are for the spouses—or, shall I say, significant others—of the participants.

"Most of the wives were here this morning. Actually, they're heading off now on a coach tour—famous gardens, Windsor Castle, a trip on the Thames. Perhaps you'd rather—"

"Wouldn't miss this for the world."

I glanced around the room. The head of Australia's Probation Services was the only other woman at the table. The chair behind her was empty. The spouse seats were almost completely deserted except for one backing up an older French Minister of Justice, whose trophy wife or mistress sat dutifully in place, and that of the Danish criminologist, whose barely-out-of-her-teens girlfriend stroked the back of his head as we waited for everyone to settle down.

Chapman growled into my ear. "You really owe me for this one. Everybody's treating me like I'm some useless appendage you've brought along to carry your luggage."

"Personally, I think you should have taken the garden tour with the significant others. You would have found someone to hit on in that group."

"Don't throw yourself at Windlethorne too quick, Blondie. I know how you fall for that kind of sensitive-looking specimen."

I looked up to the head of the table. Lord W. was chewing on the end of his wire-rimmed glasses as he debated some weighty issue with a pudgy German who kept punctuating his comments with jabs in the air. I blushed when Windlethorne caught me looking and smiled back at me. Mike was right, he was exactly my type.

Lord Windlethorne invited everyone to take his or her seat and called the afternoon assembly to order by introducing me formally to the politicians and academics who had presented papers or would be joining my panel for the rest of the day. He then proceeded to call on speakers in the order they were listed in the program.

One of the Swiss finance ministers began the session with a forty-five-minute discourse on the problems of financial frauds and the Internet. He detailed instances of multimillion-dollar swindles that had been attempted in recent months and outlined a plan for combating technological hoaxes in the next century.

The concentration then moved to interpersonal violence. Twenty-minute time slots had been allocated for each of the four speakers—the Australian woman who talked about her country's novel techniques for handling teen offenders; the pudgy German, a sociologist who studied European ethnic violence of the last fifty years, predicting and projecting trends; Creavey's analysis of terrorist tactics and how to combat them; and my slightly doctored version of Battaglia's remarks about the prospect for America's future—crime and punishment.

Lord Windlethorne lit his pipe and opened the floor to statements from everyone present. Like many Europeans, these professionals seemed most interested in the problems of urban America, which had to this point in time seemed so extraordinarily unlike their own.

"What about *your* specialty, Miss Cooper?" Professor Vicario asked, "Do you think it has much, how do you say in English, relevance to our population here in Europe?"

I had made only a short reference to the issue of sexual violence in my formal remarks but was delighted to get it on the table during the question-and-answer period. "As progressive as you all tend to be on a variety of topics, you're light-years behind on this one. One need only consider the terrible cases of child abuse in Belgium last year—the pedophile rings that involved government officials—to understand how widespread the phenomenon is. And you'll forgive me, *professore*, but your magnificent country still has some of the most archaic laws concerning spousal abuse that one can imagine in this day and age.

"I don't need to center this around my own personal interest, but it *is* just incredible to me," I added, "that you could even contemplate a meeting of this scope without devoting attention to the issues of drugs, drug treatment, and gun control."

I thought Windlethorne was squirming a bit in his seat as he tried to reignite his pipe, but others in the room picked up on the subjects immediately.

Creavey jumped in. "I assure you, Alex is right. If you don't think these are your problems yet—and I can't believe there's one of you in this room who hasn't had some exposure to them in your criminal justice systems at home—they're coming in your direction."

The Home Secretary tried to pooh-pooh the trend toward violence, sheltered in this elegant retreat that seemed a world apart from the reality of city streets. "Oh, come now, people. Let's not exaggerate this picture, shall we?" Battaglia had been right on the money. "A bit of hooliganism, joyriding—"

Chapman had been waiting for his moment. He knew, from conversations with Creavey, how aware of this issue the British had become after the unspeakable tragedy in the elementary school at Dunblane.

"You wanna know what you're facing if you don't start moving in the direction of gun control and funding drug treatment programs? You wanna know what kind of cases I work on every single day of the week?

"John, you ever have a 'dis' murder?"

Creavey frowned and stroked his mustache. No answer. Mike looked from face to face. "Any of you know what I'm talking about? Dis—that's the motive to kill another human being."

Professore Vicario attempted to inject a note of humor. "You mean, Signore Chapman, dis or dat?"

"No, professor. I mean disrepect. Last week, I got called to the scene of a homicide. The killer was fifteen years old. Deals heroin. Snoopy tabs, we call 'em. Glassine envelopes with cartoon characters like Snoopy on the label. Big seller with kids, right outside the fence at an elementary school.

"His victim? A five-year-old girl who dissed him. She stepped on his shadow after he told all the kids not to. He turned and put a bullet through her head just as a lesson to the others not to ignore him. Not to dis him."

The theoreticians were silent.

"Maybe this was a culture in which guns were in the hands of the upper class—hunting grouse and pheasants and wild boar on weekends in the country. But if you don't start acknowledging these problems today, you'll be right up there in the record books with your American cousins."

"Well, I think we'll all need a bit of refreshment, now, don't we?" Lord Windlethorne announced, trying to put a smile on the end of the day's work. He looked at his watch. "It's half past six. There will be cocktails in the library at seven-thirty, followed by dinner. Thank you all for your presentations and we'll see you later."

I pushed back my chair and turned to Chapman. "As usual, Mikey, we've added the stamp of our personal cheer and spirit to another event."

"C'mon, they needed a dose of reality. Too many ivory tower types to suit me. Let's go up to the room. I want to call the office."

It was a cloudy evening and we walked together the short distance back to the main building. I checked with Graham but there were no telephone messages, so we continued on to the suite. I went into the bathroom to freshen up while Mike called the squad. The running water had drowned out his short conversation, and by the time I emerged he was pouring us each a drink from the crystal decanters on the table in the sitting room.

I sat in one of the stuffed fauteuils and kicked off my shoes, pressing on the remote control device of the television set to find CNN.

"Turn it off a minute."

"I just want the top of the news."

"Turn it off so I can tell you something."

I pressed the clicker and looked at Mike, who sat opposite me on the footstool and rested his drink on the tray.

"Everything's fine now, Coop. But there was a problem during the night."

"What kind of problem?" I raced through thoughts of the

stabbing victim at Columbia-Presbyterian, my parents, to whom I hadn't spoken in days, my friends, and—

"Maureen—"

"Oh!" I gasped and slammed my right palm across my mouth, my left one already quavering with the full glass of Scotch. Ever since I had tried to call her earlier in the day I had assumed that she was safe at home with Charles and the kids.

"She's fine, Alex. Trust me." He placed his hand on my knee and, as Mercer had done at the airport, he eyeballed me to reassure me that he was telling the truth. "I swear to you she's okay." He took the drink from my hand and stood it beside his.

My panic turned to anger at the thought that we had left Mo in any real danger. "What happened to her?" We spoke over each other as I fired questions at him while he reminded me he would never have let us take off unless he had been assured that Maureen would be fine.

"If you calm down I'll tell you what I know."

"I want to speak to her first. I want to hear her voice myself. Then I'll listen to you."

"You can't speak to her. That's half the point. She's been moved out of Mid-Manhattan and, for *her* sake, no one except Battaglia and the Commissioner know where she and her husband are. You want to screw it up for her by making a phone call that somebody could intercept? Mercer's in the office now. He was with her this morning and she is absolutely perfect. Somebody just tried to scare her out of the hospital, not kill her. Honestly."

"What do you mean 'somebody'? I assume the video surveillance caught whoever it was, right?"

"Look, sometime around midnight, whoever it was that did this entered Maureen's room. Dressed like a nurse."

"Like a woman nurse?"

"Yeah. Uniform with a skirt. The schmuck on surveillance—don't worry, he'll be out looking for a new job in a few days—looked up at the screen, saw the nurse's outfit and cap, assumed that it was business as usual, and dozed back off.

"Mo doesn't know what hit her. She was sound asleep. But this 'nurse' covered her mouth, which is what startled her and woke her up. Then a second later she was jabbed with a hypodermic needle in her arm.

"When the real nurse went in to check on Maureen a bit later, she was completely motionless. They rushed in some oxygen, pumped her stomach, and got her the hell out of that nuthouse."

"What—"

"They're waiting for toxicology, if that's what you're about to ask. Nobody has a clue what was injected into her system but she rebounded pretty quickly, which is why they don't think it was lethal."

"And the nurse?"

"Probably one of the boys we're looking at for Gemma. A bit of late-night disguise. Found a very large white uniform—a dress and a little nurse's cap—in a garbage pail in the parking garage behind the hospital. Plus a woman's wig. Brunette, kind of a Donna Reed do from the fifties."

"Now I guess we've got to figure out how they knew she was a cop. Any ideas on how she got made?"

"Easy, despite our best intentions. Timmy McCrenna, the DEA delegate—know him?"

"Yeah." McCrenna was the squad's representative to the Detective Endowment Association.

"He heard a rumor she was in the hospital and never figured it to be on business. Sent her a huge flower arrangement and a bunch of cards with the DEA insignia all over the place sticking out of every lily and carnation. Almost got her killed 'cause he's such a fruitcake about hospitalizations and funerals. Everything's a goddamn Hallmark occasion with McCrenna. He must get a kickback from his local florist."

Mike was on his feet to pick up the phone and redial the office so I could speak to Mercer. "I called back home to the squad during the break in the afternoon session, after the German's presentation. I wasn't holding out on you, Coop, I just didn't want to upset you right before you had to deliver Battaglia's speech."

I stirred the ice in my drink with my finger and took a swallow of the Scotch while he waited for the connection to be put through.

"Hey, big guy. Coop needs to talk to you. Uh-huh, just told her now. No, no, she's not. Speak to her yourself or I think she'll be on the next flight outta here."

He extended the cord to its full length and carried the phone to my chair.

"I have had just about all the bullshit I can take, Mercer, so please tell me exactly what's going on with Mo now."

"She's good, Alex. They moved her to New York Hospital in the middle of the night right after this happened—to check her out and do some tests on her blood. I saw her there and held her hand this morning. Then they transferred her out of the city for safekeeping. None of us knows where but she's cool about that. And Charles is with her.

"Mo said that if I mentioned four little words to you, you'd know she's just fine."

I tried to think if she and I had ever discussed a code word but nothing came to mind.

"'Canyon Ranch. Your treat.' You tell me, is she alive and well?"

I smiled. We had often joked about going to an elegant spa for a week—to be pampered with massages and mud baths and facials—but had never taken the splurge. "Tell her she's on, first break Battaglia gives me."

We said good-bye and I hung up the phone, resting my head back against the top of the chair's cushion. "God, I just couldn't forgive myself if anything ever happened to Maureen. *That's* not the work of any crazy guy living in an underground tunnel. I don't know what its hook is to Dogen's murder but only a health care pro would be sticking syringes in patients—or in chocolates, for that matter—to try to scare us."

"Let's go downstairs and get some chow. Tomorrow we see Dogen's ex-husband. Creavey's going to sit in on the interview with us and have a look at the photos. Then Saturday morning we're going home. So take yourself off duty for a few hours and enjoy what's left of the evening."

I looked at my watch and saw that it was almost eight o'clock. We'd been in England more than twelve hours. The combination of jet lag and this disturbing news had hit me head on. "I'll go down with you, but I'm too nauseated to eat anything."

I splashed water on my face, reapplied my lipstick, spritzed on more perfume, and tried to smooth the wrinkles out of my yellow-and-black David Hayes suit. We bypassed the bumpy lift in favor of the staircase, and walked down toward the library.

Graham stopped us at the doorway. "Sorry, madam. Sir. They've all gone in to dinner already. To your right," he motioned us with his gloved hand. "And Miss Cooper, you had two calls while your line was engaged." He handed me the message slips. Mr. Renaud phoned and will call again tomorrow, I read. The second one said that Miss Stafford was anxious to talk to me, was on her way to the airport, and would ring back.

"You go on ahead, Mike. I want to go back upstairs and return the calls."

"But Graham just said—"

My annoyance was palpable. I hadn't meant to direct it at Mike but he was the only one in range. "I just want to go back to the room for a couple of minutes." I turned and stomped off to the staircase, taking its three tall sections on the run without missing a beat.

I opened the door to the room and stepped inside. I had no intention of returning Drew's call at that point. I simply did not want to speak to or socialize with anyone.

I went into the dresser drawers and removed one of Mike's shirts. Not expecting to be sharing a room, I had packed without bringing a nightgown. Then I called the housekeeping department and asked them to pick up the laundry I placed in a bag and left outside the door of the room, including the dirty shirt Mike had worn on the plane, for overnight service. I wanted to make sure it would be washed and ironed since I had now purloined one to sleep in. I went into the bathroom and turned on the shower until the steam poured out into the rest of the suite, then stood beneath the water until all of the tension of the day and evening ran out of me.

Dressed in Mike's red-and-white-striped shirt, I sat at the desk and wrote him a note apologizing for snapping at him and abandoning him to the crowd. I placed it on his pillow and turned down the corner of his sheet, leaving on the reading lamp so he could see his way around.

I crawled in between the tightly pulled linens of my own slender bed, separated by a couple of inches from Mike's. I wasn't thinking Tina Turner tonight, I was thinking Otis Redding. He had been right. Young girls *do* get weary. Try a little tenderness, he had advised, over and over again when I had listened to him sing to me. I wanted someone to try it and I wanted it soon. But it wasn't likely to happen tonight, so I turned off the lamp nearest to me, burrowed my head into the pillow, and convinced myself that I was exhausted enough to need a good night's sleep.

23

I am so unaccustomed to an early bedtime that I was up shortly after five in the morning and rolled around restlessly until I could see a glimmer of daybreak at the curtain's edge. I slipped into the bathroom quietly and dressed for a run. Down the stairs, a nod to the young man at the reception table, and I was outside and around back on the rear balustrade of the enormous building looking out over acres of lush green gardens and forests. I did my leg stretches against the columns that had supported Cliveden's façade for a couple of centuries, then set off through the clipped hedges to follow the paths that eventually sloped down to the Thames. In the more than five miles that I covered, I encountered only an occasional gardener or groundsman and relished the stillness that surrounded me in this peaceful sanctuary.

The last hill of the return gave me a particularly hard time so I slowed to a walk and wandered through the intricate mazes of the formal Long Garden created from boxwood hedges that had been so carefully laid out and maintained.

Mike was still sleeping soundly under a halo of stale-smelling lager as I let myself back into the suite, showered, and dressed for the day. He mumbled a greeting as I was about to leave the room and I explained that I was going to the morning program to hear the presentations on DNA that one of the forensic men from the Yard was giving.

"Geoffrey Dogen's due here at about eleven. Creavey'll meet him at the door and wait for us. He's arranged a small conference room that we can use for a few hours." His head rolled in my direction. "Hey, thanks for holding up your end of things last night, kid. I only waited about three or four hours for you—by then, I figured you really had stood me up."

"Sorry, I—"

"Don't worry about it. Creavey and I scored. Some duchess took us on."

I laughed at the idea of it.

"No kidding. A duchess—and a knockout, too. Bounced us around to a few pubs, showed us the sights."

"What time did you get in?"

He cocked an eye. "My mother's alive and well in Brooklyn, thanks. She doesn't need any backup. I'll see you at eleven, okay?"

I walked outside and over to the Churchill Boardroom, picked up some coffee and a scone, and found my place again at the table for the nine o'clock program. After apologies to Lord Windlethorne for missing dinner, I made small talk with my neighbors until the speaker finished setting up his audio-visual equipment and began his address.

The British were way ahead of us in their use of DNA and genetic data banking. And although their volume of sexual assault cases was far lower than ours in the States, they had already begun the process of developing the genetic finger-print from crime scene evidence in every single case of reported rape that occurred in the Greater London area. The lecture had some fascinating suggestions for future uses of the technology and I busied myself at note taking so I could bring the ideas back to Bill Schaeffer who had done such great work establishing and running the DNA lab in our medical exam-iner's office.

It was almost eleven when Windlethorne announced the midmorning break. I explained to him that I would be absent for the following session because of some business Chapman and I would be conducting locally. He assured me that he quite understood and I went back to the room to pick up my folder of materials on the Dogen case.

When I returned to the reception area, Creavey had just fin-ished introducing Geoffrey Dogen to Mike. I approached and Dogen extended a hand. "You must be Alexandra. Lovely to meet you. Thanks for coming over. Commander Creavey told me you're Benjamin Cooper's daughter, aren't you? I had the pleasure of hearing your father speak, uh—it must have been at the medical conference in Barcelona last year. He's a remarkable man."

"I think so, too. Thank you."

Creavey directed us to one of the adjacent outer buildings, which the staff had prepared for our use. He walked ahead with Dr. Dogen, who was smaller than I had expected, about sixty years old, thin and wiry, with a balding head and ears that were a bit too large in proportion to his other features.

"By the way, while you were in school this morning your boyfriend called."

"What—?"

"Drew. That's the guy's name, isn't it? Said it was four or five in the morning at home. Just called to say hello—said he couldn't sleep and hadn't been able to reach you 'cause of your travel schedules. Lucky he called when he did—woke me out of a deep sleep."

"Great. You told him who you were, didn't you? I mean, that you're just my fr—I mean, that we're only sharing, you know—"

"What'd you expect me to tell him? Sorry, I don't know the Wellesley etiquette. They probably taught you rules for all this kind of crap. Should I have said 'Not to worry, I'm a gay cop,' or 'Jesus, I wouldn't nail Alex Cooper on a bet, would you?' The guy woke me out of a heavy slumber, Blondie. I took a message and told him to call back. Yesterday, he pissed you off and you're thinking he's a murderer 'cause Dogen butchered his wife—now you want his calls. Go figure. Let him think there's a little competition in the field, like you're here with the Prince of Wales or Sean Connery or something. No common sense for a smart broad, really."

Forget about Drew Renaud and everything else in your personal life for the moment, I reminded myself. Get to work.

We entered a miniature duplicate of the boardroom. In it were a rectangular table with six comfortable seats, slide and video projectors with which to display our photographic evidence, and enough water and coffee to keep us afloat for days.

"Perhaps you and Alexandra might begin by telling me what you know at this moment," Dogen suggested, drawing his chair up to the table and giving us his most earnest look. "Do you know who killed Gemma?"

"I'd rather do it the other way 'round, Doc, if you don't mind," Mike replied. "It would help, I think, if you just talk to us a while about Gemma. Even what might seem to you to be irrelevancies. I don't want what *we* know or don't know to direct your thoughts. After you've sketched in more of the background for us, I promise we'll bring you up to where we are in the investigation."

That ought to be impressive, I thought to myself. Mike could bluff almost anyone about almost anything but this situation seemed beyond even his best bullshit ability. We're more confused today than we were the first time we had called Geoffrey Dogen last week.

"Understood. I'll begin, then."

He pulled his chair close into the table and leaned his elbows on it, supporting his bowed head with his hands as he recalled Gemma's family background for us. Nothing struck him as unusual about the story. Her parents had moved to Broadstairs from London as hostilities flared across Europe and Gemma was born there in '39. Only child, raised by her mother after her father's death on the battlefield—Dunkirk. I scratched notes on a legal pad, doubting the significance of this part of the conversation but recognizing that Chapman's interest would be even more engaged simply by virtue of the remote link to World War II.

Geoffrey took us through her schooling and scholarship to University, where she excelled in the biological sciences and won prizes for several experiments that captured the attention of the academic community. He met her a year later, when she entered the medical school at which he was already enrolled.

"Actually, I had seen her at the school. Couldn't miss her in those days. She was quite a striking figure then," he smiled, obviously bringing back to mind an image of the young woman with whom he had fallen in love. "But I first met her somewhere else. Tower Bridge."

I shot a glance at Mike and Creavey's sharp eyes followed as ours met.

"I was there with a group of Australian students. They were visiting our medical school, and wanted to do the usual tourist things at the weekend. Beefeaters, the Crown Jewels, the Bloody Tower, and Traitors' Gate. You've done all that, have you?"

I nodded while Mike regretted that he hadn't yet had the opportunity.

"Pity to be so close to London and not have the time to see some of it. Can't you take the weekend off?"

"Sorry, no. We've got to get back directly, after you've helped us, Dr. Dogen."

"Of course. Well, I'd almost finished showing my Aussies the sights but they were determined to climb to the top of Tower Bridge. Three hundred steps at least. Dragged me along with them. Got to the pinnacle and there's only one person up there with us. I recognized her from the medical college. It was Gemma, standing at the window and staring downriver, oblivious to the rowdy troop of us that piled in behind her.

"I introduced myself, explained the connection to school, and learned that she was called Gemma Holborn."

Mike was impatient. He didn't particularly want the love story, if that's the direction in which Geoffrey was headed. "Why was she there? Any special reason?"

"For her, growing up in the countryside, Tower Bridge *was* London. It is for many people. Sort of a symbol of this city. For some it's Big Ben or Buckingham Palace, but Gemma didn't care for those because you just look up *at* them. They didn't give that curious child an enormous structure that opened its windows onto a faraway world. The bridge did. It's a newcomer really, compared to the Tower itself, which is almost a thousand years old. But its structure is so identifiable, wouldn't you say, Commander? Sort of represents old London to lots of people."

Creavey agreed.

"It was the first place Gemma remembered visiting as a young girl after the war, climbing both of the towers to see how far up- and downstream the river went. Probably believed she could see America 'til she got old enough to know better. When she had anything to dream about or fancy, she'd take herself up to those rooms, or out on the catwalk, and wish to her heart's content."

"D'you ever go back there with her?"

"I had little choice, Mister Chapman. It's where I proposed to Gemma, two years later. That way, I knew she'd accept," Geoffrey said, smiling at us, a bit more relaxed as he continued his storytelling. "She'd go there the night before her big exams. Never mind that she'd studied more hours than all the other students combined, she needed the comfort of some moments of solitude in her tower.

"Even liked to go for the big events, with the crowds. The *Gypsy Moth* came home in '67 and they opened the bascules for it and we were the first to arrive—"

"Whoa, you lost me here," Chapman interrupted.

"Me, too."

Creavey injected the facts. "You Yanks are a bit too young to remember, but it's a good one for that quizzer you watch on the telly. Sir Francis Chichester sailed 'round the world on a little yacht by the name of *Gypsy Moth IV*. Took a year, and when 'e got home they opened the bascules—the arms of the bridge—so 'e could sail into the city. And the Queen 'erself got on board to make him a knight. Used the same sword that had tapped the shoulders of Sir Francis Drake."

Chapman was loading up on history but this conversation was going nowhere for me.

"Any idea if this interest carried through in her adult life?" I thought of Gemma's key chain that was sitting at home on my dresser and its twin that I had observed in William Dietrich's hand when he left the conference room a few days earlier.

"I'm afraid it was impossible to shake her out of it. She made a special visit in 1994 for the centenary celebration of the construction of Tower Bridge. By then I'd remarried, as you probably know, and Gemma dragged a bunch of us up to the top for a view. She must have bought souvenirs for everyone in America. Tower Bridge coffee mugs, Tower Bridge teaspoons, Tower Bridge key chains—"

"Lots of them?"

"Loads of them."

So much for the importance I was reading into Dietrich's token of affection. It was more likely one of dozens she had distributed to friends and colleagues.

"I'm sure you must have noticed things like that in her home and her office, didn't you? That remote side of her was one of the pieces of Gemma I never quite unlocked.

"We divorced less than ten years after we'd been married. Never an argument or a cross word. You can probably tell that we remained quite good friends. Saw her every time she was over here, practically. Corresponded with her, kept up with each other—professionally and personally, much as I dared. She simply couldn't let anyone into her world, into the part of it that really counted.

"She was a brilliant scientist and a fiercely loyal friend if she believed in you. But there was an entire piece of her that was hollow, that she never let *me* fill for her—and I'm quite sure no one else was ever allowed to venture in. Odd, actually, that as a physician I used to think of it as a real space somewhere within her body that I could 'cure' if only I could locate it. But I never quite did."

Geoffrey Dogen was quiet now, looking at his hands, which were clasped together on the table in front of him.

We listened to more than an hour of background information on Gemma's marriage, divorce, friends, students, and her career in England. In many of the murders Chapman worked, the access to this kind of detail from a reliable source close to the victim could have proved to be invaluable. Here, it was bringing us no closer to anything we seemed to need.

Gently, Mike tried to steer Geoffrey to the recent events

that involved Gemma's professional future. The doctor let out a deep sigh and slumped down into his chair.

He looked over at Mike. "Do you honestly think this could be connected to Gemma's work?"

"We want to consider all the possibilities at this point."

"Well, the last couple of years have been a constant battle for Gemma. I'm referring to Minuit Medical College and Mid-Manhattan, not to her personal life."

"D'you know what the issues were and who were the enemies?"

"She's created waves from her very first days there, you know. Nothing major, but she's always been a stickler for her principles. Quite a good thing in our business, actually.

"I'd say there were two things that made Gemma a lightning rod for trouble." Dogen kept looking at me now and I figured he was concerned about my taking notes as he speculated out loud. I tried to be casual about writing but met his gaze firmly to imply that I wasn't to be stopped.

"Early on, she made it clear that she was not going to accept anyone into the neurosurgical program unless the applicant met all her standards. Those were rigorous, as you might imagine. Medical school grades, references, intellectual ability, integrity, performance in the operating theater, internship ratings. No teacher's pets or favorite sons or people who'd blundered already along the way. Gemma was quite unforgiving. Certainly, some viewed that as a flaw."

"Anything going on like that right now? Was she being pushed to admit someone she didn't want in?"

"I'm sure, yes."

Mike and I both spoke at once as we asked who it was.

"Oh, no, no, no. Forgive me. I don't mean I knew of anyone in particular. It's just that there was always some other professor or one of the administrators who was promoting a candidate and he and Gemma would lock horns over it. I'm afraid I can't give you a name.

"Last time she was here, the complaint was about a head of service at your Columbia-Presbyterian Hospital. Seems one of his students had already been accepted—name like Nazareth—and then an inquiry began because the young man was involved in a rather bizarre episode. A girl he was seeing—actually, she was a patient he picked up in surgery and started dating—passed out in his apartment. This medical student let her lapse into a coma in his own living room, kept her there for hours until he finally picked her up and carried her into the hospital. She nearly died right under his nose. On top of that, it turns out that he had tried to draw blood from her—never explained why—and did so by inserting the needle in her wrist, bruising her quite badly. When the girl recovered from the coma, she was quite traumatized. Dr. Nazareth never explained what kind of needle he used or whether it was a clean one, nor what became of the blood sample. His superiors never pressed him on it.

"The young lady was convinced she passed out because he drugged her. Strange business. And the doctor recommending this medical student—"

"Do you recall his name?" I was writing down everything Dogen said.

"Sorry, no. But you fax me a list of department heads and I'll pick it out. Anyway, the doctor belittled the entire event. And the four arrests Gemma's enquiries revealed for a variety of minor run-ins the student had had with the police—most of them related to motoring offences. She thought the boy a rotten egg and a real danger to the profession, mostly because of what he had done in regard to the well-being of that young girl. I know she was successful in getting him blocked, but I couldn't begin to guess how many other unhappy candidates like that are floating around. After ten years of doing this, Gemma's rejects are probably bumping into each other at medical centers all over the States."

"You said you could think of two reasons for Gemma's unpopularity. What's the other?"

"The direction she was taking the department. There were a lot of people at Minuit who were unhappy with Gemma's view of the neurosurgical division."

"Too much emphasis on trauma?"

"Mostly that."

"In whose view?"

"Well, of course, you've got Robert Spector leading the pack against Gemma. No secret that he'd be happy to see her go so that he could step into her shoes."

"Spector told us she wouldn't want to stay in New York and be second banana to Dr. Ghajar, up at New York Hospital."

"Rubbish. She had the utmost respect for Ghajar—and he was quite generous to her. Included her in a lot of his studies and research projects. It's Spector who can't take that kind of competition. He'll never develop a trauma unit to match Ghajar's so that's why he'd like to move his staff into another forum. That's part of his problem at Mid-Manhattan. Without making brain injury a specialty, as Gemma urged, they've got three times the mortality rate for coma patients that New York Hospital does just a few blocks up the road.

"Just a lesson to you, Mr. Chapman. If you get knocked about the head, be sure you get yourself to Ghajar's trauma unit."

"Was Spector right, though, about Gemma's interests? Was brain injury her major focus?"

"Not so. Not at all. It interested her enormously but almost like a diversion. She was quite an intellectual, as I am sure you realize by now. Sounds a bit gruesome to talk like this to laypeople, but she was far more curious about the pathology of brain illness. What is it that actually causes tumors to develop? What is the effect on one's DNA when there are tumors? Is it altered or mutated? Gemma was enormously sat-

isfied when she could unscramble the brain of someone who
had been in an accident or suffered a grave wound, but she
was far more challenged by the surgical demands of a rare
tumor or blood clot."

I opened the case folder that rested on the table next to my
legal pad, lifting some of the police reports from within it.

"Ever met Robert Spector?" Chapman asked.

"On a few occasions."

"Think he hated Gemma enough to—"

You could hear Geoffrey's intake of breath as he cut Mike
off midquestion. "Every profession has its jealousies and
political infighting, Mr. Chapman. I'm giving you as candid a
picture as I can of the people in Gemma's world, but I'd say
that none of them disliked her enough to cause her any physical harm. Most of them had to be aware that she'd be out of
their hair in a matter of months, I'm quite sure."

"Because she was returning to London?"

"In all likelihood."

"Don't you know?"

"Well, she had the offer, you see. And she said she'd let the
university know by the end of this month. There was some
unfinished business she had to take care of before she could
give them her word."

"Not even you knew?"

"I wasn't the one making the offer. She had no reason to
tell me officially. Yes, I assumed she'd be coming back here by
the next term, if somewhat reluctantly. But she had no cause
to tell *me* by any deadline. I assumed she was simply finishing
the academic year and just devilishly teasing Spector and the
other people in administration who were so anxious to see the
back of her. Sort of Gemma's last stand, if you will."

There was a knock on the door and Creavey moved to open
it. A white-gloved young man had appeared to announce that
lunch had been set up in an adjacent room, should we be able

to take a short break. I thanked him and told him we were about ready to do that.

"We can go over some of the statements and photographs after we've given you a breather, Dr. Dogen," Chapman said, rising from his chair and rubbing his fingers over the lids of his bloodshot eyes.

"I just wanted to run through a few of the names of Gemma's colleagues. Some of the information we've gotten seems to conflict with what others say. If you recognize any of these, perhaps you can tell us who the good guys are, who we can trust."

Creavey and Chapman were staring out the window, looking over the pool and pavilion area while I read from a list to Geoffrey Dogen. He was familiar with some of the professors whose offices lined the hallway near Gemma's, as he was with most of the people in administrative posts, and I checked their names off with a red pen to come back to ask about later on. There was no recognition of the younger doctors, residents, and fellows—even those who had been drawn into the investigation—until I hit on the name of John DuPre.

Dogen looked at me quizzically. "Did that old codger come out of hibernation to teach at Minuit? Hard to believe that Gemma never mentioned it to me."

Chapman turned. "You know DuPre?"

"I can't say that I know him very well, but I did attend a course at which he taught—just a two-week seminar, it was, in Geneva. Let me see—Lord, it must be more than twenty-five years ago. I think he was close to retirement at that point. What is he, nearly ninety now?"

I laughed. "Wrong guy. This one's only forty-two."

"Also a neurologist?"

"Yes, he is."

"Well, perhaps he's the son, or the grandson. Do you know where he went to medical school?"

I looked at the DD5 to refresh myself. "Tulane."

"Can't be a coincidence. That's where old Johnny DuPre went as well. Those are some shoes this chap's got to fill. Johnny was one of the finest practitioners in the field—a genius, really. Became something of a recluse a while ago. Moved to Mississippi—Port Gibson, if I'm not mistaken."

The military historian in Chapman piped up, "The town too beautiful for General Sherman to burn. Spared it, you know?"

I didn't. I was closing up my files as Creavey held the door open for us to leave the conference room.

Dogen was still focused on DuPre. He seemed animated by the memory of the distinguished lecturer. "It was quite an ordeal for a young doctor like me to try to understand neurological details from a man with the thickest southern accent I'd ever encountered. Should have had a translator for us, really. And he had this fabulous shock of bright red hair, matched by his beard. Not a speck of gray in it, even in his sixties."

"Bright red hair," I mused. "Probably not related. Our John DuPre is an African-American."

"Well, then, that *is* quite an odd coincidence. He can't be John J. D. DuPre, as the old doc liked to introduce himself. John Jefferson Davis DuPre."

I pulled the cord off the folder and slipped out the DD5 again. Interview of John J. D. DuPre, M/B/42.

"Let's go, Blondie. I'm famished."

"I'll meet you inside. I just want to call Mercer before he leaves for work and ask him to check something out for us." I couldn't imagine that there were a lot of southern black men named for the president of the Confederacy.

Chapman's mind was squarely set on the luncheon feast that had been spread out in the room next to us, which I passed on my way to find the nearest telephone from which I could access an overseas line.

At the moment, all I could think about was the note that had been slipped under the door of my apartment on Sunday evening one week ago. CAREFUL. IT'S NOT ALL BLACK AND WHITE. DEADLY MISTAKE.

Had someone been trying to alert me to a fact that Geoffrey Dogen just inadvertently made clear to me? Was John DuPre not the man he claimed to be?

Mercer answered on the second ring.

24

"Saved you some quail's eggs in haddock-and-cheese sauce. The Commander says it's not to be missed."

"I'll pass."

"Steak-and-kidney pie?"

"The waiter's bringing me some grilled sole. Dover." We all took a break from the case as Dogen and Creavey lectured us on the local sights and Cliveden myths. After tea was served, I tried to get Mike out of earshot of Geoffrey to explain my call to Mercer. He was holding one of the Cliveden luncheon menus, passing it to me and telling me to put it in my folder to take back to the States.

"Did you see this? Can you believe they serve a dessert called 'spotted dick'? I gotta take one of those back for Mercer and the guys in Sex Crimes."

"I'm really proud of how well you're maturing—something kept you from sharing that thought, as they say, with Dr. Dogen."

I told Mike that I'd asked Mercer to check on DuPre's credentials and reminded him that the neurologist had been one of the doctors checking on Maureen while she was at Mid-Manhattan.

Geoffrey Dogen and I walked the short distance back to our workroom and resumed our places around the table while Chapman and Creavey went to the men's room. I had resisted the urge, in Mike's presence, to ask Dogen whether he remembered the circumstance of Carla Renaud's death in a London operating room a couple of years ago. But as we were alone, I quietly asked the question that had been gnawing at me.

"Indeed. Gemma was devastated by the event, of course. The procedure was a new one that had been developed in our program by James Binchy, one of our finest surgeons. Quite a radical operation, and a very long one—six, seven hours. That's why Binchy invited Gemma over to assist him. Unfortunately she became a bit too involved, personally, with the family. Wanted very much for the experiment to succeed—for the girl's sake and for the larger picture.

"Gemma hadn't lost very many patients on the table. Took this rather hard. Had to break it to the husband herself. He was wild with grief."

"Wild—*at* Gemma?"

"Mad at the world. One of those 'she had everything to live for so why did you let her die' tirades. Truth is, of course, that Carla Renaud couldn't have lived more than another month without an attempt at the surgery. Binchy wasn't trying this out for sport, Miss Cooper. It was the only hope for the Renaud girl and it didn't work. How does this fit into your questioning?"

Mike was standing in the doorway and answered for me. "Like I said, Doc, we're looking at every angle. Last December, right before Christmas, an ex-con found his way into a cancer clinic at New York Hospital and slashed the face of a doctor who had treated the guy's child five years earlier. The teenager had died of leukemia, despite everybody's best efforts, and the father just never came to grips with it.

"Agatha Christie here is considering whether Renaud's widower might have harbored this same kind of vengeance for Gemma."

Dogen's face puckered and grimaced as he tried to call up old conversations about the matter. "Well, I remember the husband—he was a barrister, wasn't he?—I know there was talk of lawsuits against Binchy and Gemma and so on. But I'm quite sure nothing came of it. Poor lad was disconsolate at his wife's death. Had at least expected she'd survive the surgery and die in his arms. But it seems to me he was reasoned with in the end and I'm not aware Gemma ever heard from him again. Not that I'd have any reason to know that for sure."

"You want to get back to business, Blondie, or you think maybe Dr. Dogen can help you with your horoscope, too?"

Mike and I split up the pile of hundreds of DD5s and began to go through them in detail, picking out points about which to question our cooperative witness. Creavey sat at the far end of the table, sorting through a duplicate pile of police reports, using his own skills and methods to try to reconstruct a version of the investigation.

When we reached the autopsy report, Mike passed the several-page document over to Dogen. "There's no reason to hold back these details from you, Doc. It's pretty tough stuff but at least the medical terms will make sense to you. Why don't you read it and then we can answer any questions you have."

The mild-mannered physician started at the top with the paragraph describing the deceased's physical appearance and dimensions. Before he had gotten very far, he stood up and walked to a corner of the room, slumping himself into a chair and running his hand back and forth over his mouth as he tried to absorb the information about the number of stab wounds and the frenzy of the attack.

We sat silently for almost five minutes, then Mike tapped my arm and pointed to the door. As we left the room together, Creavey followed along with us. For a quarter of an hour, the three of us walked around the pool, taking in the brisk spring air while we left Geoffrey Dogen with the haunting pathologist's portrait of his friend, his former wife. It was obvious he had been crying when we rejoined him and he blew his nose before speaking to us.

"Well, I knew Gemma was a fighter. Looks like your man didn't expect her to be, did he?"

I let Mike take the lead. "My partner thinks that's one of the reasons to assume she knew her killer. Someone who'd be aware she might be alone in her office in the middle of the night and that she wouldn't freak out to see him come in. Maybe it started as a conversation, something he thought he could reason with her about. But he was obviously prepared for the assault if he didn't get his way."

"And then she was bound and gagged?"

"That's what the ME suggested. But almost any one of those stab wounds would have disabled her. If the first thing he did was that blow to the middle of her back, he could have tied her after that and then continued the assault."

"But certainly there would have been screams—"

"And no one to hear them. It'd be easier to raise some of the dead in the morgue than anyone on that hallway at 2 A.M. once it was cleared of all its other occupants. Even if Gemma had gotten out one shriek before she was gagged, another thrust of the knife would have silenced her."

"What do you make of the attempt to sexually assault her in this—well, condition? The man would have to be insane, don't you think?"

"I think that's exactly what he'd want us to think. If you've ever seen Mid-Manhattan, you'd know it's full of lunatics—I mean, the resident population. More than likely, the killer tried to stage this to look like an attempt to rape Gemma just to throw us off course."

Mike loaded a pack of slides into the viewer. "These are some photographs of the crime scene, Doc. I don't know if you're familiar with Gemma's office but I'd like you to have a look."

"I've been there several times. Even have a few photos of it. Gemma sent them— 'Me in my natural habitat,' as she labeled them."

Mike pressed the button that rotated the slides around the carousel and the images from the first run flashed onto the wall-sized screen. Dogen's head was still as he focused on the shots, many of them repeats of different angles of the dark blood stains soaked into the carpet.

Interspersed with those were photographs of Gemma's desk and chair, then of the rows of bookshelves that stood above her file cabinets and drawers full of X-ray film.

"'Ere you go," Creavey said, breaking the silence by pointing at a large object on Gemma's desk, sitting like a paperweight atop an inch of documents. "Tower Bridge, Doc. Front and center."

"I bought her that from a stall in a market on the Portobello Road. Shape of the bridge, so she loved it. If you take us back a slide or two, Chapman, I can point out people in some of those photographs she's got on the bookshelf. Took a few of them myself."

Mike clicked the loader and reversed direction. Dogen called out names as he recognized snapshots, many of them taken in London years ago judging from the styles of the clothing. It was clearly an exercise that meant more to Dogen than it did to our investigation, but in light of the emotional

toll on him, Chapman seemed happy to indulge the gentle
man.

"Whoops. Hold it there, will you?" Dogen rose to his feet
and squinted as he walked closer to the screen. "You probably
know this—I can see you've been very thorough in your work.
You're aware that her chain is missing from the bookshelf?"

Chapman and I exchanged puzzled glances. "What chain?
What are you talking about?"

"Another of her Tower Bridge obsessions. You see this
hook on the end of the metal support?" There were pairs of
slender steel arms that held the lengths of bookshelves along
one entire wall of Gemma's office. Dogen was standing beside
the screen pointing at the curved end of the brace that protruded directly next to the side of her large office desk.

"This is where Gemma hung her spare set of keys. The
round hook fitted over the point of the arm and that way the
two essential keys she needed—her office and her home—
were always ready for her to grab in case she didn't want to
carry an entire handbag around with her. You know what I
mean," Dogen said, looking over at me.

I nodded, similarly having a spare set that I used when I
jogged or walked Zac and didn't want to deal with the bulk of
a pocketbook. Police had found Gemma's tote bag in her
drawer—untouched—and from it recovered the set of keys
that Mercer and I had used to enter her apartment.

"Are you saying you've seen a set of keys up there from time
to time when you visited?"

"I mean, she *always* kept them there, detective. It had
become a joke. Not very funny now. But she called her office
Traitor's Gate, after the part of the Tower where prisoners
were received to go to their deaths. It's where they got their
last look at the world on their way to the block. Ironic now but
she had come to view herself as an outsider at Minuit.

"So those were her keys to freedom, Gemma used to say.

LIKELY TO DIE   337

They always dangled from that spot so she could reach up and grab them and be off anytime she wanted. Go for a run, walk to her apartment, get away from the people she didn't like. I assure you—look at any photograph of this room before Gemma's death and you'll see that Tower Bridge key chain hanging from this very point." Dogen was at his most emphatic pitch now, driving his finger against the enlarged tip of the bookshelf, which wavered as the screen hit the wall behind it.

Neither Mike nor I seemed to know what significance to attach to Geoffrey's news. We let him calm down and finished reviewing the slides as I realized it was almost five o'clock in the afternoon. When he stepped out to use the telephone, Mike shrugged his shoulders and asked what I thought.

"Hard to tell. I can't imagine anyone except the cleaning staff who might actually know how recently such a key chain was in the office. But I guess we better put it on the list to ask everyone when we go at it again next week."

"Yeah, but what's the point? Nobody broke into her office just to steal the key to that very same office, right? That's kind of stupid. And it didn't appear that anything had been taken from her apartment, either."

"Maybe the killer kept it as a trophy or something."

"I'm telling you to lighten up on those murder mysteries, Coop. You're reading too many of these serial killer things and buying into all that FBI bullshit. Are we done with Dogen, d'you think?" He opened the door to look for the doctor.

Creavey, Chapman, and I walked Geoffrey Dogen out to the car park in front of the Great Hall. "Did you and Gemma ever talk about her social life, the men she dated?"

"No, no. Not the kind of thing she'd bring up with me."

"I assume you've heard the name William Dietrich, I mean, because of his position at Minuit."

"Know him for two reasons, actually." Dogen frowned. "I

knew about his professional tiffs with Gemma and I'd heard bits and bobs about their relationship from other colleagues who disapproved. Something about his financial problems and a motor car that he wanted desperately. Gemma was always a soft touch for a friend who needed money. Material things meant very little to her. The girl came from nothing, made a lot of money, and was happy to give it away. Don't know any more than that but I must say I wasn't inclined to like this Dietrich fellow."

We were struggling to make small talk by this time and Mike asked the doctor what Gemma had done for amusement or fun.

"Fun?" Dogen responded as though the word needed inter-pretation for him. "Not exactly the first thing that comes to mind about her. I mean, she enjoyed her friends, and she liked a good movie or a great read, but Gemma was quite intense about all her pursuits."

"Well, did she ever talk about American baseball or simi-lar events that she went to for diversion? Mets, Yankees, Knicks—?"

"Never heard her say the word baseball. Can't imagine she went to any games of that sort. She hated team sports."

Mike's questions reminded me of the folder I had seen in her apartment when Mercer and I had visited there more than a week ago with the file tab labeled MET GAMES.

Dogen rambled on. "Gemma loved nature. Put her in a canoe or climbing a mountain or running for miles at a clip and she was content, but I've never known her to be interested in any kind of team activity, really. And your American base-ball? Much too slow a game for her to sit through. No patience for that kind of nonsense at all."

I'd have to make a note to check out the file folder and see what it had contained. Or decide whether this meeting had been a complete waste of time because Geoffrey Dogen simply didn't know his ex all that well after the many years of separation.

Mike and I entered the reception area, having said good-bye to Dogen and the Commander. A bellman handed me the piece of paper and told me its message. I was to call Mr. Mercer back at Sarah Brenner's office. Good news, the note read, and bad news.

Mike followed me up the stairs to our room. I dropped the case folder on the desk and asked the operator to place the call to my office.

Sarah's secretary answered and put me through. "I'll give you the good news first. They've had a break in the stabbing of the doctor at Columbia-Presbyterian. A snitch led them to a suspect last night and the squad's got someone in custody right now. Tell Mike he was right. The guy saw the M.D. plates and flattened the tire himself, figuring he could at least steal drugs or a prescription pad from the victim. Then the doctor turned out to be a woman, so he tried to rape her, too. But this perp's an uptown guy. Nothing at all to link him to Mid-Manhattan. Unfortunately, his victim is still likely to go out of the picture.

"And Maureen gets a message to me, via the Commissioner, once a day. Everything's fine, so try and take it easy 'til you get back home. Here's Mercer with the bad news."

I could hear him humming in the background, doing the intro like he was one of the Platters, before his deep bass voice broke into song as he took the receiver from Sarah. "Oh—oh, yes, he's the great pre-e-tender—"

"Dammit. Will the real John DuPre stand up, please? What's the story, Mercer?"

"Keep in mind the Tulane Medical School offices didn't open until ten o'clock—that's not much more than an hour ago. Just got a call back from them. The only John DuPre who holds a diploma from their distinguished institution graduated with honors in, let me see, the year of our Lord one thousand nine hundred and thirty-three. Nineteen thirty-three—that's a wee bit before our boy was born, I would say. And I have to agree that my money's with you on the idea that no self-respecting brother is walking around with the name Jefferson Davis anywhere in his pedigree.

"Now, when are you bringing m'man home to me?"

"We're done. We're on that noon flight tomorrow."

"I'll be picking you up at Kennedy so we can compare notes then. Right now Sarah's typing me up a search warrant for DuPre's office.

"I'm not gonna call over there first 'cause I don't want to alert any of his staff. But I'll just show up and go back in to the receptionist saying I've got some more questions I forgot to ask about Gemma Dogen. Meanwhile, Sarah's looking at the statutes on practicing medicine without a license. The warrant should cover all those diplomas on his wall, some of the patient records, and his appointment book. I'm thinking maybe we'll catch a break and find something that connects him to the deadly candy or the attempt on Mo the other night."

"Fingers crossed. Keep us posted."

"Let me talk to Chapman. Can't wait to tell him how much I miss him."

25

While Mike showered and dressed for the Cliveden Conference Banquet, I wrapped myself in the crested robe, stretched the telephone line over to my bed, put my feet up, and placed a call to Washington to try to find Joan Stafford. I gave the operator Jim Hageville's number and was incredulous when it finally connected and I heard my friend's voice.

"I hate to get melodramatic but where have you been in my hour of need?"

"I tried to call you back as soon as I got your message. Drew's been phoning you over there, too, but—"

"I doubt he'll ever try again. Mike answered the last time he called and he probably thinks I'm holed up with another man. Joanie, you have to help me with this one. Can you remember exactly when it was that Drew told you that he wanted to meet me?"

"Why are you mixing him up in this woman's murder case, Alex? You're just overreacting. You've got to get over what you went through with Jed and his kind of—"

"One has nothing to do with the other. It's a bit freaky that Drew tells you he wants to meet me and a week later I find out that the doctor whose murder I'm working on was the surgeon holding the knife when Carla Renaud went out of the picture. How did the whole thing start? That's what I want to know."

There were a few seconds of silence as Joan stretched for an answer. I was thinking like an interrogator now rather than a friend and it hurt my case not to be able to eyeball her and gauge her demeanor as she tried to answer me.

"Joanie?"

"I'm not stalling. I'm looking in my date book. Remember the AIDS benefit at the Temple of Dendur in early March? Jim and I were just leaving when you arrived—you were standing right in front of that sarcophagus with the twenty-five-hundred-year-old mummy on loan from the British Museum—"

"Which one of us looked better?"

"Personally, *I* voted for the mummy, but that's when Drew told Jim he knew who you were and wanted a chance to be introduced. We were on our way out so I told him to give us a call with some dates and I'd put it together at a dinner party."

"And when did he call you? Got that in your little black book, too?"

A longer pause.

"He didn't call you until after he saw the newspaper articles about my assignment to Gemma Dogen's case? Right? Like a day or two before the dinner party that you'd already set up. And you just added an extra chair."

"What's the big deal? I mean, I certainly didn't know anything about this, Alex. But I can't blame the man for being curious about the doctor who had such a profound effect on his personal life. I've talked to him plenty since then and he's really crazy about you."

"Well, it's extremely weird to be in the middle of a love triangle with a guy who's probably trying to channel messages to his late wife through the prosecutor who's handling the murder of the woman—"

"Cut it out. I've got to go, the baby's crying and—"

"You don't have a baby."

"Well, it works for Nina whenever you're making *her* crazy with your phone calls. Maybe I'll borrow one 'til you pass through this phase."

"I'm sorry."

"Look, you've only dated the guy a couple of times. Jim's known him forever. Get through with this case and give Drew a chance."

I was lying down on my side now, with my head propped up on one elbow, holding the phone to my right ear. We made small talk for a couple of minutes before I wormed my way back to the purpose of my call. "Mike thinks this is a bit far out, but do you—well, does Jim think that Drew harbored enough of a grudge against Dr. Dogen that he might have—I don't mean that he did anything violent himself, but that he would have hired someone to—"

Joan was shouting at me across the Atlantic. "Do you remember what you used to tell me you did your first year in the D.A.'s Office, when you were assigned to that bureau where all the nuts called in with their complaints? Whenever you got stuck on the phone with a pain in the neck who wouldn't let you go, you used to reach a point where you'd say, 'Madam, I think we're about to be disconnected.' Keep talking like this, Miss Cooper, and you will be permanently disconnected."

I could hear Joan take a deep breath.

"Listen to Mike," she said. "He's got wonderful instincts about this kind of thing. I'll be back up in New York on Tuesday, then you and I can get together for a quiet dinner. Call me here on Sunday after you've unpacked and settled in."

Mike had shaved and showered during my call and emerged from the bathroom dressed in a dark blue suit. He was almost ready to go downstairs for the cocktail hour as he finished knotting and straightening his tie.

My conversation with Joan had put things in perspective and cheered me up as my exchanges with her usually did. There was no reason to write Drew off altogether, especially since I wouldn't have much time for socializing as the pace of our investigation picked up. I might as well enjoy my free hours now and figure out how I felt about him when this case was behind me.

"Is my little wallflower going to stay in her room again this evening or are we going to have the pleasure of your company?"

"Give me half an hour. I'll clean up and be downstairs—"

"That's what you told me yesterday."

I waved him out of the suite and went in to shower and wash my hair. My cocktail dress was a simple black silk with a short pleated skirt that swung when I moved. My mood was lighter than it had been in days as I stepped into my evening spikes and gave the skirt another shimmy.

It was after seven when I walked down the staircase to the Great Hall. I could see Chapman's thick dark hair amid the thinning pates of the older academics and made my way across the room to join him. Along the route I asked one of the servers for a Dewar's on the rocks and was told that the only Scotches the bar stocked were single malts. He would bring me a Glenrothes.

When I approached Mike he was standing with his back to me, facing three enormous panels of tapestry that lined most of the south wall of the Great Hall. He was shoulder to shoulder with a woman in a strapless gown whose skin glowed with the creamiest porcelain texture I'd ever seen and whose short platinum hair bounced gently beneath a diamond tiara as her head moved up and down in response to something that Chapman was saying to her.

I hovered a foot or two behind them waiting to be glimpsed instead of interrupting the conversation.

"I never knew Orkney had anything to do with this place but I sure know the story of these things." The hand with the Jameson's pointed up at the wall hangings. Chapman was telling the woman that the Earl of Orkney had been England's first Field Marshal, second in command to the Duke of Marlborough at Blenheim. The huge tapestries celebrated that victory and, as Mike was describing, depicted the arts of war.

My curiosity was overwhelming my manners and I circled around Mike's side as my drink was delivered to include myself in their conversation.

"Cheers. I'm glad you could make it, kid. I'd like you to meet my duchess."

The elegant woman shifted her glass of champagne to her other hand and extended the right one to shake mine, throwing her head back and laughing at Mike's description, introducing herself to me as Jennifer, Lady Turnbull. Enough midnight soaks in my Jacuzzi with fashion magazines made the introduction unnecessary. Her beautiful face and stunning figure had graced as many covers and articles as those of any professional model. And the stories of the American college girl who had married the elderly Lord Turnbull and shortly thereafter inherited his millions had been front-page tabloid news while I was still an adolescent.

"Jenny's fiancé is the person who underwrites this conference for the Brits every year. That's how come they're here. He's the guy over there, talking to your boyfriend."

Lady Turnbull wrapped one of her long thin arms in the crook of Mike's elbow and turned him around to face into the roomful of people. I saw Lord Windlethorne speaking to a man I recognized from the same sort of magazine articles as the British industrialist Bernhard Karl, a fiftyish man with boyish good looks.

"Your detective and I have been having a marvelous time, Alexandra. He's told me so much about you, I'm just fascinated to meet you."

"Didn't believe me when I told you Creavey and I hit all the nightspots with a duchess, did you?"

Before I could answer, Jennifer held up her finger in protest. "I keep telling Michael I'm not a duchess but he delights in calling me one. We went absolutely everywhere in the neighborhood last night and he's promised to return the favor as soon as I'm in New York."

I couldn't quite picture Lady Turnbull on a barstool at Rao's in her strapless gown and tiara surrounded by a crew from Manhattan North Homicide, but I'd seen enough politicians, movie stars, and moguls there to know Mike could make it happen.

"I feel terribly underdressed for your—"

"Don't be silly. Bernie and I just get all done up like this because we're hosting the banquet. It so suits the setting, don't you think?"

I clung to the duchess and the cop like a fifth wheel for at least another half an hour and another neat Glenrothes. I kept looking to see whether Mr. Karl was keeping an eye on his consort but he was clearly either comfortable with her style or secure in his skin.

Shortly before eight o'clock, Graham began moving among the guests announcing that dinner would be served in the French Dining Room. Lady Turnbull took Michael by the hand and led him down the corridor while I sort of shuffled along behind them trapped in a conversation about juvenile delinquency with the tedious Danish criminologist. She took her place at the head of the elongated banquet table sparkling in the reflected surroundings of gilded walls and ceiling, dangling chandeliers of all sizes, and countless tabletop candelabra.

As I slipped past Jennifer to search for the place cards bearing my name and Mike's, she pointed at the seat next to her and beckoned to him. "Since this is the French Dining Room, I'm taking the liberty of keeping Hercule Poirot right here beside me. With all the talk of crime at this meeting, I can't think of anybody to keep me safer."

"Poirot's a Belgian, Mikey. He wasn't French and neither are you. Remind her your roots are in Bay Ridge and maybe she'll give you back to me," I whispered, dreading the thought of sitting between the Australian penal expert and the Teutonic ethnologist.

"Don't be rude to my duchess, Blondie. Room service might be the answer if you're in one of your moods again." He winked at me and pinched my arm as I walked behind him.

I was two-thirds of the way down the table before I saw my name, placed between Lord Windlethorne—that must have been Mike's doing—and Ambassador Richard Fairbanks, the American delegate to the Pacific Economic Conference. A waiter pulled out the chair to help me into my seat.

Windlethorne joined me almost immediately and I was treated to a lecture on British libel law as interpreted through the most recent court cases, which outlasted the service and consumption of the starter, a Cornish crab with lime pimentos. Midway through the second course of salad smothered in truffles, Windlethorne was diverted by the woman to his left—whom I wanted to kiss in gratitude—and I introduced myself to Fairbanks, whom I had not met earlier.

The Ambassador was charming, attractive, and funny and I managed to stay engaged in conversation with him throughout the next three courses, as I lost count of the varieties of white and red wine that accompanied each dish.

When all of the desserts and champagne had been finished
and the ormolu clock had chimed midnight, Bernhard invited
the heartier participants to follow him along for cigars and
port. The Europeans with the earliest airport departures
began to peel off and say goodnight, as did a number of the
spouses who complained about the odor of all that smoke.

I would have been happy to call it a night, too, except for
my fascination with Jennifer's interaction with Mike. She was
all over him again as they headed out of the dining room, so I
reminded myself how much I loved the smell of my father's
cigars and made my way after them into the library with its
wood-paneled walls and immense fireplace. I positioned
myself next to Ambassador Fairbanks and his wife, Shannon,
and eventually Jennifer and Mike worked themselves around
the room to us. Chapman was carrying an extra glass of port
for me. "This could be the smoothest thing I've ever tasted.
You gotta try it."

Graham came over to the sofas where we had seated ourselves near the crisp fire. "Excuse me, sir," he said, leaning in
to speak to Chapman. "Your mother returned your call during
dinner, but asked me not to disturb you. She said she was just
calling back with the information you wanted and to tell you
when I saw you and that you'd understand. Mrs. Chapman
said that last night's category was Geography and that I was
to tell you the answer."

"Hold it, Graham." With a cigar stuck in the corner of his
mouth and half a load on, Mike liked the way Jennifer was
playing and flirting with him and delighted in her reaction to
Graham's cryptic message.

He started to explain to her what *Jeopardy!* is and she
squealed back at him, grabbing him by the wrist, "I know
exactly what it is. I always watch it when we're in the States."

"Ten bucks, duchess. You in it for Geography?"

"Fifty bucks, detective. How about you?" She had turned to me asking if I was still in the party.

Knowing my chances were slightly better than with the Bible or Physics, I told her I was in for fifty with her.

"Carry on, Graham."

"Madam said to tell you that the question was—" He paused as he looked down at the sentence he had written out on the back of a Cliveden postcard. "'Formerly called Mount McKinley, this highest peak in North America is known now by its Native American name meaning Great One.'"

Jennifer pounded the arm of the sofa shouting "Got it!" at the very same moment Graham was asking Mike whether he had understood the message. "D'you know it, too?" she asked me.

I smiled lamely and offered, "What is Mount Rainier?"

Her feet were drawn up under her gown now, and Jennifer shook her head at me to tell me that I was wrong. Then she looked over at Mike on the sofa next to her.

"Clueless, m'lady," he said, beaming that great white grin back at her.

"What is Denali? That's the name of it now. Bernie financed an expedition to the peak of it last summer. For an environmental group or something. Isn't that amazing?"

Truly amazing. Even more astounding was the fact that Mike was digging in his pocket for the payoff, which he'd never done so quickly with me in all the years we'd been playing together. Mostly what I got were IOUs. This dame needed his fifty like I needed another drink.

"Excuse me, Graham. Could I please have another drink—a bit more port?"

He had just returned with my glass when Bernhard made his way across the room to reclaim his gorgeous treasure and take her upstairs to bed. Mike got to his feet to accept kisses on each cheek from his duchess and promises to both of us that she'd see us in New York before very long. We thanked Mr. Karl for his generosity and resumed our places on the sofas in front of the fire as the conferees continued to trickle out of the room.

Someone had turned on the CD player that was sitting on a table in the corner. Bette Midler's voice came at me asking if I wanted to dance under the moonlight. I walked to the double doors that led onto the terrace. A few people had strolled outside to enjoy the bracing night air, escape the cigar fumes, or distance themselves from the heat of the fire.

I moved to the edge of the balcony and rested my crystal wine glass on the solid stone slab that overlooked the starlit gardens, breathing in to clear my head and my mind.

Mike joined me. "Sleepy?"

"I was an hour ago but I'm really wired now."

"Anything in particular?"

"The case, I guess. Odd to be in the middle of all this elegance, all this irrelevant excess from another age, while somebody else is working our murder case. I don't mind that they are, I just wonder what they're up to. You think it's DuPre?"

"You know me. I think it's everybody until we prove it's somebody."

Now it was a man's voice singing to me from inside the great house. In between Mike's comments I could make out phrases. "When the day—" Then Chapman spoke to me over the sound of the singer. "—and night has come—" And, in fact, the moon was the only thing I could see.

"Dance with me?" I asked. I was gliding to the music by myself across the uneven foundation of the ancient structure, imagining that all sorts of titled men and women had waltzed over the same terrace for centuries.

I was singing along with Ben E. King now, hoping my partner would stand by me. Chapman was staring at me, cigar in hand and unable to repress his grin at the sight of my intoxicated, finger-snapping dance steps.

I said it again, a bit less tentatively this time. "Dance with me, please." He still seemed to hesitate. "I'm only asking you to dance, I'm not—"

"All right, all right."

He put down his cigar, placed his glass next to mine, and picked up the beat as we swayed to King's tender voice.

"So who am I dancing with tonight, a Wili or a duchess?"

I didn't get it. "What?"

"Are you planning to dance me to death, like the Queen of the Wilis, or does 'blue collar' just look more appealing to you this evening because Lady Turnbull got such a kick out of it?"

"That's not fair. I—"

"Shhhh." He let go with his left hand and put it up to his lips. "No talking. I'm trying to figure out a way to get one of those tiaras for you. If her boyfriend had left her with me for just another hour, I could have talked that one off her head and given it to you. You know how good you'd look in front of a jury trying a case with a tiara on? You couldn't lose."

The disc had switched once more and Smokey had speeded up the pace by telling us that he was going to a go-go. Mike danced himself over to the edge of the balcony and picked up his cigar. I was swaying alone and watching my skirt twirl, backing up the Miracles with some harmony, and trailing after Chapman to find my glass of port and refill it.

"I'm pulling the plug, Blondie. Bar's closed."

"I just want to fin—"

"C'mon upstairs. Tomorrow's a long day and we got a lot to catch up on when we get back." He had me by the elbow and was steering me through the library doors and across the Great Hall.

"You didn't cut Jennifer off last night, did you?"

"She holds it a lot better than you do, kid. Stairs or elevator?"

I looked up at the three-tiered flight of stairs when we reached its bottom and the steps appeared to be rolling like an escalator. "The lift will do just fine, thank you."

It lurched its way to our floor and Mike again reminded me to lower my voice as we passed the row of suites that led to ours. He turned the knob and opened the door and I followed him inside. He gave me the shirt he had worn earlier in the day and grabbed the robe that I had left on the end of my bed. "Go into the bathroom, brush your teeth, take a couple of aspirin, and get yourself ready to go to sleep."

When I came out five minutes later, he handed me a slip of paper with my name on it that had been folded and pushed under the door of the suite while we were at dinner.

I opened the note, glanced at it, then looked up at Mike to see if I could tell from his expression whether or not he had read it. "Mr. Renaud phoned. Please call him at whatever hour you get in tonight." Joan must have egged him on and explained my relationship with Mike.

"Want me to leave the room?"

I shook my head. "It'll wait 'til I get home." I was crashing rapidly.

"Go on, Blondie. Get into bed."

The housekeeper had turned down the blankets. I unwrapped the little chocolate mint on my pillow, put it in my mouth, and slid down between the covers. I reached up to turn out the light as Mike came over and kissed the crown of my head.

"You're a lousy drunk, Coop. Harmless but lousy."

I must have fallen asleep immediately because I didn't remember anything else until the front desk rang for our eight o'clock wake-up call. I could hear a noise coming from the floor at the foot of Mike's bed. I sat up and looked, but the only thing there was the pair of pants to his suit, wriggling and buzzing as if a giant bumblebee was trapped in its pocket and trying to escape. "Good morning. At the risk of being told it's none of my business, may I ask you what you've got in your pants?"

"Whaddya mean?" He didn't look much better than I felt as he rolled over to face me.

"Something's jumping around in your trousers." I pointed at the moving pile on the floor.

"That's my Skypager," he laughed. "I had it in my pocket last night. But it's set on the vibrating mode so it wouldn't beep in the middle of dinner and make any noise. That's why it's so frisky."

Mike got out of bed, picked up the writhing pants, reached into his pocket, and pulled out the little machine. "It's John Creavey's number." He called the desk and asked them to dial it for him.

A short conversation with the commander and then he turned back to me. "Mercer called Creavey 'cause the Sky-pager doesn't work this far away and the reception desk here wouldn't put his call through during the night.

"John DuPre is on the run. Skipped town some time within the last twenty-four hours. Mercer seized some stuff from his office and they've got his house staked out, too. But the wife is hysterical. Claims she's left there on her own with two kids and no idea where her husband is. Let's get packing. Mercer'll tell us the rest of the story when he picks us up at the airport."

"Well, is the guy a neurologist or not?"

"Are you kidding? Mercer doesn't even know his real name. He's not John DuPre, he's not a doctor, and it seems he never went to medical school. He's a con artist and a scammer. And when they figure out *who* he is, maybe we'll figure out how to find him."

26

It was almost five o'clock when the announcement came that our flight was ready to depart after hours of delay caused by a mechanical problem. We were both bored and squirming as we were marched onto the plane with three hundred other disgruntled travelers and found our way to our seats two-thirds of the way to the back of the coach section. Our upgrade didn't work on this side of the pond.

Once airborne, the trip was unremarkable. We ate and read and watched Mel Gibson shoot up half the population of Los Angeles in the fifth sequel to whatever action series was on the screen. I finally came to life about twenty minutes east of JFK as we descended to twelve thousand feet and I could point out to Chapman a crystal clear view of Martha's Vineyard off the right wingtip of the plane. We were flying just to the south of the island and from the air the bareness of the trees in the early spring made it possible to pick out the distinct towns and bodies of water as well as some of the actual farms and houses that I knew so well.

Mike leaned across me and looked down through the window. "Can you see the Bite? I'm ready for a second portion of those incredible fried clams."

I tried to point out where Menemsha was, orienting him by the large red-and-black roof of the Coast Guard building.

"Have you been back to your house since last—?"

I interrupted his question before he could complete it. "Not yet."

"You know you've really gotta go—"

I didn't want to snap at him again, and I knew I had been avoiding a difficult situation for too long, but I hadn't been able to face a weekend alone in my lovely old farmhouse since I had returned there with Mike during the investigation of Isabella Lascar's murder last fall. "The caretaker closed it up for me for the winter. It'll just be easier to deal with the whole thing in a few weeks when it's springtime. The inside is being painted now and I'll wait 'til Ann or Louise are going up to their places. I have been avoiding it but I'm about ready to go back."

The flight attendant was directing us to fasten our seat belts for our initial approach to the airport. There wasn't a cloud in the sky as we circled out over the ocean and I tried to urge Mike to relax his grip on the arms of his seat before he broke them in half.

Mercer was standing on the ramp of the gateway as we deplaned through the front door. A sergeant from the Port Authority Police had taken him past security to meet us, and we were able to clear Customs and Immigration before the luggage even landed on the carousel.

We picked up our bags and went out to his car, which was parked directly in front of the terminal. The highway was jammed with the Saturday night bridge-and-tunnel crowd on their way into the city for dinner or theater or sports events. We crawled along with them, Mercer saving his stories until we could sit quietly at dinner and catch up on his news.

When we reached the Triboro Bridge, I used his car phone to call Giuliano at Primola. It was almost seven and I told him we could be at the restaurant in twenty minutes. "Got a corner table of Adolfo's that you can give three of us?"

We ordered quickly so we could get down to business. For me, stracciatelli soup and a small bowl of pasta that could just slide down my throat with barely any effort on my part. Mike and Mercer both went for veal chops. Adolfo brought over the first round of drinks as Mercer started to talk.

"Here's what we know so far. Our fugitive started life in a parish outside of New Orleans. Name was Jean DuPuy— Cajun, I guess. Graduated high school, then got a bachelor's degree in pharmacology. That's the closest his formal training ever came to medicine.

"But he's been impersonating doctors for almost ten years. Somehow he found out about the real DuPre, who's a bit of a hermit at this point. Ninety-four years old. Most folks just assume he's dead.

"You know part of his scam. Writes to Tulane and claims his diploma was destroyed in a fire. Sends 'em ten bucks for a new one along with his name and a post office box address. They're happy to give one of their favorite sons whatever he asks for. Next, our impostor starts with that one priceless piece of paper—Xeroxed a few times—and some phony letterhead, which he uses to mail off to medical societies and journals. And before you can say Jefferson Davis, he's got an entire portfolio establishing his credentials as Dr. John DuPre."

"D'you talk to anyone who knew him before he got to New York?"

"Just this afternoon. Once he had his papers, he applied for jobs in clinics in the South, working his way up—with experience, of course—to better positions at medical centers."

"What did they say about him?"

"Two of the neurologists he worked with said he acted like a real pro. They're among the many who gave him glowing references when DuPre started to make plans to move to New York. All the patients raved about his bedside manner."

Just ask Maureen about that, I thought to myself. At least, that's what she said the first few days.

"Looks like he started doing this when he lost his pharmacist's license for a Medicaid fraud. The prosecutor from the Louisiana Attorney General's Office said when they investigated him for that offense in the early eighties, all the local physicians were shocked. They used to call him Doc 'cause he seemed so knowledgeable about the profession. A real charmer. That's when he moved to Georgia and started life all over again—as DuPre."

"Get any word back on the lawsuit he told us about?" I asked between spoonfuls of steaming hot soup.

"Yeah, the malpractice case. Poor patient was a thirty-year-old guy. Came to see DuP—well, whoever he is. Described his symptoms, which were—" Mercer flipped open his steno pad and looked at the notes he had written. "Complained of sudden weight loss, insatiable thirst, dry lips and mouth, and dizziness.

"This quack orders some blood tests, fills a beaker of urine, but simply told him to stay home and rest. The medication he ordered was for vertigo. Forty-eight hours later, lady friend finds the guy in his house—dead."

"How come?"

"His symptoms, Dr. Chapman, are the classic markers of an uncontrolled case of diabetes. Any first-year med student should have picked it up. Our clown missed it completely and his trusting patient left the office and went into a diabetic coma. A completely avoidable death."

"So that drives him out of some small town near Atlanta and where better to go than the naked city? Eight million stories here and nobody'd even ask what his used to be."

"Now we got to figure out if he really left New York yesterday or he's still lurking around here somewhere."

"Update on that, too." Mercer was sliding his knife through the largest, most tender chop I think I've ever seen. "Checked with the squad while I was at the airport. American Express and Visa are helping us track a flight route, which looks like it's headed right on back to the bayou.

"Somebody's using the cards of an eighty-eight-year-old man, Tyrone Perkins. Car rental in the Bronx, gas on the Jersey Turnpike, motel in South Carolina last night."

"When were they reported stolen?" I asked.

"Haven't been—yet."

"Then I don't see—"

"The companies each called up the guy's house 'cause the cards are showing a flurry of recent activity after a very long dormant period. Problem is, Tyrone's niece says he's been in the hospital on life support for about seven months so he has definitely not been leaving home or anywhere else with his American Express card."

Mike was pointing his fork at Mercer. "And if I had to guess, I'd bet ol' Tyrone is hooked up to some machines over at Mid-Manhattan."

"The lieutenant sent someone there this afternoon to check the lockup where they store the valuables of the patients in the intensive care unit. Mr. Perkins's personal things seemed to have been 'misplaced' sometime during the past few days. So we got a trace going nationally on ATMs, restaurants, and stores 'til we find that scumbag."

"Anything else going on at the hospital while we were out of town?"

"Well, I was over there yesterday afternoon. I say starting

Monday morning we gotta bring every one of these guys down to the D.A.'s Office and reinterview them. Whoever left that note under your door—the one about black and white—was trying to point a finger at DuPre if that's what it was a reference to. Now, would they be doin' that because they knew he was guilty of murder? Or just because they knew he was a fraud? Or was it simply because they wanted to divert attention from themselves?"

"I'm with Mercer. Enough of trying to give 'em special treatment and meet them on their own turf. They're regular witnesses, like in any other case. Who'd you see there yesterday?"

"I wanted to bypass administration and go right to Spector's office. But somebody got on the horn when I walked into the lobby because Dietrich was on my back the minute I got to the reception area on the sixth floor."

I reminded Mike that we had to bring Mercer up to speed on Geoffrey Dogen's thoughts about the missing key chain.

"We're going to have to talk to Dietrich about exactly when Gemma gave him the one he carries with him."

"Yeah, and how many other people walking around that hospital got them from her as gifts. I'm not sure that's gonna be a very fruitful avenue to explore. We have no idea the last time that key ring was hanging from her bookshelf. D'you talk with Spector at all?"

"Sure. The whole bunch of 'em greet me like I'm a prospect for brain surgery when I walk into Minuit, kinda rubbing their hands together and acting like they're pleased to have me there. He was in his office with Coleman Harper and Banswar Desai.

"Desai still mopes around like he lost his best friend and Harper's got his nose so far up the boss's ass that it's gonna be a shade darker than mine is any day now."

"Cooperative?"

"Yeah. No problem with that. I was just trying to see if anybody had any ideas about DuPre. None of them seemed to know he had hit the road so I didn't tell them. Spector's real busy trying to do his own work and be anointed to take over Gemma's place, too. Real humble, now, like it's a big surprise he'll get the job."

The owner came over to offer us an after-dinner drink on the house as soon as we had taken care of the check with Adolfo.

Mike was already on his feet, pulling out my chair. "You know, Giuliano, just once I'd like you to buy me a drink *before* dinner. You're always quick to suggest one when Blondie's dragging me out the door. Next time, okay?"

"*Buona notte.* Nice to see you—Miss Cooper, gentlemen."

"*Ciao,* Giuliano."

We got in Mercer's car for the short ride to my apartment. "What's the plan, guys?"

"I'm off tomorrow," Mercer answered. "Unless we get word from one of those out-of-town departments that they've picked up Jean DuPuy. The lieutenant will give me a call if that happens. He's trying to encourage me to stay home because of all the overtime we're racking up on this case already."

"I promised my mother I'd stop by and take her to Mass in the morning."

"Then why don't we meet in my office on Monday?" I said. "I'll go over all the reports again tomorrow and set up a schedule for doing interviews. We can plan it out around your tours for the week, okay?"

The doorman came out to meet the car and help me into the elevator with my luggage.

"Want me to go up with you and make sure no one's hiding under your bed, Goldilocks?"

"No, thank you. Be sure you tell your mother about your conquest of the duchess. She'll be very proud of you."

"Hey, if DuPuy rings your doorbell tonight and wants to make a house call to take your blood pressure, don't let him in, y'hear?"

27

I was relishing the solitude of my own apartment on a rainy Sunday morning, reading the *Times* and filling in the answers to the puzzle. My telephone tape had been loaded with messages from friends but I didn't intend to start returning any of them until later in the afternoon. I had unpacked my suitcase and had nothing that needed doing other than to organize my notes and police reports for the week ahead.

Mercer's call caught me in the middle of noshing on a toasted bagel. "Hey, Alex, it's me. Two things, one you may be able to help me with."

"Shoot. You sound like you're on another planet!"

"I'm on a cell phone up in Connecticut. Drove up to my cousin's house for a family party today. Almost forgot about it. First thing is, I got beeped by a little police department in

Pennsylvania. Bluebell, to be exact. Seems like DuPuy made a U-turn somewhere near the Mason-Dixon line and reversed his tracks. Coming back north.

"Commissioner's concerned enough about it to be moving Maureen again to a different location, just as a precaution. Everyone assumes he'll start using a new credit card or ID any hour now. Steal one, buy one, con one off somebody. Surprised we've had this much of a run on him using the Perkins cards."

"Maybe he's coming back to get his wife and kids."

"Well, that's a very generous view of the weasel, but it's a point. There's a trap on her phone and the lieutenant's had a team sittin' on the house since we heard he fled.

"Which leads to my question. Peterson asked me if we had inventoried the files in Dogen's office and apartment. I told him that you and I took some notes but they were pretty general. At least mine were by topic, not by specific name. He wants to know if she had a folder on John DuPre. And, frankly, I couldn't remember. Sound familiar to you?"

"Hold on. I can look through my materials and check it for you right now. Off the top of my head, I know I was listing the categories of things she had but I don't remember even seeing any individual names." I was trying to visualize the reams of documents we had plowed through that afternoon and whether the neurologist's name would have had any significance to me at that particular point in time.

"Not that important. I tried to reach George Zotos but he's upstate fishing with some of the guys from his old squad. He was goin' through a lot of them with us that day."

"Just give me a minute and—"

"It'll keep 'til during the week. I can promise you the Chief is *not* bringing me back in on my RDO unless there's a major break in the action." Regular days off were sacred in the NYPD's high command, since the rate of a second-grade detective's overtime scale was quite costly.

"Okay. Have a good time at the party."

I hung up, refilled my coffee cup, and took it into the bed-room while I showered and dressed. I thought I might walk around the corner to the Frick Collection for an hour or so and threw on an old cashmere sweater—a pale yellow cable-stitched tunic—over some velvet leggings to dress myself up a bit for the weekend art crowd.

I poured one more hit of coffee from the pot and sat at the dining-room table reviewing the notes I had jotted down while talking with Geoffrey Dogen. It bothered me that Lieutenant Peterson had questions about the files in Gemma's apartment for which I didn't have answers, especially since I had offered myself to go there to look for information that might be rele-vant to our case. I was even more annoyed that I couldn't make a connection between some of the file names I had seen and facts that Gemma's friends had not been able to fit into her life.

I didn't have any way to get into Dogen's office at Minuit without alerting the hospital administrators, but her own house keys had been sitting on top of my dresser ever since the afternoon Mercer had taken me to her apartment almost ten days before. I had forgotten to return them and no one had needed to claim them on her behalf. Rent was paid up through the end of this month and Geoffrey Dogen had sent directions to donate her clothes to a thrift shop and have all her other personal belongings packed up and shipped home to England for distribution to relatives and friends.

I walked into the bedroom to call a couple of my girl-friends to see if anyone wanted to meet me at the Frick. It was a toss-up whether to just hang out for a few hours or try to accomplish something useful on the case by spending some time in Dogen's files. I picked up the miniature model of Tower Bridge and played with the keys as I dialed the familiar numbers. Lesley Latham's husband told me she was in Houston on a business trip, and Esther Newton was on her way out the door to a Huskies game at the Garden.

If I went down to Beekman Place and detailed information from Gemma's records, I told myself, then I'd deserve a late-afternoon visit to the museum—see the current exhibit and pick up some new postcards to send Nina—and a stop for a cup of hot chocolate on my way home. I left a message on David Mitchell's tape telling him I was back from London and asking if he and Renee wanted to come in to watch *60 Minutes* this evening. Then I called Mike's machine to pass on the news from Mercer about DuPre's change in direction.

Still undecided about which route I would take, I stuck a blank legal pad in my tote, dropped in the key chain, and put on my hooded red rain slicker. The museum was only four blocks away, but as I stood in the drizzle on the corner of Park Avenue waiting for the light to change a gentleman in a green mackintosh coat stepped out of a yellow taxicab and made it easy for me to shift course.

The cab discharged me at the entrance to Dogen's building. I saw only one doorman inside the lobby. I smiled and started to approach him to explain my purpose but he barely looked up from his *Daily News* comic section, so I continued on back to the right and waited for the elevator to descend and bring me up to the twelfth floor.

The nervous feeling I had experienced when I first came to the apartment with Mercer fluttered back as I knew it would. This time, it was just the spookiness of being alone with the keepsakes and belongings of the dead woman, which didn't seem to hold much meaning or value for any of her heirs or acquaintances. How odd for the accumulation of such an interesting life to pass with so little notice or concern.

The double locks gave easily as I turned a key in each of them. Once again I was startled by a noise behind me, but this time it seemed to be the door resounding as it slammed shut at my back. I thought of William Dietrich and the other people who still might have had Gemma's keys, so I twisted the lock and chained the bolt before throwing my slicker onto the back of an armchair.

Things were more or less as I had left them on my earlier visit. I knew that detectives had been in and out of here on a number of occasions since then on orders from the lieutenant, but whether the superintendent or rental agents had scavenged any of Gemma's belongings I doubt I'd be aware. I spent a few minutes walking from room to room looking for differences that I might notice but finding few.

The book on spinal cord injuries was no longer on the bedside table and the closet door in that room had been left open, revealing its empty innards. I put my finger on the bottom edge of a furled-up yellow Post-it someone had stuck onto the wooden trim around the closet with a handwritten arrow pointing beneath to the words, "Deliver to Hospital Thrift Shop, Third Avenue."

Back in the living room, I looked at the photographs with renewed interest. Now I could pick out the faces of Geoffrey Dogen, Gig Babson, several colleagues from Minuit, and London backdrops of Gemma's favorite setting. Books and CDs were still in place, but someone had made off with the disc player and the little television set I had seen there last time. I took out my notepad and wrote a reminder to find out whether the removals were authorized or not—a typical problem at the scene of a homicide when there was no family member to keep up a presence.

There was an old clock radio on the back of the desk and I turned it on to a classical music station to fill the room with something other than the stillness that hung in the air. People in the adjacent apartment must have been more hard of hearing than my late grandmother as the noise from their television set almost boomed through the wall at me with the shrill voices of Home Shopping Network announcers. Today was obviously Capodimonte day and prices were being slashed by the minute. The neighbors couldn't have heard me turn Gemma's little radio knob up a notch.

I sat down again in the seat I had worked in from the day Mercer and I tried to catalogue some of the property. I could remember remarking about the lack of logic of some of the files, but there were far too many cabinets to put my finger on the ones that had stood out to me at the time.

At random, I slid open drawers and started to rifle through the subject tabs, looking for names that were now more familiar from meetings with the hospital staff and the expanded scope of our investigation. I was interested in information Dogen might have had about the men we had since interviewed and especially wanted to please Lieutenant Peterson by coming up with something that Gemma might have known about Jean DuPuy.

Inches and inches gave me nothing but medical research and clippings from journals about brain injury and surgical techniques. I checked my original notes and matched the third drawer from the left with a list that earmarked her files on "Professional Ethics." Grabbing a handful of them, I swiveled around to place them on the desk and began to skim through them.

Some of them went back years, almost to her first days at Minuit, and none of the names they referenced had anything to do with the current staff or student body. With a red marker, Dogen had annotated the official school documents, commenting in the margins on the suitability of a candidate or her opinion of his worthiness to enter the program.

I pushed the pile to the side of the desk and reached back for a more recent assortment on the same topic. Fanning them out across the top of the blotter, I started from the rear of the pile. Midway through, the titles changed and I realized I had passed from the ethics folders into her personal records.

The tabs I was reading were labeled in Gemma's hand with the names of sports teams. Clipped together in one lump were the Saints, the Braves, and the Redskins. I lifted the metal clasp and opened the three packets as Gemma's filing system became obvious to me. This was her stash on John DuPre, the team name representing the city in which an academic institution or professional connection was located—Tulane was in New Orleans, his practice and lawsuit were in Atlanta, and Georgetown, where he claimed to have received his undergraduate degree, was in D.C. Somehow, she had figured the information she collected would be less obvious or desirable to an interloper if it looked like it related to a sporting event.

I thought of the briefing session at which we'd been told that one of the cops from the 17th had found file folders in a trash barrel in the hospital parking lot that bore similar labels. Perhaps this was a duplicate set that Dogen kept at home, where she had a greater assurance of privacy.

The find excited me. I dialed Chapman's number but he still wasn't there. I left him a message and told him to call me at Gemma's apartment if he got in within the next hour, reading the number off the printed slot on the base of her phone. I beeped Mercer, then returned to ferreting through the drawers for more things like DuPre's records while I waited for him to call me back.

"Who's this?" Mercer asked when I picked up the receiver.

"It's Alex."

"Where are you? I didn't recognize the number."

"Gemma's apartment. Peterson is going to smother us with kisses when we get through with what I've got here."

"You first, Coop. That's not exactly the reward I've been looking for."

I started to explain what I had found and that I was continuing to search for more pieces. "What time are you coming back to the city?"

"You tell me."

"Why don't I take a few armloads of these with me, stop at Grace's Marketplace and pick up something that you guys can feed me for dinner, and we'll start the week off with gold stars."

"What time is it now? Two-thirty. Plan on me gettin' there about seven."

"Fine. I'm still trying to come up with the one we saw when we were here together. She had labeled it 'Met Games.' Remember, I remarked how out of place it was that Laura would have refiled it in better order? Only now I can't come up with what it was stuck in between. It's got to have something to do with her whistle-blowing, too, since she never went to a ball game."

"It was close to something like 'degenerates'—that's why it stuck out in my mind."

"That's Sex Crimes for you, Mercer. *We've* got degenerates, medicine has 'regenerative tissue.' I knew you'd remember."

"I'll hold while you look for it."

I put the receiver down on the desk, scanned my notes, and found the reference to the drawer that held both a series on ethics and another on specific medical topics like tissues. I opened it up and saw that crammed right in between the two was a green Pendaflex holding the file I was looking for.

I cradled the phone on my shoulder as I separated the sides of the folder and removed a thick sheaf of papers. "Curveball, Mercer. 'Met Games' looks like it's all about Coleman Harper. This stuff goes back a lot longer than Dietrich's archives do. It's Dogen's notes from her first year at Minuit. Harper was finishing his internship just like he told us. Only these records make it clear that Gemma's the one who blackballed him from Mid-Manhattan and the neurosurgical program.

"Spector got him parked over at Metropolitan Hospital while he tried to appeal the decision." I flipped through some of the documents. "Met Games is right. Spector was trying to find supporters uptown who would go to the mat for his boy Harper, and Dogen dug her heels in to track the guy's every move. It's too much to skim through right now but it looks like she's been documenting every mistake Harper's ever made in the past ten years—and there are plenty of them."

"Like what?"

"She's got a few things circled in red ink—someone up at Met who wasn't happy with his technical skills in the operating room, another one complaining to Spector that Harper had a poor medical knowledge base. And it's clear they weren't going to keep him there, either."

I looked at Dogen's meticulous handwriting in the margin of the files. "Her notes read like Coleman Harper had something on Spector—like some secret about his personal life. At least, that's why she thinks he's backing Harper for admission, even though by most accounts he wouldn't make it at Minuit."

"Good hunting."

"Look, I'll bring these with me. And I think I'll swing by Minuit on my way home. I've got my ID with me so maybe someone from security can let me in Gemma's office. That way I can examine her folders there before Spector gets on to us during the week."

"No. That's a serious, emphatic, Battaglia-inspired capital N, capital O. There's absolutely no way of knowing who's around there on a Sunday afternoon and who you're gonna bump into. Remember, we know we've got one loose cannon running around out of control. Who knows whether DuPre left anything at the hospital that he's coming back for."

"Mercer, I can't get in there on a Sunday unless someone from security opens the door for me. It's not exactly a big risk to take in the middle of the day—"

"No! Get it? First of all, a lady was killed in that room just a couple of weeks ago, remember? Second, we don't know who to trust in that entire hospital, do we? Go directly home. Do not pass Go, do not collect two hundred dollars, and definitely do not stop at Minuit Medical College. Am I understood?"

"What if Mike gets back and can meet me there?"

"You really are stubborn, girl."

"I'll be good, Mercer. See you later." I didn't want to lie to him and tell him I wouldn't go to Mid-Manhattan. I was only a couple of blocks away and anxious to see what was in Dogen's office now that I knew what to look for. I could always get the Police Department to secure her apartment by this evening so no one could get into it even if they had keys. But we'd have far less control over circumstances at the medical school if someone wanted to purge her files, unless we acted quickly.

I gathered up the folders, turned off the radio, and walked across the room to put on my raincoat. April fifteenth was only ten days off and Coleman Harper was once again waiting for a decision about whether he would be admitted to the neurosurgical residency. I wondered how much of Dogen's determination not to tell the Board at Minuit whether she was leaving was tied to the ten-year struggle she had waged to keep him out of the program. How desperate had he been to get in this time? And were there other candidates whom she had tracked and thwarted in exactly the same way? Gemma Dogen's principles had made her a lot of enemies and I thought about how powerful a motive revenge could often be.

I reached out to unlatch the chain on the back of the door. There was a flash of movement over my left shoulder that star-

tled me and in the split second that my head whipped around
to look for its source I was slammed against the wall into the
corner where it met the door frame. A fist pounded into the
rear of my skull, blinding me with its force and causing me to
drop everything in my arms as I shrieked from pain. The second blow landed on the knuckles of my hands, which I had
instinctively thrown up behind me to cover my head. Again
my forehead crashed into the doorjamb as my arms flailed
behind me, striking wildly at the body that was pressing in
against my back.

I braced myself against the wall and turned to confront my
tormentor, hoping to reason with him when I looked him in
the eye. But my feet slipped on the shiny tops of the dozens of
folders that had dropped to the floor and spread across it like
a giant-sized version of fifty-two pickup. My left leg slid out
from underneath me as I pivoted and fell onto one knee, staring up to see Coleman Harper plowing his fist into the place
on the wall where my face had just been.

I screamed at him to stop but he pushed me onto my back
and straddled me, one of my legs locked in place beneath me,
as he pinned my shoulder to the floor and stuffed something
that smelled like a dirty sock in my mouth to muffle my
shouts. Harper's eyes were darting madly around the room
while he pressed his knee into my abdomen, holding my
throat with his left hand and trying to keep both of my wrists
in his right. It seemed as though he was searching for something to use as a weapon but hadn't decided yet what it would
be. I knew I could probably break loose of his hold but the
pain was burning fiercely in my forehead and I was trying to
conserve every ounce of my strength to counter whatever his
next move would be.

Likely to die.

My mind was cartwheeling as I tried to figure some way to
defend myself against whatever device he would turn on me.

The only person who knew where to find me—Mercer Wallace—was hours away from here with no idea that I was in any danger. There would be no one to save me from Coleman Harper if I couldn't do it myself.

I watched his facial expression change as he looked from shelf to shelf mentally evaluating the deadliness of the objects his eyes passed over. I prayed he hadn't seen the expensive set of kitchen knives I had noticed in the next room when Mercer and I first visited the apartment. Silently, I begged the neighbors to turn off their blaring television set instead of cluttering their home with more of that wretched-looking pottery that the salesman was offering. I wanted them to hear the struggle, which I knew was going to get worse.

From my twisted position on the floor, I could see the coat closet Harper had secreted himself in before my arrival. It had been emptied out for delivery to the thrift shop, too, no doubt, and had given him an ideal place to hide while I searched the files and until I left. If only I hadn't called Mercer to brag about my discovery. Maybe he would have let me walk right out the door.

Stay calm, I tried to tell myself. He doesn't have a weapon because he didn't come here to kill people. He didn't expect me or anyone else to be in Gemma's home. It isn't like the night he went to her office intending to pay her back for ruining the career he had wanted for himself.

I closed my eyes and willed myself out of the apartment with all the faith in me, but I opened them again when the doctor spoke to me and I found I was still very much in the middle of this bad dream.

"Get up." His voice was sharp now, not quavering as it did the night I first spoke with him about Gemma's death. He was standing and pulling me along with him, but the soft wool at the collar of my sweater wouldn't keep his grip. It stretched and pulled out of shape and he grabbed at my hair instead.

I was trying to spit the wool sock out of my mouth so that I could implore him to release me and get out of there but he pushed it farther in as he saw me attempt to cough it loose.

He wasn't taking me to the kitchen, I realized, which caused me a sigh of temporary relief. Images of Gemma's mutilated corpse flashed through my mind and I was almost glad that he was pulling me in the direction of the window.

Each of his hands was holding one of mine as he walked in back of me with my arms crossed behind me. We were near the corner of the desk when one of his hands released me and I saw him reach for the telephone. I knew he wasn't planning to make a call. He wanted the cord to wrap around my neck.

Likely to die.

I waited until Harper stretched one arm across the width of the table to pull the phone wire out of the wall socket. Then I swiftly bent forward from the waist, kicking back my left leg as I moved, trying to hit his kneecap with the heel of my loafer. I must have come close to my mark as he shifted his weight and cursed when my foot made contact. It hadn't unbalanced him as I had hoped and he turned back to me with a vengeance—and with the heavy telephone appliance swinging from the end of the liberated line.

I had run out of prayers moments ago and I didn't know how to whisper a more urgent one than those I'd been murmuring. I only knew that I didn't want that length of cord wrapped around my slender neck. I had tried cases of ligature strangulation and knew what a slow, torturous manner of death it was.

My head was facing away from Harper and I could only see his movements out of the corner of my eye. He was trying to free up the loose end of the long wire that had run from the base of the phone on the desktop to the floorboard outlet, and when he finally grasped it he looped it over the top of my thrashing head.

Now I pulled my right hand out of his hold and reached it up to cover my throat. He let go of my left one as well while he worked to secure the cord around the middle of my windpipe and I struggled to sneak all of my fingers between his murder weapon and my crawling skin.

Keep them in there, I lectured myself frantically. Don't let that ligature tighten around your neck.

I was rocking back and forth, kicking occasionally, tugging against the stricture of the cord while Coleman Harper looked for a place to anchor the body of the phone so he could pull its wire tighter around me.

Again my brain was doing cartwheels. Random thoughts pushed themselves to the fore and I fought to get them out of sight. When my mother and father loomed in mental view, I shook my head more violently and tossed them away, not wanting them to visit this scene. Mercer and Mike were the people I wanted to see and to have save me.

Harper was trying to pull me farther back from the bookshelf, so I tried to find something to cling to that would keep me in place, keep me apart from wherever he wanted to take me. I kept bringing up Chapman's voice inside my head.

Now I remembered what was familiar about this scene. I was almost giddy with thoughts of how Chapman would react to finding my body. I continued to twist against my captor, thinking how Grace Kelly had been attacked by the killer in *Dial M for Murder*. I'd be strangled from behind, just like Kelly almost was, and Mike would be telling the uniformed guys how much he loved her in that movie—even as they bagged my corpse.

The letter opener. I was fighting against Harper's right hand, which was trying to pull one of my arms out from under the cord so he could finish off the job. My eyes scoured the top of Gemma's desk for a letter opener or sharp pair of scissors but nothing was in sight. C'mon, kid, my voices were telling me. Grace Kelly did it. You can do it, too.

Let him take one hand out, I thought to myself, grabbing onto my throat even more tightly with the other, to protect it. As he let go of my right one to use both of his to pull on the cord, I thrust my palm up against his face and scratched at the socket of his eye with my fingers. Again a howl and a spit at the side of my head.

But I knew what I wanted now and I knew I would only need a few inches to get at it.

I was gasping for air as he jerked on me harder this time. He could see the sweat that was dripping from my scalp, stinging my eyes, and hear my irregular intake of breath. My left side was facing him and I had leaned my entire upper body away from his as I pawed at the bookshelves for support. I had few things to be thankful for at that very moment, but the rigor of my exercise over the years was giving me an edge against his greater girth and strength.

A sudden bend toward Harper, which surprised him, left me with several inches of play in the cord. With my left hand still guarding my neck, I pitched away from him and grabbed Gemma's prize surgical award from its ebony stand on the third row of shelves. I whirled back with the gold-handled scalpel in my palm and ripped it across the wrist of the mad doctor. His blood spurted everywhere from whichever artery I had cut.

The cord fell from his hand as I began to slash at him savagely. I let up only to pull the gag out of my mouth. I wanted to find a place to cripple him seriously enough for me to have time to get out of the room but I wasn't sure I could find the right spot through his clothing. As he hunched over the desk, trying to wrap his own sleeve around his most serious wound, I stabbed at his upper thigh, digging the scalpel in it repeatedly. When he fell to the ground wailing, I ran to the door and unlocked it—as I had tried to do so many minutes ago—sprinting out this time and slamming it behind me.

The twelfth-floor corridor echoed with my screams as I pounded on the few doors between Dogen's apartment and the elevator. I could hear the peephole cover slide open behind the door of the nearly deaf neighbor and I realized what a sight I presented. Two lengths of black vinyl cord were wrapped around my neck while I held up the telephone machine that was hanging from one end of it to prevent the sheer weight of it from choking me to death. My yellow sweater was drenched in Harper's blood and stretched out of shape so that it appeared to be coming off one of my shoulders completely.

No sane New Yorker was going to let me into his or her home in that condition. All I really wanted to do anyway was get a police officer to respond. I began banging on the neighbor's door. "Let me in," I shouted. "I just killed a man. I'm crazy! I escaped from Stuyvesant last night and I came here to kill him. Let me in, NOW!"

Exactly as I thought the little feet inside shuffled over to the telephone and whoever they were attached to dialed 911. Then she immediately called the doorman to complain about the madwoman who was ranting in the hallway outside her apartment. I kept the scalpel firmly in my hand and my eye on Gemma's door, for the forty-seven seconds it took the superintendent to bring the service elevator up to the floor.

I unwrapped the phone from around my neck while the two of us waited on the silent corridor for the police. The response time was less than seven minutes. I guess it was fortunate that Harper had tried to kill me on a quiet Sunday afternoon and not during a weekday rush hour. Three cars answered the call. Two cops stayed with me while the other four broke down the door to find Harper, who was unconscious on the floor of the apartment.

"We gotta take you to be checked out and examined, Miss Cooper. What hospital you wanna go to?" one of the rookies asked me when I explained to him who I was.

"After this investigation, I'm not sure there's a medical center in this city where I'd be welcome. I've got a really great internist, though. If you guys could just take me home and do your interviews there, it'd be much less painful all around. You can look up a number for Dr. Schrem with Information and his service will beep him. I think maybe he'd make a house call in this situation."

The superintendent's assistant had seen the cops arrive at the building and had followed upstairs with an old blanket. Police Officer Dick Nicastro wrapped it around my shoulders and took me down to the patrol car for the short ride home.

I sat in the backseat with my head resting against the window listening to the staccato noise from the radio as a call came over of a rape in progress on a rooftop in the 7th Precinct.

"It's gettin' to be that season, Miss Cooper."

I closed my eyes and wiped the raindrops off my hair, shaking my head at the sight of my bloody hand. "Unfortunately, officer, it's always that season."

28

Battaglia's Monday morning reaction to my unexpected skirmish was nothing compared to the whipping I took from Mercer and Mike on Sunday evening. When they arrived at seven, my doctor was just finishing up his examination, documenting his findings in detail because I told him they would be evidence at the trial. He made the guys promise not to aggravate my fragile condition with any excitement or emotional turmoil and he insisted on remaining with us while I relived for them my encounter with Coleman Harper.

"No cross-examination, gentlemen," he dictated as he left us. "She needs an early night—and a quiet one."

Mike had called in Hal Sherman from the Crime Scene Unit to take photographs of my injuries. I didn't need a mirror to remind myself what shape I was in when I saw the expression on his face. "I've photographed cadavers that look better than you do, Alex. If you were the winner, what does the other guy look like?"

Chapman lifted my hair from the side of my neck to show Hal the ligature marks. "Don't worry. She took a nice chunk out of his ass. He'll be singing soprano with the Attica boys' choir."

The flash from the camera made my eyes sting as he shot close-ups of the bruises on my forehead, then focused on my wrists and forearms.

Nobody wanted me to stay alone in case I needed anything during the night. So I accepted the invitation from David Mitchell to sleep on the fold out sofabed in his living room, where he and Renee could look out for me, with Zac at my feet. Mike and Mercer left at nine, taking my clothing along with them to be vouchered and sent to the police lab for serology and analysis.

I was determined to show up at the office bright and early before the story of the attack took on mythical proportions. It was obvious that Gemma Dogen's murder case would have to be reassigned to another assistant district attorney—along with the assault on me. I was an ordinary witness in this matter now and not a prosecutor. Rod Squires let me have a choice of lawyers to handle the two attacks as long as it wasn't Sarah or anyone in the Sex Crimes Unit. I asked that it be given to Tom Kendris, who was a friend and whose work I respected.

There was a bedside arraignment at Bellevue for Coleman Harper and I was pleased when Battaglia called me himself to tell me that Judge Roger Hayes, a sage and intrepid jurist, had remanded the defendant without bail.

Laura would need an extra week's vacation even more than I did. She spent the better part of each day dodging the calls from the press, everybody looking for an exclusive. I hated to say no to Katie Couric, so Battaglia reluctantly agreed to go on camera himself to do a *Today* show interview about the issue of violent crime as it occasionally involved health care professionals. Mike Sheehan was begging me to leak something to him for Fox 5, but I knew there were enough of the guys he used to work with in the Police Department to take care of that impropriety for me.

Most of the week I spent working with Tom Kendris and the detectives so that I could testify before the grand jury on Thursday afternoon. We devoted hours to analyzing the evidence in the case, with Gemma's voluminous records from ten years of her guardianship of Minuit's neurosurgical program spread out on every flat surface in Kendris's office. I kept coming back to the pictures of the crime scene floor trying to divine whether the dying woman had actually been writing some message to us in her blood.

Now the unfinished letter looked to me like an R, and so, in hindsight, I had her spelling out the word "Reject." Every time he saw me glance at the picture, Chapman pulled it from my hand and told me to get real. "She didn't have the strength to write anything at that point." I would always be willing to believe that she did.

Maureen and her husband Charles had been brought back from their safe house on Sunday night, so Mercer drove me out to see them after work on Monday. We hugged each other until I thought I would crack her rib cage. Then we took out our date books and picked a May weekend for our trip to a spa.

The lab results had confirmed that the "nurse" who drugged Mo had given her a massive dose of a horse tranquilizer—nothing that would kill her but something that would call to everyone's attention that she had been made as a cop.

There hadn't been any progress on figuring out who had done it, although Mike suspected it was Coleman Harper trying to divert the police from looking at him and get them to focus their attention on DuPre, who was one of Mo's attending physicians. No one was able to convince Mo, though, to blame it on her pal John DuPre. She was having trouble with the fact that he wasn't really a doctor at all since she had liked his manner better than that of the guy whom David had assigned to be in charge of her hospital admission. We imagined that John was probably cruising around the country right now, looking for a little town where he could hang out his shingle and start up a new practice. Maybe this time using some dead doctor's name that he could lift off a tombstone.

Joan Stafford had returned to New York on Tuesday evening and insisted that I come for dinner. She cornered me once she had me seated at the table. "Here's the deal. It's an offer you can't refuse. Nina's taking the red-eye in from California on Thursday night and on Friday the three of us fly to the Vineyard and help you open the house for the season. Just us girls—she's leaving the baby in L.A. with her husband and Jim has to go to Vienna to cover the summit. U.S. Air has been flying direct from La Guardia as of April first. I've booked three seats and we're not interested in any arguments from you. We take the last flight up at 5:45 Friday afternoon and come back at the crack of dawn on Monday. I'll have you at your desk before nine, okay?"

I smiled at her across the table. "It's the new me, Joanie. I'm ready."

I wanted to go home to the Vineyard and nothing could be easier than having my two best friends at my side when I drove into Daggett's Pond Way for the first time since last October.

Nina Baum took the red-eye and arrived early on Friday. I had left my spare keys with the doorman so she could shower and relax before coming down to hang out with me at the office. Our friendship had started the first day we both arrived at Wellesley when we had been assigned by lot to be roommates, and I had never found a more loyal or loving friend.

Sarah had called in early to say she was taking the day off

and fortunately, for a change, the Sex Crimes Unit had a quiet one. Nina and I went to Forlini's for a long lunch, came back to close up my desk for the weekend, and hopped into a taxi to meet Joan at La Guardia.

The flight was smooth and easy. Joan had arranged for a Jeep rental at the airport so we didn't have to bother to get my old car out of storage. The fifteen-minute ride up-island was magnificent as we caught the last light of the spring day. Green buds were starting to sprout on most of the trees and daffodils dotted the yards and roadsides with cheerful yellow fringe.

My stomach churned as Nina braked for the turn onto the path that leads to my house. Isabella Lascar had died there and I would never again be able to make that turn without thinking of that. I was pleased to see, though, that Joe, my caretaker, had planted wonderful beds of tulips and bearded iris all along the drive and placed a granite marker at the base of the tree where Isabella's life had been taken.

The little farmhouse had the wonderful smell of fresh paint, which had also removed every sign of the fingerprint powder the police had used and gave my home a cheerful accent with its hand-drawn stenciling and clean linen-white trim.

I put my things down in the master bedroom and walked out to meet Nina and Joan on the deck. "I couldn't have done this without both—"

"Shhh. I haven't seen this view in three years," Nina reminded me. "I just want a glimpse of it before it's completely dark." It was my own little piece of heaven and I sat on the railing to absorb its beauty, taking in the hillside with its fields of wildflowers, the ponds that were emptied now of all the boats of summer people, and the sea beyond.

Joan was on her feet. "Okay, ten minutes to get yourself out of that ridiculous lady-lawyer suit. We have an eight o'clock reservation for dinner at the Outermost."

"I didn't even realize they'd be open before the beginning of May."

"You haven't had time to realize anything lately. If I'd left it in your hands, we'd be having popcorn for dinner."

"Don't knock her. It *is* one of the few dishes she does well, Joan."

I went inside and changed into jeans and a blazer, then sat in the back of the Jeep while Nina drove us out to the western tip of the island—Gay Head—where Hughie and Jean Taylor built and ran the most wonderful inn on the island. A neo-Victorian house with only seven guest rooms—each made from a different kind of wood—it sat on a spectacular piece of land that rolled down to Vineyard Sound. It offered, in addition, the world's most perfect sunset.

We were too late for that feature tonight, but their chef, Barbara, was a graduate of the Culinary Institute and could do some pretty special things in that kitchen. I carried a couple of bottles of wine under my arm because, like this whole end of the island, Gay Head was dry.

We walked across the lawn to the entrance of the inn. Jeanie welcomed us warmly as I introduced my friends to her and she asked if we wanted to go out on the veranda to sip some wine before we sat down in the dining room. The bar was actually outside, on a wide terrace facing the water, and I told Joan and Nina that if they liked my view they absolutely had to see this one.

I led the way out onto the porch and froze in the doorway. Hughie was playing the piano and a chorus of familiar faces was singing "Happy Birthday" to me, champagne glasses in everyone's hand. Mike was behind the bar, of course, helping out Hollis, the regular bartender. Mercer had brought Francine with him and they were flanked by Sarah and Jim, Charles and Maureen, Rod Squires, and Renee and David. Joanie and Nina had filled every room at the Inn and the party was on.

I was radiating my happiness as I made the rounds of the crowd, kissing everyone and learning how three carloads of friends had banded together to keep the plan secret and drive up here this morning.

"Open your presents!" Mike shouted at me pointing at the pile of boxes stacked up at the far end of the bar.

"You're a few weeks early," I chided my pals. "I'm hanging on to thirty-four every minute that I can."

"Yeah, but Nina said you were flying down to visit your parents on the thirtieth for your birthday. And we figured the only way to surprise you was to start early."

I accepted a cold glass of champagne and worked my way through the group. Joan steered me to a tall vase of yellow roses on the bar with a card nestled among them that was signed from Drew. I bit the inside of my lip and promised myself to call him tomorrow to make a date for dinner and a chance to talk about the past few weeks.

While I walked on to thank Sarah and Francine and compliment them on their well-kept secret, I could hear Mike and Mercer over my shoulder, back to talking about the murder of Gemma Dogen.

"You remember that conversation we had in the precinct, about whether love or money was the motive in more cases? Well, I was right again. Coleman Harper. Can you imagine, for whatever reason the guy wasn't content to be one kind of doctor, he had to have more?"

"You'd think some of the people we've interviewed this week would have come forward before now, when she was killed," Mercer responded. "Now they're jumping out of the woodwork to tell us how resentful Harper was of Dogen, how angry he was at the way she treated him when she met him almost ten years ago."

"You should see the crap they recovered when Zotos and Losenti executed the search warrant on the guy's apartment."

I was in a great position to do an overheard since Tom Kendris hadn't wanted to tell me about any of the other evidence in the cases now that I was a witness. Mike was talking. "All kinds of disguise stuff—fake hair, mustaches, makeup. They even got a note that Robert Spector had sent him months ago saying he was doing his best, but Dogen has 'blackballed you all over the world.' Harper must have been thinking of every kind of way to get the job done.

"My guess is he went there in the middle of the night, knowing he'd find her alone, to talk her out of rejecting him again. He had Spector's support and she was the only thing standing in the way of his admission to the program. If she was leaving town anyway, she was just being a spoiler in his view. I'm thinkin' she told him to forget about it right then and there, so he stabbed her. He had come—ready with his butcher knife—prepared to get his revenge."

I couldn't pretend not to listen any longer. I leaned on the bar, and even though Mike shot me a look he and Mercer kept talking.

"You know when it all started?"

I shook my head back and forth.

"Gemma Dogen's predecessor had been the first one to have reservations about Harper's ability. That's a decade ago, kid. This Dr. Randall is the one who said he would admit him into the neurosurgical program, but only if he completed a residency in neurology first.

"Dogen took over when Randall left later that same year— only she made her own decision. She evaluated the reports on Harper's work and she flat out refused to be bound by the promise that Randall had made to him. Effectively, she ended his chances of getting into the program."

"What about the 'Met Games'?" I asked.

"That was all Spector's doing. It was his idea to park Harper over there for a year, figuring he'd have a chance to change Dogen's mind. But Harper continued to screw up. Then he went down south to practice for a while. Finally, it was Spector who got his hopes up again this last time. Told him to get back up to Mid-Manhattan by doing this fellowship thing where Spector could supervise him. Thought with Dogen leaving there'd be one last chance to get his man in before he got too old to try for that kind of residency. Harper'd be fifty years old when he finished it as it is. Trouble with that plan—Spector alerted him one year too early. Dogen just wouldn't let go."

We were all silent knowing that it was only a few days short of April fifteenth.

"Have either of you sorted out why Spector was pushing so hard on Harper's behalf?" I asked.

"Not completely. Yet. But you really hit a nerve when you found Gemma's notes on that. Both of them are mum on it for the moment, but I'm diggin' around. We'll find out. Besides that," Mercer went on, "it all just kept snowballing. Robert Spector knew that Gemma would quit—just on principle—the minute Coleman Harper was admitted to the neurosurgical program. Spector's a winner automatically 'cause he'd wind up with Dogen's job, which is exactly what he wanted."

Mike broke in. "I guess we rattled Harper in that last interview when we told him we'd be getting the hospital's records from ten years back. He knew Minuit didn't keep them that long. But what he didn't know was how long Met kept its documents—and whether his archnemesis, Gemma Dogen, had her own set of papers on him. How much you wanna bet that he's the guy who broke into Metropolitan to see if he could unload their file room of his own records? And that's why he kept Dogen's keys after he killed her. He must have slipped up to her apartment on Sunday to clean out whatever she had on him figuring sooner or later someone would find the papers that damned him."

"Why'd he let me finish that conversation with Mercer instead of just grabbing me while I was telling him all about the files I had found?"

"If Harper had jumped you while you were on the phone, no matter how far away Mercer was he just would have called 911 and the cops would have been there before Harper could kill you and get safely out of the building. Probably thought if he got rid of you *after* the conversation and made off with the only set of Dogen's files that still existed, it'd just be Mercer's word against his with no proof to back it up."

"We assume it was Harper in one of his disguises who got past your doorman and slipped that black-and-white note under your door," Mercer suggested. "He may not have known the whole story on Jean DuPuy, but like Gemma he knew something was fishy about the guy's background. Too slick, too glib. Don't forget, they had both practiced in the South. I expect Harper knew something about the real John DuPre that started him thinking.

"Anyway, he and DuPuy were both so unhappy to be anywhere near this investigation, they were each pointing fingers at the other one. They must have been so damned excited to find that bloodstained old derelict sleeping in the X-ray department that they tripped over each other to reveal him to someone else. And we actually worried about which one found him first."

"Do you think it was Harper who tried to run me down with the car?" I asked, thinking back to my near miss with Zac.

"No question about it," Mike shot back without hesitation. "He probably just freaked. A couple of days earlier, he personally delivered to us a blood-covered mental patient we all bought as the killer. Then he hears on Friday evening's news bulletins that you, Alex Cooper, exonerated the old guy.

Mercer thinks that when Harper had been sitting at the precinct for hours that first night, he heard Peterson ask for a sector car to drop you off after work and gave them your home address. May have gone there in a fury when he heard the news, never expecting to actually see you. Then he hits the jackpot—out you walk at eleven o'clock. Hey, I bet he was striking out without a plan at that point. Just desperate."

Again, we were quiet as the others reveled around us.

"Know what I can't stand?" Mike asked. "Forget that these morons don't want to help out the police when there's a murder, but somehow they can't wait to tell any reporter who comes along that they've known about the killer or his motives the whole time. Have you seen any of the clippings?"

"Nobody's shown me anything. I'm a witness, remember?"

"You got the ex-wife being quoted in some rag down South," Mercer said, "claiming Harper felt Gemma Dogen was *the* only reason he couldn't get into school anywhere else to study neurosurgery. Then there's one of the doctors he worked with two years ago who said Harper was 'obsessed' with Dogen and absolutely fixated on becoming a neurosurgeon—the one thing in life that was denied him. Even believed Dogen was the ongoing source of most of his problems ten years after she screwed him."

"Yeah, that's our shortcoming, Mercer. Cops can't pay these fools like the tabloids do. Nobody wants to tell me zilch about a suspect. But stick a microphone or a camera in their puss or offer 'em a hundred bucks for their story and suddenly everyone knows who the killer was all along."

"Not the big cheese. I saw Spector's comment in Monday's *Post*. Can't believe his man did it. 'Harper has a brilliant mind. He's done some superb medical studies for me.'"

"Yeah, well maybe Coleman can study the effects of prison on the nervous system for twenty-five years to life. Okay,

Blondie, enough of this stuff—we're all off duty and out of the jurisdiction.

"C'mon, open up my present first." Mike reached over to the pile and handed me a package. It was a red leather jewelry box wrapped in a large white bow. I pulled off the ribbon and unfastened the clasp, lifting the lid to reveal a glittering tiara. Nina grabbed it from my hand and sat it squarely on top of my head while Mike assured me that it was a fake and that he'd paid more for the box than for the rhinestones.

"Listen up, guys," Mike said. "Joanie and I have arranged a gastronomic birthday tour of the Vineyard—my itinerary, her pocketbook. We start here, of course, at the Outermost Inn, where I recommend you begin the evening with the crab cakes followed by the lobster and then the homemade peppermint ice cream.

"Tomorrow is breakfast with Primo—coffee and bagels on the porch of the Chilmark Store. Good food, good gossip. Lunch, the amazing Flynn sisters and the world's best chowder and clams at the Bite. Dinner with Tony and David at The Feast—don't miss the *pasta fra diavolo*."

I kicked off my shoes and walked to the edge of the steps that led down to the wide, rolling lawn bordered by Vineyard Sound.

Mike was touting Sunday breakfast at the Inn, Primo's pizza for lunch, and a farewell dinner at the Red Cat—the tenderloin with caramelized onion. He truly had explored all the best local options for food.

Hughie's brother, James, was quietly singing about fire and rain in the background while Mike continued to entertain the troops. He was telling them that their weekend assignment was to look for the tallest staircase on the island if they really wanted to see me do my Tina Turner imitation.

I had come to the bottom of the gently sloping hillside where I stood with my feet in the icy water looking off at the not-too-distant spot where it flowed out to meet the Atlantic. I smelled the salt spray of the ocean as I looked over at the flashing signal of the great lighthouse—warning ships away from the rocks of Devil's Bridge as it had for two hundred years. The sound of the waves lapping against the shore soothed me almost as much as the laughter of the people I loved coming from behind me. I could blow out the candles on my cake at the end of the festivities later tonight and everyone would be urging me to tell them what I yearned for. But as I stood here alone and stared up at the millions of stars that showed themselves from high overhead to the farthest point on the horizon that I could see, I privately made all my wishes for the year ahead.

ACKNOWLEDGMENTS

Every crime described in this book is based on an actual event.

Once again, I am profoundly grateful to all the usual suspects for their love, friendship, and sustenance throughout the period in which this book was written.

Alexandra Cooper thrives on the support of her great friends, some of whom borrow traits like their humor, wisdom, and loyalty from a few friends of my own. Alexandra Denman, Lisa Friel, Joan Stanton Hitchcock, Maureen Spencer Forrest, Karen and (the other) Alex Cooper, Susan and Michael Goldberg, Sarah and Mitch—and Casey—Rosenthal all contribute to the cast. Joan and Bernie Carl provided the very generous introduction to Cliveden. The real Dr. Robert Spector, whom I have known and admired since we were both fifteen, is not the model for the character who borrows his name in this book.

Bob Morgenthau continues to be my professional inspiration and hero. This, the twenty-fifth year I have served in the Office of the District Attorney of New York County, has remained as challenging and rewarding as all that came before. My colleagues and partners there are the best in this business and continue to work on the side of the angels for survivors of violent crime.

Perhaps the nicest part of my new career as an author has been the time spent in and around people who love books—the librarians and booksellers who place them so carefully in peoples' hands, and the readers who devour them with such eagerness.

My great fortune in having Susanne Kirk as an editor cannot be overstated.

Esther Newberg is an extraordinary agent, but she is an even better friend.

All of the Fairsteins contribute to the spirit of my work, as they always have. My newest sources of inspiration—small but mighty—are Matthew and Alexander Zavislan.

My husband, Justin Feldman, continues to be my muse and my greatest joy. And my mother, Alice Atwell Fairstein, will always be the very best.

FINAL JEOPARDY

Linda Fairstein

The days of Assistant D.A. Alexandra Cooper often start
off badly, but she's never faced the morning by reading her
own obituary before.

It doesn't take long to sort out why it was printed: a
woman's body with her face blown away, left in a car
rented in Coop's name in the driveway of her weekend
home. But it isn't so easy to work out why her lodger – an
acclaimed Hollywood star – was murdered, or to be sure
that the killer had found the right victim.

As Coop's job is to send rapists to jail there are plenty of
suspects who might be seeking revenge, and whoever it is
needs to be found before her obituary gets reprinted.

'Raw, real and mean. Linda Fairstein is wonderful'
Patricia Cornwell

POSTMORTEM

Patricia Cornwell

A serial killer is on the loose in Richmond, Virgina. Three women have died, brutalised and strangled in their own bedrooms. There is no pattern: the killer appears to strike at random – but always on Saturday mornings.

So when Dr Kay Scarpetta, chief medical examiner, is awakened at 2.33am, she knows the news is bad: there is a fourth victim. And she fears now for those that will follow unless she can dig up new forensic evidence to aid the police.

But not everyone is pleased to see a woman in this powerful job. Someone may even want to ruin her career and reputation . . .

'**Terrific first novel, full of suspense, in which even the scientific bits grip**'
The Times

CRUEL AND UNUSUAL

Patricia Cornwell

At 11.05 one December evening in Richmond, Virginia,
convicted murderer Ronnie Joe Waddell is pronounced
dead in the electric chair.

At the morgue Dr Kay Scarpetta waits for Waddell's body.
Preparing to perform a postmortem before the subject is
dead is a strange feeling, but Scarpetta has been here
before. And Waddell's death is not the only newsworthy
event on this freezing night: the grotesquely wounded body
of a young boy is found propped against a rubbish skip. To
Scarpetta the two cases seem unrelated, until she recalls
that the body of Waddell's victim had been arranged in a
strikingly similar position.

Then a third murder is discovered, the most puzzling of
all. The crime scene yields very few clues: old blood stains,
fragments of feather, and – most baffling – a bloody finger-
print that points to the one suspect who could not possibly
have committed this murder.

**'Chillingly detailed forensic thriller confirming
Cornwell as the top gun in this field'**
Daily Telegraph

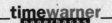